FLYABOUT

An Adventure Novel of
Survival, Romance and Mystery
in the Australian Outback

comma

by

Robert W. Campbell

This is a work of fiction. Names, characters, organizations, places, events other than those clearly in the public domain, are either the product of the author's imagination or are used fictitiously. Any resemblance to actual persons, living or dead, events or locales is entirely coincidental.

ISBN-13: 978-1-7323559-0-3

Table of Contents

Dedication

This book is dedicated with love and thanks to the two most amazing women in my life, my wife Alice Campbell, and my daughter, Leah Murthy. They stayed by my side offering encouragement, support, and understanding for years on end as I completed my Doctorate Degree, in spite of the fact that I often was so preoccupied that it seemed to them that I wasn't there at all. And later their support never wavered as I pushed ahead with this novel which, at times, seemed like I'd never finish. I especially thank my wife for encouraging me to take flying lessons in order that I could write the flying sequences in this novel with authority. Thank you both for your lifetime of support. Love to you both!

Acknowledgements

I wish to thank the following individuals for their invaluable help, support, and advice that allowed me to write this novel with clarity, accuracy, and precision.

Captain Richard Abers, a university colleague and former DC-10 Captain. Richard's help and technical expertise were invaluable to me. He used his experience and official DC-10 Flight Manual to coach me in writing accurately about the emergency procedures that took place during the airliner disaster sequences in this novel.

Mr. Brian Mahoney, former flight instructor, Beverly Flight Center, Beverly, MA. I would never have been able to write the flying sequences in the novel without his expert instruction in both the single-engine airplane and twin-engine airplanes that are part of the story in this novel.

Dr. Charles B. Howard, Belle Meade, NJ. Dr. Howard is a caring, highly valued, friend and family member. His medical/technical advice proved to be invaluable in allowing me to deal with the characters' injuries in a realistic and accurate way.

Mrs. Louise Wallbank, The Villages, FL   I sincerely thank Louise for all the work and effort she put into editing this novel. Her skills and support were greatly appreciated.

CHAPTER 1

Whoa, what an old looking plane, thought Derek Hunter, as he boarded the aircraft. It looked to be a big old DC-10 that had long since seen better days. Still, it was an imposing sight as it stood on the tarmac with its doors wide open. As he entered the cabin, he was greeted by a stunning flight attendant. Derek noted her nametag read *Michelle*. He spotted an empty row of seats near the rear emergency exit door, and selected window seat 26A. It was just above the main baggage door. Gazing out the window, he enjoyed a panoramic view of the area surrounding the aircraft. He watched in fascination as an armada of people and equipment darted about preparing airplanes for departure. Smiling, he recalled his childhood and how much he loved being around airports and airplanes. He recalled vividly how his parents had given him a flying lesson on his 18th birthday. He actually got to do a landing--with the instructor's help. The instructor encouraged him to get his license and consider a career in aviation. The instructor said he had a 'natural talent' for flying. Although he promised himself that one day he'd get a flying license, he never did find the time or money to do it. Instead, he found pleasure in reading about airplanes whenever he could. Happy thoughts.

Derek felt a slight 'thump.' Shifting his gaze down to the left, he saw the baggage crew busily loading luggage into the cargo hold directly beneath his seat. Tired now, he reclined the seat and tried to relax.

Across the aisle he overheard a newly-wed couple chortling about how wonderful their wedding reception had come off and what a great honeymoon they were going to have in Alice Springs. The giddy young couple cooed and kissed then repeated to each other *"till death do us part."* Mercifully, they would never know that the wedding vow they'd just reaffirmed would come to pass very soon.

At 7:00 p.m. Derek checked his watch and recounted how lucky he'd been to catch the flight. It was supposed to have departed at 6:00 p.m. but when he called to confirm his reservation he'd been told that the flight would be delayed an hour, and that was good news for him. A scheduling mix-up at the Computer Science Conference he'd just attended had put him behind schedule. But the flight delay allowed him to make his flight. For once in his life a flight delay actually worked to his advantage.

He'd come from Boston, halfway around the world, to make a scholarly presentation in Sydney. And now that the 'business end' of his trip was over he was looking forward to a short vacation. The trip to Alice Springs, then on to Ayers Rock and the Outback, would be a welcome diversion and a pleasurable end to his first visit to Australia. He was really looking forward to a guided jeep tour into the Outback that he planned to take. That, he thought, would really help him get back on his feet after his recent break-up with his longtime girlfriend.

He reminisced how they'd been together for several years while he struggled to balance his heavy workload at the university and the grueling years of study to complete his Doctorate Degree. Their relationship couldn't hold up under the strain. She'd felt neglected and, in his heart, he couldn't blame her. It was a classic case of relationships vs careers and something had to give. Sadly, he unconsciously let the relationship suffer and he'd paid the price. He was tired now and tried to put the sad situation out of his thoughts. He let the matter go.

Derek stretched his arms over his head and let out a long sigh. He reviewed how his day had begun. '*Doctor* Hunter,' the moderator announced as he introduced him to the assembly. The lofty title, *Doctor,* sounded like music to his ears. He'd received his doctorate degree only three months earlier. And now here he was presenting his first scholarly paper, in *Australia* of all places. Although the presentation '*Artificial Intelligence and Its Impact on the Workforce*' was a success, the 'follow-up' discussion period had to be rescheduled. And that caused delays, frustration, and anxiety. But now, luxuriating in the reclined seat, he felt all those issues melt away.

A loud 'thump' from the baggage compartment below his seat shook Derek out of his reverie. He straightened up in his seat, then quickly scanned the cabin. He was surprised when he didn't see many passengers. It was a very large airplane and even though he couldn't see all the way down to the front, it was clearly apparent that the plane was far from being full. Derek checked his watch and noted that the flight was still delayed. He wondered if the delay was caused by mechanical problems. "Ah, I'm just being ridiculous," he mumbled to himself. Dismissing the idea, he shrugged his broad shoulders and settled back into his seat.

Still, even though he tried not to, Derek was beginning to have second thoughts about having used the Internet to get the cheapest fare possible. For a moment he feared that he may have chosen an air carrier that uses old aircraft and cheap maintenance for the sake of profit. With a shudder, he shook off his depressing line of thought.

A moment later Derek was jolted out of his thoughts by a more welcome 'thud.' This time the sound came from the cabin door as it swung shut. Twisting around in his seat he caught the sight of a pretty young flight attendant moving the door locking lever down into position. *That must be Michelle getting the cabin ready for departure*, he thought. He'd remembered seeing her name embossed on the gold-winged badge that was pinned to her blouse. He was surprised that he noticed the badge at all because Michelle was so strikingly beautiful that one could hardly notice anything else. Had it not been for her airline uniform one might have thought that she was a cover girl flying off to a photo shoot. Her long beautiful blond hair and gorgeous blue eyes certainly made her look the part.

He remembered her warm, friendly greeting as he entered the cabin. Although he could never explain it, her infectious smile and warm sincere *'welcome aboard'* made him feel like he had just been kissed by an angel. He reflected that the golden wings of her badge would have been more appropriate had they been affixed to her back because she truly did look like an angel.

Hearing an engine start up outside, Derek looked out in time to see a motorized luggage conveyor moving away from the aircraft. *Ah,* he thought, *that means all the luggage is aboard and we'll be departing any minute.* He was even more convinced that departure was imminent when he heard a muffled 'whining' sound. The baggage handler had just pressed a switch activating the cargo door's control motor causing the big baggage door to slowly move down into the closed position.

But trouble was brewing. Below Derek's window, the ramp baggage handler stood waiting for the motor to stop—that would mean that the cycle was completed and the door was ready to be locked. He cocked his head and listened, but he didn't hear the click that normally accompanied the mechanism moving into its secure position. Though he should have waited, he went ahead and pushed on the lock handle above the door. That movement was supposed to complete the locking procedure. That done, an indicator light should have lit up in the cockpit of the plane signaling that the baggage door was locked and secure. But something was wrong—the door lock handle wouldn't move into place.

In the cockpit, the 'door locked' indicator on the flight deck remained as dark as the mood of the flight crew. They were already behind schedule and eager to do the engine startups but couldn't do so until the cargo door was secure—and that meant more delays. Like other flight crews who flew for 'cut-rate-fare' airlines they were under constant pressure to maximize their productivity by maintaining rapid flight turnarounds and on-time service.

The baggage man grumbled at the problematic latch. He re-checked his work and noticed that the lock handle wasn't flush with the fuselage and its small 'vent door' hadn't shut properly. He knew that the vent door operated simultaneously with a set locking pins in the cargo door to prevent cabin pressure buildup if the big cargo door wasn't properly locked. He was furious about the delay and having to deal with the aircraft that many of his colleagues thought was a *'Russian built piece of crap.'* The man scowled at the latch, gave out a loud curse, then slammed his barrel-sized fist against the side of the cargo door. With that, the little vent door slowly moved into place. An instant later the "door closed and locked" indicator light winked on in the cockpit. Derek, oblivious to the cargo door drama, drifted off into pleasant thoughts of his long-awaited vacation.

Derek was startled out of his daydream by the sudden impact of a man pounding into the seat beside him. The scruffy young man appeared to have just dropped right out of the sky. He landed in the seat with a tremendous *'whump'* that shook the whole bank of seats.

"Hey man, what's going on out there?" he asked, as he rudely thrust himself across Derek to gape out the window. He glared at the baggage crew outside. "No way! What's holding things up. We should have been out of here by now—we're never going to take off!" Moaning in displeasure, he flopped back into his seat. The man's agitation, Derek hoped, was only due to the flight delay.

Looking more closely at him, Derek couldn't help but note how closely his appearance resembled that of the legendary *Unabomber*, Ted Kaczynski. He had the same look about him with his disheveled clothing, unkempt beard, and strange disposition. *Of all the places on the plane he could sit, he picks here—lucky me*, thought Derek.

"I don't know what's going on," Derek finally responded. Hoping to lessen the man's agitation Derek said, "they must have had a little trouble with the loading but I just heard the cargo door close so we should be on our way any minute now." The man seemed calmed by Derek's remark. But he soon renewed the conversation.

"Well they better not mess up my camping equipment," he grumbled.

"So, are you're going camping in the Outback?" Derek asked.

"Yeah, I sure am—and hey, what's ya' name."

Oh God, thought Derek. *I should have kept my mouth shut—this is why you don't talk to people on the subway.* Hoping to keep his apprehension from showing, he simply said, "Derek."

"Yeah? Well, I'm Shawn and I'm from a lot of different places. I sort of move around a lot, ya know." Derek didn't respond—he just nodded his head while thinking, *I'll bet you move around a lot--probably trying to keep one step ahead of the people in the white coats.* He found himself wishing the man would move along to a different seat, or better yet, a different airplane.

The uncomfortable silence that followed was broken when the man started talking again. "Yeah, I'm gonna go camping in the Outback, man. I got a pile of stuff packed in my luggage. I'm gonna camp my way all the way across the Outback in six months. Everyone says I'm crazy. But, hey, that's me!" He laughed, in an unsettling way. *Crazy, how nicely put,* thought Derek.

"And I got a lot stuff with me too," he rambled. "I can live off my supplies and after that I can live off the land. I used to be in the U.S. Army Rangers. We're some kinda crazy kick-ass tough dudes, I'll tell ya man."

"Got a psycho discharge no doubt." thought Derek. He dared not ask for details because even as the man boasted about being in the Rangers, his expression changed in a very disquieting way. Then as abruptly as Shawn had arrived, without a further word, he leaped up and headed to another seat at the rear of the plane.

The mood in the cockpit changed quickly when Flight Engineer, Jean, called out, "That's it on the cargo door. They've finally got it. We're good to go."

I'm glad of that," chortled Captain Ed Johnson. "And I've got some great news. I just made a final weather check and winds aloft are really in our favor. I figure with the tail wind we'll shave 20 minutes off the flight. We won't make up the full hour and a half we lost with that compressor replacement and baggage door problem but we may wind up being only a little over an hour late if our luck holds."

"Sir, if you call *this* luck we're in a world of hurt, I'll tell ya," chuckled his First Officer, Dan Billings, who was serving as copilot on this trip.

Turning to his right, Captain Johnson called over to his female second officer, Flight Engineer Jean Sears. "Okay Jean, let's begin the engine startups. Number 1 then number 3."

"Yes Captain," she promptly responded.

A minute later the cabin was filled with the welcome sound of the jet's engines spooling up. Even though the plane was less than full, the passengers gave a remarkably loud round of applause to indicate their approval after such a long hot wait for departure. Derek happily joined in the minor celebration. He felt the tension in his body melt away as a bright yellow tow-tractor pulled into place and hooked up the aircraft. He was on his way and feeling great.

In the cockpit, Captain Johnson was alert to follow the line crewman's directions. The line chief walked backwards and gestured to the flight crew with his batons. He signaled the crew to make a right turn out of the holding area. The captain complied and maneuvered the plane towards his assigned departure position. He glanced over at his First Officer and called out. "Okay Dan, there's the signal—We've got permission to taxi. Let's roll out onto the taxiway for departure on Runway 06 Left."

Once the big jet started rolling, Captain Johnson began the startup sequence for the number two engine. "Okay Jean," he called out. "Start number 2." The delayed startup of the big engine, perched high up on the tail, was a standard cost cutting measure that was intended to save fuel and engine wear. Jean, a highly competent perky, and bright-eyed mother of two quickly configured the appropriate pneumatic and pack controls that allowed the number 2 engine to start. "Duct pressure at positive 30 PSI," she called out, indicating that the engine start procedure could now begin. A moment later she announced, "panel items complete." Now the last of the big three jet engines spooled up. "Final items to go," she called out just as the crew completed the last item on the long and complex checklist. Two minutes later the big jet slowly lumbered down the taxiway.

In the cabin, Derek was delighted to see Michelle move into position to begin her emergency evacuation presentation. *"She's in the wrong profession,"* he thought, as he watched her move gracefully down the aisle. As he stared into her beautiful face and sparkling blue eyes he fantasized that she'd be more at home on the runway of some exotic Paris fashion gallery. He fell into a daydream and imagined her cruising along in a Rolls Royce convertible with her golden silk hair flowing out behind her as she maneuvered the big Rolls through picturesque streets along the Mediterranean coast.

Derek suddenly noticed that Michelle had a quizzical look on her face. With a start, he realized that he must have been staring directly into her eyes for several minutes. Greatly embarrassed, he blushed deeply. While Michelle continued her safety presentation Derek snatched up a magazine. He opened it wide in front of his red face hoping to shield it from her view, not realizing that he was holding it upside down.

"And if there is anything that you need during the flight please don't hesitate to ask," Michelle added, as she concluded the emergency evacuation demonstration. Suddenly a man's voice rang out from the back of the aircraft. "Yeah you can do somethin' for me babe!"

Michelle wasn't sure who made the remark. Choosing to ignore it, she walked towards the rear of the plane to begin her duties. As she moved down the aisle, the scruffy young man who'd made the remark leaned forward as she passed. He mockingly held his arms out wide while making a ridiculous attempt at putting a lecherous look on his face. "You can give me some *luv'n,*" he blurted out.

Though startled by the outburst, Michelle thought that the scruffy little man hadn't really meant any harm. While his preposterous mock lecherous look made her want to laugh out loud, she followed her training and ignored him—she wouldn't be baited. Without breaking stride, she continued on, thinking that it really didn't matter anyway because she was planning to leave her job at the end of the month. Yet somehow that thought just didn't seem to please her the way she thought it should.

As Michelle passed by seat 26A, she couldn't help but glimpse over at the young man who had blushed with embarrassment a moment ago. How odd, she thought, as she came abreast of his seat. She noticed that he was holding the magazine upside down. She stopped and looked down just in time to catch Derek sneaking a peek at her over the top of the magazine. Much to his delight she shot him a stunning smile. He eagerly returned it.

Michelle leaned over gracefully, and whispered, "Pardon me Dr. Hunter. I couldn't help but notice that you're holding your magazine upside down."

Embarrassed, yet pleased that she'd addressed him, Derek blushed again and with an impish grin said, "That's because I'm in the land down under."

"That's cute," replied Michelle with a genuine smile on her face. She straightened up. "Well if you think you're in the land down under then you must be an American."

"You're right," smiled Derek. "And I really apologize for staring at you like that earlier. I didn't even realize that I was doing it—it's very embarrassing and I'm really sorry."

Michelle took an instant liking to this man who was so easily embarrassed and with his clean shave, big brown eyes, dark brown hair, and impeccable business suit, he appeared to be quite a gentleman as well. "Don't be embarrassed," she said, "I certainly wasn't. And I can assure you it was a more pleasant diversion than the incident I just had with a scruffy little character a moment ago."

"That just *has* to have been be Shawn," said Derek.

"I had the misfortune of meeting him earlier—he's not playing with a full deck that's for sure."

"Not playing with a full deck?" she repeated quizzically.

"Not all there, screwy, a little crazy," Derek explained. "Sorry, I guess that's an American expression."

"Well it certainly seems to fit in this case," she chuckled. "No argument there."

To Derek's disappointment Michelle's attention was drawn away by the sound of clanking jewelry. An elderly lady vigorously waved her heavily jewelry laden arm in the air and called out for service. As she was about to respond to the call, a male flight attendant, Jerry, took the call instead.

A moment later, Michelle's ears perked up as she heard the electronic 'bong' of another service call. "Sorry, duty calls," said Michelle. Turning back to Derek she added, "Enjoy your flight Doctor Hunter. We'll be in the air in just a minute."

"Thanks. I will," replied Derek. An instant later he started to add, "But how did you know my name......." His voice trailing off in mid-sentence. Michelle had already flitted away with the grace of a butterfly.

CHAPTER 2

While Captain Johnson continued taxiing towards the assigned runway, the flight crew monitored their instruments and ran through the preflight checklists. The captain glanced over at his First Officer, Dan, and thought, *he'll make a good captain in a couple of years.* Scanning the flight deck, Captain Johnson's eyes fell on his flight engineer, Jean Sears. He smiled as he thought about the charming and intelligent young woman. She had graduated at the top of her class and was known to be a top-notch second officer—the best he'd ever flow with. After bringing the big airliner to a gentle stop at the hold-short-line the captain awaited takeoff clearance. He called to Dan for a last-minute weather check before takeoff. A minute later Dan responded, "Sydney is at 87 degrees Fahrenheit, winds are from the southeast at 12 MPH, with medium cumulus clouds between 3500 and 4000 feet, and visibility 20 miles, but there's heavier cloud cover 30 miles to the west of Sydney."

While the aircraft sat at the 'hold-short-line' the crew completed the mandatory checklists and prepared for takeoff. With all in readiness, the captain made a final check that the flap setting was at 19 degrees and that the slat handle was locked into the 'extension range.' He keyed the mike, and in the professional tones that seem reserved for airline pilots, he contacted the tower. "Tower, this is Australian Outback Air flight 604 ready for departure, request takeoff clearance."

While he waited for a response from the tower, Captain Johnson completed the last item on the checklist. He called to Jean and asked her to conduct a final scan of her panel. As expected, she reported all her checklist items were at specifications.

"Thanks for the confirmation," he replied. "All set then Jean. You can make the departure announcement now."

"Right Captain," she replied, as she picked up the intercom. Speaking crisply into the handset she announced, "Flight attendants please be seated for departure."

The captain was adjusting his seat belt harness when the radio squawked to life. *"Tower to Flight 604. You're cleared for takeoff on Runway 06 Left, maintain runway heading to 5,000."*

Captain Johnson keyed his mike, repeated the clearance back, and thanked the tower. *"Thank you, sir and have a safe flight,"* replied the tower.

The cockpit remained quiet as the captain made one final scan of his panel. He nodded to Dan and Jean that all was ready.

"Okay, we're good to go," the captain called out. He reached to the center pedestal, placed his hand on the thrust levers, and smoothly moved them into a near vertical position. The engines roared as they spooled up to full thrust. He released the brakes and the plane started its takeoff roll. The lumbering jet's speed increased with each passing second.

Back in the passenger cabin the engines were reaching their highest pitch. The jet careened down the runway. Without warning Shawn suddenly screamed, *"Scottie! I need more power and I need it NOW!"* Then in a thick Scottish brogue he yelled, *"Aye Captain, but I'm give'n her all she's got!"* Michelle, seated nearby, was startled by his exclamation. Though Derek recognized the voice and the classic phrase from old Star Trek episodes, he didn't respond, nor did Michelle.

Derek thrilled to the lift-off as the huge jet began its rapid climb away from the airport. Looking downward he was delighted by the spectacle unfolding below. He'd been cheated out of an aerial view of Sydney caused by his earlier inbound nighttime arrival. But now his daylight view was superb and his spirits were high. As the plane continued its climb out over Botany Bay, Derek happily gazed out the window taking in the full beauty of the bay below. He was amused by the beehive of activity below with the pleasure boats and yachts skimming in every direction like a huge crowd of water bugs darting about.

A moment later he spied the Sydney Harbor Bridge. Far from being a mere access route to the northern side of the city, the unmistakable record-breaking bridge with its eight lanes of traffic, two railway tracks, a footpath, and cycleway, is a popular tourist attraction as well.

16

Derek made a mental note to visit both the Opera House and the bridge before returning home to Boston.

A moment later Derek's view was obscured as the plane moved through a layer of scattered clouds. But Derek didn't mind—he'd already gotten an impressive view of most of the city.

As the plane continued its climb and moved through 5000 feet, Captain Johnson looked out the cockpit window. The scattered clouds at the lower altitude were rapidly building up into a thick cover. But that was as predicted and he was unconcerned. He turned his attention to the flight announcement. He picked up the handset. "Welcome aboard," the captain announced cheerfully. "This is your pilot, Captain Ed Johnson, and I'd like to apologize for our delayed departure time. But I have some good news for you. It appears that the winds aloft are much in our favor and that should help us make up for some of the time we lost. I'll be back on the intercom in a little while to give you some more information and expected time of arrival in Alice Springs. Till then, please enjoy your flight and thanks for choosing Australian Outback Air where value *counts*." He then switched off the microphone.

Dan called over to the captain. "Don't you hate making that *'value count's* advertisement. It feels like we're salesman not pilots."

"I hear ya," said the captain. "But it pays the bills Dan. Come on let's do our final checks and get settled in for the flight."

Robert Campbell

As the plane climbed through 10,000 feet the flight crew made the final course adjustments for their flight path that would take them to Alice Springs heading directly over the Strzelecki Desert in southwest Queensland—an infamous and brutally harsh section of the Outback.

Though there was only a minor bit of turbulence during the climb, Captain Johnson decided that it was no longer necessary to require the passengers to stay buckled up. He reached to his panel and turned off the 'seat belts on' light. As he completed his announcement a hint of turbulence shook the plane. The nearly imperceptible bounce caused a microsecond flash of the 'cargo door warning' light—an instant later it returned to its normal 'door safe' mode leaving all instruments reading 'flight normal.' Though none of the flight crew perceived any abnormality, all was decidedly 'not normal' in the cargo hold. Unseen and unheard by the flight crew or passengers, a tiny hiss of high-pressure air burst out for a microsecond through the cargo door vent, before finally seating it in place. As it seated, it put tremendous pressure on the jammed and improperly secured cargo door mechanism. There was no inkling that the door was still not properly latched and locked. All cockpit flight instruments continued to display normal readings. The flight crew pressed on in anticipation of better weather and a smoother ride at higher altitudes.

CHAPTER 3

A muted 'bong!' caught Derek's attention. A moment later he noticed that the seat belt sign had winked off. The cabin air was stuffy after the long wait for the takeoff. Thinking that a cool splash of water on his face would feel refreshing, he made his way to the nearest lavatory.

Derek passed by Shawn's seat, noticing that he'd changed it again. This time he was in a window seat next to a middle-aged woman. Derek took her to be an American tourist. For some reason Shawn kept trying to get the woman to look out the window. His odd persistent gesturing outside the aircraft seemed to distress her. A moment later she got up and moved off to a different seat. Derek dismissed the incident and entered the lavatory.

Derek looked around the small compartment marveling at its compact yet efficient design. He always admired good design and sometimes wished he'd gone to engineering school instead of entering the field of education. Still, he smiled to himself as he reflected on something his high school guidance counselor had once said. '*Derek, I can't see you going on to college but with your strong mechanical aptitude and interest in working with your hands, I bet you could do all right as an auto mechanic—remember you need to strive to reach your full potential.'* He clearly remembered how hurt and offended he was by that remark. He badly wished he had the courage to say what he was thinking. *Well, if you were living up to your full potential you wouldn't be just a guidance counselor.* Chuckling aloud, he turned on the sink spigot, cupped his hands full of water, then splashed the cool refreshing liquid onto his face.

At just a whisker over six feet tall, Derek had to scrunch down to see his full face in the mirror. The harsh fluorescent light of the lavatory lamp made his normally well-tanned skin appear pale. Unconcerned and feeling greatly refreshed, he dried his face and hands. Another glance in the mirror revealed that his dark hair was unkempt as usual. A few passes of his comb made it presentable. Pleased with the result he carefully adjusted his tie and exited the lavatory.

Derek was almost back to his seat when the passenger intercom crackled to life. "Hello again, this is your pilot speaking. Hope that you are all settled in now for your flight. Our planned arrival time is now 10:30 P.M. It's presently 60 degrees with clear skies over Alice Springs, and a light southwesterly breeze. The temperature tomorrow morning is expected to be in the 80's with crystal clear skies. Should be just perfect for sight-seeing. Also, you're in for a really unusual sight when we reach the halfway point in our flight. There's a large band of thunderstorm activity in the area and that should produce some spectacular views in the night sky as we pass over. And don't worry, there is no need for concern, because we will be flying miles above the storm. It's unlikely that we will experience anything but mild turbulence. But to be on the safe side, please watch for the seatbelt sign, just in case we have to turn it on for a short time. Thank you and enjoy your flight." Derek was pleased with the pilot's weather report. But, just in case, when he reached his seat he buckled his seatbelt anyway. He was looking forward to seeing the lightning storm. He recalled startling images he'd once seen on the Learning Channel of lighting as seen from space. *Should be quite a show*, he thought. He looked out the window but saw nothing of the thunderstorms that were still to come.

Derek stirred in his seat. Far below the sky was rapidly darkening with the setting sun and there was nothing to see. With little else left to do, he reached into the seat pocket in front of him and pulled out a magazine. To his delight he pulled out a back issue of *Flying* magazine that some passenger had left behind. He looked wistfully at the Cessna 172 that graced its cover. Then, as he'd done hundreds of times in the past, he recalled his birthday 'orientation flight' and again about someday learning how to fly. *One day—one day,"* he promised himself, *"I'm really going to do it."*

While putting the magazine back into the seat pocket he noticed the standard plasticized Aircraft Safety Procedure card sticking up. He pulled it out and, to his surprise, the card identified the aircraft as a *Russian built TC10*. He was taken aback by its astounding resemblance to the virtually identical looking Douglas

DC-10—right down to its distinctive third engine mounted high on the tail. Derek had never heard of such an aircraft before. His thoughts returned to his earlier concern that choosing such a cheap airline ticket may have been riskier than he thought. *Had this airline cut costs by using old cheap Russian airplanes?* Not wanting to dwell on such unpleasant thoughts, Derek unceremoniously shoved the card back into the seat pocket. Dismissing the unpleasant experience, he looked out the window. Though the sun was down he was still surprised at the utter blackness below. He marveled that at such a high altitude, and only a few hundred miles out of Sydney, that he couldn't see any lights at all. Perhaps, it's just cloud cover he thought. Meanwhile the plane continued on its flight path crossing high above some of the most desolate and inhospitable territory on earth.

Derek's boredom suddenly vanished. He saw Michelle coming down the aisle heading his way. Looking for a pretense to talk he called out. "Excuse me Miss."

Michelle turned towards him and smiled. "Yes? Is there something I can get for you?"

"Ah, not really, but I was just wondering. When we spoke earlier you called me by my name. How did you know happen to know my name? You have a very intelligent look about you, but surely you didn't memorize the passenger list by seat number."

With a quick smirk, Michelle simply pointed to the nametag stuck to his suit jacket.

"Oh God, of course. I feel so ridiculous," Derek replied. He looked down at the name badge that clearly read *Dr. Derek Hunter*. Characteristically, he blushed. In his rush to catch the flight he'd neglected to remove the nametag that identified him as a symposium participant at the Sydney Conference Center.

"Oh, that's okay," said Michelle. "At least we know there's a doctor on board if we need one."

"Oh no, I'm not *that* kind of a doctor," Derek quickly added. "I'm not a *medical* doctor. I have a doctorate degree in Computer Science. But it's 'sort of' like medicine because my 'patients' are computers and they do get *viruses*." Michelle smiled at the silly remark. Derek continued, "I'm a Computer Science professor at a university in the states. And please, the name is *Derek*. I just got my Ph.D. and it's nice to be called *doctor* and all that, but I'd really be pleased if you'd just call me Derek."

"Okay, Derek it is, but if I do that, you'll have to call me Michelle," she said as she tapped the nametag pinned to her breast pocket that read *'Michelle.'*

"Deal," replied Derek as he happily followed the finger pointing towards her beautifully formed breast.

"Okay then, *Michelle.* I'm pleased to meet you." He extended his hand across the empty seat and took her hand. He found both strength and warmth in her smooth soft hand. Her handshake had a gentle yet sincere firmness to it.

"A pleasure," said Michelle.

"The pleasure's all mine," said Derek. He immediately felt a little foolish for using such an old cliché—yet he truly felt that way. He wanted to put the silly remark behind him. "Say, I think I missed out on drinks when they came around earlier. Is there any chance I can get a Coke?"

"I'd be happy to get that for you," she replied. "I'll be back shortly."

"Thanks," said Derek. His voice trailed off as Michelle flitted away. He hoped she would return soon. The brief encounter left him feeling as if a refreshing ocean breeze had just passed over his body. Michelle's beautiful blue eyes helped reinforce an idyllic image that was running through his mind. A short time later, Derek turned away from the window and reclined his seat. A big smile spread across his face. He even forgot about the stuffy cabin air—but his forgetfulness didn't last long. A moment later he heard the familiar clanking sound of an 'out-of-tune' tambourine. The clatter continued unabated as the elderly lady with the ton of jewelry on her arm waved wildly in the air. Michelle's friend and colleague, Debby, quickly appeared at her side asking if she could be of help.

"Indeed, you can dear," she huffed. "I spoke to a nice young man named Jerry ten minutes ago about the air being stuffy in here, but nothing seems to have been done about it. My doctor keeps telling me that my heart isn't good, and this stuffy air is not good for me. And drafts, I'm quite affected by drafts too," she added.

"I'll check with the flight crew," Debby replied. "I'll certainly tell them about your condition as well. He'll probably turn up the air conditioning."

"But not too much dear. I don't want to get a chill. I'm quite susceptible to chills at my age you know. Yes, quite susceptible indeed."

"I'll be sure to tell the captain that too. You just sit back and relax and I'll take care of everything," Debby smiled and left to answer a call from the galley.

As Debby entered the galley area she met Michelle coming out. "Michelle, the elderly lady with all the bracelets up in 19B is complaining about the air being stuffy. She says she spoke to Jerry about it ten minutes ago and, if I know Jerry, he certainly would have called it in. Anyway, she's right, it does seem like the air is stale and stuffy."

"Well the air does seem a bit unusual, doesn't it?" responded Michelle. "But it's only been ten minutes since Jerry reported it and that's not enough time for the cabin air to be fully recycled. Let's give it a little while longer and if things don't get better we can report it a second time, okay?"

"Sure," Debby replied. With that, Michelle moved out of the galley to deliver Derek his Coke. A minute later she reached his seat.

"Coke, just what the *doctor* ordered," quipped Michelle, with a smile. To his immense pleasure her silken hair brushed against the back of his hand as he reached for the drink. *Her hair flows as easily as the air itself,* thought Derek. He returned her friendly smile.

"Thanks, very much."

"You're most welcome." She lingered by his seat while she surveyed the cabin. It was clear that no passengers required any attention. She watched as Derek took a sip of the Coke.

"It's kind of quiet right now," she said. "Mind if I sit down here for a minute." She motioned to the empty aisle seat beside him.

Derek had to force himself to keep from spraying the drink as he enthusiastically sputtered, "Ph--please, please do!" He quickly recovered, while dabbing his chin with the napkin that had been provided with the drink.

"You're funny," laughed Michelle as she sat down. "Do I make you nervous?"

"No no. Not really." He regained his composure.

"Things seem to have settled down and I just wanted to get off my feet for a minute."

"Well it's my pleasure Michelle. And please don't go, I really like you being here—but won't you get into trouble for sitting down with the passengers?"

She turned to Derek and put on a mock-serious face. "Frankly Derek, I don't give a damn!" she quipped, in remarkably funny imitation of Clark Gable's classic line from *Gone With the Wind*. Derek laughed out loud.

"And you say *I'm* funny!" he laughed. "Really though won't you get into trouble?"

"No, I'll be leaving the company at the end of the month anyway. So, it wouldn't matter even if someone did complain."

"Oh, I'm sorry to hear that you're leaving. You're doing a great job and you seem to like it, except for Shawn, the scruffy guy back there, that is."

"I like it just fine. But I'm going to be working in a corporate finance office at the start of next month."

26

"That seems a world apart from this job. Why would you want to take a desk job like that—this job must be far more exciting."

"You're right, but my fiancé works for that same company in Sydney. He's an investment analyst and he thinks it would be a good idea for me to stay closer to the ground and nearer to home. We're getting married in a couple of months," she added. But, to Derek, her statement about her upcoming marriage seemed to be lacking in the enthusiasm one might expect from such a happy pronouncement.

"Oh," replied Derek. He hoped she didn't notice the intense disappointment in his voice upon hearing that she was engaged. The news dashed any hopes that he had about asking her out—a fantasy he'd entertained many times over the last hour.

Though crestfallen, Derek quickly recovered. Wanting the conversation and the pleasure of her company to continue, he prompted, "So you're getting married soon?"

"Well we haven't set an exact date yet, but it will be pretty soon. As soon as I get settled into my new job my fiancé, John, and I will make all the arrangements. He's got everything all planned out for us. He's what you Americans call a *'mover and shaker.'* He's gone now. He's off for two weeks, on one of his regular trips to New Zealand. He's going there to put together a big corporate merger."

"He's got everything all planned out all right," thought Derek. *"Everything but the wedding date! What a jerk he must be. If she were my fiancée I'd set a date—*

27

like right now! I'd have the captain of this aircraft marry us. Wonder if airline captains have the power to marry people on planes like ship captains do," he thought. A smile came to his face as he ran the fantasy through his mind.

"What's so funny?" asked Michelle.

"Oh nothing," replied Derek, quickly trying to change the subject.

"Opps, I've gotta go," said Michelle as she looked up the aisle. Debby was signaling to her. "Duty calls, I better see what's up. Thanks for the chance to chat." She left the seat with a gentle swish.

"Thank *you!*" said Derek. He instantly missed her company.

Michelle quickly learned from Debby that Shawn had been acting up again. He'd kept changing his seat ever since the seatbelt sign went out. And now he was annoying other passengers with his incessant chatter, whether they wanted to listen to him or not.

"He's been bothering a few people with some stupid story that there's somebody outside on the wing," said Debby. "Now, he's agitating about the stuffy cabin air. I tried to get him to quiet down and stop bothering the other passengers. He says he'll think about it, but only if *you* come up to see him. He says you're so beautiful he'll do anything you ask."

"Sure," Michelle replied. "Don't worry about it. I'll go up and take care of it."

"Oh, and Michelle, there have been other complaints about the stuffy cabin air. I think that maybe we should call it in now. What do you think?"

"Yeah, I think it's time to do that. It's only gotten worse. You go ahead and call it in and I'll take care of our friend up front." Michelle moved to the forward part of the cabin.

As Michelle approached Shawn's seat, she was greeted with a display of his theatrical antics. He had his hands clutched around his throat while he squirmed in his seat pretending to gasp for air. She nearly laughed out loud at his pathetic attempt at suffering but dared not—she knew that was what he wanted. Instead, retaining her professional composure, she asked, "Do you need something Mister.......?"

"Shawn—just Shawn," he replied with a silly smirk.

"Okay, Shaw, are you having some kind of problem up here?"

"Yeah, I'm dying, can't you see that? I'm suffocating. Can't you do something?" He smiled as he removed his hands from around his throat.

"Yes, Shawn. We've just notified the captain and the problem should be taken care of shortly. And, Shawn, I'd appreciate it if you would find a seat and remain in it for the rest of the flight. Your constant movements are causing a disturbance. And, some of the passengers are getting upset with your routine of someone being outside on the wing of the plane. I'm afraid this behavior will have to stop."

"Ah, you Aussies can't take a joke. It's funny. Don't you get it?" he said chuckling.

"Afraid not, Shawn," she replied stern faced. "You'll have to stop. And according to airline policy I'm supposed to make you sit in the seat you were assigned but I'll tell you what I'll do. Since the plane isn't very full, I'll let you stay here. And I'll bring you an ice-cold beer on the house if you promise to stay here and not act up anymore. Deal?"

"Deal—I'll do anything for *you!*" He flashed her a big grin and settled down.

Again, forcibly holding back a smile, Michelle replied, "Okay then, I'll be right back." She quickly turned and left. As she walked away she couldn't help but think that he was really an overactive 12-year-old wrapped up in an adult body.

Shawn turned his head and watched Michelle disappear down the aisle. Though he enjoyed the lovely sight and dearly wanted to keep his bargain with her, he couldn't quite force himself to fully comply. *"There...out there...on the wing....there's someone out there on the wing,"* he whispered. Chuckling to himself, he reclined his seat, settled down, and quietly relaxed.

Debby was about to pick up the cockpit intercom phone when Michelle entered the galley area. "Oh Michelle," she said. "I'm calling in the air quality problem right now. Can you cover for me for a few minutes?" Michelle willingly agreed.

Debby picked up the cockpit intercom telephone. It automatically activated the 'attendant call light' in the cockpit. Captain Billings answered.

"Captain, we've got a problem here in the cabin with the air," she declared. "Quite a number of passengers have been complaining that the air is hot and stuffy. We noticed it a little while ago and waited to report it to see if things improved but it actually seems worse now."

"Ok, thanks," he replied. "Jerry called it in earlier and our flight engineer is checking it out right now. We should be able to do something about it soon. And keep me informed if it continues to be a problem. Thanks Debby."

A few minutes after Debby completed her call to the captain, Michelle re-entered the galley. "All set Michelle," Debby reported. "Captain Johnson says that the flight engineer is working on the problem right now and that we should keep him informed if the problem gets worse. Oh, and how'd you make out with the nutty guy up there?"

"Pretty good. I made a deal with him. He gets a free beer if he quiets down for the next hour or so until we get to Alice Springs. Actually, I was amazed that he could be bought off so easily. And he seemed to settle right down. He's certainly a bit antsy but he seems pretty harmless—just wants some attention that's all. I think he'll be okay. God help me, but I think he likes me."

"Lucky you," said Debby.

"Well at least there are other passengers that more than make up for the odd ones like him," Michelle added.

"You mean like the nice young girl with the baby up front?" asked Debby.

"Yeah, isn't she a nice person to deal with," said Michelle. "And that gorgeous baby she has on her lap. Isn't she a doll? Oh, how I'd love to have a beautiful little girl like that for my own. She smiles and giggles at me every time I pass by—I love that! I warned her mother not to turn her back because I might scoop the little muffin up and put her in my flight bag and spirit her off to my house."

"Put a baby in a flight bag! Don't you know *anything* about taking care of babies?" Debby teased.

"Oh, go deliver some drinks," Michelle added in mock seriousness.

"Babies in a flight bag, babies in a flight bag," Debby happily chortled before heading off to answer a call.

Captain Johnson called to his flight engineer. "Jean, the flight crew is still reporting uncomfortable air quality in the cabin. They say it's getting worse. You having any luck with that yet?"

"I'm still working on it," she replied.

A quick scan of her instrument panel revealed unusually high cabin temperature readings in the rear section of the aircraft. "Captain, the temperature levels are still high in the aft cabin. I've tried regulating it downward but it doesn't seem to have any effect. Though the temperature still remains high, everything on my panels register as normal. I don't know what's causing the problem. I'll have to do some further checking."

"Okay Jean. Get back to me on that."

Returning to the procedures manuals she stopped at a passage relating to corrective steps to take when an overheat is sensed in any of the air conditioning packs. But even after conducting a series of systems checks and diagnostic routines she was no closer to solving the problem than when she first started. But just to be on the safe side she ran another complete diagnostic check on the system.

Fifteen minutes later Captain Johnson checked again with the flight engineer. "How's it going over there, Jean?" he called out.

"Captain, I suspect that we have one or more failing—or at least weak—air conditioning packs. But since I don't have any system faults showing up I think we'd be best off to just sit this one out for a while. Maybe the system will clear and reset itself. In any case, we've only got another 90 minutes of flight time left so it shouldn't be too much of a problem."

"Okay, Jean, thanks. But keep a watchful eye on things and keep me informed."

"Yes, sir" she replied just as the 'aft attendant call indicator' glowed once again.

Captain Johnson picked up the phone to hear Debbie's voice explaining that several more passengers had begun to complain about the stuffy cabin. "Okay, thanks, Debby," he replied. "I think I'll come back there myself and check it out. I could stand to stretch a bit anyway—I'll be down in minute." Before leaving the flight deck he called over his shoulder to his copilot. "Dan, I've been keeping an eye on that unusual band of thunderstorms that were predicted along our route. Keep monitoring it and if things start to get bumpy don't hesitate to put the 'Seatbelts On" warning notice."

Captain Johnson was a commanding sight as he entered the passenger cabin. His impeccable appearance was a matter of personal pride to him and it served him well in his career. He was tall and handsome and with his black hair that was graying at the temples he was the very image of an airline captain. He was well liked and respected by all those who flew with him. And now with this new start-up, economy fare airline, he was the most experienced captain in the company—and many said, the most professional, as well.

The captain immediately noticed the difference in the air quality from that of the cockpit which was controlled separately. Checking further, he moved to the rear of the plane, smiling and nodding to passengers. He stopped occasionally to ask passengers how they were enjoying their flight. Not surprisingly he heard a number of complaints about the stuffy cabin, but otherwise people were quite pleased with the flight. In answer to questions about the stuffy air, he simply told them that he'd do the best he could to remedy the situation as soon as possible. The captain worked his way to the food galley at the rear of the airplane where he met with the flight attendants who were not out on calls. He advised them of the current on-going repair attempts then returned to the flight deck.

"The air is certainly a bit of problem back there," said Captain Johnson as he re-entered the flight deck. He turned to his flight engineer and asked, "Jean, have you been able to come up with anything on the problem yet?"

"No Captain, but I just got 'overheat lights' in air conditioning packs 1 & 2 and a flickering reading on pack 3. I don't understand it. That's not supposed to happen—let me look at......ah, now there goes 3. Now we've got failure on all three packs."

Without waiting for a response from the captain Jean said, "I'll get right on this Captain." After rechecking several manuals, she reported, "Sir, it looks like the problem is that we've got abnormally high temperatures going into the air conditioning packs. When that happens the 'air cycle machines' automatically shut down the faulty pack's control valves. And that's already happened as indicated by the three fault lights that just came on," she added as she pointed to the three glowing lights on her panel.

"If the system cools down enough it's supposed to turn the individual pack's airflow back on again—and if that occurs we should be okay. But if it stays hot, the fuses blow and the ACMs shut the packs down for good. Then there's absolutely nothing we can do until ground maintenance can repair the system. So, if the fuses blow we'll be forced to use the ram-air distribution system." An instant later, as if the system heard her words, it spat out its nasty reply with a panel indication that the fuses have blown—all three. Sadly, Jean reported, "Sir, I can now confirm ACM shut down—air conditioning is completely out now."

"Okay, thanks Jean. Stand by."

Captain Johnson considered the situation. He was well aware that the failure of the air conditioning packs themselves was not a critical problem. If they simply did nothing the worst that would happen was that the airplane would stay uncomfortably hot until they landed. *Besides,* he thought, *at this point in the flight there are no alternative airports that could handle this big aircraft anyway. No, we'll just have to tough it out until we reach*

Alice Springs Airport. Just as he was about to announce his decision to continue the flight to Alice Springs Airport, the 'attendant call light' blinked on.

"Captain Johnson," he answered. It was Debbie again.

"Captain, I'm sorry to report but we have a real problem here. We have an elderly woman who has been complaining for some time about the stuffy air. She says she has a bad heart—among other ailments. Anyway, she's so upset now that she's on the verge of hyperventilating. I was able to quiet her down with a cool towel. But now the stuffy air seems to be getting worse and I don't know how much longer I'll be able to keep her quiet."

"You'd better check to see if we have a doctor on board."

"Yes, sir I've already done a discrete check, but there isn't any medical doctor on board. She's putting herself into a frenzy. We're afraid she may force herself into a real heart attack at this rate. We're really getting worried back here."

"Ok Debby, do what you can to make her comfortable and keep a close eye on her. If there's any change call me back immediately. Stand by, I'll get back to you in a few minutes." Captain Johnson knew he needed to update his flight crew on the situation.

Captain Johnson quickly assessed the situation. He knew he had to do something about the air quality—and fast. And that meant using the aircraft's ram-air induction system. Although it was intended for use only under emergency conditions and would quickly solve the problem, he hesitated to employ the unit. His decision was complicated by the fact that since it was designed to bring in ambient outside air, that meant it couldn't be used at their present cruising altitude of 28,000 feet. The outside air at 28,000 feet was so thin that it was unbreathable. That meant he needed to get the plane down to a lower altitude where the air was thicker and more breathable. Under normal conditions with clear weather below the aircraft that wouldn't have been a problem. But with a thunderstorm already boiling beneath the plane he was having a hard time justifying a move that would take the plane so dangerously close to the storm. It was a decision he didn't want to make unless there was a dire and compelling reason to do so.

Sighing heavily, the captain scrutinized the radar images displayed on his panel. The screen showed the area of the storm front that still lay ahead in the aircraft's path. He had been keeping a watchful eye on the storm as soon as they entered the area of thunderstorm activity. But now, he noted with satisfaction, that the end of the storm appeared to be in sight. The radar showed that they were rapidly approaching the outside edge of the thunderstorm. He stroked his strong square jaw as he evaluated his options. Things are looking up, he thought. He began forming a plan of action. '*Looks like if we start a gentle descent to 16,000 we'll just barely glance the outer edge of the storm and yet we'll still be well above it. At the worst we'll just experience a short period of some turbulence. Still, he thought, if we could just hold on just a little longer we won't have to..........*'

His line of thought was broken as the 'attendant call light' flashed. He took the call immediately.

"Captain. This is Debby." There was a clear sense of urgency in her voice. "Things are not going well with the elderly lady. We've got her quieted down but her color looks very bad. We're really concerned now. *Really* concerned!"

"Okay, Debby. We'll be taking care of that in less than one minute. We're going to make a decent to a lower altitude to pick up fresh outside air. I'll get back to you in a minute."

Debby's call had forced his hand. The decision had to be made. He would order a descent and activate the ram-air system as they neared 16,000 feet where the air was breathable. Given the medical situation on board and the relatively low risk involved in glancing over the outer edge of the storm, he felt confident that the decision was a good one. It was time now to get clearance to descend and alert the cockpit and cabin crew.

Captain Johnson turned to his right and called over his shoulder. "Jean, we're going to descend. Please look up your procedures to activate the ram-air distribution system and then stand by. I'll be back to you very shortly." Jean reached up to an overhead bookshelf and pulled down a heavy flight manual.

The captain turned his attention to his first officer. "Dan, I'm afraid we've got no other options here. We're going to have to begin a descent to 16,000 while Jean configures the ram-air distribution system. Hang in there while I get clearance to descend."

"Okay, Captain." He let out a heavy sigh. "Well, there goes any hope of making up for lost time with those tail winds. We'll have to drop our airspeed in the thicker atmosphere in order to activate the ram-air system."

"That's right Dan. But at least the procedure will cure the hot, stuffy cabin-air problem. The old girl's condition should improve quickly. We, for sure, don't want a heart attack situation with no doctor on board." Dan nodded in agreement.

The captain calmly put on his headset and keyed the radio button to raise Alice Springs Airport where their flight was being monitored. After establishing contact, he reported, "Australian Outback Air flight 604. We're at flight level 28,000 and we have an Air Cycle Machine failure and a passenger who is at risk to our poor air quality. Request clearance to 16,000 feet so we can activate our ram-air system."

The center control responded immediately. *"Center Control Flight 604. Descend and maintain 16,000 to flight termination at Alice Springs Airport."*

Captain Johnson repeated his instructions back to center control. He turned to his first officer. "Okay Dan, we're cleared for the descent to 16,000. Let's start to take her down." Dan immediately began the descent.

A few minutes into the descent, Captain Johnson picked up the flight attendant call handset. Debbie answered.

"Debbie," explained the captain, "we're descending now to a lower altitude to activate the back-up air distribution system. You should see a dramatic improvement in the cabin very shortly as soon as we pick

39

up fresh outside air. I haven't announced our descent because I don't want to alarm the passengers, especially the elderly lady. In any case, it's pitch black outside and nobody is likely to notice anyway. I expect that we'll hit some turbulence at the lower altitudes as we skirt the outer edges of the thunderstorm so it would be a good idea to check to see that everyone buckles up when I put the seat belt signs on. I'll be doing that shortly." After Debby acknowledged the instructions, the captain hung up his handset.

As the plane continued its gradual descent, Captain Johnson kept a careful watch on the altimeter until it finally read 18,000 feet—it was time to start the activation process.

Okay, Jean," called the captain, "we're coming up on 18,000 feet. You can begin your ram-air procedures now. When we reach 16,000 feet I want the system to come on line. Can you do that?"

"Yes sir," she replied. A moment later she unfastened her seat belt and shoulder harness and moved behind Captain Johnson's seat to where the ram-air's floor-mounted access panel was located. As they passed through 16,000 feet she activated the system. The unit was now in automatic operation. Fresh outside air was already flowing into the cabin.

"System is activated Captain," Jean called out as she returned to her station. After making some control adjustments on the flight engineer's panel she rechecked the cabin pressurization and airflow readings—they were within the specified range. "Captain, I'm letting the fresh air in to balance at 1 atmosphere of 14.7 psi. exactly as the manual indicates."

"Good work. Thanks Jean."

The captain turned to Dan. "Looking good. If we keep the descent slow and gentle and we should clear the outer edges of the storm nicely."

"Yes sir," he replied. He checked his vertical speed indicator to ensure a slow steady descent.

Hoping to spot some lightning flashes below, Derek glanced out the darkened window. Up until now he wondered why he bothered to look outside at all—there had been nothing to see. Then suddenly, as if the storm read his thoughts, Derek watched a series of lightning flashes below the aircraft. As he continued gazing out the window he had the odd and disconcerting sensation that the plane was descending.

While Derek sat reclined in his seat, he pondered the possibility of asking Michelle to join him for a cup of coffee or a drink at the airport before she headed out on her next trip. He started to formulate a plan about how he might make it happen. *Maybe she's staying overnight in Alice Springs*, he fantasized. *I could ask her to be my guest and have her show me around the town. We could hit a few nightspots and have a great time.* A smile spread across his face. *That's what I'm going to do. I'm going to ask her to show me around town.*

Though Derek knew Michelle was engaged and that he shouldn't be asking her out he thought of the cultural aspects of making such a request. *After all*, he rationalized, *I'm a stranger in a strange land and I'm*

41

just asking a native to point out some places of cultural interest in their homeland. He smiled as he played the silly fantasy over in his mind.

Several minutes later, much to his delight, Derek spotted Michelle coming down the aisle. "Hi ya, how's it going?" he asked as she approached his seat.

"Not bad." She stopped at his seat to chat. "But I did have a little issue again with your friend, Shawn."

Wanting to keep the conversation going Derek asked, "What was his problem this time."

"Oh, he was acting like a baby. And he apparently had been bothering people with some dumb routine about someone being out on the wing, or something like that."

"You're kidding," Derek laughed. "Well I guess we've got a real *William Shatner fan* on board," he chuckled.

"What do you mean?"

"You remember that bit Shawn did earlier about *'Scottie I need more power?'* Well that's a classic line from an old science fiction series called *Star Trek*. It was popular in the United States during the 60's. William Shatner played the captain of the Starship Enterprise and he often used that line when the ship was in trouble. Shatner got his start in television on another classic TV show called *The Twilight Zone*. In one of the shows he played an airline passenger who was convinced that he was seeing a man out on the wing of the airplane in mid-flight. Shawn was just pulling that gag from *The Twilight Zone*. It's funny in a way, but if you don't know the background behind it, then it doesn't make sense. And, for someone who didn't get the joke, it sure must have made Shawn look like a really crazy person."

"You've got that right," said Michelle. "Thanks for the explanation. But he wasn't really that hard to deal with. I gave him a cold beer and he's been quiet ever since. He's just like a kid who can't get enough attention."

Michelle saw that Derek's Coke was empty. She asked if he wanted a refill.

"No thanks," replied Derek. He was afraid that she'd leave if he said 'yes.' "Oh, by the way are we descending by any chance? I had the odd sensation that we were descending a few minutes ago."

"Aren't we the perceptive one?" she said with a smile. "Yes, the captain notified us a short time ago that we're going down to a lower altitude to pick up fresh outside air. The air quality problem should be cleared up in a few more minutes."

Derek was becoming increasingly concerned about the apparently worsening storm below. "I've been looking out the window occasionally and now I can see a lot of lightning flashes from the storm. The Captain said we'd be seeing some activity along the route. But it seems to be getting worse now. Think that storm will cause us any problems as we descend towards it?"

Oh, I doubt it. We'll still be way above it—at least I hope so! There shouldn't be any problems. It'll still be a nice smooth flight." Still standing in the aisle beside Derek's bank of seats she hesitated a moment then asked, "Sure I can't refill your Coke before I go?" Before Derek could answer, the captain turned on the Seat Belt

Warning sign that was immediately followed by an announcement. It began, *"All passengers and crew are to immediately return to their seats and snugly buckle their seat belts."* Derek couldn't help himself. "Oh, *Miss Nice Smooth Flight,* what exactly does *that* mean?" He smirked as he pointed to the lighted sign above his head, that read, 'Seat Belts On.'

"That," she responded with a *gotcha* smile, "means, no more Coke for you, *Mister Afraid of Storms!* A second later a jolt of turbulence suddenly knocked Michelle off balance. With a yelp of surprise, she willingly tumbled into the seat beside him. Then added, "Now that's a bonus for you. After *that* slam I'm going to buckle up right here, right now. I've got to obey that sign too," she smiled as she snapped and tightened her belt. Derek immediately checked his own belt. An instant later the aircraft shuddered from another jolt. This time the sudden shock caused a disturbance directly below their seats. *Once again, unseen and unheard by Derek, the crew, or the passengers, the cargo door directly under Derek and Michelle's seat gave another microburst of high-pressure release. At 16,000 feet the improperly latched mechanism, strained to the brink, a catastrophic failure was imminent! Then....*

BLAM!!! An enormous blast roared through the cabin as the cargo door locking mechanism disintegrated! *The explosive decompression blasted off the cargo door and ripped a huge ragged hole in the floor beneath the bank of seats that held Derek and Michelle in place.*

"Gahhhhhh...." was all that came out of Derek's lungs as he and Michelle were violently sucked down through the ragged floor opening out into the gaping hole that was once covered by the huge cargo door. Derek instantaneously lost all sense of comprehension and reality as their bodies tore through the opening. Mercifully, Michelle was knocked unconscious as her head took a glancing blow from cargo debris.

CHAPTER 4

Explosively ejected from the aircraft, neither Derek nor Michelle felt the incredibly frigid and solid force of the slipstream of air that hit the bottom of their seats. The force hit them like a brick wall moving at over 300 miles per hour. Momentarily knocked unconscious, Derek awakened in a state of total disorientation that prevented him from thinking or reacting. In a state of detached awareness, he lost all sense of feeling.

In his nightmare dream state, Derek couldn't see what was revealed below by sudden lightning bolts as the storm moved rapidly across the desert plain that lay in its path. The occasional blazing bolts lit the broad plain below unveiling momentary glimpses of its stark beauty. The light revealed a desert plain below but it was unlike that of the Sahara with its endless oceans of sand. Instead, the luminescence flashes unveiled vast rolling stretches of green, red, brown, and gold colored terrain all tinted an eerie electric-blue by the hysterical lightning bolts. In total chaos, their bodies continued spinning and tumbling through a long and terrifying downward spiral.

They raced downward through the black void towards the waiting earth nearly three miles below.

With a sudden gasp, Derek momentarily 'came to' dizzily trying to form thoughts that might make sense. *"What's happening, what's happening???!!"* In touch with reality for barely a moment, he was wildly disoriented. His brain raced with confusion. Creepy, and crazy thoughts flew through his mind which refused to comprehend what was going on around him. Drenched by a deluge of rain, he continued spiraling downward through the heart of the thunderstorm. Forcefully pinned to his swirling seat, he gasped for air. In his distorted thoughts he felt certain that he had somehow fallen off a boat and was drowning in the darkest depths of a violent ocean.

A disembodied Derek looked down from above and watched in detached horror as he saw himself and Michelle falling and falling deeper into the black sky. Yet then, in a sudden weirdness, he felt warm and comfortable and was at complete peace with himself. He watched as they spiraled and pirouetted through the sky below and marveled at the beauty of their gentle dance that was spotlighted by occasional electric-blue flashes of light. In total contentment he watched Michelle's beautiful blond hair streaming upwards as if a million tiny angels were gently pulling on each strand as they tried to reverse her fall and bring her up into Heaven.

An instant later peace and contentment were ripped from his mind and replaced by red-hot pokers of pain and confusion. *Michelle, Michelle!! Where is Michelle!!* He screamed without sound. *Michelle? Michelle?* he cried out through a fog-clouded mind. For an instant he remembered that she was with him, that she was sitting beside him. *Michelle! I must reach her, must touch her, must save her*, he thought, as he tortured himself with the impossible. With superhuman strength he tried to will his arm to move, to reach out, to touch Michelle, to bring closure to his thoughts and to his life. Instead, he was tormented further by his inability to move any part of his body or to comprehend the utter chaos that assassinated his senses. The tremendous forces of the fall held him paralyzed in his seat unable to move and unable to see Michelle or the incredibly steep slopes of a mesa that was racing up to meet them.

To ease his suffering at this moment of despair, a merciful and gentle God reached out and touched Derek. He released him from his torture and bestowed upon him the same peaceful unconsciousness that He had earlier given to Michelle. Now the pair could continue their journey together to meet their destiny which lay so far below.

Through a wall of darkness, the storm intensified. Suddenly its ground-level horizontal winds gusted furiously across the huge barren plain. It seemed impossible that anything could stand against the terrible forces of this storm. But now a mesa, some 150-feet-high, stood solid and unmovable in its path. With nowhere else to go, the powerful hurricane winds blasted against the unyielding slopes of the mesa creating inconceivably powerful updrafts which roared upward into the face of the mesa. The vegetation strained against the immense forces of air being driven up at them.

The mesa's slopes were densely covered with small trees and low scruffy shrubs that were anchored in soil. But the roots were rapidly losing their holding power as the storm continued inflicting harm upon the mesa. It continued to pound its surfaces with even more rain, high winds and huge updrafts as it moved rapidly across the plain until it engulfed the mesa.

A brilliant lightning flash brought into momentary view an amazing sight that lay directly at the base of the mesa. The anomaly revealed by the flash took the form of a miniature marsh pool that was filled with murky water and tall green reeds. Invisible to a distant observer were the dozens of tiny bush crawfish crawling around the narrow muddy shore. The little creatures welcomed the rare and desperately needed downpour that kept them and their micro marsh alive. The crayfish, happy in their pool, cared nothing about the erosion that was beginning to take place on the slopes of the mesa that rose directly above them. And higher up, back inside the storm, violent updrafts continued roaring upward, all the while decreasing the speed of the bank of seats that was hurtling toward the base of the mesa.

Suddenly a bolt of lightning froze in time a preposterous, inconceivable sight—two humans strapped into a gang of six airline seats attached to a ragged section of flooring was racing downward towards destruction.

The storm seemed to react as if it were a sentient being, almost as if it were seeking vengeance against intruders that dared enter its domain. Gathering all the force it could summon up, the storm erupted with a gigantic blast of updraft air as if to vent its anger and to send the intruders back up into the sky and out of its private domain. The *tornado-like* force of the gigantic updraft was a miracle for Derek and Michelle. As it struck their seats it not only dramatically decreased their descent speed but it rotated the gang of seats into a rearward position.

Neither the most brilliant NASA engineer nor Oscar winning Hollywood stunt coordinator could have perfected a more outlandishly effective survivable impact. In the last split second of their fall their seat bank made one final rotation. At the last instant before impact, the empty row of seats behind Michelle and Derek rotated just enough to strike the steeply sloping face of the mesa first. The crumpling action of the unoccupied seats behind them acted like a gigantic shock absorber, instantaneously cushioning the violent blow onto the mesa's slippery slope. The tremendous rearward hit slammed Derek and Michelle into their seatbacks like astronauts, but with a powerful *deceleration* force instead.

The gang of seats careened backwards down the side of the mesa's slippery mucky slope as if it were part of some horror movie amusement park ride. They tore down the slope through small trees and low vegetation as the crumpling bank of seats continued to shock absorb their rapid deceleration. As they neared the end of the wild ride their speed diminished more rapidly as their seat bank encountered heavy patches of dense underbrush. The brush's water-logged roots easily gave way helping to absorb much of their remaining speed. In the final seconds of the fall their seat bank slowly rolled over coming to rest upright where they tottered precariously at the edge of the marsh pool's murky water at the base of the mesa.

Unconscious and bleeding, Derek and Michelle lay slumped in the twisted remains of their seats like two broken rag dolls. But their fall was not yet complete. One last gust of wind hit the back of their bank seats and forced the delicately balanced seats to fall forward. Derek and Michelle's bodies plunged face first into the slimy water.

"Garrragh," roared Derek as his face hit the water. Gasping and choking he instantly came awake! He was horrified to see Michelle, beside him, face down in the water! Without thought, his body fought to prevent drowning. A rush of adrenalin provided a surge of energy and focus. After a second, that seemed like a lifetime, he found and released his seatbelt and drunkenly stood against the mangled seat bank. In an adrenalin enhanced state, Derek found a foothold in the muddy pool at his feet and called upon every fiber of muscle strength in his entire body. With super human strength, he forced their seat unit up and back enough to raise Michelle's body out of the muddy pool of water. An instant later, with a final mighty shove, he forced their crumpled seat upright out of the water. The wrecked seats teetered for a moment at a crazy angle until Derek finally anchoring them safely into the muck.

Michelle remained slumped and unconsciousness in her seat.

Derek was spent. He collapsed back into his seat. Eyes closed, dazed and disoriented, he muttered confused phrases as he tried to come to grips with the chaos surrounding him. "What's happened!" he cried out. *"Where's the plane? Where am I? Can't be right, I'm outside. No, no, there is no plane. What's happening! What's happening!...I'm...Ahh!......"* His ravings were cut off as he slipped back into unconsciousness.

The night wore on. Derek continued to slip in and out of consciousness. But slowly his confused and clouded mind began to clear. He remembered Michelle. *"She was with me. Yes, I was with Michelle,"* he mumbled though not yet fully conscious. *"But where is she now?"* Just as his mind started to come alert, a great tiredness swept through his entire body and he fell back into a deep stress-induced sleep.

Hours passed before Derek once again returned to consciousness. His eyes slowly began to open but, his senses were assaulted by incongruous data that his mind couldn't process. There was darkness, the water, dizziness, confusion and Michelle. Derek was starting to regain consciousness. Half-awake he called out, "Michelle! Michelle!" His head bobbed as he tried to focus his mind and eyes on the limp form beside him. It took a moment or two before he was able to comprehend that it was Michelle in the seat next to him. In spite of his pain, grogginess, and confusion, he forced himself out of his and struggled towards her. For an instant, he was struck by terror. He thought she might be dead. He reached out and touched her face. An indescribable wave of relief swept over him when he heard a soft moan—she was alive!

"Thank God, Thank God." Derek repeated over and over. He frantically released her seat belt and gently removed her from the wrecked seat. Nearly spent from his efforts, Derek willed himself to drag Michelle the few yards out of the water and darkness up onto the narrow shore of the marsh. With all the gentleness his body had left to give, Derek lowered the unconscious Michelle onto the soft damp beach, stumbled a few steps, and collapsed nearby as he softly called out her name. At that moment his body once again took him back into the peace and tranquility of unconsciousness. Then, as if reacting to the end of the chaos, the shoreline of the pond screamed with quiet---dead quiet. Finally, its power exhausted, the storm lost its ability to sustain itself. A short time later it disappeared into nothingness.

CHAPTER 5

A loud BLAM roared through the airplane! The entire plane lurched violently as if a gigantic sledgehammer had just slammed into the plane. "What the hell was that?!!!," yelled Captain Johnson. First Officer, Dan Billings, had barely opened his mouth to form the first syllable of a word when the cockpit door was violently ripped open and nearly torn off its hinges. It hung at a crazy angle, held by a single distorted hinge. The instant the door exploded outward a gigantic cyclone tore through the cockpit sucking out decades worth of accumulated dust, dirt, maps, charts, and every manner of indescribable debris. The sound was as deafening as if a jet engine had torn off the plane and was roaring through the cockpit itself. Second Officer, Jean Sears's, headset was ripped from her head and sent ricocheting around the cockpit where it struck Dan full in the face, gashing his forehead and nearly knocking him out.

Captain Johnson's years of training and experience kicked into overdrive. His eyes darted over to Dan who'd been flying the plane when the blast struck. He saw that Dan had streaks of blood oozing between his fingers as he attempted to stop the bleeding from a deep cut over his eye. Dan caught the captain's glance. Although still injured, Dan remained in control. He yelled out over the chaos in cockpit, "I'm okay Captain!! I've got a cut over my eye! I can still see, but I need you to take over for me while I see if I can stop the bleeding." Captain Johnson reacted immediately and took over.

The pilot's first rule of survival flashed through Captain Johnson's mind. *Fly the plane! Fly the plane! That's what was always drummed into a pilot's head during training. That's the first thing to do whenever there is an emergency—fly the airplane!* His heart thumped heavily. *Okay, I've got her—still got control—sluggish though—but we're still flying! God! Now the memory list.*

Thoughts raced through his head as he recalled the emergency procedure memory list that all captains were required to recite orally, without error, every six months in order to retain their Captain's Rating. The long complex list was an enormous task to commit to memory under the best of circumstances. But now, caught up in the chaos of an unknown emergency, remembering it all correctly would be the challenge of a lifetime. He knew his life and the lives of all on board depended upon his performance--he was up to the task. He ran flawlessly through the list performing all the visual and manual checks rapidly and accurately in spite of the chaos in the cockpit.

"List done," the Captain said to himself. His mind furiously searched for answers. He knew from the first second of the event that there had been an explosive decompression. *But what had caused it?! And where*

did it occur?! How bad was the damage?! Was it a bomb?! His eyes flew over the instruments amid the terrific roar and chaos. He could hear alarms and warning sounds blaring all around the cockpit. He had the plane under control—just barely. But he needed answers, and he needed them *right now!*

"Jean," he yelled above the din. "What the hell's going on!? What's happened here!? What've you got that you can confirm on your panel?!"

Jean screamed back. "We've got a bunch of stuff going off all at once! I'm sorting it out now! But, for sure, we've got decompression! Her eyes flashed to the flight recorder panel and picked up two glaring amber warning lights. "I think we've blown the rear baggage door—I've got both warning lights on the panel for the aft cargo door." He fired another glance at Jean.

He had no worries there. He watched for a moment as her eyes and fingers darted furiously around her panels checking and resetting switches and dials in a blur of activity. *Great job,* he thought with pride as his eyes went back to his own panel. *I've seen male second officers fall apart under lesser circumstances. She's all right!*

Barely a moment had passed before Jean called back, "Captain, I can confirm an explosive decompression. The aft cargo door must have separated from the aircraft. I'd say it just exploded open and blew right off the plane. No fire control lights, so it probably wasn't a bomb. No matter what caused it, there's a breach in the fuselage and it must be a big one. Cabin pressure is falling at a terrific rate!"

Cabin pressure! The words raced through his mind. Cabin pressure was their lifeline in the rarefied air miles above the surface of the earth! Losing cabin pressure at such high cruising altitudes meant that without oxygen masks passengers would be forced to breath the thin outside air that lacked enough oxygen to survive. Passengers and crew would become unconscious in less than a minute and would quickly die of oxygen deprivation. That was why aircraft had pressurized cabins—to keep the air thicker and more breathable like the air one might breath at low elevations near the surface. The only problem with pressurizing the cabins is that the only thing holding the pressure inside the airplane is the thin aluminum shell of the aircraft. And when that shell is breached, the high pressure inside the aircraft explodes violently outward through the breach. The explosive force has all the furry and destruction of a tornado—viciously sucking everything out of the aircraft that isn't tied down. *"And sometimes big stuff that is tied down as well,"* he thought with a shudder. He prayed that the destruction caused by the explosive decompression wasn't enough to bring his aircraft down.

"Decompression confirmed," repeated the Captain. "Deploy the oxygen masks NOW!" he shouted through the cockpit din. "We've got to get to a lower altitude-- and *fast*. Get ready for a push over," he yelled. With that, the captain immediately pushed the control wheel forward to steepen the aircraft's rate of descent. Simultaneously, he pulled the throttles backwards to keep the plane from going into a supersonic dive that might tear the aircraft to pieces if he didn't cut its speed.

The maneuver caused a momentary sensation of weightlessness that he knew would terrify the passengers as the plane began its rapid descent. But there was no choice. He had to get to a lower altitude right *now!*

"Thank God," said the captain as he watched the altimeter spiral down. He called out to his crew, "We were at 16,000 feet at the time of the rupture and the oxygen masks deployed. The air in the cabin will still be thin for a minute or so but at least it will be breathable." He watched the altimeter continue its downward spiral. "How you doing now Dan?" asked the captain through the din of the cockpit noise.

"Shaken, but not stirred," he replied as he continued putting pressure on the cut over his eye. "This will stop bleeding in a minute. I'll survive." Captain Johnson gave him a thumbs-up. He was proud of his crew.

Though they were only into the disaster barely a few minutes, to the crew it seemed to have been a lifetime. But now the din of the decompression was finally starting to abate. Still, Captain Johnson could tell from the distressing sounds coming through the open cockpit doorway that the passengers were terrified. A moment later he was relieved to see that the altimeter read 9800 feet. He began leveling out procedures and adjusted the airspeed to 300 knots to maintain control of the aircraft and to reduce the possibilities of further damage to the plane.

A moment later he glanced over at Dan. He was immensely relieved to see that he was coming around to full awareness. He turned to check on Jean. She was still working furiously about her panels and reference manuals. Though he badly wanted to leave her alone, it was apparent that he needed more information on the state of the aircraft than could be determined from the engineer's panels. He needed someone to do a physical check on the aircraft and he couldn't send Dan—he needed him badly. It would have to be Jean. He turned to her, and as he was about to speak, Jean called out. "Captain, I can get a better picture of what's going on and how badly we're damaged if you can release me to do a physical check of the plane."

"Okay, but be careful back there!" yelled the captain. "I can't have you getting hurt."

"Yes sir!" Jean replied. An instant later she hurriedly flung her seatbelt harness aside, rose from her seat, and headed towards the tangled cockpit doorway. She nearly cut her hand on a sharp piece of jagged aluminum that was jammed into the doorframe.

Jean looked on in awe. The immediate results of the explosive decompression were clearly evident. The decompression had hit the passenger cabin hard with a sound and fury that defied description. Some passengers had frozen in their seats, unable to comprehend the horrific chaos erupting around them, while others were still flailing their arms wildly fending off the dirt and flying debris of all sorts that blasted about them from everywhere. Overhead compartment doors and loose luggage had combined with ceiling and wall panels to create a hell storm of danger. All that had torn loose had been hurled, like missiles, towards the gaping hole in the cabin floor at the back of the plane. All tenaciously gripped their seats in intense fear, terrified that they might be sucked out of the aircraft.

Even the flight attendants who had been trained in decompression emergencies were dumbstruck by the violence of the event. Yet, while the horrific sound and fury overwhelmed and overloaded everyone's senses, it was Shawn who was instantly galvanized into action. Almost as if a switch had suddenly been flipped on in his head he came to full alert status.

He acted the part of an Army Ranger whose company commander had suddenly been killed right in front of him in a surprise enemy attack. As if in combat, he took command and leaped instinctively into action. While others remained immobile in terror, he was already out of his seat to assist the injured. In an adrenaline-induced state, Shawn looked up and took in, with great clarity, the situation and what needed to be done. He immediately started aiding the injured.

For the passengers and cabin crew the seconds passed like years. Finally, the vortex of horror slowly began to abate. But as the jet engine-like roar diminished, new sounds of horror began filling the stricken cabin. Passengers were now becoming aware of the situation and their injuries. Some were screaming in terror while others screamed in pain from wounds inflicted by flying debris.

Flight attendant, Debby, also came to immediate alert. Quickly surveying that there was a breach in the rear of the cabin she shouted above the din that passengers were to move to the front of the aircraft away from the gaping hole. Shawn looked up as he was attending to a passenger's injury. He understood the cabin crew's needs. He knew they couldn't tend to the injured and move the passengers to safety at the same time.

Shawn turned to Debby and shouted with forceful assurance, "I can help! I've been fully trained in emergency medical care by the military. I can help these people!" he added. His eyes flashed with concern as he scanned the passenger cabin. He noted at least a dozen more people in need of help. "And it sure looks like you could use some help right now."

"You're on," she yelled. "Go to the front of cabin and start working your way down to the rear! Tell the other flight attendants you're working with me! I'm going to get some help to move passengers forward away from the breach," she yelled above the noise. *"Now Go!"*

She didn't have to repeat the order, Shawn was already headed at a dead run towards the front of the cabin grabbing up scattered cloth dinner napkins for bandages in mid-stride.

Shawn's ears exploded with the sounds of screams and moans as he sprinted forward down the aisle towards a man lying crumpled on the floor just outside the cockpit doorway. "I'll get them out! I'll get them *all* out this time!" he yelled. "This time I'm going to save them *all.*"

Second Officer, Jean Sears, forced herself to remain calm as she tried to assess the carnage in the passenger cabin. She'd only gone a few feet into the cabin when she came upon an unconscious male passenger sprawled in the aisle. A large chunk of ceiling panel lay beneath his head. She held onto the arm of a seat as she bent down to check on the injured man. An instant later she was nearly knocked off her feet as Shawn lurched to a halt directly in front of her.

"I'll take over here ma'am'!" Shawn shouted. "I've been trained in emergency first aid by the Army!" He immediately bent down and checked the man's pulse. He was alive. "I'm working with the cabin crew," he added as he applied a napkin compress to the man's head wound. "I'll take care of this man."

Jean was astonished by the cool professional manner of the scruffy young man, who despite his own injury, was in complete control. *Appearance aside, s*he thought, *he has the sound and manner of an emergency room staff doctor—all that's missing is a white coat and a stethoscope.* She watched, momentarily fascinated, as Shawn went about caring for the man as if he were a battlefield medic under fire. She was astounded when a moment later the man moaned and regained consciousness. It was clear to Jean that the young man was highly skilled in emergency first aid and was clearly up to the task of caring for the badly injured passages. She decided to leave the man to do the job he apparently knew well.

Jean moved to the rear of the passenger cabin where she was certain the decompression had originated. As she continued down the aisle she feared that she might find that the elderly lady who had been at risk of a heart attack might not have survived. Her fears were well founded as she spotted the 'lady with the bangles' on her arm. As she approached her seat she could see even from a distance that she was dead. Still, when she reached her seat she instinctively reached down to check for a pulse—there was none. She got up to continue her inspection when she saw a male flight attendant rushing up the aisle with a portable oxygen bottle, obviously intended for the elderly lady. She put up her hands and stopped him.

"It's no use. She's dead," she said above the rushing sound of air that still filled the cabin. "I want you to go up to the front of the cabin instead and help out the bearded man who's working on the injured up there!" He complied immediately.

As she moved towards the rear of the cabin she stood at the brink of a huge ragged hole that had been savagely ripped out of the cabin floor. While holding tenaciously onto a bank of seats far enough away from the hole for safety, she played her flight engineer's flashlight over the devastation below.

Jean shuddered as she surveyed the enormous amount of damage. The floor was buckled and warped and a huge gaping hole lay in the floor where several banks of seats once stood. They had been ripped right through the floor and out of the aircraft through the gaping hole that had once been the baggage compartment door opening. Cables and wires were exposed and hydraulic fluid was spraying from somewhere in the void below. *It's a miracle we're still in the air*, she thought as she played the light over the damage. She nearly lost her balance as the plane suddenly lurched. *No time to waste here. Nothing can be done. To her engineer's mind, the plane was doomed.* It was only a matter of time now, minutes or an hour it wouldn't matter. Jean returned to the flight deck to give her report. It would be a dismal one.

God, I hope Jean gets back fast, thought Captain Johnson. His mind was racing as he continued his struggle to keep the stricken airliner flying. *I need three more sets of hands to fly this thing and make radio contact. Can't do it all now. Jean will have to work the radios now. Ah, damn--these rudder pedals are stiff and heavy and the controls are murder.* He searched his mind for answers as to what was wrong. Decompression, of course, he knew that. But why were the controls so hard to move. And why had the rudder pedals shuddered so violently the instant the decompression blast hit the plane. Maintaining control of the airplane was getting more difficult by the minute. He desperately hoped that Jean might have some answers that would help them deal with the situation. *Where is she?!* Just as he reached down to pick up the handset in an attempt to contact her, she came through to the cockpit door.

"Ah! Jean. Give me a quick status report then get on the radio, *whh—what the hell.............?!*" He stopped in mid-sentence as he felt the controls stick solid.

"Dan get on the controls with me fast!" he commanded. "I need help here! The controls are stuck!"

Dan's hands blurred with speed as they flew to the controls. An instant later under the strong force of both men, the controls came free but the aircraft was just barely under control.

"Damn," Dan blurted out. "This is scaring the ever-loving hell out of me. What the hell is going on with the controls."

"I don't know Dan. Maybe Jean can help." The captain turned to his second officer. She had just finished strapping herself back into her station. "Jean, I need that report now! What did you see back there? Can we keep this bird flying or not?"

Jean responded immediately. "The cabin floor above the aft cargo hold door is badly buckled and there's a big gaping hole where a couple of banks of seats got torn out of the aircraft. As I suspected, the cargo door separated from the aircraft. The cabin floor couldn't take the enormous instantaneous pressure differences when the door blew off. The floor structure collapsed and was sucked out of the aircraft along with the two banks of passenger seats. It's bad. Really bad. There are exposed control cables and wires in the damaged area. And hydraulic fluid is spraying around. A catastrophic fire or failure could occur at any moment." Her voice was heavy with emotion as she described the seriousness of the damage and the loss of the elderly lady due to a heart attack. "And I hope to God nobody was sitting in those seats that got torn out," she added heavily.

"Okay, Jean—thanks. Now get on the radio and raise Alice Springs........."

"*Damn,*" he thought, as he waited for Jean to complete radio contact. "*A ragged hole, collapsed floor, missing cargo hold door, and severed hydraulics lines—*

lines that provide the power to the flight control systems to keep us flying." Captain Johnson barely had a second to process that information when a blaring alarm went off on his panel. The panel alarm now got his full attention. It was the 'hydraulics failure' warning. The alarm indicated that the fluid levels for controlling the aircraft were dropping fast. Their situation was now bad—very bad!"

The Captain continued trying to process the enormous quantity of information that was thrust at him. He was aware that decompression alone, even one severe enough to cause a major breach in the fuselage, generally wasn't enough to bring down a big airliner--*unless, the decompression caused damage to the hydraulic flight control systems!* And he knew from the flight manuals that the plane he was flying did have vital fluid control systems that ran under the floor. Those systems activated the flight control surfaces which gave them their ability to fly the airplane, and he knew there was damage—severe damage. That was clearly evident by the extraordinary forces it took on the control wheel to maintain what little control he now had over the aircraft.

For several long minutes Jean worked the radios. "Not doing very well here, Captain," she reported. "I don't know if they can hear me or not. They '*may*' be getting at least part of what I'm saying. But I can't understand anything of what they're saying back to me. It's just garble and static. Far as I can tell all they know is that we are having radio communications problems, nothing more. I tried all the radios and used different frequencies but it doesn't help. How the hell can that be?! That's not supposed to happen!"

"Planes aren't supposed to explosively decompress either," responded the captain. "Who knows what damage that flying cockpit debris could have done up behind those radio panels. Some wires or connections may have torn loose and are making intermittent contact. Just do the best you can."

Captain Johnson turned his attention back to his panel and intently scanned the instruments. *At least we're still flying right side up with a little measure of control,* he thought. A moment later his thoughts turned to what Jean had reported earlier. Something about a couple of banks of seats being torn out and that it might have been possible that they were occupied at the time of the decompression. It hurt him deeply to think about such a possibility. But then, he reflected on their own situation and what may lie ahead. *Perhaps they're the lucky ones after all,* he thought. *At least their troubles are over.* Captain Johnson was gravely concerned now. Yet under his command, in spite of the grievous damage, the aircraft continued flying into the night sky. But for how much longer?

CHAPTER 6

*I*n the pre-dawn darkness of what was to be their first full day on the ground, Derek slowly began to stir. He forced himself to open his eyes. What he saw around him seemed so unreal and unnatural. All he could perceive were weird shadowy shapes like something out of a bad dream. He shut his eyes hoping it was all a nightmare and that the chaos and hurt that was swirling around him would be gone when he awoke. But it didn't go away, and a stabbing pain that suddenly shot through his left arm assured him that he was not dreaming. Moments later, the pain and confusion were more than he could stand. He shut his eyes tightly until sleep once again took hold of him.

As the hours passed, the sun climbed steadily into the sky. The mid-morning temperature, already into the mid 80's, soon soared into the 90's. Derek and Michelle lay unmoving in a small shaded area caused by the unnatural position of their seat bank. But the moving sun acted like a thief wielding a knife, little by little slicing away their protective cover until its burning rays reached Michelle's exposed leg. Slowly, she began to stir and came awake.

Somewhere in the dark recesses of his mind, Derek began to sense the light, a moving light, he thought. Without comprehending, he knew the light was important, vital, and he must go towards the light. It was bright and warm and calling out to him. He had a frightening thought. *Wasn't this exactly how people who have had near-death experiences describe reaching the brink of death?"* That thought was blasted from his mind as an intense pain shot through his head. "Arrhhhhhh!!!," he shrieked. For an instant he welcomed the stab of pain because he knew that he wasn't dead—at least not yet.

His foggy thoughts began to clear. He was both stunned and awed to find himself staring directly into Michelle's face. "I must be in heaven," he mumbled to himself.

"Lie still, you're hurt," Michelle called out. As soon as she had come awake, her airline crash and first aid training kicked in. In spite of her own injuries, she went immediately to his aid. "We crashed," Michelle croaked. She removed his neck tie to help him breathe then reached over into the marsh pool to soak the tie. Then, kneeling beside him, she applied the cooling compress to a cut over his eye. Wincing at first, Derek felt immediate relief.

Derek's vision slowly cleared. He was appalled by what he saw. Michelle's face was scratched and scraped and streaked with blood! Her hair was matted and caked with dark dried blood. Her appearance looked even more horrifying where blood contrasted against her light

69

blonde hair. Taking a moment to force out the words, Derek spoke haltingly. "What's happened! Where are we?"

"I simply don't know," replied Michelle. "One minute were in the air then a *BLAM*, and now we're on the ground beside a muddy old pool. I can't conceive of what happened. We'll have to try to figure things out later. Right now, you need some fixing up. Stay still." Derek didn't comply. He attempted to rise but instantly abandoned the effort as an intense wave of dizziness and pain forced him to lie back down again. His head spun in pain. He clutched his left arm in pain. He'd injured it during the fall but at least it didn't feel broken.

"Easy big boy, easy," said Michelle as if she were trying to calm a horse. "I'll try to fill you in on what's happened and where we stand right now. So just lie there for a bit and let me tell you what I know. First of all, I came awake a little while ago and I found you here, still out cold. I saw that you had a cut over your eye and from the look of all the bruising and swelling in your left forearm it might be broken. I needed some kind of medical supplies so I struggled around the area looking for something to use as bandages. But instead, I was lucky enough to find one of our Airline First Aid Kits. It smashed onto the ground a little way over there," she pointed to the marsh pool. It was broken open where I found it but the supplies inside were intact. Someone up above must surely have been watching over us I'll tell you," she proclaimed. Michelle gently lifted Derek's injured arm. "Hold still while I check it," she ordered.

After gently probing the injured forearm she asked, "Can you move your wrist?"

"Yeah, I can but it hurts when I do that." His raspy reply was a better indication of how much it really hurt than his answer implied.

She continued to probe the area and manipulated his fingers causing only mild complaints from Derek. "It really seems to be either a badly sprained wrist or a mild fracture at most," she reported. "But I've got some Velcro splints in the first aid kit that should fix you right up." A few minutes later she finished applying the splints to his injured wrist and forearm. Moving on to the cut over his eye, Michelle used two butterfly bandages from the kit to act as temporary stitches. Considering their astounding fall, Derek was in amazingly good shape. A moment later she called out, "Dr. Sherry hereby declares you, Dr. Hunter, cured!"

Quite confused, Derek mumbled, "Dr. *Sherry*? But I thought your name was Michelle," he croaked.

"It is Michelle, but Sherry is my last name."

"And you're a doctor *too?*" he asked.

"Well, right now I am. I'm *your* doctor. I'm a flight crew member, fully trained and certified in emergency first aid. You're a passenger, and this is an emergency situation so, *yes*, I am your doctor and you'd better do as I say, or else."

"Or else, *what?*" asked Derek. "Or else you'll throw me off your plane? Well it looks like that's already happened so what can you do to me now?"

Grimacing and wiping her own face with the still wet tie, Michelle replied. "Ah, the patient has a sense of humor—how nice. But, in any case, it's still a *sick* sense of humor and I'm going to make you call me *Doctor* Sherry."

"Pleased to meet you *Doctor* Sherry," said Derek. He foolishly raised his arm to shake her hand. "Arghh!" he cried as a shooting pain forced him to drop it back down. "Okay," he moaned. "You can play doctor and take care of me." He hesitated a moment. "But you wouldn't take advantage of me while I'm incapacitated, would you? *I'd like that!*" He snickered then winced with a stab of the pain.

Michelle started to laugh at Derek's ridiculous statement but it triggered a stabbing pain in her rib. She felt as if a white-hot poker had just been jammed into her side. She tried unsuccessfully to hold back a wail of pain. Derek was alarmed as he watched her clutch her ribs. In spite of a shooting pain in his head, Derek forced himself up to help her. "What's wrong," he shouted.

"It's my rib," Michelle cried. "I may have bruised a rib or two. It's possible I may have a broken one but I don't think so. God, it hurts when I move in a certain way. I'm sure I'll feel better once my ribs are wrapped but I can't do that myself. It looks like we're going to have to work on each other. Do you think you are up to wrapping my chest?" she asked. "There's large elastic bandages in the first aid kit for that purpose."

"Yes," Derek replied instantly. Though in pain, he struggled to sit up. Michelle handed him the large first aid kit.

Michelle grimaced for a moment then recovered. "And it was that stupid joke you made that set off my pain. That humor of yours is going to kill me—literally."

"I'm sorry Michelle. I'm so sorry," Derek pleaded. Then, in spite of his own discomfort he gently stroked her cheek. "Are you hurt anywhere else," Derek asked.

"Yes. I think I have a pretty badly sprained ankle too," she replied. "It hurts an awful lot but only if I put any weight on it. So, if you don't mind, I'd like you to take care of that injury first. There's another Velcro splint in the first aid kit that should work on my ankle." Derek found the splinting device and easily applied the Velcro unit to her ankle. Michelle found that the even pressure the splint provided over the injured area provided considerable relief. "Before you help me with my ribs, let's get out of the sun over to the pond where there's a little bit of shade cover in the shadow of the mesa. And there's water to clean up our cuts and bruises." Derek agreed and the pair struggled to the water's edge. Michelle clutched her ribs to control the pain until they settled into a small band of shade. Though it had only been a short distance both felt drained from the effort.

"How's your rib?" Derek asked."

"Somewhat better, as long as I hold it," she replied. "But I think we need a break for a while," said Michelle with a grimace. She lowered herself into a reclined position on the sandy edge of the pond. A moment later she let out a groan of relief then paused. "Derek, I think we both need a break before we do anything else. My ribs are okay as long as I lie still. And we can wait a bit

73

to finish fixing up our scrapes. Rest is more important right now." A moment later she fell into a fitful sleep.

She didn't need to convince Derek. He badly needed to rest his throbbing head. But first, he scavenged a few articles of clothing that were strewn around the wreckage site. He fashioned a couple of 'make shift' pillows then gently slid one under Michelle's head then one under his own. He moved close to Michelle's side and both fell into a fitful sleep.

CHAPTER 7

Hours later **Derek awoke with a start.** He was momentarily confused and unaware as to where he was or what had happened. An instant later a sharp pain in his left arm jolted his memory back. He remembered, all too well, about the crash, Michelle, and their injuries.

In spite of the pain in his arm, Derek pushed himself up to a sitting position and glanced up at the sky. He was nearly blinded by the brilliance of the sun. Worse yet, even though they had moved back into the shade earlier, the sun was again reclaiming the shade. They were in serious danger of being burned and dehydrated by the sun's blistering rays and what little shade remained wasn't going to last much longer. Derek knew he had to construct some kind of shelter right away. Knowing that Michelle would be better off resting, he left her sleeping. A moment later, he forced himself up to his knees. Cradling his painfully throbbing arm close to his chest, he dizzily rose to his feet. After a few halting steps, he shakily set across the short area of beach in search of anything that he might find useful in building a shelter.

Derek walked unsteadily across the narrow shore line. His progress was impeded by his damaged shoes.

One had lost its heel and the other had its back seam ripped out. Considering the terrible consequences of going barefoot on the searing surface, Derek put up with the awkwardness hoping that he might find some appropriate foot covering among the debris. He moved on in search of materials for the shelter. Before he began to search in earnest, he found himself inexplicably drawn to the spot where their twisted seat bank lay cockeyed in the muddy water. The seatbacks were caked solid with mud and roots from uprooted shrubs and debris. Turning his gaze upward, he focused on the steeply sloping face of the mesa that towered above him. Something caught his eye. He noticed that a long groove had been torn out of the slope from top to bottom, ending at the mesa's base where the torn and twisted airliner seats lay. His gaze remained transfixed upon the scene. In a sudden flash-back, he weirdly recalled an unworldly blast of air roaring into his face, then tearing down the slope backwards in his seat. As quickly as the flash-back hit him--it vanished. He shook his head at the impossibility of the idea. *Had we actually fallen down that slope?* He thought.

Something caused him to again survey the mucky groove that had been torn down the mesa's face. He thought for a moment. *Could it be that the plane crashed on the mesa top and just our seat bank fell over the edge?* Derek's heart skipped a beat when he considered another possibility. *Could there possibly be survivors on the mesa's top?* Cupping his hand to his mouth Derek yelled, "Hello, hello up there! Down here! We're down here! Is there anybody up there! Anybody?!" Derek's cries were answered by total silence. The silence hit Derek hard. It didn't take a genius to figure that the likelihood of other survivors was virtually zero. Their only hope now was that they would be found by rescue search crews. The wreckage shouldn't be hard to locate in the featureless landscape. He prayed that help would come soon. He prayed too that he was not hallucinating. Everything had seemed so weird and dream like. He dismissed his thoughts.

With nothing more to be accomplished, Derek turned his attention back to the task of finding suitable branches for a shelter. It was an easy task because their bank of seats had torn many small trees from their roots during their descent down the slope. He readily collected a large number of branches from among the debris then carried them to a small sheltered area a dozen yards down the beach. He carefully wove the long branches together as best he could. He then fashioned them into a reasonably sized 'stick-frame' structure. Next, he covered the frame with a large number of assorted articles of clothing he'd recovered from destroyed luggage bags that littered the area. A short time later he stepped back and looked approvingly at the makeshift shelter that would easily accommodate two people.

Michelle came awake just as Derek had put the finishing touches on the shelter. She struggled to sit up as he approached.

"How are you feeling now," called Derek out to Michelle. After a momentary yelp of rib pain, Michelle regained her composure.

Robert Campbell

"I'll be okay," she replied. "My ankle feels better but I still can't put much weight on it. And once my ribs are wrapped I should be a lot more mobile." Derek's spirits improved with the news.

"Don't worry," he replied. "I'll take care of your ribs and finish cleaning you up as soon as we move over into the shelter. I built it while you were resting. What do you think of the it?"

"Looks a little an igloo," she laughed. "But it looks nice and shady inside there. I think we'd better move over into it right now. The sun is awful."

Derek helped Michelle up. With one arm around his strong neck, she limped along beside him. She managed to keep her sprained ankle up as they moved the short distance across the beach to the shelter.

"We're home honey," proclaimed Derek. He gently helped her into the modest structure.   Michelle grimaced as he helped her down. "If you call this place home it's a clear indication that you've already been out in the sun too long. You better get in here yourself before you fry what's left of your brain."

"I will in a minute," Derek replied. "But first I've got to go wet some more cloths so I can clean your cuts and bruises, not to mention my own. I know it's murderously hot out there but hey, I'm a hero I can take it. I'm *Mr. Macho Man!*"

"If I had the strength I'd bop you one and you'd have one more injury to fix. Go now," she replied insincerely, while trying unsuccessfully to look annoyed. But she finished her send off with a big smile while adding, "Ya done good!   Being inside the shelter completely

78

surrounded by shade is a blessing. Nice job Derek!" He smiled in return.

Moments later Derek, wet cloth in hand, re-entered the shelter. The two found the full shade of the shelter a huge relief from being outside. Derek needed to rest for a while from his strenuous efforts to build the shelter in the searing sun. They both felt it would be better to stay in the shelter for a while until the sun was lower in the sky when the high temperature would begin to abate. While they waited, they pondered what could have happened to cause the accident and where the main wreckage fell.

After an hour's rest, Derek and Michelle felt calm enough to discuss their situation. Derek's head was filled with questions about the accident. He broke the silence with a question. "What happened?" He asked Michelle. "Do you know where we are and if there are any other survivors?"

Michelle replied. "First off, all I know is that we're stranded somewhere in the middle of the Outback. Thinking back, I know we were about half way into the flight and that would have placed us near the south west corner of the state of Queensland. And I hate to say it, but it's likely that we are somewhere in or near the Strzelecki Desert. That's one of the worst and most desolate parts of the Outback." Michelle appeared to be shaken by her own words. Clearly struggling to compose herself, she continued. "As far as survivors go, no I haven't seen any other survivors. It's weird. I didn't see anyone else and I haven't heard anyone cry out. I mean if we survived the crash in halfway decent shape then there must be others around too. I think they must be over on the other side of that big mesa or maybe even on top of the mesa itself."

Derek glanced through the shelter's opening and looked up at the mesa. "It looks sort of like the kind of mesa you might see in New Mexico in the United States," he said. "But this one's really different because it has so much vegetation on its slopes and it's not really very big. It' looks to be about 150, maybe, 200 feet tall but not too wide. Whatever happened there, I'll bet that mesa has a story to tell."

"I have a theory," said Michelle. She continued, "Do you think that since the plane is so huge and the mesa top is so small that it's possible that the front of the plane hit at the top of the mesa's far side? And if that happened the plane might have cartwheeled and broken up. Somehow, our part of the seat wreckage may have been flung across the mesa top where it fell over and down onto our side of the mesa with us still in it." Looking up at the mesa she added, "You can see the groove in the slope from where our seats fell down it. So maybe the rest of the wreckage, and possibly other survivors, are stranded on the mesa top.

Derek considered Michelle's theory and thought it was a scenario worth checking out. "I think you could be onto something there, Michelle," he replied. "I'm going to hike up to the mesa top and see if you're right. There may be some survivors up there after all." He tempered his statement by revealing that his calls to the mesa top earlier were unsuccessful. "But, no matter," He proclaimed. "I'll hike to the top anyway. I know it's steep but it isn't very high. I should be able to make that climb.'

Michelle looked out of the shelter's opening and up at the mesa. "That doesn't sound like a very good idea. It's very steep and you're in no shape to do that anyway. So, let's slow down a bit. If help doesn't arrive soon, then maybe you can try. Right now, neither of us is in any shape to do much of anything just yet. And don't worry, when the rescue crews come they'll certainly know enough to look over this side and find us. They should come anytime now."

"Yeah. You're right," Derek sighed. He lay still for several minutes then asked, "Michelle, do you remember anything about what happened? How'd we get down here on the ground? I mean the last thing I remember was we were descending then we hit a bit of turbulence. But hell, we had to be nearly 3 miles high at the time." Derek shifted his eyes towards the mesa. "How could we possibly have crashed into that thing. It can't be more than a couple of hundred feet off the ground! Do you think we had a mid-air collision or something? What the hell could have brought the plane down?"

"I don't remember a thing about crashing," said Michelle. "The last thing I remember was serving sodas, remember you wanted a Coke? Then the next thing I knew I woke up here on the ground. And what a creepy experience that was! It was pretty dark when I first came to and I thought I'd died. I called out again and again but nobody answered. Just total silence—it was awful. I must have drifted off again or something because the

81

next thing I knew the sun was up—and it was burning my leg. Then I looked around and saw what I thought was a body lying beside me. Thank God it wasn't a body—it was you." Forcing a grin, she added, "In spite of your fancy degree I guess that really makes you a '*no body*' after all. 'A *Nobody*', get it?"

"Yeah, I get it, but that remark shows that you need help more than I do. And besides, how come you can crack jokes now and I can't."

"Oh, be quiet," she said. "Anyway, was I ever glad to find you here alive." She sounded more and more anxious as she continued talking. "There's absolutely no one around. I don't understand it. But we have our theories and in time we'll find out for sure. But, no matter what, I'm glad you're here with me I'll tell you that."

From the look on Michelle's face, Derek sensed that it would be better to move away from discussing the crash. Looking for an easy way to change the subject Derek declared, "I need to step outside for a stretch. Be back in just a minute." The full heat of the sun struck him as he left the shade of the shelter. He stood up and stretched, with only a small amount of pain, then raised his hand to shade his eyes. Once again, he surveyed the nearby terrain. He spied some objects not far off.

"Hey Michelle," Derek exclaimed. "Looks like there's some broken suitcases and more loose clothing scattered all around us and there's even more off in the distance. I think I'll check that out right away because the sun's already getting lower in the sky. What do you think?"

"That's okay," Michelle called out from inside the shelter. "As long as you're not gone too long, I'll be fine. My ribs are all right for the moment and I can wait till you get back to wrap them." Derek bent over into the shelter opening and blew her a kiss." She caught it! Derek immediately set off.

Derek was encouraged by the fact that the intense heat had already abated, if only slightly. He shaded his eyes as he scanned the sky in hopes of spotting a search aircraft or helicopter. Sadly, he saw no aircraft. Instead, all he could see was an empty sky and a sun that was now even lower in the sky. He knew from his readings about the Outback that sunset only lasted a half-hour or so. An article he'd read earlier had warned tourists that nighttime temperatures in the dessert sometimes fell to near freezing. Both he and Michelle, were not in any condition to face that kind of cold without protection. Derek was aware of the dangers of facing such cold temperatures without proper clothing. With sense of urgency, he headed out towards the bag he'd spotted earlier. He dearly hoped he'd be able to gathering enough appropriate clothing to cover themselves for the night.

As he struggled across the hot barren surface an odd thought came to Derek's mind. He called into question the scene of the wide spread debris of clothing and smashed bags around. He thought, *this is pretty odd. Why in the world would there be so much baggage debris way out here' beyond the mesa.' How could this happen. If the plane crashed into the mesa then the crash debris should be at the base of the mesa.* Too tired to process his own questions, Derek focused on a specific bag and picked up his pace toward it.

Just a few minutes later, his short walk was rewarded with the discovery of a rather large bag. It was a dark-green, soft-sided, suitcase that had small wheels on one end and a sturdy metal collapsible handle on the other. He was greatly disappointed to see that the bag had been severely damaged on the left side rendering the wheels useless. Just to be sure the bag contained useful items before he dragged it off, he opened it. A quick cursory look indicated that it was likely worth bringing back to the shelter.

Using his good arm, he strained to lift the heavy over-stuffed bag. It proved to be far too heavy for him to carry any distance. He let it drop to the ground. *Too heavy--I've got to try something else*, he said to himself. He examined the bag more thoroughly and found that even though the top of the bag was damaged its extension handle came up with surprising ease. With the extension in its fully raised position he found that he could drag the bag a lot more easily than he could carry it. But even though dragging the bag was easier, his arm ached as he dragged the bag the short distance back to the shelter.

Michelle heard Derek struggling as he approached shelter. She called out to him. "Are you all right Derek?" He responded enthusiastically that everything was great. Michelle was excited. "Come in and show me what you've found," she cried out happily. Derek moved the bag inside the shelter then gasped for air.

"Whew, what a hot job that was," he huffed. It took a moment for him to catch his breath. "Give me a minute then we'll go through the bag. I just can't believe it," he huffed again. "I thought that during my hike I'd spot a rescue party or at least some search plane flying overhead to pinpoint our location. Don't all big commercial planes today have emergency locator beacons on board?"

"Yes, they do," Michelle replied. "And I can't understand it either. I don't know why there hasn't been any sign of help. And it's so creepy that we still haven't seen or heard a single sign that anyone else survived here with us." She lowered herself to a sitting position just outside the entrance of the shelter. "It just doesn't seem right." Her voice quivered as she spoke. "I'm beginning to think that we're the only survivors and that everyone else may be dead on the top of that mesa." Derek sat beside her and put his arm around her to bring comfort.

"We don't know that, Michelle," Derek replied trying to sound confident. "Remember, I called out to the top of the mesa a while ago and although I didn't get any response, that doesn't mean anything yet. Maybe others *are* up there and they're just farther away from where we fell. They couldn't know we're way down here," he explained. "If there are survivors up there they are probably huddled together some distance back from the mesa's edge thinking that they're the only survivors too. Don't worry, help has to be on the way. We live in an era of modern technology and giant airliners don't just disappear without a trace. They'll find us soon. Besides, it hasn't even be a whole day since the plane went down. I'll bet they'll be here later in the day or tomorrow, for sure." Though he desperately wanted to believe what he said, he knew in his heart that an early rescue was not very likely. Yet his words seemed to give Michelle some hope. And that's something they both needed. Derek sat with his arm around Michelle for several minutes. Although he didn't say it, putting his arm around her gave him comfort too. He figured that right now he probably needed her every bit as she needed him.

Derek decided it would be a good idea to cheer themselves up so he enthusiastically suggested that they open the big bag together to see what they might find. "Come on, Michelle," he proclaimed with great enthusiasm. "We're going to open this bag up. Maybe there's a bottle of gin inside—that would make us feel better!"

Michelle put on a brief smile then reached towards the bag. But as her hand reached the clasp she hesitated. "Maybe you better do it," she said. "This doesn't feel right, even though it's an emergency situation I'm still airline personnel and somehow it feels wrong for me to be opening up a passenger's private bag."

"Okay then," Derek replied eagerly. "Then I'll open it. But I don't think you should feel that way. In a situation like this we have to use everything at our disposal to take care of ourselves till help arrives. Let's see what we've got."

Derek reached for the bag then grabbed a shiny metal ornament that served as the bag's zipper pull. He yelped in pain. The zipper pull was searing hot from its exposure to the blazing sun. It was a stark reminder of just how dangerously hot the sun could be out there in the open. Derek wet his fingers and tried again. This time the zipper was cooler and it slid easily around the bag. He lifted the top to reveal its contents.

"This is too neatly packed to have been a man's bag," said Michelle. She fingered the airline luggage tag and read off the owner's name. "Janice Foster is the name on the tag but I don't recall that passenger's name." The top layer of the suitcase was made up of an assortment of short, fashionable, dresses and skirts in a variety of prints and solids. Michelle held up a couple, looked at the labels inside, and quickly proclaimed them to be from an expensive young women's clothing store in Sydney.

Derek liked the fashions and though he couldn't tell, it seemed to him that the dresses were almost the same size as Michelle would wear.

"Ah! Here's something we can use," said Derek, pulling out a brightly colored package of beef jerky that he'd found in a side pocket of the suitcase. The package contained six separately packaged strips of dried, spicy, seasoned beef. "Would you like one of these, you must be hungry by now," he asked.

"No thanks. My head hurts and I think if I have to chew something hard and dry like that I'd feel worse-- maybe later. You go ahead."

"Nah, I'll have one later too. To tell the truth I'm not very hungry either right now," Derek lied. "Maybe we better save them till morning."

The two turned their attention back to the suitcase. They continued to search deeper into the bag where they found a collection of informal play clothes, shorts, tops, and a variety of T-shirts along with a pair of sneakers, flat dress shoes and a ladies' shaving kit in a pink case.

"Opps, looks like our young lady friend has a bit of larceny in her blood," said Derek as he pulled out several plush towels embroidered with the name of an expensive Sydney hotel. "I think I'll use them when I take my morning shower," he added in a poor attempt at humor. Michelle didn't react. It was clear that they both were nearly exhausted.

"Let me look a bit," said Michelle, warming to the idea of searching the bag. She quickly felt better as she started removing more of the high fashion clothing. "Cool!" chirped Michelle as she held up an elegant piece of exotic lingerie. Momentarily forgetting their plight, she held the incredibly sheer and enticing garment up against her body. A quick glance at Derek clearly indicated that the thrilling one-piece undergarment had not escaped his attention. She giggled with delight at the expression on his face. Before he could respond she dug deeper into the bag. Her efforts were rewarded when, much to her delight, she came across bottles of hair shampoo, hair rinse, body wash, and some beautifully scented soap in expensive looking foil wrappers.

Michelle was pleased with her find. Now she would be able to clean up her hair and make use of the soap to cleanse their wounds. And she was delighted, too, when she uncovered a zippered bag of toiletries. She smiled, knowing that it would help make the morning more tolerable. And even better, she found a 16-ounce bottle of sunscreen.

Delighted with the success of her search so far, she turned the rest of the bag over to Derek. He turned up some more useful items which included a small disposable flashlight and a zippered plastic travel kit. Inside, he found that the double-sided case contained a small sewing kit on one side and a travel first-aid kit on the other. The sewing kit came complete with an assortment of needles, threads, and scissors. The first-aid kit contained assorted sized Band-Aids, first aid cream, and a number of antiseptic cleaning pads sealed in foil packets. "Here's something you can add to our first aid supplies," said Derek. He handed her the small kit.

"But here's one thing we *will* need right away," Derek added, as he held up a full 20-ounce bottle of Evian spring water. The pair readily shared the badly needed water. Derek retained the bottle so that he could refill it with water from the nearby pond, should it come to that. He hoped it wouldn't.

After the refreshing water break Derek went back to searching the luggage for useful items. "I found a travel flashlight, Michelle he proclaimed. "We can certainly use this. It's going to be getting dark real fast. The sun will be down in no time." He fingered the on button on the light and was gratified to see that it gave off a small but brilliant beam of light. "Ah, great, we've got light, but we don't need it just yet," he added as he switched it off. After the search of the bag was complete, the two lined the floor of the shelter with excess clothing to avoid having to lie directly on the bare ground.

Robert Campbell

With sunset only a few minutes away, Michelle wanted to rest for the night. She insisted that her ribs could wait until the morning when they could tend to their wounds in the daylight. Besides, she was especially looking forward to washing her hair in the daylight. In spite of Derek's protests, she won out. Sunset indeed came quickly and with it the temperature quickly fell and they needed warmer clothing. Using the flashlight, Derek dug through the clothing he'd salvaged. He came across a pair of khaki men's pants. "Here's something for you Michelle," he said. "They're not exactly a fashion statement but the pant legs are pretty big and they should fit over your ankle splint. But if that doesn't work I'll just slit the leg up the side until it does."

Michelle tilted her head, put on a quizzical face and looked at Derek. "You know what? I think this could turn into a beautiful friendship," she replied in a deep voice while trying to imitate Humphrey Bogart's famous line from Casablanca.

"Bogart!!! From Casablanca—I love that movie!!" Derek shot back.

"I loved it too. I cried when Bogart made Ingrid Bergman get on the plane. My fiancé, John, thought I was such a dope when I cried. But I couldn't help it, I found that part so moving."

"You and millions of others, excluding John, of course," Derek added, hoping she didn't detect the note of jealously in his voice.

"Well it's bedtime now Michelle," said Derek. "Let's see if we can get you into your wardrobe for the night. We'd better move quickly. I don't want to have to use the little flashlight unless we really have to. We may need it to signal the rescue crew if they show up tonight. In the darkness, Derek suggested that they sleep as close together as possible to maintain their body heat through the cold night. Without a word of protest, Michelle tugged him closer towards her. Derek didn't even feel his aches and pains. He willingly slid over until their bodies touched. They fell instantly asleep, oblivious to the many, varied, and strange sounds and shrieks emanating from the unseen desert life all around them. So ended their first full day on the ground.

Michelle and Derek came awake as the early morning sun came up, bringing with it, quickly rising temperatures. Sounding like patients in an old age home the two groaned and croaked as they came awake. Derek laughed and commented on the absurdity of their waking. Michelle wasn't amused. "Speak for yourself you *old* person," quipped Michelle. It took her a moment to organized her thoughts and check her injuries. She knew that she was in remarkably good shape for someone who had just survived a plane crash.

"Let me take a look at you," declared Michelle. "Wow, what a face," she chortled. "You look like a disaster. You should see your hairy old face," she teased. "You need a shave, wolfman!"

"And you, Michelle, need emergency attention," replied Derek. "If I had a cell phone I'd call the Fashion Police to save you from that outfit you're wearing before it's too late!"

"Enough of your silly jokes Derek," Michelle huffed with a smile. She slid out of the shelter. Raising herself up to a standing position, she shaded her eyes then squinted off towards the horizon. She called over her shoulder, "I'm sure help will arrive today but I don't see any sign of rescue crews yet." Derek struggled to pull himself from under the shelter. He joined Michelle. The pair continued scanning the horizon.

"I predict help will arrive by noon today," Derek pronounced. Though he wouldn't admit it to Michelle, he didn't have much confidence in what he'd just said. He, too, couldn't understand why they had not yet been found. It seemed impossible to him that search and rescue crews hadn't been dispatched to cover their known flight path. And it seemed inconceivable that emergency locator beacons hadn't already been activated to indicate their current position. *How could rescue personnel possibly not find the wreckage of such a large airliner in such a featureless place*, thought Derek.

"Until they come, we're just going to have to take care of ourselves," mused Michelle. "And right now, I'm hungry and thirsty. With the Evian gone we can strain the pond water, so at least we've got the water situation taken care of for the time being. And, speaking of hunger, I think I'm ready for one of those dried beef things you found. How about you?" Derek readily agreed. Though salty and hard to chew, the nourishment raised their spirits. The two moved off to the pool to wash up and tend their injuries. "We'll take turns and wash each other up," giggled Michelle.

Together the pair gathered up clean towels, shampoo, soap, and the first aid kit. Derek snatched up the pink shaving kit they'd found and stepped over to the water's edge. Derek wore only briefs as he entered the shallow pool. Michelle wore only her panties and bra. Though neither would admit it, they both enjoyed a sense of erotic pleasure as they bathed themselves in the murky water. Although Derek tried to hide his enjoyment from Michelle--he was not successful. An embarrassing and inescapable bulge in his shorts betrayed his excitement. Michelle could not help but notice. She simply smiled, a pleasurable smile at that.

Michelle was at a loss to explain to herself the thrill she was experiencing. *I should be ashamed of myself,* she thought. *Here I am, I'm injured, I hurt, I'm stranded after a bad accident with a man I hardly know; yet I have this thrilling feeling! What would my fiancé, John, think?* She arranged her bathing supplies and pondered her brief relationship with Derek. *It doesn't make sense,* she thought. *But I feel I know, and care more about Derek after only one day, than I do about John after our three-year relationship! But this isn't right,* she pondered, *it's a fluke, an accident, that we were thrown in together like this. It doesn't mean anything.* She forced herself to think…*I've got John and he wouldn't approve of this behavior no matter what the circumstances.* She resolved to behave herself.

But Michelle's resolve was stressed to the breaking point. She glanced at his, now soaked, white briefs. The wet coverage left little to the imagination. "What have we got here?" asked Michelle. She wore a big grin that she could no longer control."

"I'm sorry Michelle. But it's all your fault. In spite of your scrapes, you still look beautiful. I just can't help it. I'd be lying if I said I didn't like it."

"You think I'm beautiful when I look so all messed up?"

"I think you are beautiful no matter how you look. There's something about you Michelle. You have beauty inside and out, that's all I can say. And I'm sorry for saying that. I know you're engaged, but I just had to say it."

"Thanks, Derek. I've had my share of guys telling me I'm beautiful, on the outside—but *never* on the inside. It's nice to hear that." As Michelle spoke, Derek immersed himself in her deep blue eyes. Then a big smile came across his face as his mind drifted off into an involuntary fantasy.

"Derek," Michelle called. His delightful daydream popped as Michelle called his name. "We better finish cleaning up before the sun gets too hot to search the area for anything." Though she enjoyed their brief thrilling interlude, she felt an urgency to bring it to a close. Derek sensed, and regretted, that the enjoyable episode was about to end, but he knew it was for the best. He'd known Michelle for barely one day and he knew that she was engaged. It wasn't right to take advantage of their desperate situation. *She has her own life,* he thought. *I have no right to interfere.*

Michelle returned to her task of cleaning up and found it a great luxury to shampoo her hair. The very thought of having all that dried blood washed out of her hair buoyed up her spirits. After she was done, Derek inspected her scalp. He applied first aid ointment to her small cuts and scrapes. Derek's spirits lifted when he watched the beauty return to Michelle's hair. Michelle's spirits lifted as well after Derek's shave revealed a handsome man's face under the scruffy two-day beard growth.

The time had come for Derek to address Michelle's injured ribs. She sat near him while he searched through the aircraft's First Aid kit. He pulled out a long and wide stretch bandage for Michelle's ribs.

Before I start wrapping your ribs Derek said, "I've got a story to tell you. And I'm not *'ribbing'* you."

Michelle responded, "If I have to put up with any more of your puns there won't be enough bandages left in the first aid kit to patch *you* up!"

"Seriously though," Derek replied. "I once broke a rib when I hit a car during a huge snowstorm in Boston. We got over three feet of snow. And some of the snowdrifts were as high as ten feet. It was a couple of days before I could get to a hospital and I was amazed that all they did was to bandage up my ribs and send me home. I expected some big chest cast or something but the doctor just wrapped me up, showed me the door, and shouted *next!"*

"God, you got hit by a car? You were lucky it was just a broken rib."

"Well, not exactly," he hesitated. "I didn't say I was hit *by* a car. I said I hit *a* car. You see the truth of it is that I couldn't have been lucky enough to have been hurt doing something noble like making a heroic rescue or delivering a baby in the middle of the blizzard. No. I'm afraid that I broke my rib when I fell off a five-foot-high snow bank onto the fender of a parked car as I scurried over to my neighbor's house to beg for a six pack of beer."

"That's a dumb story. You're kidding, aren't you?!"

"I wish I were but that's really what happened. Anyway, the purpose of the story, and there *is* a purpose you know, is that all they do for broken ribs is bind them up and send you home. So, I think once I get you all wrapped up you'll be safe until we can get some professional help for you."

"Our first step is for you to take off that bra," said Derek as he unsuccessfully tried to suppress an uncontrolled blush. Michelle just smiled. "Seriously I need to see if you have any other injuries."

"Yeah, and you'd better not try to take advantage of me!" Michelle retorted with a smile. She started to laugh at her own little joke then yelped in pain.

"See, God's punishing you," replied Derek.

"You're right, He put *you* down here with me didn't He?"

Failing to rise to the bait, Derek blushed and replied. "I'm sorry I really do think it's best to remove the bra if I'm going to wrap you up properly."

"I know--it's all right," replied Michelle. "I can understand your pain in having to do that. But I think somehow, you'll rise above it," she added with smirk. With that, Derek reached behind her back and began fumbling with the bra clasp. Michelle smiled and wondered if his face was still red from embarrassment or was it due to the exposure to the sun.

Finally, the clasp came undone and the bra fell from her soft beautifully shaped breasts. Derek let out a low involuntary moan as her breasts emerged. He couldn't believe that in spite of his physical condition and their critical predicament that he could still enjoy such a pleasurable sight. Derek's unintentional soft moan gave Michelle an unexpected and welcomed thrill. Like Derek, she too, couldn't believe that she could feel such pleasure amid their present turmoil. Though she couldn't understand her feelings, she thoroughly enjoyed the pleasure of the lustful event. It was obvious to Derek that his unintentional moan had caught Michelle's attention. He was greatly embarrassed by it yet didn't know what to say. Finally, after a conspicuous pause, he decided that it would be best to say nothing more about it.

With the gentleness of a surgeon, Derek softly probed the rib area that Michelle described. When he touched the third rib down she yelped. From the deep purple coloring in the rib area it was apparent that area was the one causing her the most discomfort. A minute later he completed the examination. He was satisfied that her rib injuries were likely due to bruising, not fractures. With Michelle still in a sitting position, Derek reached down and picked up the elastic bandage and wound it around her chest. A moment later he leaned back, surveyed his work, and smiled while he once again admired her beautiful breasts.

"What are you smiling about," asked Michelle. "Admiring your work, are you?" she quipped. Derek didn't comment. Michelle looked down at the neatly done job that had left her breasts completely exposed.

With the job done, Derek held up a man's long sleeve flannel shirt and said, "Here, you'll need this. Your blouse is ruined and the sun's getting hotter. You'll burn your skin if you don't get covered up." Derek dearly hoped that his disappointment at covering up such a vision of loveliness didn't show on his face. It did, but Michelle never said a word. Derek helped her into the shirt and fastened the buttons with his one good hand.

"You'd better lie down now," said Derek as he gently helped her recline. "How do you feel now?"

"That's a lot better," said Michelle. She pecked his cheek.

Derek looked up at the sky. It was approaching full noonday sun, and it was much too hot to be unnecessarily exposed to the sun. Derek suggested they return to the shade of the shelter. On the way over Derek discussed his plan to conduct another scavenger hunt. He hoped to find additional useful items among the bags and debris that still littered the area. He told Michelle how he was planning to leave later in the day when cooler temperatures would make the search easier. Michelle liked the plan. Derek and Michelle ambled off to the shelter in good spirits.

CHAPTER 8

Arriving back at the shelter, **Michelle** and Derek again sorted through the clothing items and supplies from the recovered luggage they'd previously found. They needed more suitable clothing if they were to survive out on the burning hot terrain. Though long pants would have been more practical, Michelle chose a pair of rugged shorts instead. She was pleased that when she tried them on that they were a perfect fit. Derek flashed a smile of approval. Her lovely long legs looked beautiful and graceful in spite of the ankle splint.

After an extended rest break, the two went back to sorting and arranging supplies. Derek knew that they both would need more water if they were to make it through their wait time for a rescue. Although he had the Evian water bottle they had emptied earlier, he needed more containers. Not wanting to head out into the blazing sun searching for containers, he scavenged through items they had earlier set aside as un-wanted. There he quickly found a, mostly empty, large plastic bottle of shampoo along with a similar size bottle of hair rinse. After gathering up the three containers and a clean white tee shirt, Derek stepped out of the shelter and moved over to the pool. There, he rinsed and refilled all the containers using the tee shirt as a filter. After holding one of the bottles up to the sunlight, he cringed a bit. Though the water was somewhat cleaner than that of the pond, he wasn't looking forward to either of them having to drink it. *Not to worry*, he told himself. *Help should arrive pretty quickly now and it probably won't come to that anyway.*

Before heading back to the shelter, Derek glanced over his shoulder at the pond. Something didn't seem right. He was taken by surprise when he looked more closely at the pond. He suddenly realized that the water level in the pool was lower than it was earlier in the morning. This was not good news. He thought it would be best to keep the news to himself for the time being.

As he approached the shelter with the water, Michelle called out. "Here, I think you should put these on, before you go out scavenging." She held up a pair of durable baggy cargo shorts from the suitcase. "And try this on too," she added, while holding up a white long-sleeved shirt. "I know it won't fit well but it has long sleeves. It will protect you better in the sun than the short sleeve one you're wearing." Derek took the proffered clothes then stepped outside the shelter to more easily change into them.

Michelle was right, the shirt wasn't a great fit. It was too small to button up all the way and his ample supply of chest hair was clearly evident. But the cargo shorts fit well due to the generous stretch in the elastic waistband.

A moment later he caught a chance glint of light flash off an object. It didn't appear to be too far out from their shelter. He leaned under the shelter and called to Michelle. "I see something shining in the sun a little way off. I'm going to hike over there to check it out. I should only be a few minutes."

"I thought you were planning to conduct a search later when it's cooler," declared Michelle.

"Well, I was, but whatever it is that's catching the sun is fairly close."

"In that case, I'm coming with you," Michelle said. "I'm in decent enough shape with the splint on to make a little trek. I need to get out of the shelter's cramped space anyway." Though Derek protested, Michelle won out again, but only after Derek insisted that she use the hastily made crutch he'd constructed out of a forked branch of a tree. For comfort, he wrapped the arm placement with towels.

But Michelle had a demand too. "Since your shoes are in terrible shape, you have to put something better on your feet," Michelle protested. She rummaged through the suitcase that was within reach and found what she was looking for. She handed Derek a pair of sneakers through the shelter opening. "Try squeezing your foot into these. I know they're look small but if you don't lace them up there may be enough room to squeeze into them. In any case, you'll have to make-do with them until we can find something more useable. The sand out there is getting so hot now, you'll burn the soles right off your feet, if you don't cover them with something." Derek readily agreed. He generously loosened the laces and worked the sneakers onto his feet. He smiled with

101

satisfaction. They actually felt pretty good. A moment later the two began the short trek across the plain.

Small insects buzzed around them but they pushed on. They found it necessary to keep brushing the pesky critters aside. Fortunately, they didn't seem to bite--they were just a nuisance. Derek observed how well Michelle maneuvered her crutch without complaint. In fact, after an awkward start she wound up using it more as a walking stick instead. That was a good sign that the injury wasn't as serious as they thought earlier. About two hundred yards out from the shelter they reached the source of the glint they'd set out to investigate.

"It's a piece of the plane! We've found the wreckage!" Derek shouted. He looked down at the torn and twisted remains of, what had once been, the cargo door of the aircraft. His elation went cold an instant later. His mind recalled an earlier thought he'd had about the luggage that was strewn around the area. Earlier, it had occurred to him as very odd that there wasn't *any plane wreckage* in sight around the shelter—just ripped open and destroyed luggage bags! He stood in disbelief, staring down at the wrecked cargo door at their feet.

As Michelle looked on in stunned silence, a hundred questions flew into her mind. She struggled to understand what was going on. "Derek!" she called out. *"Where's the plane? ...where is the rest of the wreckage?"* They both furiously scanned the horizon. *"Where's the rest of the plane and all the debris that should be around an airplane crash site? The plane was huge it can't have vanished. God! It just doesn't make sense! There's nothing else around anywhere!"*

Derek's brain screamed for answers. He looked down at the wrecked cargo door in disgust and confusion. *Where is the rest of the wreckage?* he screamed to himself. He tried to run through his mind what happened on the aircraft. But everything had happened so fast. He strained to recreate the event in his mind but came up blank. *Then it suddenly hit him!*

"*But that's impossible--no it can't be!*" he shouted into the air. For several moments Derek stood rigid. Nearly in shock, he replayed in his mind what had happened. Suddenly he slammed his palm solidly onto his head! "*NO WAY*," he shouted. His head spun as his mind tried to process his thoughts. "*The door, that's it! It was the cargo door that caused the crash!*" Derek's heart raced as his thoughts suddenly fell into place. He took a moment to calm down then began to speak. His voice was shaking from his revelation. "Michelle, we'd better sit down while I tell you what almost certainly happened. *You're not going to believe it, but please hear me out first.*"

"Michelle," he began. "There's no other wreckage and there are no survivors--at least not *here* because I'm certain that *the plane didn't crash here at all*. Michelle was crestfallen. She shook her head in confusion. "But what are you talking about? What do you mean that *the plane flew on without us?*"

While Michelle battered Derek with a host of questions, he worked to calm her down. "Here's my theory," he explained. "The cargo door must have blown out from the side of the aircraft causing an explosive decompression." He told her how he thought that the floor under them, along with the seats they were buckled into, must have gotten torn out of the airplane and blasted out of the cargo door opening into the slipstream along with luggage from the cargo bay.

Michelle appeared shaken but Derek continued. "I remember vividly how the crew kept having trouble with the cargo door. I had selected a window seat that happened to be directly above the cargo door. I couldn't help but see that the crew was having a lot of trouble with it. Then a minute ago when I saw that cargo door sitting on the ground in front of me *it suddenly hit me like a ton of bricks.*"

"I don't understand," said Michelle. What are talking about?!"

"Please, let me explain," Derek continued. "For years and years, I've always had a real interest in flying. I even took a flying lesson one time. Anyway, articles about flying and aviation news always gets my attention. The instant I saw that cargo door lying at my feet I immediately recalled something about DC-10's and their cargo door problems when the aircraft was first introduced. I like the History Channel's aviation channel on cable TV and I remember learning about it from the show. They had interviews and old aviation news videos about it." Derek continued, "when the DC-10's first came out there was a series of cargo door accidents that happened because the doors wouldn't latch properly. In two cases, the planes landed without loss of life. But then, even after modifications were supposed to have been made, one of the big DC-10's crashed in France killing everyone aboard. It caused the greatest loss of life in a single aircraft accident in history up to that time—that's why I recalled it."

"But the crucial thing about that accident is that when the cargo door exploded, it severed most of the flight control cables and ripped a huge hole in the cabin floor. Six passengers, still strapped into their seats, got sucked out of the cargo door hole and died from the fall. And after the door blasted out, the plane continued flying for many miles before it went down into a forest and exploded. Michelle, I honestly think that's what happened to us---*with one big difference. We survived!* Something happened that caused the cargo door to explode and we got sucked out. That's it Michelle. That's what happened. The door blew off and we fell from the sky and landed here. We survived because our seat bank took a diagonal blow down the muddy mesa slope--you saw the seats and the groove down the mesa. That miraculous slide down the slope saved our lives."

Michelle pondered Derek's theory. "But that doesn't make sense Derek," Michelle responded. We weren't flying on a DC-10. *It was a Russian built Tupolev TC-10.*"

Derek's mind went into a wild spin. *That can't be,* he thought. It all made so much sense to him about the cargo door explosions on the DC-10's and what had just happened to them. *But Michelle was right about the plane being a TC10. It couldn't be a coincidence,* he thought, *or could it?* Then, in a flash of insight it all came to him.

"I'm sure I've got the answer," declared Derek. After pausing for a moment, in deep thought, he began again. "Although we weren't on a DC-10, I believe we were actually on a virtually identical copy of the DC-10 whose design was stolen by the Russians, and built in Russia, and designated as a TC-10 instead. Michelle was confused. "How could that be," she asked. Derek quickly responded.

"Russians have a long history of stealing U.S. aircraft designs spanning decades from WWII up to and including the U.S. Space shuttle designs into the 1990's. During WW II the U.S. designed and built a plane called the B-29 Superfortress. The Russians had no aircraft like it and were desperate to get it. During a mission one of our B-29's had to make a forced landing in Russia. The Russians refused to return the aircraft to the United States. Instead Stalin's engineers reverse engineered an exact copy of the plane, rivet by rivet, then manufactured a fleet of the phony B-29's for their own air force. They used them well into the late 1960's. And that's a historical fact right out of the history books."

Michelle was not convinced. But Derek continued. "That's just one instance of Russian's stealing aircraft designs. Here's another. Back in 1968 the Russians built a virtually exact copy of the British/French designed Concorde Supersonic airliner. They called it the TU-144 and it took to the air just 90 days before the Concorde. Aviation experts around the world were certain it was built through industrial espionage stolen from the Concord designed systems. Much to the Russian's embarrassment, the plane was even dubbed the

'Concordski.' And through industrial espionage they even made a near exact copy of the U.S. Space shuttle, right into the 1990's. All this information is historical fact and was reported worldwide.

"But there's more," Derek explained. "The moment I boarded the plane, I thought it was a DC-10, that's how similar it appeared. "I have no evidence to support this, but I'll bet our Russian built TC-10 was virtually an exact copy of a DC-10. The Soviet's aircraft industry was on the rocks back in the 1970's when the DC-10 was first designed. And I believe that there's a good possibility that they used industrial espionage to appropriate much of the DC-10's design features to cut development time and costs. Given their historical record of stealing aircraft designs it's just a small leap of faith to believe that they so closely copied the DC-10's design that they even copied the deadly cargo door system. Again, I have no facts to cite and no proof. But, you have to admit, it's a *very* likely possibility."

Michelle sat stunned for some time while she pondered Derek's proposal. But after some deliberations, she thought, *"with no other information to go on it certainly is a plausible explanation. And that's the only explanation that we've got that fits into place."*

Michelle ended her silence. "I really have to say that your explanation makes good sense and all that. But, even if it's true about our TC-10's cargo door decompression, how can that explain our survival. It can't be," responded Michelle. "That would mean that we fell out of the plane from some three miles up. And you mean to say that we landed here with just some nonthreatening injuries and only minor cuts and bruises? *It just isn't possible, nobody could survive a fall from such a high altitude--nobody."*

"Oh yes they could Michelle," challenged Derek. "I know of a real case where a person survived a fall from almost two miles high. A 17-year-old girl and her mother were among the passengers onboard an airliner that had departed from Peru. The aircraft was around 16,000 feet, over the Peruvian jungle, when the accident happened. The plane was struck by lightning which caused a devastating explosive decompression. The airliner blew apart in mid-air, scattering pieces of wreckage and passengers over a wide area into the dense jungle below." Derek continued, "When the young girl came alert, she found herself hung-up in the fork of a tree dangling ten-feet above the jungle floor--still strapped in her seat. And incredibly, she was virtually uninjured— all she had was a broken collarbone!

Days later, she stumbled out of the jungle into a work camp. A work crew took her to a hospital where she made a full and complete recovery. *"This is a true, documented story, that got world-wide press coverage,"* stressed Derek. "Incredibly, she's still alive and well today and is working as a librarian in Germany."

Michelle listened intently as Derek went on. "Later, crash experts, meteorologists, and scientists, theorized that her fall was broken by vicious updrafts from the storm and by the cushioning effect of the dense jungle canopy. All those factors combined, scientists concluded, helped absorbed the shock of the fall which resulted in her incredible survival."

"Michelle, fantastic as it may seem, I think we survived our fall very much the way she survived her fall. I think that when we fell into the thunderstorm that severe updrafts slowed our fall. Then when our seat backs hit that scrub-covered mesa slope it must have acted like a shock absorber slowing us down to a survivable impact."

Michelle sat for a long time without saying a word. She played the scenario over and over in her mind and each time it made more sense.

"My God Derek. It seems so impossible, yet that must have been what happened. It must have happened just that way! Everything fits." Though she was certain she knew the answer, Michelle asked, "But if that's true what happened to our plane?"

Derek reached over and put his arm around Michelle, as much to comfort himself as her. "It's gone Michelle. I'm really afraid that it continued flying after the door exploded. It could have flown on for ten miles or fifty miles or five hundred miles. We may never know how far it flew on without us, but we've been left behind.

Michelle's voice began to quiver and choke with emotion. "I know you must be right. If it had landed safely they would have sent out rescue crews by now. And even if it did fly on for a while before it finally crashed, they must not have been able to report our position. If they sent out planes or helicopters they would have followed our flight path and arrived here within hours. It's been over two days now, and no rescue is in sight because nobody knows we're here and they never will."

Then, no longer able to hold back the emotion and stress, Michelle broke down and burst into tears. Her body and mind were wracked with pain as she spoke in halting sobs. "We're here and we're stranded, but at least we have a chance to survive. But what about all those passengers, my friends on the flight crew, that beautiful little baby girl that was on board, I loved her so. And she's gone—they're all gone."

Michelle let herself go in a flood of emotions. Derek cradled her in his arms and comforted her as best he could. As her sobs were gently absorbed by his chest, Derek found that, he too, was torn apart inside. Everything seemed to crash down on him as the enormity of the situation finally hit. He too, was struck by the loss of all those lives on the plane. But most of all he feared that he might lose the chance to win the love of the beautiful angel he held so dearly in his arms. He felt love for Michelle like he had never felt for a woman before. He loved her and he needed her so much. But now he was afraid that he would fail. He was frightened that he would not be able to save her from a terrible end in the inhospitable Outback. He couldn't bear the thought of something happening to this girl he loved so much. He was certain that, if necessary, he'd give up his own life for her to see that she survived this terrible ordeal.

The stress and emotions he was trying to hold back were breaking him apart. Finally, he could no longer hold back the torrent. He held Michelle gently in his arms and he wept. Together they tightened their embrace and wept as one. Shortly the pair recovered. Knowing that it would be pointless to grieve in the blazing sun, the pair put their emotions in check. With Michelle's arm around Derek's shoulder, and her crutch under her arm, they headed back to the shelter in sorrow.

Simply because they didn't know what else to do, Michelle and Derek decided to continue searching for more luggage that might contain useful items. During a moment of rest, Michelle brought her hand up to her face and scanned the area. She wiped rivulets of perspiration off her forehead. Then something caught her eye. She squinted and focused more clearly on what appeared to be an intact bag lying off a short distance just off to their right. They set off to investigate.

Derek's heart skipped a beat as they approached the bag. He looked down in disbelief--it wasn't a bag at all. At their feet lay a large aluminum framed backpack that looked to be crammed full with camping equipment. Tied securely to the bottom of the pack was a tightly rolled sleeping bag. His high hopes were rewarded when he opened the pack for a quick look. Inside, there was a treasure trove of needed supplies, including a new Coleman 2-man pop-up tent! Derek slapped Michelle on the back in hearty congratulations for her find. Because the heat was rapidly building the pair put off any celebration. They headed back to the shelter—their spirits suddenly soaring. Derek hefted the pack onto his good shoulder and set off with happy thoughts of preparing a *real* campsite.

Back at the shelter neither could contain their delight when they opened the backpack. As far as they were concerned it was a complete camping store stuffed in a bag. Michelle squealed with delight when she examined the two-man popup tent. But there was much more. They uncovered: two battery powered lanterns, a mess kit, water purifying tablets, compass, signal mirror; large bottle of bug repellent; a complete professional hiker's first aid kit; a Swiss Army knife that bristled with a marvelous assortment of blades and tools; a large assortment of Natural High brand freeze-dried meals, along with a host of other useful items and gadgets. Derek was thrilled to find the water purifying tablets. He made a note to put some tablets into the water he'd just strained from the pool. It might not make the water cleaner, he thought, but it sure would make it safer to drink. Both their minds and spirits whirled with delight from the recovery of the back pack.

Derek checked out a side pocket in the pack and pulled out a paperback book titled "Camper's Guide to the Outback." Stunned for a moment, it suddenly occurred to Derek that he knew the owner of the camping equipment. He was certain that it belonged to the odd young man on the airplane. He'd told Derek that he was going to camp his way across the Outback. That explained why there was so much food and other survival equipment inside the pack. Saddened for a moment, he couldn't help that think that Shawn was likely dead now, and he was truly sorry for that. Yet he had a peculiar feeling that the strangely likeable character wasn't gone from their lives. He had a premonition that through Shawn's 'backpack gift,' he and Michelle were really going to survive their ordeal. But if they were to survive they needed to head back to the shelter to get out of the brutal sun. With a mixture of happiness and sadness the two headed back.

Upon their return to their make-shift hut Derek placed the camping backpack on the ground. He stood for a moment silently looking down at the bag. He pondered its contents and the fate of Shawn and all the others that were on the plane. He said a silent prayer for them.

Michelle picked up on Derek's silence. "Is there something wrong."

"No, nothing," Derek lied. He didn't want to reduce their high spirits at this time when they needed it so much. "I'm just beaten from the hot hike back here. That thing must have weighed a ton and I'm still sweating gumdrops from carrying it."

Trying to change the subject, Derek asked, "Can you let me have a look at that package of water purifying tablets?" Michelle handed them to him. He took the package and read the directions on the back. "We need to use them right away if we're going to drink that pond water," he declared. "I'll take care of that right now, and as soon as I'm done, we'll put up the tent together," he said enthusiastically.

The light nylon tent was a marvel of engineering. It was brand new and the directions inside clearly illustrated how to set it up. The umbrella supports were made of ultra-light carbon fiber and they threaded easily through the slots on the sides and top. In a matter of minutes, the tent was up. Together they unrolled the sleeping bag inside the tent. Michelle tested it out and proclaimed it to be perfect. Compared to their primitive shelter, the tent site looked like a luxury suite in an expensive hotel. With purified water and snacks from the back-pack, Derek and Michelle quickly quenched their thirst and hunger. Despite the heat, they luxuriated in their new campsite to await the cooling evening weather which was still hours away. It was going to be a very good evening.

CHAPTER 9

Derek and Michelle emerged from the tent into early evening sun into yet another day of their ordeal. Though their rescue situation had not improved, both felt a sense of renewal after their discovery of the tent and life-giving supplies. Derek stretched in the sun and proclaimed, "God, I feel better now." His announcement was contradicted as he punctuated the statement with a series of moans and groans.

"If that's how you act when feel *good,* I sure don't want to be around when you feel *bad,*" Michelle replied.

A bit embarrassed, Derek quickly changed the subject. "I think I'd better get over to the pool and collect some more water." He ducked back inside the tent and gathered up an empty container and some water purifying tablets. "I'll be back in a minute," he said as he emerged from the tent. "Oh, and if you're going out shopping while I'm gone, please leave me a note so I'll know where to find you when I get back," he chuckled.

"OK, dear," Michelle replied. Then she stuck out her tongue at him. After he left, she moved outside the tent into the cooler evening air. She found it refreshing and relaxing. And, now that they had a suitable shelter and food, her spirits soared. For no reason that she could identify, she suddenly had a 'special feeling' that they would come out of their ordeal alive and well. Though she was feeling good about herself and about their situation, she knew that there was something more involved than those feelings of safety and well-being. She was beginning to have feelings about Derek, too—strong feelings.

To Michelle, Derek was more than just a shoulder to cry on when she desperately needed someone. He seemed so much more of a person than anyone she'd ever met—and that included her fiancé, John. It wasn't that Derek seemed to genuinely care for her, and it wasn't that she was starting to care for him just because they were thrown into this situation and needed each other for survival. *No,* she thought. *Derek was a person she wanted to be with.* Unlike her fiancé, John, Derek made her feel more capable and confident about herself. Now that she thought about it, John always seemed to be pushing her around. She now sensed that he was starting to consider her as nothing more than a 'piece of his property' and not capable of doing any thinking for herself--or doing anything else in life that mattered. *I'm never going to be a 'sit at-home' trophy wife,* she fumed. Suddenly she realized that for the first time in her life she felt a great deal of confidence in herself and in her own abilities.

"We're a great team, we'll get out of this together," she whispered aloud without even realizing it. A moment later she became aware that Derek just arrived, water in hand.

"What's that? You said something as I came up?" asked Derek.

"No....it was nothing," Michelle said with a smile. "I know it's a long shot but do you think there's any possibility tomorrow that help will arrive?" she asked as she looked up to the sky.

"We can always hope," replied Derek as he turned his eyes towards the horizon. But as he gazed out over the plain it wasn't the sky and land that he saw before him. Instead his mind drifted into thoughts of Michelle. And a beautiful face it is, thought Derek, as he enjoyed his daydream. In a pleasant daze he thought about Michelle and his feelings towards her. He knew for certain that he was falling in love with her. He could tell when he held her in his arms that she was more than just someone who needed comforting at a difficult time. He felt her sorrow and pain more than he felt his own. He was in love with her and he wanted to be with her always.

While he continued his aimless gaze at the horizon, he thought about how Michelle had earlier called her fiancé a 'mover and a shaker.' Well I'm going to shake *him* up, thought Derek. *So, you better watch out 'Mr. Mover and Shaker.' You've got competition now-- Derek's here and you're going to be history!* Derek burst into a wide grin.

Like Michelle a moment before, Derek abruptly felt certain that they were going to break themselves free from the deadly Outback's grip. For some unexplained reason, he was elated by a feeling that he was on a *'mission'* in which he was not only going to ensure Michelle's safety; he was going to win Michelle as the

117

spoils of his victory over the desert and that sleazy character she called her fiancé. Derek looked down at the tent and the hiking and camping supplies that lay before him. He knew they had the means for the victory. We're going to make it--me and Michelle--the two of us *together,* he resolved. He smiled. It was a tough and hardened smile.

As if on command, Derek and Michelle turned to face each other and both simultaneously blurted out, "We're going to make it. *Together!"*

"Ahh, that's weird," squealed Michelle. "How'd you know I was going to say that?!"

"And how'd you know *I* was going to say that," Derek laughed. "We're a pair of matched bookends I guess. I feel great and I know we can make it through this. Look at all the stuff we've got, and besides I've got *you* to make it all work. We're going to be fine, I just know it."

"Me too! We'll stay here for as long as we can, just in case they come looking for us. And if they don't come for us we'll just do a *'walkabout'* and get out of here on our own.

"Do a *what?"* asked Derek.

"A *walkabout,"* Michelle repeated. "That's a walking journey that Aboriginal boys do around the outback as a test of their manhood, it lasts for months."

"Whoa! I get the idea but I sure don't want to wind up roaming the Outback for months!" whined Derek.

"Oh, stop being a baby, you know what I mean," she said as she punched his good arm.

Derek feigned excruciating pain but his efforts were wasted. Michelle just laughed, then reached around his neck, pulled him close, and kissed him solidly on the lips. Michelle found the kiss immensely pleasurable and sexually arousing. But her moment of pleasure was suddenly interrupted by a stabbing rib pain. She let out an involuntary yelp. Concerned, Derek released her immediately.

"I'm okay," replied Michelle in response to Derek's concern. "It's just a passing pain. I'm all right now." To change the subject, she looked up at the sky and said, "It's getting late now. I think we'd better look further into that camping stuff and pick out something to eat for supper before the sun goes down completely." Derek readily agreed.

The freeze-dried meal that Michelle picked for supper was surprisingly good. Though the chicken was a little chewy, the flavor of the noodles, mushrooms and white sauce, more than made up for any shortcomings of the chicken. Together they ate every last morsel. It was their first real meal in over two days.

After the twilight meal, Derek gathered up the dirty cooking utensils and mess kits and took them down to the water's edge to clean them. His high spirits took a sharp dip when he observed the pool's water level. Though he'd noticed it earlier, this time it was evident that the water level had dropped *significantly* since his last visit. The water wasn't going to last long, that much was clear. If the pond continued to shrink at this rate they had only a few days at best before they would be forced to hike across the plains in search of more water.

But 'where' he thought. He once again surveyed the barren wilderness as far as he could see. He shuddered at the prospect of such a hike. He knew that their lives were going to depend upon how much water they could carry. "Better start building a water supply right now," he thought. With that, he washed out the plastic bag and foil outer wrapper of the meal they'd just finished then filled them with water. A moment later he headed back to the tent. He knew he'd have to tell Michelle the bad news.

"What's up?" Michelle asked as Derek entered the tent. Derek knew he couldn't hold back the dismal news about the falling water level in the pool. Without any alternative he shared the bad news. He briefed her on their precarious water situation. He explained that it was clearly evident that they only had a few days of water left in the pond before it dried up completely. They needed to move on seeking a new water supply and shelter elsewhere. Both understood the gravity of the matter. Their fortunes had taken yet another downturn. They'd need to make quick use of both day and night working times to lay out and execute a plan to move on.

CHAPTER 10

After a fitful night's rest, the two began to stir. The brilliant rays of the sun that awakened them marked the beginning of their third full day in the hot, barren, and inhospitable Outback. Derek stretched as he rose. He was both pleased and surprised at how much better he felt. His leg felt good and his arm gave him only a little discomfort. In preparation for their trek Derek pulled out the "Outback Handbook" they'd found earlier. As he opened the book an old news clipping from the Ohio Sun Times fell out. Michelle saw it fall first and picked it up. There wasn't any date on the yellowed clipping but it appeared to be at least a few years old. Intrigued, Derek and Michelle read the clipping.

The article was headlined, 'Local Man Is Honored: Hero Of Army Training Disaster.' In the upper left corner of the half-page article was a picture of a clean-shaven Shawn wearing a U.S. Army Ranger's uniform. The story explained how the young man had saved the lives of six of his fellow soldiers when an engine failure caused their helicopter to crash. The aircraft burst into flames on impact. Shawn, single-handedly, pulled five injured men from the flames. He then re-entered the flaming craft and managed to free and save a sixth man before the craft finally exploded. The blast threw him to the ground causing near fatal head injuries. Four more injured rangers were still trapped in the wreckage at the time of the explosion. After a long hospitalization he was discharged from the Army. His injuries were such that he was no longer fit for active military duty.

After finishing the article Derek felt a sense of guilt about how he had so unfairly judged the young man when he first encountered him on the plane. Now he had an understanding as to why Shawn had acted so flighty. His strange social behavior was no doubt directly linked to the head injuries he'd received when he'd risked his life to save others.

The two sat in deep thought. It seemed so unfair that after Shawn had given so much to save others only to have his own life likely taken away by this aircraft accident. Bowing their heads, both made a Sign of the Cross, and prayed that Shawn and the others on the plane might have survived after all.

But reality quickly set in again. The sun was rising rapidly and they had much to do before they could move on in hopes of finding help or at least a more reliable water supply. Both exited the tent. Once outside Derek asked Michelle, "How are you feeling?

"Actually, pretty good," Michelle replied, "my ankle is better and even my ribs are a little better."

"Glad to hear that," Derek replied, "because, I've got a bit of a mission to complete today and, if you feel up to it, I'd like you to come along." Michelle agreed.

Although she didn't need a reminder, Derek reviewed their need to prepare to move out of their camp. He'd already made another quick check of the ever-shrinking pond. He reiterated that unless they moved out within a day or so, their water supply would likely be exhausted. Dehydration and death would quickly follow. He explained how he was planning to scavenge the debris field in search of any type of containers that could be used to carry water. Their only hope was to carry enough water with them to survive as they moved across the plain in hopes of finding a more reliable water source. Michelle felt up to the task. After consuming a hastily prepared breakfast, the pair moved out to begin their critically important scavenger hunt.

The hike started out well. Michelle ankle was much improved. And she was pleased that her crutch worked better now if she used it as a walking stick instead. Fortunately, Michelle remembered to carry the bug repellent—it worked great. After hiking a short distance, Derek stopped for a moment. He spotted a bag a short distance off. "Over there," Derek called out. "That bag looks promising. Let's take a look." They headed off to the bag. As Derek continued hiking he happily noted that the ankle injury was no longer a problem. *Things are looking up,* thought Derek.

They approached the bag. It lay upside down on top of a small scruffy shrub that had been thoroughly crushed by its impact. Derek looked down at the large soft-sided bag and was astonished to see that it looked to be in perfect condition. Like the bag he'd found earlier, this one too, had wheels built into the bottom. But the wheels on this piece of luggage were larger and more substantial than the other. That meant the bag would make a useful 'wheeled transport' to carry water containers and supplies on their trek towards civilization.

Derek pulled the bag free from the tangled shrub. "Let's open it up now," suggested Michelle. "No sense hauling a full bag back to camp if there's nothing useful inside." Derek readily agreed. After a quick unzipping of the bag, the top layer exposed what looked to be a typical packed piece of luggage. They pulled out lots of clothing, men's underwear, a pair of men's black wingtips which were just about Derek's size, typical toiletries and more. But the most valuable item found at the bottom of the bag was wrapped up in a towel. Michelle unwrapped it and squealed. "Derek, look at this!" She held up an expensive looking Nikon 35 mm camera complete with a telephoto lens.

Derek wondered at her enthusiasm. "Okay--so we can take pictures of our ordeal in the Outback and that's going to help us, how?"

"Don't be silly," Michelle said. "Don't you see. It's not the *camera* that I'm excited about it's the *telephoto lens* that I'm so happy about." She checked out the telephoto lens and proclaimed it to be intact. She proudly held up the lens. "We can use it as a periscope!"

"Ahh...a *periscope*?" Derek repeated. "I think you meant a *telescope*!"

"You know what I meant," sputtered Michelle. She playfully punched his wrist. "Of course, I meant a *telescope*!" Derek laughed at her in spite of a brief stab of wrist pain. A moment later she handed the camera and its lens over to Derek. He attached the telephoto lens to the camera, held it up to his face and looked into the viewfinder. After taking a moment to adjust the lens, the distant terrain leaped into focus with astounding clarity.

"This is great," Michelle. It's just like a telescope. Someone must have been going to use it for long-distance wildlife photography or something," he guessed. "Wow, this is amazing," Derek practically shouted. "Michelle you're a smart one. I'd almost dismissed the camera as not having any use but you saw the, *big picture*, pun intended," he smirked. "All kidding aside Michelle, this is a terrific find!"

Derek hefted the camera to Michelle. She looked through the viewfinder. "This is fantastic!" she proclaimed. "It should be especially useful to us as a telescope when we start hiking out of here. Let's take good care of this little beauty," she added as she carefully placed it on a soft pile of clothing.

Wanting to continue searching the bag, Michelle unzipped a side pocket. With great surprise she pulled out a cellphone. Both stared at the phone in disbelief. They held their breath as Michelle's shaking finger tapped the 'talk' button. "My God, it works!" she screamed as the phone beeped into life.

"Quick, dial 911!" yelled Derek.

Michelle never heard Derek. She was already dialing '000,' the nationwide Australian emergency help number. Their elation turned to bitter disappointment when the only display that appeared on the lighted window was the instruction to enter a PIN code in order to use the phone. Without the 'personal identification' code the phone was useless and since there were thousands of possible PIN codes the phone could not be used.

There was no way Michelle could hide her disappointment. She sadly placed the phone aside, carefully laying it on a soft pile of clothing to protect it, "just in case," she said. "I'll try random numbers when I'm bored," she proclaimed, "you never know."

Derek's disappointment was evident as well, but it didn't matter, it was time to continue their scavenger hunt. Due to the fact that they were already well supplied with articles of clothing they only placed a few items, including the camera, the phone, and the man's shoes back into the wheeled bag. Michelle made sure the carefully wrapped camera was safely stowed back in the bag and securely zipped up. After another hour of searching the area they found only a few more useful items beyond a number of bottles and containers that, once rinsed, would serve as water carriers. They headed back to the campsite towing the wheeled bag behind them.

Back at camp, Derek took out the camera and surveyed the horizon. The only thing that caught his attention at all was an odd-looking mesa, way off in the distance, and the hills beyond it. Frustrated by his inability to see anything that resembled civilization, Derek turned to Michelle and said, "You know what? I'm going to climb up that slope behind our shelter after we've eaten. First, it will put to rest whether or not any of the wreckage is up there. But most of all I'm hoping the higher vantage point might give me a better view of what lies off into the distance. I'll be able to see in every direction. And the camera's telephoto lens will provide remarkably better distance viewing. Maybe I'll be able to spot something within striking distance out there."

"Agreed," replied Michelle. "But it wouldn't hurt to rest for a while until it's later in the day when the sun isn't so hot," she suggested. With a good meal and a rest, you'll feel better and you'll be able to make the climb more safely." Derek readily agreed.

In the protection of the tent the pair selected dehydrated lasagna for lunch. This time, in order to ration their supplies, they only cooked one quarter of the contents. The meal was small but filling and both felt better after resting and having had something to eat. Late afternoon arrived all too quickly. The time had come for Derek to make the climb up to the mesa top. They stood together at the base of the mesa, looking up.

Derek turned to Michelle. "It really doesn't look that high," he declared. "The furrow we cut out as we crashed down the slope may actually help me climb. The ground is loose in there but I think I'll be better able to hold onto the trees and small shrubs. I should be able to work my way up through it okay."

"Wait," called Michelle. "You don't want to forget this" she said as she placed the strap of the Nikon camera with its huge telephoto lens around his neck.

"It feels like an albatross around my neck," quipped Derek. "But that's okay, I feel like the 'ancient mariner' right now anyway. But instead of a barren sea of water, we've got a barren sea of hot, dry, red dirt." Michelle gave Derek a kiss and made him promise not to be gone too long. He gave Michelle a quick kiss in return and headed off to begin the climb.

The first twenty feet up went well but then the climb became more difficult. The steep slope and the looseness of the dirt caused his feet to slip out from under him. He had to move slowly and carefully to keep from falling. At about the 60-foot level he suddenly lost his footing and slid a dozen feet back down. His heart raced as he grabbed wildly for a handhold. An instant later, using his injured arm, he snared a shrub and stopped the fall. He was thankful Michelle had the foresight to double wrap his splinted wrist support before the climb. He didn't dwell on what might have happened had she not done that.

Michelle called up to him asking if he was all right. He responded that all was well, though he doubted his honesty for that remark. After a few minutes rest, he checked the camera to be sure the telephoto lens hadn't been damaged. He let out a sigh of relief when he found that it worked.

Derek resumed his climb. But this time he was more cautious with the loose footing in the gravel-like soil. He stayed very close to the vegetation, going from bush to bush keeping handholds at every opportunity. At times he felt he was climbing a ladder because the closely packed shrubs served as 'steps.' He continued his ascent up the slope.

Derek knew that he shouldn't put so much stress on his injured arm before it was properly healed, but he had no choice. Though it throbbed in pain, he was committed to the climb. And he was getting closer to the top as each minute passed.

With a final groan, Derek pulled himself up to the top of the mesa. He gasped for breath, then doubled over and rolled over onto his back. The trip up was far more exhausting than he had expected. He lay on his back for a moment, panting heavily. He could hear Michelle's faint calls from below. He simply didn't have enough energy to call out a response.

It was a long moment before he was able to push himself up onto his hands and knees. He stayed in that position panting and huffing for breath like an exhausted old dog in the summer heat. Finally, he forced himself to his feet. He took a few halting steps towards the edge and called down to Michelle that he was okay.

Michelle was relieved to hear his voice. She was certain that he was exhausted by the time he reached the top. She didn't comment on why he took so long to answer her calls. She cupped her hands and yelled up to him. "What about wreckage—can you see any wreckage up there?"

"Give me a minute." Derek huffed as he caught his breath. He scanned the area but here was not the slightest evidence of any aircraft wreckage. As he looked around, he had the feeling that no man had ever set foot on top the forbidding place since it was created by some freak of nature millions of years ago.

"No, nothing!" he called down to Michelle. "It's real flat up here and I can see for quite a distance in every direction but there's no sign of anything that looks like airplane wreckage. It's really desolate up here. I'm going to scout around for a while to see if I can get a better vantage point to look around with the telephoto lens. I shouldn't be long. I'll check back in about 10 or 15 minutes."

Derek was surprised by the flatness of the mesa-top. For some reason, he'd expected it to look different. But it didn't. Like the terrain below, it was almost completely flat. The whole mesa-top was covered with the same type of dry grasses, shrubs, and small clumps of scraggly trees that filled the plain below. But a short distance across the mesa top he spotted an unusual formation in the form of an odd-shaped outcropping of rock. It stood out above a clump of small trees. After a few minutes' walk, Derek stood atop the outcropping and took in a panoramic view of the plain below.

Delighted with his vantage point, he shaded his eyes and scanned the horizon in every direction hoping to see some sign of civilization. He was greatly disappointed by what he saw. Everything out across the plain in every direction looked as barren and devoid of life as it had from the ground. No airplane or wreckage in sight anywhere. Even though he checked the opposite side of the mesa's base there was no sign of aircraft wreckage at the bottom. He shook his head in dismay. He couldn't help but think, *I can't believe it. Desolation as far as I can see. God, how I hate this place."*

Derek put his disappointment aside. He hefted the heavy camera up to his eye and began scanning the horizon with its telephoto lens. A slow pan through the south, east, and west turned up nothing. All the telephoto lens revealed was just a closer and more detailed version of the same desolate endless plain he'd searched a hundred times before.

Undaunted, Derek turned his attention to the north. As he moved through a slow pan, his heart suddenly skipped a beat. Something caught his eye! A tiny but brilliant glint of light had just reflected off something in the distance. It appeared to have come from the base of the odd looking, flat-topped mesa he'd spotted earlier. He was so surprised by the reflection that he lost sight of it. Though he was determined to locate it again, and eagerly panned back and forth over the area, he was unsuccessful. After several minutes of fruitless search, he was nearly convinced that his mind had just played a cruel joke on him. *He was about to give up in disgust when he caught sight of the flash once more.* Though he knew Michelle couldn't possibly hear him, he shouted aloud, *"There it is! I've got it! I see it! "Yes! Right there at the base of the mesa! It's flashing!"*

For several minutes Derek kept the telephoto lens focused at maximum resolution on the spot. As he watched the flashes, he searched his mind for what little he knew about signaling and Morse code, hoping to recognize the flashes as a form of communication code. Thoughts raced through his head. *Maybe it's more survivors. Maybe that's where the plane really went down. Maybe they're trying to signal others, who might have survived the crash.* But no matter how much he tried, he couldn't recognize anything that resembled a signal code. The more he watched, the more the flashes appeared to be random. But random or not, he thought, *there's something out there causing the flashing.* Natural or man-made, he knew something was out there. And that was the first encouraging sign of hope they'd had since the crash.

Though he still couldn't detect any pattern, Derek kept the lens focused on the distant flashing. But as suddenly as it had appeared, the flashing stopped. Derek put the heavy camera down and searched his mind as to what could have caused the flashing and why it had stopped. Over the next ten minutes he checked and re-checked the location but no more flashing emanated from the spot. Although he wanted to stay longer and investigate further, he remembered his promise to Michelle that he'd keep track of time. He placed the camera strap around his neck and onto his shoulder. It was time to leave. He climbed down from the rock ledge and headed back. As he neared the ledge he had a lingering feeling that something was odd about the site off in the distance. He couldn't put it out of his mind. He knew *something* was out there---but what?

Derek heard Michelle calling out to him as he approached the edge of the mesa. He moved cautiously to the edge, leaned over, and shouted down to her. "I'm okay Michelle. And I've got some great news! I saw something out there! There's a flash of light off in the distance! I can't tell what it is but it could be something important! I'm coming right down and I'll tell you about it!"

"Tell me now!" Michelle yelled up excitedly.

"Hold on! I'll be down shortly. I'll tell you as soon as I get down there!" Derek yelled back.

Though Michelle could hardly contain her excitement, she didn't press the issue. She knew Derek needed to put his full concentration into the climb back down. She resigned herself to wait until he got safely to the bottom before demanding the full story of what he'd seen.

"Okay then. I'll wait," she yelled. "Just be very careful coming down. You scared me when you slipped going up the first time. Take it slow!"

Michelle needn't have warned Derek. The near disaster during the climb up was still fresh in his mind. He'd learned a lesson from that. As he threaded his way back down he showed a greater respect for the dangerous slope. He descended slowly and cautiously. With gravity on his side the climb down was much easier than the climb up. He soon reached the bottom without mishap.

"Well tell me what you saw!" Michelle demanded. His feet had barely reached the surface.

"In just a second," Derek huffed trying to catch his breath. He was winded and perspiring so heavily he looked like he'd just taken a shower with his clothes on. A minute later he began talking again. His enthusiasm was evident as he spoke.

"I saw a flashing light reflecting off something in the distance. It flashed for a while then stopped. It could have been just a natural phenomenon, like sunlight glinting of a shiny rock. Or…..," he hesitated.

"Or what?" asked Michelle. "Come on, tell me!"

"Well….." Derek hesitated again. "I don't want to get your hopes up but it's possible that it could be coming from the wreckage of our plane. And if it is the wreckage, maybe there are survivors out there trying to signal for help. Of course, they couldn't know that we're way out here, but maybe they were just signaling randomly hoping to attract someone's attention--or even a high-flying plane. That makes sense doesn't it?" he asked hopefully.

"It sure does," said Michelle still trying to contain her excitement. "Tell me what happened when you tried to signal back."

Derek's jaw dropped. He was dumbfounded. He slapped his hand against his head. "God, what's the matter with me. I never thought of that. Damn! Why didn't I think to try to signal back?" He shook his head in disgust. "Hey, wait a minute—I remember seeing a signal mirror in the camping equipment! I'm going to go get it and climb right back up there and try to signal back!"

Michelle quickly reeled him in. "Calm down a minute. You can't do that right now. The sun is already going down and by the time you get back to the top there won't be any light left to make a signal with." Derek couldn't argue with her logic, especially when she pointed out that it would be courting disaster to attempt the climb back down in the dark.

"You're right of course," replied Derek. "And you know what, that may be why the flashing stopped. The sun was going down while I was up there and it's likely that it stopped because the sun's angle wouldn't allow anymore reflection as it went down."

Derek was full of enthusiasm as he spoke. "You know, Michelle, I think there's a good chance that the flashing may be coming from the wreckage. Maybe it didn't fly on as far as I thought, and if it is the wreckage then it would cover a wide area. And if that's true then there's a good chance that searchers will be able to find it."

"Of course, they'll have a big target to search for," said Michelle. "Maybe there's hope for rescue after all! We should start hiking over there first thing in the morning," Michelle added with great enthusiasm.

Derek readily agreed. "And," Derek went on, "there's still the possibility that there really are survivors out there. That flashing light certainly is a hopeful sign. Maybe we'll get out of here without having to walk our way out after all. Although," Derek added with a note of concern, "we'd still have to hike across the plain to get to the other mesa."

"If it means rescue," added Michelle, "I'll walk on water if I have to!"

"Calm down," cautioned Derek. "I'm not trying to be a wet blanket but let's not forget that it could be just a natural reflection, nothing more."

"Even if it turns out to be nothing it's still the best news we've had so far," said Michelle as she threw a hug around Derek's waist. "Anyway, you can forget about climbing back up there to try to signal back. It's too dangerous to try that again. You nearly fell already. We can't stay here any longer. We simply have to move on anyway. Our one best choice has to be to head towards that flash of light on the horizon." Derek knew she was right. There was nothing to be gained by procrastinating, it was now or never. It was time to move on. They both agreed. Tomorrow *was moving day*.

"We should have a celebration supper," chortled Michelle. "We'll have a *full meal* tonight and make a party out of it. I'll even make dessert. There's a chocolate cherry mousse in the inventory of freeze-dried foods." Derek heartily agreed. Their spirits soared.

As the temperature cooled with the setting sun, Derek and Michelle enjoyed a hearty meal of creamed tuna casserole. It tasted exquisite and they enjoyed it immensely.

After the fine meal Michelle set about preparing the rich mousse dessert she'd promised. Since the dessert needed time to set, they decided to retire to the tent until it was ready. While Derek held the tent flap open for Michelle, he couldn't help but notice how easily she moved through the opening.

"How's that ankle doing?" Derek asked. "It looks like you're moving better on it now."

"It's doing much better. As a matter of fact, I'm going to take off the splint for a while just to see how it feels."

"I'm not sure that's such a good idea, Michelle," Derek protested.

"Nonsense, it's just a sprain. We know that now. Besides it's already a lot better and I need to start moving around on it. The sooner I'm ready to walk on it the better." Derek considered her logic and decided to take off his own wrist splint. It felt reasonably pain free in spite of his escapade climbing the mesa. *It was probably just a sprain after all,* he thought.

Derek helped Michelle out of the splint and the two made themselves comfortable. Their talk soon turned to the subject of the light Derek had seen. Though both knew the glint of light might prove to be nothing, it offered them a ray of hope in a desperate situation and they took full advantage of it. They decided to use it as a focal point for the final course of their *'dinner party.'* They laughed heartily as they took turns creating fantastic scenarios of what the reflection was. Michelle's favorite was one that Derek had come up with. He suggested that it was portal to another universe where the land was green and filled with beautiful blue lakes. In his fantasy world, the air was always cool and refreshing and everyone was required *'by law'* to be naked with the one they loved. Michelle smirked. Judging from his unmistakable arousal he was taking his fantasy seriously. And as she savored the view, she was beginning to take the fantasy seriously herself.

"It's very hot in here," said Michelle, with a sultry smile, "maybe I'd better take some of these clothes off." Though Derek eagerly offered to help, Michelle refused. Instead she chose to tantalize him. Slowly and gracefully she removed her clothing. Derek found her beauty indescribable. She stood nearly naked in the soft glow of the of the setting sun that still filtered into the tent. All that remained covering her fantastic body was the wrapping around her ribs.

Michelle moved over to Derek. With the softness and elegance of silk, her hands caressed him with a gentleness he'd never known. Derek sighed softly in anticipation of what he hoped was about to take place.

"Now it's time for me to take these awfully hot clothes off you," said Michelle. Without protest Derek let her undress him completely. When she was done he reached up to pull her down to his side but she held back.

"No. Not yet--not *inside!* Like in your fantasy, we have to go through the portal," she said as she pointed at the doorway of the tent. "We have to have our pleasure *outside* so we don't *break the law*," she giggled.

Though Derek was hot with anticipation, he willingly took her hand and they exited the tent through the 'portal.' Once outside, Michelle took a moment to lay a large beach towel on the sand for them to lie on.

As they stood in the now cool refreshing night air, Derek embraced her in a passion he'd never known. As he drew his lips to hers in preparation for what he knew would be the finest experience of his life, she suddenly pulled away.

"Not yet," she whispered. "Take this," she said as she handed Derek the end of the rib wrapping she'd started to undo."

"Now pull gently on the wrapping," said Michelle.

As Derek gave a gentle pull, Michelle began to pirouette with the grace of a ballet dancer as the wrapping unwound from her gorgeous supple body. With a final graceful turn, she wound up naked in his arms with her sweet lips caressing his.

Moaning in unison, Derek and Michelle entwined as one. They slowly sank down onto the towel. The pair thrilled as their combined sweat lubricated their bodies heightening their pleasure. Pain and worry dissipated into pleasure and joy.

Nearly a thousand miles away the quiet of an air-conditioned room was broken. "More! More! More!" a woman's voice shrieked! "Come on you bastard! Don't make it lousy again. All you ever want to do is get your own pleasure! You rotten bastard...I hate you! I hate you!" she screamed as she pummeled his chest.

Before he could respond to the attack, he was rescued from the confrontation by the ringing of his bedside telephone.

"Yah! This is John! Whadda ya' want!" he growled angrily into the phone.

"Oh!..... Mrs. Sherry, I'm so sorry," he stammered. "I–I didn't know it was you." He listened intently. "What's wrong.....what's the matter? You sound so upset. No... no I didn't check my messages. I've been out of the country for a week and just got back in the middle of the night. What's happened?!"

Michelle's fiancé listened in disbelief as her mother explained. She had been calling him for days to tell him that Michelle's flight to Alice Springs had ended in fiery crash a hundred miles from Alice Springs. News report said there were no survivors. Devastated by her daughter's loss, she broke down, and sobbed uncontrollably as she tried to speak. She continued sobbing and talking incoherently about the upcoming wedding. Her mind was in a daze and her thoughts were distorted. Weeping, she rambled, as to what she was going to do with the wedding dress she'd ordered as a surprise for Michelle. She was tearing herself apart in her grief.

John didn't know how to react and his well-intentioned responses only made matters worse. His conversation with her ended abruptly when Michelle's father took over the phone. He apologized for his wife's condition and explained that she was taking Michelle's loss very badly. From the man's tone, John suspected that he was not taking his daughter's loss very well either. The conversation quickly ended.

John sat naked on the edge of the bed holding his head in his hands trying to accept that Michelle was gone.

"Enough of that phone call," his frustrated female companion chimed in. "Get back here and finish what you started."

In an angry voice, John commanded her to put on her clothes and get out. As she quickly dressed, she hurled a flurry of profane insults at him. "You suck! And you've got a tiny dick anyway!" she screamed, slamming the door as she left.

John was confused and upset. He sat in silence. He was truly saddened by Michelle's loss. He really did like her. But deep down inside he couldn't help but be happy that there would be no wedding after all. All through his business trip he kept thinking of ways he could get out of it. He'd even had a couple of panic attacks when he'd thought of what his life might be like when he actually got married and had to settle down. There would be no more secret women on the side. He wasn't sure he could handle that.

Yes, he thought, he'd miss Michelle and do all the right things for her family. He would show his grief because it was the right thing to do. But inside, he was glad that he was off the hook.

It wasn't until days later that he felt well enough to call his female companion back to explain why he'd thrown her out so abruptly. He hoped she would accept that his bad behavior was due to his sudden shock and grief in learning that his fiancée had just been killed. He sincerely hoped she'd come back to his bed and pick up where they had left off.

After the most pleasurable experience of his life, Derek pulled Michelle over close to him and in a loving embrace, he soon fell asleep. But as Michelle lay beside him she couldn't fall asleep. She lay awake thinking about how much her life had changed in the short time since the crash. What bothered her most was that she couldn't explain why she felt no remorse for the wonderful sex she'd just enjoyed with Derek. She thought she should feel guilty about having sex with someone she hardly knew--after all she was engaged to be married. But the more she thought about what she'd done, the more intense her memory of the experience came back to her. Her heart thumped with pleasure even as she tried to shake the thoughts from her mind. She tried to be ashamed of what she'd done. But in her heart, she knew she wasn't ashamed. She had loved it and she loved this kind, gentle, and caring man. Her lips curled up into a pleasurable smile. She snuggled closer to Derek and fell fast asleep.

CHAPTER 11

Michelle awoke at sunrise. She looked over at Derek—he was sound asleep and snoring heavily. He was exhausted after the previous day's hiking, climbing, and carnal activities. She thought it better to just let him sleep. They both needed all the rest they could get if they were to cross the unforgiving Outback in search of the glint from the far-off mesa. Tired, but unable to sleep any longer, she sat up, looked down at her ankle, and wiggled her toes. *Still feels pretty good even without the cast* she thought. *Doesn't even hurt.* She wiggled her toes again and tried to rotate her ankle. *Opps, that smarts a bit!* thought Michelle. *"Better take it more slowly. But it certainly is getting better.* A short time later the sun came up. Michelle decided that it was a good time to practice walking without her crutch. She haltingly hobbled to the pond to fetch water. She was shocked to see how much the water level had dropped overnight. It was dreadfully low now, and what water remained was very cloudy. She hoped that the water purification tablets were up to the task of making the water drinkable. She shook her head as she looked down at the pathetic sight. It was readily apparent that if the water continued dropping at the same rate it would be completely dry in only a matter of days. Greatly dismayed, she filled an additional bottle full of water and returned to the tent. It was a lifesaving decision that they'd made earlier to gather up and purify as much water as they could carry before starting their trek. The decision to move on offered their only hope of survival.

Michelle placed a water-filled pan on a flat rock that had been exposed earlier to the searing heat of the day. Although the sun had just come up, the rock still generated enough heat to warm up the water in the pan. When the water was warm enough, she made a pot of coffee from one of the freeze-dried packets. While the coffee stayed warming on the rock, Michelle retrieved the camera and telephoto lens. She held the big camera up to her eye and searched off into the distance where Derek had earlier seen the glint of light. She panned all around the area but saw nothing.

She heard Derek coming out of the tent. Pleased that he was still naked she playfully turned the telephoto lens on his body.

"Wow! *You're huge!*" she chortled playfully while focusing in on his manhood.

Unflapped, Derek teased her back by striking a body builder's pose.

"Any other observations," he added with a grin.

Michelle became serious but still smiled as she put the camera down. "No, not really. I was checking the mesa out there but I haven't seen anything more of that flashing light you saw."

"I'm sorry to hear that. But that may because you can't see it from this angle. I was a lot higher up and that may have had something to do with it. Anyway, we've no choice now. We've got to head out sometime in the late afternoon in order to get some daytime traveling done. The night will be our best time to travel but the darkness will make navigating difficult. We'd be in a real jam if we hadn't found that compass in the camping gear. Don't let me forget it, please," said Derek with emphasis. "And please remind me to bring the signal mirror too, I don't want a repeat of yesterday's fiasco when I forgot to bring it up with me on my climb to the mesa top. If we see any more of that glinting on our trek I want to be able to signal back immediately."

"Going up naked?!" chided Michelle. "Don't even *think* about it, naked or clothed. We already talked about that. It's not worth the risk. So, forget about it and let's start to organize our stuff and start packing for our hike."

Derek laughed as he hugged her. "It's only been a few days and already you seem to know what I'm thinking half the time. But, no, I wasn't thinking of climbing up there again. At least not naked. I don't know what would happen if I fell on your favorite part of my anatomy—*huge as it is.*" He laughed, then reached into the tent, retrieved his shorts, and pulled them on. "How's your ankle doing?" he added.

"Oh, that," Michelle responded. "I'm happy to inform you that my ankle's much better."

"You sure," Derek asked. "It's still swollen a little."

"I know, but I can move it all right. I even took a short walk earlier. I wasn't enthusiastic about doing it, but I don't have a lot of choice. I need to get mobile as soon as possible. You'll see what I mean when you take a look over there," she added as she pointed towards the marsh pool. "It looks like we're going to have to be moving on sooner than we expected."

"Whoa, I see what you mean," said Derek. He spied the greatly shrunken marsh pool. "Let's go check it out." He took Michelle's arm and the two walked over to the pool.

Derek couldn't understand how so much water could disappear overnight without the sun to evaporate it. Michelle suggested that the problem might be that whatever underground spring that kept it replenished must have, itself, dried up. They were both deeply concerned and agreed that they should immediately fill up every remaining container they could find.

Derek and Michelle thoroughly searched the campsite looking for anything that was capable of storing water. In Shawn's camping equipment they found a plastic collapsible water storage container that had a capacity of one full gallon. Michelle found more plastic bottles among the luggage. Rinsed and refilled with water, they were added to the collection. When they were done, they had collected nearly four gallons of water. That, along with the assorted other containers of water they'd collected the day before, gave them a total of six gallons. Michelle knew very well of the dangers of dehydration in Australia's hot and dry climate. She knew too, that six gallons of water, even if carefully rationed, was barely enough to complete their upcoming hike. Both prayed that it would be enough to get them across the searing heat of the plains out to the distant mesa. Neither wanted to even think of what they would do if the mesa didn't have a supply of water. In preparation for the hike, they brought the water supply into the tent. Michelle loaded additional water supplies into the big wheeled piece of luggage they'd found earlier. To her satisfaction, the bag rolled easily in spite of the weight of the water.

The sun moved across the sky as Derek and Michelle prepared for their departure. Although he knew it was too soon to strike out, Derek hiked out a short distance from camp to get a better vantage point to survey the route of their upcoming trek. He spent some time using the telephoto lens camera to survey the distant plain. Just as the day before, the only thing of possible interest was the occasional flash of light emanating from near the base of the distant mesa. Despite a number of attempts at using the signal mirror to make contact with the randomly flashing light, Derek had no success.

Scanning the mesa once more, Derek focused in on something intriguing. For the first time he was able to make out a dark band of what appeared to be shadows at the mesa's base. The limited power of the telephoto lens prevented him from identifying exactly what was causing the shadows. Scratching his head, he reluctantly put the heavy camera down.

After an hour's fruitless search, he sat on a rock and took a much-needed break. But he couldn't rest-- something was bothering him. Something just didn't make sense about the shadows he'd spotted. Derek lapsed into in deep thought. *And what about those shadows? They looked so out of place at this time of the day. Hmm, maybe they're not shadows at all,* he thought. *Okay, so they're not shadows then. So what are they?*

With a sudden flash of insight, it dawned on him! *"Damn!"* he cried aloud. *"It's those shadows! They're not shadows at all. The dark area is vegetation. It's trees and foliage!"* he shouted aloud. *"Growth like that just has to mean that there's water over there. I'll bet it's got a marsh pool just like this one! Please God, make it a full pool!"* He jumped to his feet and thrust the camera back up to his eyes. *"Damn! If I had just a little more magnification I could tell for sure!"* He put the camera down but a moment later thrust it up again. *"Yes, that's it! It just has to be vegetation and where there's vegetation, there's got to be water."* Derek was elated by the possibility of the existence of another marsh pool within striking distance. He hurried back to the shelter to share the news with Michelle. Though both knew that undefinable shadows alone were no guarantee that water was present, they had no choice but to bet their lives on it.

For the next two hours, Derek and Michelle carefully went through all the items that they had scavenged, taking only the most essential items. In the end, they made sure they had enough clothing to keep themselves warm during the cold nights, water, the big first aid kit, the remaining food supplies, a few basic toiletries, telephoto camera, camping equipment, including a compass, and two final '*luxury*' items.

Michelle decided that they each should pick one last item that each wanted to bring. It didn't matter if it was sensible or frivolous—there was to be no argument about it. Michelle picked the cell phone. But despite the *rule* that there would be no arguments about what luxury item was selected, Derek protested. He tried to convince her that the phone was useless without the PIN code; but Michelle prevailed. To get back at him, she issued a protest against his choice to bring along a safety razor and a bar of soap. She playfully harassed him that he was breaking the rules because he was really taking *two* luxury items, not one. He took the mock harassment in stride. Minutes later, after generously applying sun-tan lotion, Derek and Michelle were ready for departure. Everything was packed into the big rucksack and the large, wheeled, suitcase. "I guess it's now or never," Derek proclaimed. "We should move out."

"Yeah. It's time," acknowledged Michelle.

"Okay," replied Derek. "I've got the compass. And I found directions on how to use it in the Outback Survival Guide. But I don't think we're really going to need it anyway. All you can see on the horizon is that far off mesa so it's unlikely we could miss it."

"And what about the hiking we'll have to do in the pitch-black night?" asked Michelle? "Don't you think we'll need it then?" Michelle asked while flashing a silly grin. Derek felt a little foolish.

After making one last final check that they had everything they needed, Michelle helped Derek heft the heavy rucksack onto his back. It contained all their camping equipment and supplies including the light weight tent. Once balanced properly, Derek felt that he could easily handle the load.

Despite Derek's protests, Michelle decided to walk on her leg without the aid of the crutch. She preferred using it as a hiking stick instead. She insisted that she would be all right. They had decided earlier that each would carry only one thing. Derek got the rucksack-- Michelle got the big-wheeled case. She reached down and pulled up the extension on the wheeled suitcase and the two headed off towards the distant mesa.

The late afternoon sun was low in the sky as the pair walked past the marsh pool. It was virtually empty now. It was clear that by the next morning it would be completely dry. They knew they were making the right decision to move on.

Derek had estimated that their destination was some 15 or so miles away. He figured that if they traveled 7 miles a day that they should arrive at the mesa in two days with food and water to spare—as long as they rationed their supplies. But both knew that if the trip took three or more days, their chances of survival would be slim to none.

They mutually agreed to set as brisk a pace as possible their first day out because that would be the time when they would be at their best. They knew, too well, that their progress would be slower for each day they remained out on the open on the plain. It was imperative that they reach the mesa in two days--two and a half at most.

Before they left, Derek took a compass reading on the mesa at the point where he'd seen the glinting light. Then after one last look back at their former campsite,

Robert Campbell

they kissed each other and began the long trek across the
barren outback towards the distant mesa.

CHAPTER 12

A fter two full days of painful hiking, the pair were nearly spent. Michelle's voice was thick with weariness and exhaustion. "We have to stop and rest for a while!" she croaked. She let go of the suitcase handle letting it drop to the ground. Winded and huffing for breath, she called out again. "It's time to stop Derek. Let's do it! Stop now!" A moment later she eased herself into a sitting position atop the overstuffed suitcase—she could hardly move.

Derek, weak from fatigue, turned and shuffled back a dozen yards to reach Michelle. He nearly fell over as he lowered the huge rucksack from his aching back. He stood for a moment savoring the release from the oppressive weight of the pack, then settled heavily to the ground beside Michelle. The two perspired profusely as they gasped for breath. It wasn't until several moments later that Michelle found the energy to move. She struggled down to her knees and unzipped the big-wheeled suitcase she'd been sitting on. With some difficulty, she opened the big case and pulled out their last jug of water and that was only three quarters full. They had carefully rationed the water over the past two days sipping only minimal amounts at a time. But now, that was all that was left.

"Time for some water Derek," Michelle croaked. With great care, she poured out a small cup of water and handed it to Derek. The two shared the immensely refreshing life-giving liquid.

"Although our water supply is low I think we can hold out for one more day, if we really stretch it" said Michelle. "I'm astonished that we used so much, even with rationing." There was a clear note of concern in her voice. "I can't believe it's taking so long to reach the mesa. It's been *two full days now.*" Looking up at the sky, she declared wearily, "Make that two and a half days. And it still looks a long way off."

"We're getting there slow but sure," Derek replied in a voice that hardly convinced himself let alone Michelle. "One more day, that's all, a day and a half at the absolute most," he panted.

Michelle was unconvinced. She was becoming gravely concerned for their survival. They had clearly underestimated how long it would take to cross the huge desolate plain to reach the far-off mesa. While Derek's estimate of 15 miles may have been accurate, they simply hadn't bargained on how slow going it would be.

"Do you want another drink?" asked Michelle.

"No, thanks," said Derek though he badly wanted another swallow. "You go ahead, you look like you need it more than I do."

"I'll wait till later," she replied. After replacing the precious water container back into the safety of the bag, she stood up and scanned the surrounding area. Her eyes

152

fell upon a long dead shrub a dozen yards distant. She suddenly had in inspiration.

"Hey Derek, I've got an idea on how to make us some shade without having to set up the tent. I'll be right back. In spite of her exhausted state she ambled off towards the shrub. A moment later she snapped off four of its brittle branches.

Derek was too exhausted to participate. He just lay down beside the rucksack and put his arm over his eyes to protect them from the sun. A few minutes later Michelle returned with the branches. She sat down beside Derek and went about the task of stripping off all the extra shoots from the branches. When she was done she had four short poles which she stuck into the ground behind her. A moment later she opened the suitcase, retrieved two large beach towels, and draped them over the four poles. The result was a simple but ingenious solution to their lack of shade. Derek sat up and slid himself under the tiny shelter.

Michelle stepped back and admired her work. "There," she said with a touch of pride. "It isn't much but at least there's enough shade to cover our heads and shoulders."

"*Head and Shoulders, above all the rest,*" Derek mumbled.

"Huh?" asked Michelle.

"Gahhh!" Derek moaned as repositioned himself. "Ah, it's nothing. I'm just fooling around. I was quoting an old television slogan for a dandruff shampoo. The name of the product was '*Head and Shoulders*'."

"Humph!" replied Michelle. "You sure you aren't delirious? It sounds like your brain is fried already."

"This egg is your brain," said Derek, pretending he was holding an egg above an invisible frying pan. "This frying pan is drugs," he continued, as he tried to create the image of a frying pan in his other hand. Then, pretending to drop the egg into the frying pan, he added, "Sssssssssttt, this is your brain on drugs!" He laughed heartily. Michelle didn't get it.

"What are you talking about?" she insisted.

Derek laughed again. "Oh, I was just quoting another old TV commercial they used to run in the states. It was supposed to encourage kids to stay off drugs. I thought it was a perfect come back to your line about 'frying my brain.'"

"A minute ago, you were dying. Now you're telling jokes—if you can call them jokes," she added with a touch of insincere sarcasm. "If that's what happens when you take a drink of water, remind me not to give you any more. If your throat gets dry enough you won't be able to talk and torture me with more ill humor." She paused. "And wouldn't that be nice?" she laughed.

"Oh, I'm just trying to raise your spirits," Derek added.

"If you want to raise my spirits then move over and make room for me. Don't hog all the shade!" She gently prodded him with her foot.

The two sat quietly under the small patch of shade. As they sat, Michelle recalled their trek so far. Although it was hot at their time of departure, the temperature soon cooled as the sun moved lower in the sky and darkness fell. Michelle's ankle stood up well and both remained in good spirits as they slowly worked their way through the darkness. But as the night hours dragged on, they found it more difficult to traverse the difficult terrain and a number of sandy patches bogged down the wheels of the suitcase. She'd found dragging the bag extremely taxing and that required a lot of water consumption.

Derek found the going difficult as well. The heavy weight on his back, coupled with the soft sand, made negotiating the loose surface difficult and exhausting. And he too, had consumed more water than planned. By the end of the day they had covered less than half the distance they had planned.

Michelle knew how important it was that they travel at night but she found it impossible to sleep in the sweltering hot tent during the searing heat of the day. To her, it felt like hell on earth. *At least*, she thought, *back at the old campsite the tent was in the shade of the mesa for a good part of the day.* But out on the plain, without shade, the unrelenting sun beat miserably down on the tent. She couldn't help but recall how dreadful and insufferable those past days had been.

Now, after nearly three days hiking she wondered just how much more she could stand. One more day might be all she could take. She feared that a day and a half more might kill them both. She wearily moved into a reclining position. A minute later she dozed off.

After the short rest break under Michelle's make-shift shade cover, Derek lifted his head. He noticed that Michelle had somehow managed to fall asleep. He wished he could do the same. Derek watched her as she slept. Though she would have looked tired and haggard to an objective bystander, to Derek she was as beautiful as ever. He found that her beauty always surfaced, just like her intelligence. He was proud of the 'instant shelter' she'd created on a moment's notice just when they needed it the most--he didn't have it in him to set up the tent yet again. Knowing that Michelle badly needed rest, he decided to leave her alone. He let her rest.

While Michelle slept, Derek sat up and turned his head towards their destination. The more he stared at the mesa the more determined he became that he'd get Michelle safely across the rest of the plain. He *knew* there was shade, a recent check with the telephoto lens confirmed that. He believed deep in his soul that they'd find water there.

Derek shifted his gaze up to the sky. With dread, he calculated that they still had another two hours to go before they could end the day's march and set up the tent. He cringed at the thought. He wasn't at all sure he could stand one more 'night' in the daytime sun in that steaming torture chamber called a 'tent.'

Michelle came awake an hour later. Their short rest stop ended all too quickly. Michelle broke down the sunshade and picked up the towels. As she was returning them to the bag, her eyes fell upon the remaining jug of water. She asked Derek what he thought about having a drink before they left. The two had a short discussion then decided to share another drink of water before setting out. Michelle carefully filled a cup. The two shared the refreshing liquid, drinking it slowly and savoring each mouthful. Both knew that, what they

156

thought would be 'plenty' of water when they started out, was now 'barely adequate' to cover even half the remaining distance to their destination. Neither mentioned that once this last jug was gone, unless they found more water very soon, death would come swiftly out on the desert plain.

Michelle safely stored the jug away and rose to her feet. She shaded her eyes and surveyed the distant route they intended to follow. While Michelle picked up the handle to her bag, Derek struggled to hoist his rucksack up onto his back.

"Ready, to move out now?" he asked. "We've still got another hour or so left before the sun gets so hot that we'll have to stop for the 'night'. What do you think?"

Michelle had a quizzical look on her face. "Before we do that, Derek, let me have the camera for a minute. I think I see something out there." He handed it to her.

She searched an area off to the left of their intended route. Still looking through the telephoto lens she said, "I see a small clump of trees off in the distance. It looks like we should be able to make it in about an hour and it's still mostly on our way. Why don't we try for there--no further? The trees aren't very tall and they look pretty scraggly from this distance but maybe they'll offer at least a little shade over the tent to help cool it down. It probably won't help much but I'm all for *anything* that will help keep us from baking us alive in that tent when we stop."

Derek borrowed the camera from Michelle. He was dubious about diverting even a little way from their set route. But after a brief discussion, he relented. They'd take the slightly longer route. He hoped it would be worth the risk. A minute later, they moved out heading north, towards the clump of trees off on the horizon. Michelle took the lead.

Though the trek out to the trees was uneventful, their final steps were rewarded beyond their wildest dreams. Michelle arrived at the clump of trees a moment before Derek. She stood stark still when she reached the shade. She couldn't believe her eyes. The shade before her had a glimmer on its surface. Michelle thought, for a moment, that she was experiencing sunstroke. A moment later she suddenly comprehended that the glimmer was from *water.* Stunned, she realized that a tiny oasis stood before her, hidden under the shade of the trees. With Derek wearily plodding along in a daze, some twenty paces behind, Michelle screamed. *"Water, water, Derek it's water!"* Her screams rang out across the plain. She stood at the water's edge still looking down in disbelief at the shade-covered pool before her. It was nearly ten feet across but barely a couple of feet deep. Though it was hardly more than a big puddle, it was truly *water!* Michelle stood transfixed at the edge of the pool. Afraid that it was all a mirage, she closed her eyes and took a halting step into the water. She knew it was no mirage the moment she felt the divine water caressing her feet. She screamed with delight!

Michelle's shrieks snapped Derek out of his daze. Fearing she might be hurt he ran to her side. Arriving at the edge of the pool he was astounded to see Michelle standing in a pool of water. In an instant, he was in the water with her. They both excitedly stripped themselves naked, and whooping for joy, they lunged full body down into the water. As surely as a dry sponge sucks up water, their spent bodies sucked up life and renewal. Neither knew how long they played in the water, but neither cared. It was a luxury sent from Heaven--they stayed in the pool and enjoyed it immensely.

Eventually, the fierce sun forced them to set up camp for the 'night.' Greatly refreshed, and still naked, Derek set about the task of choosing a place to erect the tent while Michelle, at his insistence, remained luxuriating in the life-giving pool. To his surprise, the little oasis offered a lot more shade than they had anticipated. He selected a well-shaded spot under the largest of the few trees, raised the tent, and then rushed back to join Michelle.

A short time later their frolicking ended. It was time to get out of the sun and into the tent to begin resting for the next day's trek—but not before they refilled their water bottles with the cloudy liquid from the pool. After adding water purification tablets, they set the newly filled containers back in the wheeled bag.

Derek and Michelle entered the tent. Even though it was still hot inside, the tent was not nearly as oppressively hot as it had been the previous days. But Derek and Michelle didn't mind. Once inside the tent the heat, their nakedness, and the joy of their reprieve, no matter how small, struck them with passion. The heat of the tent was no longer a problem. They had a *very enjoyable* 'night.'

Michelle awoke for the start of what was to be their last day of the trek across the plain. But she was struck with confusion. There wasn't any light outside—that wasn't right—if it was early evening then there should still be some sunlight. She pawed around in the darkness and found her watch. By the glow of a small flashlight she checked the time. It was nearly 9 p.m. She was shocked. They had gone to bed at 11 a.m. and had slept through the entire day and into the evening. It was already dark outside! Though they had gotten some badly needed rest they had lost several hours of cool early evening travel. She woke Derek immediately. He too, was dumbfounded as to how they could have overslept. They had to move out quickly. Through the glow of a flashlight they rushed to break camp.

In no time they were ready to move out. Derek pulled out his compass and under the glare of a flashlight he checked his heading. He wanted to make sure they were lined up towards the base of the mesa where they'd seen the flashing light. The trek resumed. The long rest and cooling temperatures of the night time air put a spring in their step. Their route took them downward along a gentle slope. It made the hiking easier. And their trip was made easier too, because their physical and emotional conditions had improved immensely after their bath and extended sleep. Things were going so well that Derek removed the restrictive splint from his arm. Though it showed some swelling it seemed to be healing just fine. And Michelle's ankle was much improved after her luxuriating soak in the pool the day before.

Their spirits remained high and they felt confident that things were looking up.

But as the hours wore on, they soon found their weariness returning. Hiking conditions had deteriorated and they found themselves forced to continually change course to circle around or crawl over obstacles. Despite their weariness their confidence remained high and they continued pressing onward.

The pair hiked throughout the entire night. Morning was almost upon them. Once again, they were reduced to the point of exhaustion. Had it not been for their desperate situation they might have marveled at the vivid colors that painted the bush ahead as the sun peeked above the horizon. As morning's first light played upon the plain, instead of marveling at the beauty, Derek missed it all. His mind was on the rising sun and the rapidly rising temperature. At least the rising sun meant that he could use the telephoto lens again. Mechanically he took out the camera and once again panned the horizon.

Though his scan of the horizon didn't reveal the glint of light they'd seen earlier, he spotted something else that pleased him. Now that they were getting close to the mesa he could clearly see that he had been right all along about the dark band of shadows along the base of the mesa—there was vegetation, and lots of it. He happily shared the confirmation with Michelle. She was delighted by the news and insisted on having a look.

Michelle had no sooner put the lens to her eye than she cried out. "Hey! Derek! I can see that glint of light and it's dead on ahead of us among the trees. Nice navigating. I'll have the airline put you on the payroll when we get back!"

"Forget the airline. Here, let me have a look at that blinking light," he added eagerly as he took hold of the camera. "Yeah, I see it too." He paused. "I still can't tell what's causing it. Ah, now it's gone again," he added in frustration. Derek put the camera down and looked out at the mesa.

"How far away do you think it is?" asked Michelle. Derek tried to calculate its distance. "It looks to be at least four miles off--maybe less," he added hopefully. "Though I dread one more rest stop in that tent during the heat of the day we really should stop now. It would be a foolhardy risk to try to make it all the way to the mesa during the searing heat of the day. It's too far, especially since we don't know what we'll find when we get there. If there's any sign of life at the mesa I still haven't been able to spot it. So, I vote for moving on for just two more hours. No more! Then we set up camp to get out of the sun. We'll start out again a little before sunset. I'm almost certain that we can make it when the sun begins to come up tomorrow. What do you say? Is that a deal?"

"Deal," Said Michelle as the words croaked out her mouth. Dripping with perspiration she added, "Time for a drink. Want some?"

"Absolutely," replied Derek. His raspy voice was a clear indication that he very much needed some water as well. Michelle stooped down, opened her bag, and took out a jug of water. She poured Derek a cup and handed it to him. He drank it right down. For some time, they sat side- by-side on top of their respective bags gazing blankly off into the desolate Outback surroundings. Neither had yet recovered enough strength to start the hike back up again.

Some twenty minutes later Derek broke the silence. "Well, sitting isn't going to get us any closer to the mesa. I guess it's time to go," huffed Derek. "Only two more hours to go for today."

Derek wearily struggled into his backpack. Michelle prepared her bag, and in a remarkable display of energy, she fairly jumped up to her feet all ready to move out. A moment later Derek, now fully loaded up, joined Michelle and the trek resumed. There was no need to check anything with the telephoto lens for now. The mesa stuck out like a sore thumb directly ahead of them.

Though they had not quite finished the 'agreed upon' two hours hiking,' the pair felt as if they had been marching for days.   Reaching her travel limits, Michelle's thoughts turned towards the next day's goal. She knew that neither of them could take much more punishment. *If we don't reach the mesa by tomorrow*, she thought, *we're done for.* Her mind was churning. Their situation was desperate. Despite her misgivings, the two hours finally passed. At that point, both happily dropped their gear and slid heavily to the ground. Derek insisted that Michelle remain still and quiet while he quickly went about setting up the tent.

CHAPTER 13

While Derek set up the tent, a very weary Michelle sat on a rock and picked up the telephoto camera. She planned to see if anything more had become visible since their last check on the mesa. Something in the telephoto lens immediately caught her eye. She couldn't believe what she was seeing. She put the camera down for an instant, blinked, rubbed her eyes, and returned the viewer to her eye. This time there was no mistaking what she saw!

"Derek! Derek!" she screamed. "Come out here quick!!"

Derek, fearful that something dreadful had happened to Michelle, lunged out of the tent. His heart pounded as if it were sitting on an anvil being hammered by a burly blacksmith. An instant later, washed in a sea of relief, he realized that Michelle was uninjured. She stood, camera in hand, waving her arm frantically and pointing off towards the mesa.

"Derek! I can see buildings! Here look quick," she squealed with excitement. She thrust the telephoto camera into his hands. "Look you'll see. It's really buildings."

Derek's hand was shaking. He took the camera from her and placed it up to his eye. "Where, Michelle, I don't see any buildings," he replied with great disappointment. "Are you sure. I don't see anything."

Michelle was momentarily shocked. She began to wonder if she had been seeing things. She quickly took the camera back and looked again. For a heart-stopping minute she couldn't find them at first but quickly located them again.

"Right there! Look right there!" she cried excitedly. She handed the camera back to Derek and helped him aim it in the right direction.

"My God Michelle! You may be right. They could be buildings at that," Derek said hopefully. But as he continued looking through the telephoto lens he began to have second thoughts. "But you can't tell for sure," he continued, "because whatever is out there is mostly hidden among the trees. I guess they do look something like the outline of some man-made structures but I can't tell for sure." He continued looking. "And I don't see any signs of life around the area," he added.

Michelle was undeterred in her excitement. She took back the camera and inspected the area once again. "I think my eyes are better than yours," she replied, "because I can definitely make out the outline of a small building and maybe a big one too. And it's true, I don't see any signs of life there, but that doesn't mean anything. The sun's already up now and people would be inside. I know the structures are hard to see, Derek, but they're out there all right. I can just barely make them out."

"But if they are buildings, what are they doing out here in the middle of nowhere," asked Derek, still skeptical of her find.

"It must be a station," replied Michelle, the excitement still evident in her voice.

"A station? What do you mean a *station*?"

Michelle kept the lens to her eye. "A station in the Australian Outback is like what you Americans would call a ranch out West. The Outback is famous for its remote stations. This could be one Derek! There could be people at the station and maybe they have a radio or a truck. Come on Derek," she squealed. "Let's pick up our stuff and keep going. Let's go *now* please." Derek wasn't convinced that continuing on was a good idea during the remaining heat of the day.

"But Derek," she pleaded. "I know we're tired but we've still got plenty of water left since we refilled our supply, so water is no problem. Besides, even an abandoned station will almost certainly offer better protection from the elements than our sweltering tent. Michelle's argument about not having to spend another full day inside the sweltering tent was all that was needed to sway Derek.

"You're absolutely right," Derek called out. Let's pack up and go right now."

Without a moment's hesitation, Michelle cried out, "Yes! Absolutely, let's close up camp right this second." The pair enthusiastically embraced. A moment later, the two prepared for departure. Derek stored the tent and packed the rucksack. Michelle set about the task of straining some more of the dirty oasis water through a cotton shirt. Before sealing the storage containers, she added their remaining water purification tablets. A short time later, she held up a bottle of processed water for Derek to examine. "Well, what do you think Derek" she asked.

Derek frowned. "It's looks awful and unappealing right now. But, when the time comes that we need it, we'll think it looks and tastes like ambrosia. Anyway, the purification tablets should work. It'll be safe enough to drink." Michelle stored away the precious water and the two completed the task of closing up the camp site.

"I think that's everything Michelle. I'm ready now."

"I'm all ready too," she replied as she snapped up the extension handle of her bag.

"Okay, then. Let's head 'em up and move 'em out," Derek called out as if he were a cowboy starting off on a cattle drive. Michelle was unimpressed by his attempt at levity but smiled anyway. They picked up a heading directly towards the mysterious landmark on the horizon. Both were in high spirits, full of excitement and anticipation.

For the first hour their progress was disappointingly slow as they headed out across the treacherous plain. Almost immediately the terrain became difficult to navigate. Derek quickly became frustrated. It was a daunting task to work their way around rock outcroppings, clumps of waist high shrubs, and sharp scratchy branches. And, the searing sun was taking its toll on the pair.

Finally, reaching the point of exhaustion, Michelle called out to Derek. "We need to stop! I'm exhausted! We've got to take a rest break." Derek didn't have the energy to respond. He simply dropped his pack and sat down on it. A moment later Michelle joined him. The two sat silently as they caught their breath. It wasn't until several minutes later that Michelle decided to check, just one more time, on the distant 'station.' Finally, they were getting close. Michelle put the telephoto camera up to her face and wearily looked through the viewfinder.

An instant later she screamed, "*Derek! I see it! I see it! It's there; it's really there! I'm right, I'm right, I'm right!!!* We're close enough now that even *you* can see the buildings!" she continued excitedly. "Here, take a look!" She thrust the camera at him.

Derek was astounded. "My God! There really are buildings there after all!" he yelled. You were right all along! Come here 'eagle eyes'!" He threw his arms around her and gave her a bear hug.

Derek laughed. "You were right!" He gave her a long wet kiss. "All right now 'eagle eyes.' Put those baby blues back to the lens and see if you can see any signs of life among the buildings! Michelle searched the site for several minutes but saw no one. Then it occurred to her that something didn't seem right. It was more than just the fact that there was no sign of human life, it was something about the station itself. Though they were still too far away to make out specific details about the buildings, she could see that there was heavy growth around them. There were trees and shrubs growing in odd places almost as if the outback was trying to reclaim its territory. Concluding that the station must be abandoned, she lowered the camera and broke the news to Derek.

She was surprised and pleased by his reaction—he took it well. Though he readily admitted that he would have rather that it had been inhabited, his spirits remained high. The two talked excitedly about the implications of their find. It mattered only a little to them that there were no signs of life. The fact that the station actually existed buoyed their spirits and recharged their souls. They were excited and wanted to press on with only a short resting period. Despite their dog-tired weariness, they quickly shared a cup of water, got to their feet and eagerly set out across the plain towards the station that was rapidly getting closer.

To Derek and Michelle's delight, the next two hours went very well. The terrain had become nearly flat. There were fewer obstacles now and they were able to make steady progress. But the fast-paced march, sapped their energy quickly. Another hour later, breathing heavily, Derek called a halt. He couldn't take the pace any longer. Michelle was relieved when Derek lowered his pack and sat down. She dropped her bag and sat down beside him. Derek held her in an embrace for several minutes. In spite of their exhaustion and thirst, both maintained good spirits—their destination was finally real and it was close. After a long and satisfying drink of water they felt revived. Derek's confidence of their success was such that he used a cup of fresh water to pour over Michelle's head. The look of pure refreshment on her face was worth every ounce of water. Michelle returned the 'favor." They laughed in spite of their predicament.

After a short rest period, Derek helped Michelle to her feet. They started hiking again, this time side by side. The two marched together with an air of confidence. The going was easy now. With their goal in sight, nothing could stop them now.

Breathless and bone weary, Derek and Michelle stood 200 yards out from the main house of the well camouflaged station. They stood stark still, momentarily fearing that it might be a mirage. Derek could barely speak. "Do you see what I see?" he asked, just to be sure.

"Yes Derek, I see it too," Michelle croaked. "It's really there," she cried through parched lips. The two embraced and shared tears of joy.

After their long and joyful embrace, both wearily settled to the ground. They badly needed rest, water, and some food. Michelle opened wheeled bag and removed a jug of still-cloudy water and a couple of granola bars to share. She examined the water and noted that the water purification tablets had not yet had time to completely process the contents of the container. With no other recourse, she filled a cup from the mess kit and handed it to Derek. He quickly downed it. She poured some for herself and, like Derek, immediately drained the cup. Neither noticed the unpleasant odor or taste. They were delighted with the welcome relief it provided to their parched throats and weary bodies. Michelle stared down at the still cloudy water and snickered.

170

"What's so funny?" asked Derek.

"I was just thinking about back at the oasis. You said that when the time came to drink this awful looking stuff that it would taste like 'ambrosia.'" She motioned with her cup. "Well, Derek, you were right. This tastes like 'nectar of the gods' to me right now."

Derek nodded in approval. "Let's just hope that the station has lots more *clear ambrosia* when we get there."

"And we won't get there if you're a decrepit old wreck," replied Michelle." She rolled Derek over onto his stomach and did her best to massage his aching shoulder. Several minutes later the massage, the rest, and the water, loosened up his tight muscles." Derek felt much better as he hefted the backpack onto his shoulder. With daylight still remaining, Derek and Michelle struck out one last time to their destination.

The station loomed dead ahead! Michelle and Derek picked up their pace in great anticipation. For the first time they could clearly see what appeared to be a small main house with several small outbuildings hidden among the trees nearby. And on closer inspection they could see a very large building that looked to have been made out of rusted corrugated panels. *Must be a barn of some sort*, Derek thought.

Derek noted that all the buildings had been constructed close to the base of the mesa among the heavy vegetation and tall trees. He had no idea of what kind of trees they were but they were much larger and lusher in their foliage than those at their crash site. It didn't appear that the heavy vegetation and trees had grown up around the buildings randomly. Rather, it seemed that the buildings had been carefully constructed among the trees and heavy foliage in order to take advantage of the natural camouflage they offered. It almost looked as if someone had gone to a great deal of trouble to hide the station, and its huge barn, from view. Exhausted and dripping with sweat, Derek lowered his head from the horizon and kept walking forward.

A flash of light caught Michelle's eye. She screamed!!! "Derek! I can see a truck! That's what's been causing the glinting light. There's a truck almost completely hidden in the trees up against the side of the barn. The sun is reflecting off the windows or something. I can't tell exactly where, but it's coming from the truck all right."

Derek forgot his aching body and came alive. He ran to her side. Enthusiastically they picked up their pace. They desperately wanted a closer look.

"Does the truck look like it might run? It isn't a wreck, is it?" Michelle called out as they ran forward.

Closer now, Derek stopped in his tracks as he approached the truck. Sadly, he gave Michelle his opinion. "It looks kind of like a wreck. It looks old and rusted. One of the doors is missing. The hood is up and it must have flat tires on the back because it doesn't sit level on the ground." Greatly disappointed, Michelle easily confirmed Derek's observations. There was no hiding either's disappointment. The hope of finding people and transportation to civilization wasn't going to happen for them. But their choice had been made. There was no turning back because there was no other place to go. They continued toward the buildings.

With the main house barely one hundred yards away, their deep disappointment began to dissipate. Now that they were close, they could see that the buildings actually appeared to be in remarkably good condition. Michelle pointed out immediately that there were no broken windows in sight and all the doors appeared to be intact and solidly shut. Derek took note that the roofs of the buildings were in remarkable shape. In fact, were it not for all the heavy undergrowth around and lack of people, one might have thought it was a working station. Michelle's spirits picked up as he shared his observations with her.

Derek and Micelle stood for a moment, transfixed on the station. "Here's some good news," Derek reported. "The terrain looks a lot better at the station. There's a lot of flat level ground stretching far out onto the plain across in front of it. I don't see much undergrowth there and I can't see any signs of rock outcroppings either. *I wonder why that is?*" he asked with a note of curiosity in his voice." Michelle had no suggestions as to why there was a long smooth stretch out beyond the big barn. They dismissed it as natural ground formation. The brief stop in the sun brought them back to their task. They were ready now. It was time to enter the station.

"My Lady," said Derek. He made a graceful bow and extended his hand to Michelle. The pair, arm in arm, moved off towards the station with high hopes of finding water and shelter.

CHAPTER 14

Derek and Michelle found themselves filled with hope, anticipation, and fear as they moved across the last hundred yards toward the front door of the station. Up close they could see that the house and outbuildings that made up the complex were in remarkably good condition. And they were certain that, for some unknown reason, someone had purposefully built it hidden among the trees and foliage to make it difficult to spot.

Aside from the relatively new undergrowth, and young trees that were growing up in patches all around the station, the whole complex looked to be in excellent condition. The main house, though it looked unusually well-constructed, was oddly shaped. The front of the structure looked like a typical outback station. It closely resembled an old Texas ranch house. The main house had a typically utilitarian square shape and gently sloping metal ridged roof. But the back of the building had a strange, square-shaped addition attached to the rear of the house. Derek thought it looked architecturally out of place. It was taller than the rest of the structure and looked odd.

Putting any further architectural concerns out of his mind, Derek focused on the station itself. He marveled that it looked so well kept. It was hard to believe that somebody wasn't living there. That aside, there was no sign of life. As they got closer Derek felt compelled to announce themselves. They stopped. Derek yelled, "Hello! Hello the house! Anyone there?!" They heard nothing but the sound of a hot breeze blowing past their ears. They moved closer and Derek called out again. Still no answer, they stood directly in front of the house. The front door was located inside a large screened porch that ran halfway across the front of the house. Like everything else, even the screens were in excellent repair. Though they could see in through a curtained window beside the door, the house still appeared to be unoccupied. Derek pulled open the unlocked screen door and entered the porch with Michelle behind him. They stood on the screened porch catching their breath. Both were nearly afraid to enter, even though they were certain it hadn't been inhabited for some time. Stalling for a moment, Michelle maneuvered the big wheeled bag over to an open area on the porch, near the front door. Derek took the heavy rucksack off his back, nearly falling over in the process, and placed it beside the bag. Anxiously he reached for the door. He put his hand onto the old brass doorknob of the well-constructed but weathered door. He started to turn the knob. Michelle stopped him. She suddenly placed her hand on top of Derek's and whispered, "Wait Derek. Somehow it doesn't' seem right to just walk right in. This is someone's home. Please.... let me knock first. It seems like the right thing to do." Derek complied.

Michelle knocked briskly twice and called out, "Hello is anybody home?! Hello! Hello!"

A moment later, she tried again. Again, there was no answer. As she was about to try again, Derek assured her that it wasn't necessary. Michelle felt her heart pounding as Derek turned the doorknob. To his amazement, the unlocked door opened easily. He gently pushed the door, just a crack, before calling out their presence once more. Still no answer. Now that both were confident that nobody was home, Derek opened the door. Both were taken by surprise as an unexpected current of cool air flowed out from the tree-shaded home. With the door now fully open, they stepped inside.

It was several moments before either of them spoke. They stood, transfixed in silence, gazing at the spacious but austere main room that lay before them. Though a fine layer of dust covered everything in the room, it was otherwise so neat and tidy that it looked as if someone had methodically prepared it for company before going off to the market. The kitchen table that stood directly in front of them was perfectly set, upon a white-laced tablecloth. Fine china and silverware was set out and neatly folded napkins had been placed beside each setting. The room was such that it would have seemed quite natural if the owner just walked right in behind them carrying a bag of groceries calling out, G'day.

Suddenly Derek exclaimed, "Michelle! Look there's a sink with a hand pump!" He rushed over see if it worked.

Michelle immediately came out of her daze and hurried to his side. She watched with great anticipation as he pumped the old cast iron handle up and down half a dozen times. Yet, no water came out.

"Maybe you should wait a minute and try again," she said.

"That probably isn't a good idea," said Derek. "That may damage the pump seal. I think the problem is that the old leather valve down inside the pump is all dried out and if I keep pumping the handle it may break it. When the valve dries up from lack of use it can't suck up the water anymore." He looked around the room. "And from the looks of the layer of dust on everything in here, I'd say nobody has been inside this place in at least a couple of years."

"Is there anything we can do about it," asked Michelle.

Derek examined the old pump carefully before answering. "This pump is very old," he said. "I'm betting that the pump valve is made of *leather* like the ones used a long time ago. If that's the case, I may be able to make it work if I can prime it."

"Prime it? What does that mean?"

"That means we have to pour some water down the opening at the top of the pump. When the water reaches the leather pump seal it causes the leather to swell up and make a tighter seal. Once that happens, we should get suction back in the pipe and the water should start flowing again when the handle is pumped."

"How do you know so much about these old things?"

"When I was a kid I used to spend a couple of weeks with my family each summer at my grandparent's camp in Maine. There was no running water but they had a hand pump in the kitchen just like this one. Every season we'd have to prime the pump to make it work. My grandfather taught me how to do it. It's easy and there's usually no problem unless the seal is so dried up that it's all cracked and broken. Hold on a minute, I'll be right back," said Derek "I'm going to grab a jug of water from the bag outside."

While Derek went to retrieve the jug, Michelle surveyed the room once again. It was so very unlike what she imagined it would be when she'd first seen it from a distance. She expected an old station, even a working station, to be far more primitive. It looked more like a retreat house than it did a station. Her thoughts about the curious make-up of the room were swept from her mind as Derek hurried back inside with the water jug. He placed it in the basin of the old soapstone sink.

Michelle looked at the old cast iron pump with dismay. "How much will you have to put in?" asked Michelle nervously.

"I'll put in about a quart and then we'll wait a while before I try it." With that, Derek poured the water down the top of pump. They both waited anxiously to see what would happen.

"I sure hope this works Derek," said Michelle. "Our supply of water is really getting low now. I'm afraid we're in deep trouble if the pump doesn't work."

"Don't worry Michelle. I'm certain this will work." He slowly looked around the room. "From the look of this place somebody took really good care of everything. I can't imagine that they neglected or abused the pump. I think it just needs to be primed."

"Hmmm, this is curious," said Derek as he examined an odd-looking pipe and valve setup that was attached to the side of the pump."

"What's so interesting," Michelle asked.

"Oh, this pump. It's mounted strangely high and there's a pipe running out the side of it that travels off to the right. See where it disappears into the wall. I'll check it out as soon as we see if the priming job worked."

Several minutes passed. "I guess it's time to give it a try," Derek announced. His mind churned as he nervously reached for the pump handle. He'd put up a brave façade for Michelle with his determination that the pump would work but he knew there was a chance that it wouldn't. And he knew, as well as Michelle, that if they couldn't get water out of the pump their lives would be in grave danger. He was deeply concerned because he'd taken notice that there did not appear to be any surface water nearby. He'd been watching for signs of water as they approached the station, hoping that they would find another marsh pool. But there was no marsh pool and there was no sign of a wind driven pump or anything else that might indicate another source of water. If the pump didn't work and they couldn't find another source close by then they would only be delaying the inevitable. He didn't even want to think about that. Derek curled his hand around the pump handle and momentarily froze.

"Well come on, Derek, pump it!" urged Michelle.

Derek's mind returned to his task. He tightened his grip on the pump handle and pulled it through several smooth strokes. His heart started to pound as the handle moved up and down without resistance, a clear indication that it wasn't working. Again, he went through a series of several smooth strokes when he suddenly began to feel some resistance. Eagerly, he continued his smooth strokes until his efforts were rewarded with the glorious sound of cool clean water gushing from the spout and splashing into the sink basin.

"Ye-haaa! Yeah! Auh Right!!!! Look at that!! It's beautiful!!" he yelled.

Michelle screeched with delight as the water surged from the pump. She immediately thrust her cupped hands into the cool stream and splashed it onto her face and chest. Again, and again, she splashed herself, luxuriating in the experience.

"Here let me pump now! You get under it!" Michelle shouted excitedly.

Michelle didn't have to say it twice. Derek eagerly turned the handle over to her. He placed his head directly under the flow of water drinking it in and letting let it surge over his hair and down his face. For a moment, he raised his head up and let the water flow down his back before thrusting it back under the cool refreshing stream.

"That's enough, it's my turn again!" cried Michelle, as she tugged his shoulder. Derek pulled back from under the stream and shook his head. He sent a torrent of water flying from his hair. They switched places. Michelle thrilled to the pleasure of having gallons of cool water gushing over her head and down her back.

"More, more," giggled Michelle as Derek continued pumping.

It wasn't until several minutes later that they came to their senses. They recalled, all too vividly, how their last two sources of water had dried up unexpectedly. It was foolish to be wasting so much water. Michelle suggested that they put a stopper in the sink to collect some water--just in case.

As soon as the sink was full, they sank slowly to the floor and sat right in the middle of the huge puddle they had created. As if the weight of the world had been just taken off their shoulders. Michelle and Derek, in unison, let out an enormous sigh of relief. Barely a minute later the pair drifted off into blissful sleep.

Derek came awake with a start. He didn't know how long he'd been asleep in the puddle with Michelle, but he savored every minute of it. He felt enormously refreshed as he rose to his feet.

Michelle woke up as she felt Derek move. She thought she was dreaming until she felt Derek's strong hands helping her up off the floor.

"Welcome to Paradise," he chortled as he got her to her feet. "Your palace, My Lady," he said as he swept his hand around displaying the grand room.

"My God, Derek, we made it. We really made it!" said Michelle as if to confirm to herself that it wasn't a dream.

While Michelle stood wordlessly surveying the wondrous room around her, Derek's attention returned to the strange pipe that was attached to the pump. "Hey,

Michelle—check out this pipe." Michelle paid no attention. Something much more important had caught her attention.

"Forget pipes. Look over here," she shouted. She pointed to a tall open food storage cabinet over in a corner of the room. "That's food over there! Real food!" She darted across the room and thrilled to the sight of the wide assortment of canned goods stored there. "My God! Look at this Derek! There's beef stew, vegetables, corn, potatoes, all kinds of soups, peaches and pears. There's some of everything here. There's even oil for the oil lamp I saw on the kitchen table. We hit the jackpot!"

Derek felt a little ridiculous at having mentioned the strange piping mechanism. He dismissed the idea and hurried over to join Michelle in front of the storage rack. They delighted in going through the canned goods. Michelle had great fun pulling down and lining up selected items that she wanted to eat right away. Thought their diet of dehydrated food over the past days had been adequate and nourishing, they welcomed the opportunity to taste real food again.

While Michelle continued going through the food supplies, Derek walked over to the stove that stood under a curtained window near the door. It was a gas stove top, without an oven, and it appeared to be more than thirty years old. On the counter beside the stove, he found a large box of Diamond safety matches. Though he never expected it to work, he turned on the left burner, struck a match and put it to be base of the burner. He was taken utterly by surprise when he heard a loud 'poof' and a big blue flame shot up from the burner.

Michelle was delighted when she saw that the stove actually worked. It meant they could have a real meal and sit down at a table and eat like civilized people for a change. She was surprised at how she felt. *After all*, she thought, *we've had only been stranded for about a week. Yet it feels like a century since I've been inside a real home.* With thoughts of food, she called to Derek, "Do you want something to eat now?" she asked, while holding up a can of beef stew.

"No. Not right now," he replied. "Come on, let's check everything out first." Michelle readily agreed. She was too excited about their find to eat anyway.

"Okay," she chortled. "You take that side of the room and I'll take this side."

Derek began his search by taking in the construction of the room. He marveled at its simple yet effective design. The wood floors were smooth and level. The nicely shellacked walls and ceilings appeared to have been made out of thin sheets of wood paneling that had been nailed in place and covered with strips of custom molding. The overall effect was that it gave the place a comfortable rustic elegance that required little maintenance.

Moving around the room, Derek stopped in front of a large piece of furniture. The big, comfortable looking, overstuffed chair sat beside a handsome writing desk. Upon the beautifully crafted desk rested a marvelous old oil lamp, a fine pen and pencil desk set, and a large gold key. To the left of the desk was a large bookcase that had been nicely hand made out of pine boards. It was basic and unfinished but reflected a high quality of craftsmanship.

Derek's attention next focused on an old recliner chair that sat near a bed on the far side of the room. It had the look and feel of being someone's *favorite* chair. It didn't look very good but it had the charm and feel of a personally loved possession. Beside the chair was a simple table with an old and ordinary looking oil lamp sitting atop it.

"Boy, does that look comfortable," said Derek as he stared longingly at the recliner. He couldn't resist. He fell, rather than sat, into the comfortable chair. An instant later, he reached down and pulled up on the footrest lever causing the chair to go into its fully reclined position.

Michelle watched Derek settle into the chair. "Don't strain yourself as you investigate," teased Michelle.

"I can do just fine from here," Derek chortled. "As a matter of fact, I have a better view from here of that pipe that runs from the sink through the wall into the room beside it." He was intrigued. "I'll check that out now." With a big groan, Derek struggled out of the recliner. He needed to satisfy his curiosity about the odd plumbing that entered that room.

While Derek went off to check the plumbing, Michelle turned her attention back to her own inspection of the room. Like Derek, she too, was impressed by the nicely crafted and well-maintained wood floors. But the floor was not fully exposed wood. A large piece of linoleum covered the dining area where the nicely set table was situated. The flooring displayed a quiet muted pattern that seemed to give the room a simple, understated atmosphere.

Michelle decided to take a closer look at the table and the dishes that were set upon it. She picked up one of the dinner plates. Using a napkin, she wiped away a fine layer of dust to expose its hidden beauty. The elegant bone china depicted woodland scenes featuring delicate hand painted renderings of birds and flowers. Each place setting depicted different feathered creatures among floral displays. The individual settings created a table that exuded grace and simple elegance. She replaced the plate exactly where she'd found it then continued her inspection.

Off in the far corner of the room a humidor caught her eye. It looked just like the one her father still used at home. She was drawn to the object. It sat upon a low table next to the recliner. She lifted the lid and was pleasantly surprised by the aroma of the tobacco inside--it still smelled fresh. The delicious scent brought back instant memories of her childhood days at home. The simple whiff unlocked a flood of wonderful memories as she relived Sunday mornings when her dad played board games with her on the floor. He'd have to stop playing every so often to refill his pipe. That's when he'd open the humidor and release the wonderful tobacco smell. She loved it so and she missed him. After replacing the humidor's lid, she admired the half dozen well-used pipes that filled the pipe rack beside it. The pipes brought back sweet memories of home. She picked up a dust covered but highly polished pipe. Tears came to her eyes as she held it. It looked so very much like the one she had bought her dad for his birthday. She was twelve at the time and the pipe had been expensive—too expensive for her to pay for on her own. But her mother knew how much she wanted the gift for her dad. She came to the rescue and gave her enough to buy it. But she insisted that money was just an advance on her allowance so she could honestly claim she'd bought it with her own money. But her mom still paid her allowance anyway. Mom always took care of her. She was proud of her mom and dad. It troubled her to think of what they must be going through. She dearly wished that the cell phone had worked.

Michelle let the bittersweet memories fade and continued her search. Behind the recliner and up against the wall stood a rather large cherry finished cabinet with brass trim. Opening the door brought a surprise--it was actually a liquor cabinet. Though there wasn't much inside, she did spy a quart bottle of Scotch. She was about to call it to Derek's attention to it when he called out to her.

"Michelle, come in here a minute. You're not going to believe this!" He yelled, obviously pleasure by whatever it was that he'd discovered. She hurried across the room and entered the doorway where Derek stood.

"A bathroom!" Micelle exclaimed. She was taken totally by surprise. She never expected that. Like Derek, she expected that any bathroom facilities at the station would consist of a primitive outhouse of some kind. Instead, before her lay a bathroom complete with a flush toilet and an old claw foot bathtub.

"Look at this setup," Derek said excitedly. He pointed to the piping system. "There's a diverting valve on the side of the pump in the kitchen sink. In order to send water into the bathtub, you just flip the valve in the kitchen. Then, when you pump the lever, the water flows here into the bathtub instead of into the sink. And to fill the toilet tank, you flip the bathtub diverting valve, which then sends water into the toilet tank instead of the bathtub. Then you just flush the toilet as usual. It's cleverly set up so all the water flows downhill. And everything works. That explains why the kitchen pump is mounted higher than usual—that way the water flows downhill into the bathroom fixtures." It's all done in an elegant manner. Clever, simple, and effective." Derek smiled with pride, as if he'd designed it himself.

"I'm impressed," said Michelle. And she really meant it.

"What do you say?" asked Derek. "Like to join civilization," he added as he gracefully bowed in preparation to exit the room. "I already turned the lever and filled the toilet tank in case you might like to use the facilities." Michelle was pleased to take him up on the offer. She gently ushered him out and closed the door behind him.

A short time later Michelle emerged from the bathroom only to find Derek sound asleep in the recliner. She decided to let him rest while she continued exploring about the house. She opened a door which led into a small bedroom. A dresser next to the bed caught her attention. She softly opened a couple of drawers and noted that they contained only men's clothing. Sliding the drawers shut, she tip-toed over to a door near the foot of the bed. It looked very much out of place. It was considerably taller and wider than the rest of the doors leading into other rooms of the house. She suspected it led into the large addition that they'd seen attached to the back of the house. Out of curiosity, she turned the knob but found the door locked. *I'll have to check that out later*, she thought.

Another door caught her eye. She walked back towards the bathroom where she'd earlier noticed a door off to right. This time the door opened easily but it didn't lead into another room. Instead it opened into a pantry full provisions. It appeared to be well stocked. There were large sacks of flour, sugar, full cases of canned goods and a huge variety of other supplies. There was even a full case of canned beer over in one corner. Michelle looked at the food supply and estimated that they could live for months on what was stored inside. She was certain Derek would be delighted by her find when he woke up.

Michelle was intrigued by an unusually large can of food. Because of its large size she thought it might make a hearty meal. She reached up to remove it from the shelf but lost her grip on it. An instant later, the can tumbled from her hand and crashed onto her foot. She cried out in pain!

Her shriek startled Derek out of his slumber. He leaped out of the chair to see what had happened. He found Michelle sitting on the floor of the pantry holding her foot and sobbing in pain. Both were relieved when, a few minutes later, the pain subsided. It was apparent that there was no real injury to her foot. At best, there'd be just a black and blue mark for a day or two. Once Derek helped her to her feet she insisted on showing him her discovery. They both delighted in taking a visual inventory of the pantry's contents. Their spirits picked up immensely as they savored the foods and planned their next meal.

Michelle offered to start cooking right away but Derek insisted that she soak her injured foot. Despite her protests, he helped her over to the recliner chair. He demanded that she stay put while he filled the tub. It didn't take long. A quick flip of the diverter valve and a period of steady pumping put enough water in the tub to give Michelle enough water to bathe her foot and soak her tired body.

"Tub's ready," Derek called out.

"Are you sure we should do this?" Michelle asked. "Aren't you worried about wasting the water?"

Derek thought about that for a moment. "No, I think it's all right. It's most likely a deep water supply. The building has obviously been here for years and it still works so I guess we're safe enough. But, just in case, we'll want to be alert to conserve water from now on."

Michelle was ready for her soaking bath now. Derek helped her out of the recliner. She put her arm over his shoulder and the two shuffled to the bathroom. Derek eased her down onto a small stool that sat under the bathroom window. He quickly left, closing the door behind him, so she could get undressed in private. "If you need more water, just give a yell," Derek called as he left. "I'm going to leave you in peace for a little while I bring our bags in."

Derek returned with the bags and placed them just inside the front door. A moment later he heard Michelle call out for more water. He promptly returned to the pump and added more water into the tub. That second refill was all it took. The tub was full.

"Ahhhh...this is great!" Michelle called from tub. "Why don't you come on in and join me?"

Derek willingly complied. He hurried to the bathroom, stripped off his clothes and slipped into the tub with her. After all they had been through, nothing could compare to the simple luxury of a cool bath after so many days in the searing sun. The tub was slightly larger than standard size and it offered just enough room for the two of them. Derek sat with his legs outstretched and his back against the sloping rear of the tub while Michelle sat between his legs with her back reclined on his chest.

"You make a nicely padded backrest. With all that chest hair it feels like I'm leaning on a bear rug," she snickered.

"And you feel exquisite," returned Derek, wearing a smile of immense satisfaction. He closed his eyes, absorbing the luxury of the tub. He thrilled to the feel of Michelle's cool soft body squirming against his own.

Michelle was deeply into the pleasurable experience when Derek ran a wet hand through her hair. "Ouch!" she yelped. Derek's hand, caught up in a knot of hair, had broken the spell.

"Ohh. That hurt," said Michelle. She sat up.

"I'm sorry," Derek apologized.

She ran her fingers through her hair and looked down in disgust at several twigs that came out.

"It's not your fault. But I've just got to wash my hair. I can't stand this tangled mess."

She recalled, with dismay, how much she had wanted to bring her shampoo and rinse on the seemingly endless hike to the station. But they needed to keep their load to a minimum and the dearly missed the toiletries that had to be left behind. Though Derek had argued that she should bring them along anyway, she prevailed in the argument by insisting that it was simply extra weight that they couldn't afford to carry.

"Do you mind if I have the tub to myself for a while I do my hair?" she asked.

Disappointment was clearly evident in his voice. "Sure, it's all yours," he replied as he grabbed the sides of the tub and pushed himself up. "But before you start your hair, I've got to go get you something."

A moment later he returned. "A present for My Lady," he chortled as he produced the glorious bottles of shampoo and hair rinse that were supposed to have been left behind. Michelle squealed with delight when she saw them. She thrust herself up and threw a luscious wet hug around his still naked body.

"Meet you in bed after I do my hair," she said with a coy smile as she slid gracefully back into the tub. Derek responded with a smile of anticipation. He dried himself and hurried off to turn down the bed. He lay there hoping Michelle wouldn't be long.

A short time later Michelle stood naked beside the bed, radiantly beautiful in spite of the ordeal they had been through. But Derek didn't see the gorgeous sight. He was dead to the world, sound asleep, and snoring loudly. Michelle was almost glad. She wanted him but she was every bit as exhausted as he was. She slid under the sheet next to him and instantly fell asleep.

CHAPTER 15

It had been late afternoon when Derek and Michelle had fallen, exhausted, into bed. They slept throughout the rest of the day and on into the night. Michelle came awake around 8AM. She had slept nearly eighteen hours. Michelle's aching muscles caused her to stretch and groan. Her sounds caused Derek to stir himself awake. Groggy as he was, he managed to raise his head to confirm his surroundings. Seeing Michelle beside him in the bed was all the confirmation that he needed. They were safe, and together. He smiled at Michelle, then instantly flopped his head back down onto the pillow. His last thought, before immediately falling back asleep, was that of savoring the simple pleasure of being in a real bed with someone he loved. It was a delight.

Michelle looked over at Derek. His tossing and turnings in the night caused the sheets to uncover most of his body. For several minutes Michelle enjoyed the exotic pleasure of watching him sleep. Her mind drifted to the wonderful sex they'd enjoyed the day before. A smile of pleasure spread across her face. A moment later, reality set in. She was starving for something to eat and she knew that Derek was hungry as well. It was time to get up. She quietly exited the bed then pulled the sheet back to cover up Derek's fine-looking body. The movement caused him to come awake for a moment.

"Derek," she whispered, "why don't you stay in bed for a little bit while I clean up and get dressed. There's only one bathroom anyway. Afterwards I'll get us something to eat." She needn't have bothered to tell him to stay in bed. He'd already fallen asleep again.

When he awoke again, a half-hour later, the air was filled with the grand smell of fresh coffee brewing on the stove. *It's going to be a great day*, he thought. He propped himself up on one arm and stared at Michelle. She was wearing a short, floral print, silk dress. The sun coming through the window made the dress glow. Her exquisitely beautiful silhouette showed through. Yes, thought Derek, this is going to be a very good day indeed. He groaned, stretched, and got out of bed.

"There's a whole dresser full of men's clothing beside you," Michelle called over to him. "I checked, there's underwear, socks and everything. Why don't you pick out something to put on after you get cleaned up?"

Derek hopped out of bed and pulled open the top dresser drawer. "Yuck," quipped Derek. "There's only boxer shorts in here." Suddenly he realized what a ridiculous statement he'd made. They had reached safety barely twenty-four hours ago and here he was complaining about the choice of underwear.

"Poor baby, I'll call up Sax Fifth Avenue in New York and order you satin britches," Michelle called out.

"Going to use that silly cell phone to make your call," he teased. "Got that PIN code solved yet?" he

194

laughed. Derek smiled. He recalled how Michelle had whiled away the boring hours in the steaming tent by entering PIN codes into the cell phone in hopes of getting it to work. She started by entering 0001 and continued entering codes in ascending order hoping she'd eventually get the working PIN code. Whether or not the battery would last that long, or whether it would work once she got the PIN code, didn't matter to her. Derek chuckled to himself. He knew it was her way of maintaining hope during a desperate situation. And too, there was a real chance that she might make a connection. No matter, he thought, it offered her a much-needed diversion and it made Derek happy to see her spirits so high.

Sensing Derek looking at her, she smiled and said, "Don't laugh. I'll get it sooner or later. I'm already up to 1260. You'll be sorry when I get it. I'll order pizza and I won't let you help pick what kind. In the meantime, you should finish getting cleaned up and dressed. I've got coffee and I'm making scrambled eggs and Spam. I found powdered eggs on the shelf. They won't be great but it should be a lot better than our rehydrated meals made with dirty water."

"Be there in a minute. I'm starved," replied Derek. He quickly selected a kaki short sleeved shirt and a pair of dark green cargo shorts. Still naked, he was about to head off to the bathroom when he dropped the shirt. As he bent down to pick it up, he noticed a pair of heavy-duty work shoes under the bed. He pulled them out and slipped his foot into one of the shoes. Although it was at least one size too big, he laced it up. With a smile of

study

approval, he decided he'd wear them later. After dressing he pulled on both boots, laced them and found them comfortable enough to use. He thought the study boots would serve him well.

A moment later, Derek prepared to shave. He looked into the mirror above the bathroom's small sink and examined the cuts and scrapes on his face. They were healing nicely. Out of curiosity, he made a quick check of the plain wooden medicine cabinet. It contained a few assorted items along with some old-fashioned shaving cream in a tube and a straight razor. He picked up the razor and examined its deadly looking blade. Knowing that discretion is the better part of valor, he decided to abandon any idea of using it. Instead he returned to the rucksack and retrieved the razor and shaving cream they'd found and packed earlier. He quickly returned to the bathroom where he took great pleasure in removing the heavy beard growth from his face.

Michelle was taken aback when the dressed, clean-shaven, and well-groomed Derek emerged. "Well you look like an outback rancher dressed up like that," she said smiling. Derek smiled in return.

The breakfast looked and smelled exquisite. They were so hungry that they drank a whole pot of coffee and ate all the scrambled eggs and Spam that Michelle had cooked. When it was all gone Derek got up and cooked another full can of Spam. It also quickly disappeared.

With the meal finished, Derek sat contentedly in the kitchen chair looking about the room when his gaze fell upon the very large door off the bedroom. In his exhausted state the day before he hadn't noticed it. He became curious. For no apparent reason, it was a great deal larger than any of the others in the house. While he examined the door, he suddenly remembered the addition at the back of the house. Just as Michelle had done, he stepped over to the door and tried to open it.

"It's locked," said Michelle. "I tried it yesterday but it wouldn't open."

"That's okay, we'll check it out later," Derek replied. "Anyway, right now I'm anxious to get outside to see what we've got to deal with. Maybe there's a new four by four truck sitting out back with a road map on the seat and a full tank of gas. Come on let's go check it out."

"No, not just yet. I want to sit down for a while and get off my feet. I'll be out in a little bit. You go ahead."

Derek hugged Michelle. He put his hands on her shoulders and gently massaged her neck. He delighted in the way her silky-smooth hair flowed over his forearms while he peacefully continued the massage.

Michelle reached up and put her soft warm hands onto his wrists. "That feels real nice but I know you're anxious to get out there. It's okay. Go ahead. I'll be along. Yell if you find anything interesting." Derek kissed the top of her head, turned and headed out the door.

The high temperature outside struck Derek immediately. Inside, the house was much cooler by comparison. Though nobody would have ever suggested that the house was air-conditioned, it certainly was a great improvement over the outside air temperature.

Oblivious to the heat, Derek strolled across the front yard. He felt as if the weight of the world had been lifted from his shoulders. For the first time in days his body was free from the constant crushing weight of the rucksack. And for the first time since the accident he felt safe. *I didn't let Michelle down after all*, he thought with pride. He felt good about himself and their current, greatly improved, situation. Things were looking up.

Once he was some distance away from the house, Derek turned around to take in a full view of the station and its surroundings. Up close, without his vision and senses clouded by weariness and desperation, he could see that it was far lusher than he had first thought. He marveled at the heavy vegetation and large healthy trees that covered the house providing it with cooling shade-- *nature's own air conditioning*, he thought. He wasn't surprised to note that, in spite of the lush vegetation immediately surrounding the station, there was no open pool of water like the one at the crash site. *Who cares if this one doesn't have a marsh pool*, he thought with a smile. *This one comes with running water and a bathtub to boot!*

Derek's smile quickly vanished when he turned around and gazed out across the plain they'd just crossed. Hell, on earth, he thought. He shook his head in disbelief. It seemed impossible that they could have made it across that roasting hot desolate stretch of terrain. A momentary flashback of their treacherous journey caused him to shudder. He shook his head to clear his mind and bring himself back to the present.

Happily putting away the dreadful reminder of the awful trek that had nearly cost them their lives, Derek turned his back on the plain and headed briskly towards the large building he presumed was a barn. It lay some distance away from the main house.

On the short hike to the barn, Derek examined the mesa which rose behind the station. It appeared to be somewhat smaller in size than the one back at the crash site. But it differed too, in that the sides of this mesa tapered down to the plain at a far less steep angle. *This one will be far easier to climb*, he thought. *And maybe I'll be able to see signs of civilization from the top this time*, he said to himself, even though he didn't believe it. He made a mental note to consider climbing it sometime when he was more rested.

Derek continued his purposeful pace. But his mind continued to focus on the mesa behind him that protected the station and its buildings. He was struck by the thought that this mesa, with its lush base, appeared as an island of hope floating amid a sea of desolation. He marveled and wondered at the sight. How could it be, he thought, that the mesa that stood only meters behind him could be so lush and inviting, when only a short distance out from its base the terrain became dry, desolate, and foreboding.

Stopping for a moment's rest, Derek turned his attention to the northern plain out beyond the station. There, the area was virtually flat as far as the eye could see. But the terrain differed from the region they'd hiked through earlier. It lacked the scattered islands of low scruffy trees and big outcroppings of rock they'd passed through on their trek to the station. Instead, the northern plain was covered with coarse, green grass peppered with clumps of darker and taller grasses. Among the grasses sprang occasional clusters of low leafy undergrowth. Though rare, one could see an occasional solitary tree standing way off in the distance. Other than that, the view was only broken by sporadic patches of low, leafy plants with slender stems, some of which displayed delicate, sparkling white flowers.

A few minutes later Derek neared the barn. He looked back at the house to see if Michelle was outside. She wasn't. But as he stared at the house he noticed a large propane gas tank mounted on the outside wall. It suddenly occurred to him that such a tank would have to be filled on a regular basis. Even if it were only seldom used, it would eventually run out and have to be refilled. That meant that either the owner had to load the empty tank onto a truck to exchange it, or he'd have to have someone come out to refill it. Since it was only a remote possibility that someone would come out this far into such desolate territory to service a single tank, it seemed even more likely that the owner would took care of the job himself. So that meant that he must have a truck. And hopefully, thought Derek, that truck may be inside the barn.

Just outside the entrance door to the barn sat the old truck Michelle had spied earlier. *This couldn't be the truck the owner used to shuttle gas bottles with* thought Derek. It was an old Ford stake-body truck with a big long-range fuel tank bolted to the cab end of the truck's bed. It looked to be about 25 or 30 years old. Its dull green paint was worn down to the brown primer on most of the flat surfaces. The driver's door was damaged and it was easy to see that it was a right-hand drive truck, typical of Australian vehicles. It had the look of a hard driven, overused, beat up old bush truck that had long ago given up its usefulness.

As he strolled past the truck a slight breeze picked up. Suddenly Derek was struck in the face by a blinding glint of light. He put his hand above his eyes to shade them, then saw the cause of the glint. It was coming from the side mirror of the truck as it dangled from a piece of wire that had been intended to hold it in place on the rusted door frame. It had long since fallen loose and flapped whenever an infrequent breeze struck it.

So that's it, Derek mumbled to himself, *that's why it only flashed occasionally.* The sun had to be just right when a puff of wind struck the mirror. The mirror would then catch the sun and it would send out a glint or two.

Derek stepped over to the truck and looked at it more closely. It was clear that there was virtually no hope of ever getting it to run again. The dual real wheels on the left side were flat and the tires hopelessly cracked wide open at the bottom. He lifted the huge hood enough to remove a stick that had been holding it partway up. He raised the hood into the full open position. A quick check under the hood revealed that the engine appeared to be intact. And although the critical radiator hoses were hopelessly cracked open, the rest of the engine compartment looked pretty good. But even with Derek's mechanical prowess, there was no hope of reviving the vehicle without the required parts. It clearly offered no hope of ever being a source of useful transportation.

Deciding that he'd been side tracked long enough, Derek turned his attention to the large barn that stood before him. It was well-constructed out of corrugated steel that had at one time been painted a flat gray. Most of the paint had long since been worn away by the elements and had been replaced by various muted shades of rust. But the building still appeared to be strong and sound. The door itself was especially strong. It appeared to be made of heavy grade steel. He grabbed the door handle and tried to open it. It was locked.

Looking for another way in, Derek inspected the barn. *This is an odd shape for a barn*, he thought, as he observed that it was much wider than it was long. And two other things made it particularly unusual. It had an enormously wide front door that spread across the entire front of the building. Derek's pulse raced as he had an uncanny thought. *This structure looks more like an airplane hangar than it does a barn*! He had no idea what that might mean to their predicament if it was, in fact, a hangar. But it offered some hope of unique possibilities. He was more eager than ever to enter the structure. But there appeared to be no way to open it from the outside.

Derek was determined. He continued his circuit around the building. He noted that the only window openings that existed, were covered by moveable, hinged, corrugated steel panels. But the covers were placed high up on the building with no access from the outside.

With the only way into the building securely locked, Derek decided to try opening one of the steel covered windows. He remembered seeing a long pole sitting in the back of the derelict truck. He retrieved the pole and used it an attempt to push open one of the steel window panels. It wouldn't budge. He tried another, without success. Short of smashing the door open there would be no way in without a key.

With nothing to lose, Derek tried the door again. It still wouldn't budge. *How strange*, he thought. Normally a door has at least some small amount of play in it, especially a barn door. He examined the lock closely. The lock was unusual in that, unlike typical barns that are usually secured with overlapping hasps and sealed with a padlock or chain, this one had solid locks built right into the windowless door itself.

Derek yanked at the rock-solid door one last time. It remained absolutely unyielding. He couldn't help but compare the tightly closed structure to a sealed vault. Since nothing more could be gained without figuring some way to get inside, he decided to leave that task till later. Leaving the fortress-like structure behind, he met Michelle on his way back to the house.

"Hi!" Michelle called out with a cheery wave. With her hair cleaned and brushed and the pretty dress displaying her gorgeous figure, she looked the picture of health as she strolled towards him. He gave her a big hug as they met.

"Hi yourself! How ya' doing. Feel better after your rest?" he asked. She assured him the foot was just fine. She attempted to prove it by doing a slight hop into the air. She landed with a small yelp of pain. The pain of embarrassment from the silly display was far greater than her actual pain. Her face was as red as the tiny roses in the print of her dress. As soon as he was certain that she wasn't hurt, Derek laughed and put his arm around her waist.

Trying to change the subject, Michelle asked if he had come across anything interesting or useful in the barn, like the four-wheeled truck he had so fancifully conjured up.

"No, I'm afraid not," he responded. "In fact, the whole place is locked up tight as a drum. There was no way I could get in."

Michelle thought for a moment. "Wait a minute. Didn't I see a key on the table by the front window? I went over to check out what was in the bookcase when I noticed it. Do you think that might be the key to the barn?"

"Perfect! I'll bet that's it!" He gave her a big kiss. "You stay right here for a minute, I'm going grab that key and give it a try. And no dropping things on your foot while I'm gone," he chortled over his shoulder. He took off at a dead run towards the house.

A moment later he was back, key in hand. They both were full of anticipation as they hurried off towards the barn to try the key in the lock. Sadly, the key wouldn't open the sturdy door. Disappointed, they decided to search the house again later and try again. The walked hand-in-hand back to the main house.

For no particular reason, Michelle glanced up at the roof of the barn as they were turning to leave. "What's that wire up there," she asked, pointing to a strand of electrical wire that came out of the back of the barn. The wire ran from the top of the barn out to one pole then on to several others all the way over to the house. Derek hadn't noticed it before because the wires and poles were almost completely hidden by the heavy leaf cover of the low branches that hung close down over the roof of the house and barn.

Michelle had Derek's full attention. "That's an electrical service wire." He thought for a minute. His face lit up. "I'll bet that wire comes from a generator that must be located in the barn!"

"But that doesn't make sense," said Michelle. "We didn't see anything that ran on electricity in the house. There aren't even any lights, just oil lamps. Unless..... unless... that room! Yes, I'll bet that wire goes to the room that's locked. Maybe it's a radio room or something like that," she added excitedly.

"Aha, and I'll bet that this is the key to that room," Derek added while he tightened his grip on the key that had failed to open the barn. Come on. Let's go try it!"

The two hurried back to the house to see if their theories were correct.

A moment later Derek and Michelle stood in front of the huge door. They were full of anticipation as Derek slid the key toward the lock. To their immense satisfaction, the key fit perfectly and gave a satisfying 'snick' as the lock mechanism clicked open. Derek turned the doorknob and eagerly pushed against the door. It wouldn't open at first. He had to give it an extra hard push to break it free from the tight weather seal that surrounded the door edge. The door swung fully open. The two stood breathless as they stared in disbelief.

CHAPTER 16

The door opened into a gorgeous colonial style bedroom that looked as if it had been transported in from one of the grandest homes in colonial Virginia. Though the light was subdued by the heavy tree cover that shaded the windows, it didn't hide the fact that everything in the room was exquisite and that no expense had been spared on even the smallest of details. The hardwood floors shined mirror bright and the thick Oriental rug on the floor looked like it must have cost a fortune. The huge four-posted, canopied bed was covered with ornate hand carved figures and made of the finest cherry, as was the museum quality highboy that graced the corner of the room. The perfectly plastered walls were covered with grand antique oriental wallpaper that looked to have been hand-painted centuries ago.

Derek and Michelle remained speechless for several minutes before they entered the room. It was so utterly fantastic. It seemed so impossible that such a room could exist within the same structure as the house. Though the main house was well-built and well-maintained, it was austere and basic in the extreme when compared to this room, which was such a grand masterpiece of construction and beauty.   While the main part of the house would have cost only a modest sum to build--this room, with its beautiful fixtures and expensive antique furnishings, must have cost a fortune to build. Considering that whoever had constructed it had to bring all the materials and workers deep into the Outback, Derek figured that the cost of the completed structure must have reached a staggering amount. He figured that the antiques and artwork alone might be worth many hundreds of thousands of dollars.

Michelle moved into the room in awe, pointing out exciting and wonderful things.

"Look at this piece," Michelle said excitedly, as she sat down on a period settee that was upholstered in exotic embroidered fabric.   "I feel like a queen," she said wistfully as she surveyed everything around her. "And look at this," she continued. She called Derek's attention to the fine hand-carved figures on the bedposts and wall moldings. Then she looked up at the ceiling--it took her breath away.   "Derek, look up, look up," she said excitedly.   Derek quickly gazed upward.   He immediately understood her enthusiastic cry. Together, the pair marveled at the beautiful and fanciful murals, that were painted on the ceiling. The incredibly realistic clouds and sky were perfectly balanced with angels, surrounded by cherubs, in each of the four corners.   It was a masterpiece worthy of the Sistine Chapel.   The masterwork soared over twenty feet above the floor giving the observer a huge sense of space, as if it were as high as the Sistine Chapel itself. The pair stood in awe of the stunning and inspiring, artwork. They remained transfixed, marveling at the work of art for some time, before turning their attention back to the room itself. A magnificent antique secretary across the room caught Michelle's attention. On it stood a 24 caret, gold-framed, photograph. She strolled over and picked it up. The ornate golden frame housed a photo of a beautiful young woman in a grand wedding gown. She was smiling in blissful joy while embracing a handsome, distinguished looking, older man dressed in regal attire. Though the man looked old enough to have been her father, Michelle thought it more likely that he was the groom—and a strikingly handsome groom at that. The wedding photo was remarkable in that the bride and groom were embracing as they sat together on the wing of a pristine white twin engine aircraft. It appeared to be brand new. The cabin door was open and the tops of a number of suitcases were just barely in view in the bottom of the photo. And just to the right of the bride's tiara the name "Lisa-Marie" appeared in large gold leaf lettering just below the cabin door.

"Look at this Derek." She held the photograph up for him to see. "They look so beautiful and happy together, don't you think?"

"Yes, very beautiful. It looks like they're getting ready to fly off on their honeymoon."

Michelle carefully replaced the photograph exactly as she had found it. She returned to examining the contents of the room. A moment later she called to Derek.

"Look up there," she said, pointing to an elaborately framed, near life size portrait, hanging on the far wall at the end of the room. It looked as if a Dutch master had painted it. She walked up right up to it and examined it closely. "That's the girl in the photo."

Derek looked up at the portrait. "If you hadn't just shown me that wedding photograph, I'd have sworn that it was a museum masterpiece," he replied. He walked up to admire it more closely.

Michelle gave Derek a questioning look. "What do you think this is all about? This place, this room, it's all so out of place."

"I don't know Michelle. The only thing I can think of is that maybe they got married and the bride wouldn't come into the Outback unless she had a room that would make her feel at home. Maybe she was from a wealthy family from the United States and was homesick, so the husband built a room to remind her of home. Could be anything. But it sure is as strange as it is magnificent. Just think of the huge fortune that was invested into the construction of this place."

"I'll bet he loved her a lot," Michelle replied wistfully, as she gazed at the fine portrait amid the grandeur of the room and all its elegant furnishings.

Though enthralled by the room, Derek's mind soon returned to his original task--looking for evidence of a two-way radio. Almost immediately, his eyes fell on a gorgeous, ornate, hand-painted, ceramic light-switch plate near the open door. He stepped over to it and flipped it into the 'on' position. It didn't work. His eyes next swept the baseboards of the room. Encouraged by the sight of other ornate ceramic wall outlet and switch covers, he began checking the room for power cords. A moment later he spotted one. It was plugged into a wall outlet behind a truly handsome carved table that sat beside the bed. Following the cord back from the wall he saw that it entered the back of a small antique walnut chest. The two vertical doors that made up the front of the chest were inlaid with mother-of-pearl set in intricate designs. The beautiful workmanship on the doors was enhanced with highly polished brass hinges and elegantly painted porcelain handles. Derek gave a gentle pull on one of the doors.

His heart jumped when he discovered that the cabinet contained a radio. But the delight of his discovery quickly turned to dismay when he discovered that it was simply a radio receiver, not a radio transmitter as he'd hoped. As expected, it didn't work when he switched it on.

Undaunted, Derek examined the radio more closely. Though it was in perfect condition it appeared to be a long out of date model. He noted that in addition to having an AM and FM band that it also had a short-wave band. Thinking about the short-wave band, he concluded that its owner had likely selected the radio for its short-wave capabilities because without that feature it probably wouldn't have gotten any reception at all out in the desolate Outback.

Derek continued checking the room for any more signs of electrical wiring. He soon noticed a similar, but much larger, elegantly crafted chest standing at the far end of the room. It too, had a cord running from the wall up inside the chest. He opened the chest.

"What the heck!" exclaimed Derek. "Look at this Michelle. It's an older model of a color television!"

"Let me see," said Michelle. She hurried over. "Turn it on, let's see if it works," she added hopefully.

"I'll give it a try," replied Derek. "As soon as I can figure out how to turn it on. There's no remote control." He got down on his knees to examine it more closely. "It must be pretty old. Look here, there's actually color adjustment dials up on the front of the set. Ah, here's the *on* knob." He gave it a twist but the set refused to work. Derek sighed with disappointment and rose to his feet.

"Imagine how much money it must have cost to have commissioned a highly skilled cabinet maker to build a chest of such museum quality just to install a television set," said Derek, shaking his head.

"Or maybe it's a genuine antique," offered Michelle. "Maybe it was adapted to house the television set."

"You may be right Michelle. But either way, someone sank a fortune into this place."

"I wonder what we'll find behind that door next to the television cabinet?" said Michelle.

"It's probably just a closet. You go ahead and check it out. I'm going to keep searching for a two-way radio."

While Derek set off to continue his search, Michelle opened the door.

"Hey, Derek! If this is 'just a closet,' then the great pyramid is just a pile of stones. You should see all the stuff in here!"

Derek didn't respond. His head was under the bed following a wire and all he heard was something about it being a closet. He continued following the wire.

Michelle was enthralled with the enormous walk-in closet. It was full of beautiful clothes and shoes that could only have belonged to the young woman in the wedding photograph. There was a startling array of expensive dresses and evening gowns. She wasted no time in going through the beautiful array of clothing. Almost immediately she found a short gold dress with a deep plunging neckline. Removing the dress from the rack she held it up against herself. Just perfect, she thought. She turned and came out of the closet.

"Derek," she said cheerily. "Look what I found." She held the prize dress up against her body.

"Ahh, perfecto! It's as gorgeous as you are! That's the dress I want you to wear when I take you out to dinner at the finest restaurant in Sydney upon our return to civilization. I don't care what it costs, I'll reimburse the bride for the dress, assuming we can find out who she is, of course."

"And I'll buy you a tuxedo. You'd look a little silly going into a fine restaurant dressed in those silly cargo shorts!"

"Hey I thought you said I look good in them."

"Well yes, out here, but not in a fine restaurant."

Derek puts on a hurtful face. "Well how about if I wear dress shorts to the restaurant. I'll even put on a tie. How about that?"

"You get us out of here and you can wear anything you want!"

"Deal," said Derek. "But fashion problems aside, I'm going to go back to find more evidence of electrical appliances or that two-way radio." He went back to work while Michelle returned to the closet. She continued on with her pleasant diversion by inventorying the contents of the enormous closet.

A short time later, Derek concluded his search. In the end, he was more confused than ever. He puzzled over why anyone would have gone to such great efforts to build such a place and then install electricity in only one room of the house--nowhere else. It didn't make sense that there wasn't at least an electrically operated water pump in the kitchen, and there wasn't even a single electric light in the main part of the house. He was beginning to think that the outlets and wall switches in the bedroom might be just dummies. Maybe it was all a façade. Perhaps there wasn't a generator in the barn after all—but he bet there really was one out there. He decided then and there to make it a priority to get into the barn, *or was it really a hangar after all*, he wondered.

Derek shrugged his shoulders. There was nothing more to be gained by searching the room. Just as he was about to call Michelle, she came out of the closet. She too, had completed her task.

"Well how did you make out?" asked Michelle.

"No two-way radio," Derek replied. "And the few electrical items I found didn't work. But that isn't necessarily a bad thing. It could simply mean that there's a generator out in the barn that obviously isn't running. But unfortunately, there's another possibility....." he broke off in mid-sentence.

"Another what?" Michelle asked.

"Oh nothing. Forget it. It doesn't matter," Derek replied brushing the issue aside. He'd changed his mind about sharing his theory that there might not be a generator at all. It would be better, he thought, to wait and see what their search of the barn turned up.

"Okay then," Michelle replied. "Why don't we go back to the main room and search for a key to the barn."

Derek nodded his head in agreement and the two headed towards the bedroom door. Michelle was the last to leave. She placed her hand on the doorknob and was about to close it when Derek called her attention to the door's construction.

The two sides of the door were dramatically different. The bedroom side of the door was a masterpiece of woodworking, rich in carvings and intricate designs that enhanced all the other ornate trim in the room. But the side that faced the kitchen was plain and basic having been made of the same basic materials used in the rest of the main house. When the door was closed, the effect was that the bedroom remained grand and perfect on the inside while the main house retained its sense of quiet, comfortable, austerity on the other side.

When Derek was finished examining the door, Michelle carefully closed it behind them. She was certain that the room held special meaning to its owners and felt that such a private place deserved respect.

Michelle and Derek returned to the kitchen. But after a thorough search of the house they still were unable to find a key to the barn. A bit frustrated, Derek suggested that they go back outside to continue their reconnaissance of the station. His thoughts had turned to the small outbuildings. Inside one, he hoped to find some tools that might help them get into the barn. After their amazing find behind the locked bedroom door he couldn't imagine what they might find inside the vault-like barn. He was impatient to get inside. Off to the right of the big barn, almost completely covered with trees and underbrush, they found an outbuilding about ten feet by twelve feet. Derek tried the door. It was locked. While Derek put on a frown, Michelle's face lit up. On a whim, Michelle slid her hand across the top of the door frame. Her finger hit something and she instantly heard a 'clink' as something metalic tumbled to the ground. Both looked at the ground in stunned silence. Unbelievably, at their feet lay a key ring holding two weathered keys.

Derek spoke first. "I can't believe it. That's something you see on the movies. I know some people really do hide keys like that but I'm astounded that they were really there."

"Well done you," said Derek. He gave her a solid pat on the back then picked up the keys. He examined the keys with great enthusiasm. "With any luck one key is probably for this shed and the other," he said with a big sigh, "will, hopefully, open the big barn door." Derek thrust the first key into the shed's lock. It didn't budge. He switched to the other key and the door easily opened. "Success," he proclaimed. "let's check it out." They stepped inside.

Compared to the many astounding surprises and oddities they'd encountered in the main house; the shed was positively ordinary. It contained exactly what one might expect to find in an old farm type shed. It was littered a bunch of rusted pipes, weathered garden tools, a double-wheeled wheelbarrow, dull axes with broken handles, and old empty cans and containers of all descriptions. Derek did notice some hand tools that he may have occasion to use, but clearly there was nothing of any real value here. With nothing more to accomplish, Derek and Michelle closed up the shed. The two turned their attention to the barn and the second key. Both were eager to give the key a try.

CHAPTER 17

As they approached the barn, Derek had a thought. "You know Michelle, I've been wondering. I'm not sure if this is a barn at all. I think it's an...."

"*Airplane hangar,*" said Michele, completing his sentence.

He laughed. "When did you come to that conclusion?"

"Just a few minutes ago. As we walked over here I recalled that huge door across the whole front of the building. Then I recalled the airplane that was in the wedding photo. I'll bet that's what's inside."

"I guess great minds think alike because I'm betting that's what's in there too. We'll know in a minute or so if, this second key works in the door lock. Derek eagerly inserted the key into the lock. Both held their breath as he twisted the key. A smooth 'click' and the tumbler rotated. Both were filled with anticipation as Derek pulled down on the door handle and yanked on the door. It wouldn't open! They both stared in disbelief. *The key worked, so why isn't it opening,* Derek pondered. He tried again, this time using both hands he gave it a heavy yank and it still would not open. In frustration, he tried one more time. After placing his left foot on the outside wall of the hangar and both hands on the door handle lever, he readied himself to give it one more yank. Michelle looked on with great concern. She could see that he was wound up like a coiled spring ready to explode.

"Careful Derek," she yelled. "Don't do it. Let me help." Before her words could reach his ears, Derek sprang into action. With a twist of the lever and a final mighty yank, and *BLAM*, the door flung wide open! Derek's world went black.

Minutes later a huge *splash* brought Derek to his senses. His body was drenched. Michelle had doused him with a bucket of water. Sputtering, and gasping, he spit water out of his mouth.

He sputtered in disbelief, *"Whad'ya do that for?! You nearly drowned me! I wasn't even knocked out and you tried to drown me! Give me that bucket and I'll drown you next!"*

From Derek's reaction, it became instantly clear to Michelle that she had no reason to have been concerned about his well-being. *After all*, she thought, *he only fell on his head.*

"Maybe I'd better give you another dose to cool down that hot head of yours! You were out like a light and you know it," she scolded.

Derek held his arms up in front of his face. "Forget it. You're dangerous with a bucket of water!" he cried. He leaned his head down onto his chest and felt the back of his head with his hand.

"Ouch! That hurts." He shook his head trying clear his mind. What happened anyway?"

"In case you didn't notice, the door sprung open wildly when you yanked on it. You instantly lost your grip on the door lever and went flying over backwards, hitting your head on the ground. You were knocked out cold. That's when I ran back to the house for the bucket of water to wake you up. You must have given it a heck of a yank because you flew over backwards so hard I thought you'd broken your silly skull. Clearly, I was foolish to have worried. After all, it was *only* your head. But don't be concerned. I checked the door and there's no damage to it. Aren't we lucky," she chortled. She hoped her attempt at humor hid the fear and concern she really felt when she saw him lying on the ground out cold.

"Very funny," pouted Derek. "He put his hand up to the back of his head where he felt a lump forming." Finding no blood on his fingers, Derek simply groaned. They were both relieved that the accident resulted in only a minor injury. "Been inside yet," Derek asked as Michelle helped him to his feet."

"Not really," Michelle replied. "I was more concerned about you than what's inside. I'm just glad you are okay."

Derek, gave Michelle a brief hug and let out another short moan. "Okay then," he replied. Once again there was an air of optimism in his voice. "Well let's see what we've got." Together they looked through the open doorway.

The entry to the building was heavily shaded by overhanging trees. Even though the door was wide open, little light penetrated the interior of the otherwise tightly sealed building. But with the little light that prevailed, they could clearly make out the wing of an airplane just inside the door.

They entered the building together. Michelle, without thinking, automatically reached for a light switch. To her surprise she actually touched one.

"Derek there's a light switch here. No, there's two." She flipped both switches but neither worked.

"I'm not surprised they don't work," said Derek. "But it's interesting that the barn, oops make that 'hangar,' is wired for electricity but not the main area of the house. In any case, we're not going to see anything in here until we get that big door open. I checked earlier and there's no outside lock so it must unlock from in here. Can't see anything in the dark though. We'll need more light to find the door lock mechanism. Wait here, I'll be back in a minute. I'll go get the flashlight from our supplies," declared Derek.

"No," said Michelle. "*You'll* be the one to wait here while I go get the light. I can see that you're still woozy from that whack you took to the head. Stay here, I'll be right back." She called over her shoulder as she left, "and don't go wandering around tripping over anything in the dark. I don't want to find you sprawled unconscious on the floor when I get back."

"And you don't want to find me drowned either, so leave your water bucket behind when you come back," he chortled. Michelle hurried off. While Derek waited in the doorway, he spotted a red-handled lever leading to a window frame above. Curious, he pulled on the handle. To his surprise it simultaneously unlocked and pushed opened one of the steel covered windows. Light spilled into the building. In the light, he could see the clever window opening mechanism in more detail. He determined that if he pulled the lever further down, it would simultaneously unlock and open all the windows across the top of the left side of the hangar. A similar lever mechanism operated the windows on the opposite side of the hanger. He'd just finished opening all the windows, when Michelle returned with the flashlight.

"I see you managed to open the windows," said Michelle. "Guess you don't need it now. But, just in case, she handed him the flashlight."

"Thanks," said Derek. "Now let's see if we can open the big front doors."

He found that he still needed the flashlight to guide them as they worked their way to the front of the building. They soon found the interior locking mechanism for the door. Derek pulled on its red handle—the door unlocked. Together they shoved the big door outward. It was remarkably well balanced and opened readily. Likely, for the first time in many years, bright rays of daylight filled the hangar.

Once again, the pair stood in awe. Just as the grand bedroom was entirely out of place in the middle of the Outback, so too, was the airplane hangar. And this was no ordinary hangar, as its rusted and weather-beaten exterior suggested. This was a very expensive modern aircraft facility. Its smooth cement floors were painted a shiny gray and the walls were gleaming white. A long row of fluorescent lights stretched across the top of the structure. The facility resembled a sparkling corporate aircraft hangar straight out of California.

They stared in disbelief. Before them stood not one airplane, but two. The plane in front was a light blue single-engine low-winged aircraft—the badge on the fuselage indicated that it was a Piper Warrior. A wide dark blue stripe ran the length of the fuselage. It was the one they had first seen in the dim light after they had forced open the side door of the hanger. It appeared to be in excellent shape, but from the look of the chipped paint around the cowl and obvious wear on the propeller, it was evident that the plane had seen frequent use at one time.

Just beyond the tail of the single-engine plane stood another aircraft. It was a much larger one and was completely covered. They walked over to it. Derek marveled at the fact that the airplane was completely draped with a cover made from pure white silk.

"I'll bet it's the plane in the wedding photo under that cover," said Michelle. She looked in awe at the mysteriously draped aircraft.

"I know some people have expensive custom car covers made for their exotic cars," said Derek, "but I've never heard of anyone making up a custom *silk* cover for an entire airplane. This is a big plane too. It's a twin-engine. Let's take a look at it." He tugged at the fine silk that draped the aircraft and watched as it flowed effortlessly off the top of the cockpit.

Once the cover had fallen it exposed the gleaming white aircraft—a Piper Seneca.

Derek stared at the awesome aircraft. "It's beautiful and it looks like it's hardly ever been used," he said, as soon as he could form the words. He ran his fingers across the glassy smooth fuselage then crouched down to look at the underbelly. "Hey, it's got retractable landing gear too. I'll bet this thing is fast!"

"And look here," said Michelle, pointing to the tall gold leaf letters that spelled out 'Lisa-Marie' on the fuselage just below the cabin door. "This is definitely the plane that's in the wedding photo all right. But I wonder why it's all covered up. It's a much nicer plane than the other one. Why would they choose to use the small one rather than this one?"

"I don't know the answer to that," Derek replied, glancing over his shoulder at the worn single-engine plane. "It wasn't a decision just to save gas, I'll guarantee you that. Whoever owns this station has piles of money and can do anything they want." Derek shrugged his shoulders. "This whole place is a mystery to me--we should just pull the cover back in place for the time being. We can check the planes out in more detail later. Right now, we should go down to the back wall where you spotted the power line coming out. Maybe we'll find a generator--and maybe even a two-way radio to contact an emergency rescue unit."

Michelle spotted a door near the back of the hanger labeled, Service Area. She pointed it out to Derek. "That's probably where the generator is," said Derek, hopefully. "But when we get to *that door* I'd better have *you* open it instead of me," he joked.

Just outside the door to the Service Room, Derek found two switches but, like the others, they didn't work. Flashlight in hand, Derek opened the door to a darkened room. He slowly panned the room with the light. To his delight, he spotted a large four-cylinder generator mounted on a raised concrete base. The control panel on top of the machine contained several gauges, a start button, a fuel level indicator, that read 'full,' and electrical outlet connections. To his relief, Derek noticed a set of 'Generator Starting Directions' on a label attached to the machine's control panel. Like everything else they had seen so far, the generator looked to be in excellent condition. It looked as if it were simply waiting for someone to press the start button. Though Derek gave it a try, the battery was dead and there was no response from the machine.

"The battery is dead Michelle," Derek called out. "I'm not surprised. The generator looks to be in good shape but it probably hasn't been started in years."

"Can it be started without a battery?" asked Michelle.

"I think so," Derek replied. "These things usually have a pull starter or crank device to get them going when the battery's dead. After we check out the rest of the hangar I'll come back and see if I can get it going. But first, I want to look at the generator more closely."

Using the flashlight's beam to focus in on the back of the machine, Derek crouched down at the rear of the generator. He noted that the exhaust pipe from the piece of equipment vented to the outside. He played the flashlight beam over the rear of the generator. There, he located the unit's battery that was supposed to provide the power to start the engine when power was needed. The battery looked to be in good condition but when Derek checked the cable attached to the positive terminal post he found that it moved. A close inspection of the battery case showed that it was cracked. *This is a hopeless case*, Derek said to himself. *No chance of this ever holding a charge again.*

Derek got to his feet and shined the light around the room. He halted the beam when he spotted several electrical circuits coming out of the back of the generator's electrical panel. One circuit led up the wall and exited the building. That, he thought, would be the one that feeds into the grand bedroom. The other two circuits led up the wall and out into the hangar itself.

"I'm all done in here for now," Derek called out to Michelle. "Let's go back out into the main hangar area. I want to follow a couple of wiring circuits."

Once they were back inside the hangar area Derek followed the circuits that ran out of the generator room and up the wall. One line ran up to the ceiling where it fed into the long bank of fluorescent lights that were strung across the top of the hangar. The other ran from the wall behind the generator and around the building where it fed a number of evenly spaced electrical outlets. Much to his dismay, he didn't see any sign of radio equipment with which to contact the outside world.

Derek finished his survey near the big open hangar door. He switched off the flashlight. There was no need for it near the front of the hangar. But still eager for more light, Derek went to the other side of the hangar and opened the remaining five windows that were evenly spaced around the structure. Though the additional light helped them see better, it didn't shed any more light on the mysteries of either the hangar or the station.

In the full daylight Derek stared forlornly at the uncovered single-engine aircraft. "That could be our ticket out of here Michelle," he said with a heavy sigh. "If only I knew how to fly. Hey! How about you! You're into the airlines. You ever flown a small plane before?"

"Sorry, believe it or not I hate small planes."

Derek laughed, he couldn't help himself. "Yeah, big planes are so much safer...just look at us." He was immediately sorry for his remark. She didn't see it as a joke. His humble apology was quickly accepted. "But I did take an introductory flying lesson once about twenty years ago. I wouldn't dare risk trying it now. We'd have to be far more desperate than we are now for me to chance our lives like that."

Michelle changed the subject by suggesting that they look around the hangar together. "I'll check out that alcove," she said, pointing towards an office area that had been set up along the wall at the back of the hangar. While Michelle headed off to the office area, Derek stood staring at the airplane fantasizing about flying their way out.

An enormous desk caught Michelle's attention the moment she entered the alcove. Like the furniture inside the house in the grand bedroom, the desk appeared to be an expensive antique. Its handsomely carved mahogany legs, beautifully crafted top, and drawer fronts were exquisitely inlaid with floral marquetry. The rich leather top was ornately decorated in gold leaf. The desk looked as if it belonged to the chairman of the board of a Fortune 500 company.

Michelle ran her fingers over the elegant surface of the desk then over onto the back of a highly decorative and richly padded chair that stood in front of the desk. She eased herself into the grand and exceedingly comfortable chair. Like a child in a fantasy world, she slowly swiveled the chair around and marveled at her surroundings.

To her left was a bookcase which contained a dozen or more volumes. Pushing off with her foot, she glided the wheeled chair over to investigate its contents. Among the neatly arranged books she found assorted aircraft maintenance manuals and a collection of instrument flying texts. Considering them unimportant, she rolled over to the right side of the desk where an ordinary gray filing cabinet stood. She pulled out the first two drawers and examined their contents but found nothing of consequence. She opened the bottom drawer and was delighted by what she found.

"Derek, come look at this!" Michelle called. "There's maps and stuff inside this filing cabinet!"

Derek hurried over and the two eagerly examined the maps. Their initial joy at finding them quickly turned to disappointment. The maps turned out to be aeronautical charts of Western Australia. Though useful to a pilot who knew where he wanted to go, none of the maps gave them any indication of where the station was located. Without a starting point, the destination maps were useless. Michelle put them back and opened another drawer where she found a large map.

"Maybe this will be more useful," she said. She pulled it out and they unrolled it together. They both examined the sectional aeronautical chart. It covered a large geographical area that included the Northern Territory, where Alice Springs was located, and the state of Queensland

"I suppose this could be somewhat helpful," said Derek, "but we'd have to know where we are right now."

"I've got a pretty good idea of where we are," chortled Michelle. After looking at the map she remarked that the explosive decompression occurred half way, or two hours, into the flight. "And that," she said, "means we would have covered about one thousand miles. And I know that our flight plan had us crossing the south west corner of the state of Queensland. And that's almost exactly at the half way mark." She carefully looked at the big map and placed her finger on that exact spot. "There," she said. "I'm almost certain we're in this general area of southwest Queensland." Her pride in figuring their likely location was quickly tempered. "Unfortunately, "she continued, "that puts us right in the middle of the Strzelecki Desert. And that's one of the most desolate and hostile places in all of Australia!" Both stood in silence as the deadly seriousness of their situation sank in.

Michelle finally spoke. "Well at least we have some general idea of where we are now." "True," replied

Derek. He stared at the map. He noted that a few rare settlements were indicated on the vast area covered by the map. But, even if they knew how to get there, those settlements were hundreds of miles from their present location. He vividly recalled their hike from the crash site out to the station. *That*, he thought, *was only a twenty-mile hike, at best, and that nearly killed us.* He knew, and Michelle knew, that hiking out was now out of the question. Both knew that any further attempt to hike the across the desert was a death sentence.

Michelle and Derek sat in silence at the big desk. Both pondered their fate and what to do next. Shortly, Derek reached out to Michelle and held her hand. "Don't worry Michelle," he said. "We're not licked yet. We're safe and secure for months now anyway. We've got food, water, shelter, and each other. We'll think of something or someone will find us, you'll see." Though neither believed it, at least there was some hope that something would come their way to get them out of their situation.

"Well," sighed Michelle, "we really don't have any other options right now but to carry on with what we're doing. We've done great so far, let's just keep at it," she said in an upbeat way. With that, Derek went back to work searching the office area looking for anything that they might find useful. Michelle went back to searching the desk.

A moment later she reached into a lower drawer and pulled out a pristine copy of a Flight Manual. The cover sported a bright red, white, and blue logo for a Piper Seneca aircraft. Clearly it was the Flight Manual for the big twin-engine aircraft. Quickly perusing the Table of Contents, she found that it provided a wealth of information about the aircraft, its operating procedures, engine starting procedures and takeoff checklists. She looked wistfully over at the big aircraft. For a moment she daydreamed that they had just climbed into the aircraft and flown right out of the station to safety. *If only, we knew how to fly it*, she lamented. A moment later, her thoughts returned to the reality at hand. Calling out to Derek, she held up the publication and handed it to him. He too, perused it for a few minutes before handing it back. Though interesting, he regretted that it was of no value because neither knew how to fly. A moment later, in deep thought, Derek looked over at both airplanes. But his gaze focused more on the smaller, single-engine plane.

"You know Michelle," he said hopefully. "If you can find the same kind of manual for the single-engine plane maybe we could use it in a final ditch effort, to get out of here." Though neither of them believed that, a tiny fraction of hope was better than none at all. After replacing the Seneca manual to the drawer, she returned to her searching. A short time later she beamed with pride. "Derek," she called. "I think I found what you're looking for. She handed him the flight manual for the single-engine Warrior.

"Good job, Michelle, this is a great find. He happily accepted the manual and immediately scanned the table of contents. Unfortunately, the manual was much like an automobile manual in that it tells the reader *about* the automobile but *not how to drive* the car. So too, the

230

flight manual gave specific information *about* the plane but no specific instructions on *how to fly* it. But Derek was not dissuaded by the manual's lack of specific flight instructions. While thumbing further through the manual something immediately caught his attention. He came across the Checklists, section of the manual which provided detailed 'check off' boxes for the pilot's use before and during flights and landings. The lists covered Preflight inspection, Engine start-up procedures, Takeoff procedures, Flap settings, and Landing procedures. He also located detailed information concerning takeoff and landing speeds, stall speed, and more. Though he found the lists interesting and useful, the manual was of little use to them. Nevertheless, he thought it would make for interesting reading while waiting for rescue—*as if that's ever going to happen*, he mused. Derek stretched and put the manual aside. Leaving Michelle happily searching the office area, he wandered off into the hangar.

Once he was back out on the hangar floor, Derek decided that it was time to begin a systematic search of the building. Walking to the wide-open hangar door, he stopped when his toes reached the floor's edge. He stared down at the spot where the concrete ended and the Outback began. He couldn't help but think that, *this is where 'civilization' ends.* He turned his attention back to the hangar. The first thing that caught his eye was a large, silver fuel storage tank. It stood near the open hangar door. The specifications printed on its side indicated that it had a capacity of 300 gallons of aviation fuel. Attached to the tank's side was a hand pump connected to 60 feet of flexible fuel line hose. The line was clearly long enough to reach either airplane. Derek noted with satisfaction that the fuel gauge at the top of the tank registered nearly full.

Beside the fuel tank was a smaller storage tank labeled 'Aviation Oil.' And, like the fuel tank, it too had a hand pump attached to its top. Though there was no gauge on the tank to indicate how much it contained, Derek estimated its capacity at a hundred gallons or more. Grabbing it by the top, he tipped it towards him. By its weight, he concluded that it was about half full.

Continuing along the far wall, he inspected a work area where he found a long, oversized workbench. It was spotlessly clean and neatly organized. Assorted tools were precisely laid out on the upper level while the lower level was piled with clean shop rags, all neatly folded and stacked to one side.

To the right of the workbench Derek saw a large red fire extinguisher. It was mounted to the wall in a quick release mount—a similar extinguisher was mounted on the opposite wall. He checked them both, hoping to find fire department inspection labels that give a clue as to their location but there were none. Derek got the feeling, more and more, that whoever owned the station simply wanted to cut off all contact with the outside world. Continuing his search, Derek located an electrically operated air compressor. Neatly coiled nearby was a long air hose with a tire inflation fitting attached to its end. His search completed, he joined Michelle back at the big desk.

"Derek," Michelle called out. She held two manila file folders in her hand. One was labeled 'Warrior' and the other 'Seneca.' She opened the Warrior folder and handed it to him.

Derek examined the single-engine Warrior folder. He pulled out the aircraft's original title and carefully examined it. "Check this out," he said to Michelle. "The plane was bought brand new in the United States, so I suspect its owner is an American. It's made out to a Mr. Abraham Winston from Alexandria, Virginia, and it's dated August 16, 2005. And I see in the maintenance records that it was serviced a few times in Innamincka, South Australia, as recently as three years ago. So, I guess that means that we're in flying range of Innamincka, wherever the heck *that is*. The only problem is that we don't know how to fly and we don't even know what direction we'd go to reach it. Besides, since the probable range on the plane is about 250 miles, that's way beyond our hiking abilities.

"I know that place," Michelle responded after a moment's thought. "There's something historic about it. I recall reading something about that place recently, in an Outback tourist flyer. It's noted as being *literally* 'in the middle of nowhere' and the population is only about two dozen people. Back in the 1930's the Royal Flying Doctor Corp operated out there to help provide medical service in an area that was barren of medical help. The Doctor Corp ceased to exist in the 1950's, but I understand there's a handful of tourists every season who like to go there just so they can claim that they were once in 'The Middle of Nowhere."

"Oh great," huffed Derek. "So, I guess we're stuck 'in the middle of nowhere too.' Or, as we say in the States, 'we're up the creek without a paddle.' We still don't know exactly where we are and it's a sure bet we can't walk out of here. God, we only hiked twenty or so miles across the Outback and it dammed near killed us. That, in spite of the fact that we had a tent, food and water, and could actually see our destination. Derek looked longingly over at the airplanes. "God, I wish we knew how to fly one of those planes."

"Well at least we're safe for now," added Michelle cheerfully. "Think about it, we have food, clothing, shelter, and best of all you've got me!"

Derek cheered up immediately. He gave her a big hug from behind the chair and kissed the top of her head. "Ah, and you've got *me!*"

Michelle feigning shock and distress. "My God, you're right. I forgot about that. Please, help me, we need to get out of here! I'm trapped here with *you*! A fate worse than death!" She flopped onto the desktop and played dead.

"Now it's time for *you* to cheer up," chortled Derek, "because when we get back to civilization you won't have to work as a flight attendant anymore. You'll get top billing as a comedian instead. You'll make a fortune. Then, to reward me for getting you out of here alive, you can support me in grand style for the rest of my life."

Michelle rose her head from the desk, grinned, and said, "I'm that good huh?"

"Could have fooled me. I thought sure you were dead. It was so convincing it was scary! Anyway, enough play-acting, let me look at what you found in the other folder on the twin-engine plane."

She handed him the folder. "You won't find much in there. There's just a title made out to Mrs. Lisa-Marie Winston from Alexandria, Virginia. It's the same date of purchase on both airplanes. It looks like they purchased a set of 'his and her' airplanes for wedding presents to each other. She got the best deal though. Her airplane is the nicest."

Derek studied the title document then glanced over at the big twin-engine plane. "That's really odd. They were both purchased at the same time but for some reason, her plane looks like it was hardly ever used. The single engine plane obviously is the one that was being flown up until the time the owner abandoned the station." Derek shook his head. "It's inconceivable that someone would just up and abandon such valuable airplanes and furnishings. It just doesn't make sense. None of it does. I mean, what the heck is this place anyway. A station that has no purpose. It's not a ranch, it's not a mine, it's not a farm—what is it?"

Michelle could see that Derek was getting depressed. "Hey, I just got an idea!" she said enthusiastically. "It's apparent that there's no radio in the house or in the hangar, but the airplanes have radios. Maybe we could get one of them to work!"

Derek snapped out of his brooding. "Why not," he quickly replied. "The batteries in both planes are probably long dead but we've got nothing to lose. Let's give it a try!"

The pair hurried over to the Warrior. Derek quickly climbed up onto the wing and entered the cabin. Michelle hopped up behind him.

Though both doubted they would have any luck with the radio, they were encouraged to find the keys still in the airplanes. Derek turned the key in the Warrior but, as expected, nothing happened. No sounds or lights came on in the cockpit. Nothing happened on the instrument panel to indicate even the slightest amount of power. Clearly the battery was dead.

"No, I'm not getting anything Michelle," he reported. In spite of the fact that he was sure the battery was dead, disappointment clearly registered on his face.

"Maybe you have to push some of the other switches or something first," suggested Michelle.

"Could be," replied Derek. "But I'm clueless as to which one or ones that might be." He scanned the complicated panel in front of him. "What the heck, I'll just flip a few and see what happens." A moment later after he had pushed a number of switches into the 'on' position, he tried the ignition key again. Again, the cabin remained silent. He flipped the switches back to the 'off' position.

Derek let out a sigh. "Well we gave this one a try. What the heck, why not give the twin-engine plane a try as well?"

"Sure, why not?" Michelle replied.

The two climbed out of the Warrior and headed over to the Seneca where they clamored into the cockpit. But their luck was no better there. Clearly the battery was dead.

As they climbed out of the cabin Michelle was struck with an idea. "Do you think we could charge up the airplane batteries if you can get that generator going?"

"Not likely. Even if I can get it going, it probably puts out standard household 120 volt current. If I tried to connect wires to the battery posts it would probably just blow up the battery. No, that wouldn't work. We'd need a battery charger that was designed to do that."

Derek thought a moment. "Hey, that gives me an idea. I'll do a search of the storage cabinets around here. Maybe there is a battery charger in here. After conducting a thorough search of the work cabinets Derek came up empty handed on a battery charger. He returned to Michelle a short time later and reported his lack of success.

Derek's voice indicated his disappointment. "I guess we've checked out everything that we can in here for now," said Derek. He let out a big sigh, "I wish we had found something more useful to help us get out of here—like my mystical four-wheel drive vehicle. Mr. and Mrs. Winston must surely have had a vehicle like that in order to get in and out of this place. But unfortunately for us, it looks like they took it with them. My plans for a four-wheel drive trip back to civilization are gone for good."

"So, what do we do now?" she asked.

"I'm going to check out that generator to see if I can get it going. I'm certain there is a manual start procedure. With any luck I'll get it started and we'll have some electricity to run that radio in the house, which I doubt works, because it's so ancient. But, who knows, it might work. We'll give it a try if I can get the generator going." Their spirits picked up at that prospect.

"We've been out here for hours," said Michelle. "I'll go inside and get us something to eat while you look at the generator."

While Michelle left for the main house, Derek picked up his flashlight and returned to the generator room. He played his flashlight over the big machine. He was disappointed to see that it was not equipped with a built-in pull starter. But a closer inspection revealed a short shaft extending out the front of the engine. It was a 'hand crank' connection. Derek's heart skipped a beat with this find. After a quick search of the wall behind the generator, he found the crank hanging from a wall hook. Removing it from the wall, he slid it easily over the end of the engine shaft. It was a perfect fit.

Pleased with his bit of luck, he focused on the control panel's 'manual start procedures' that were stenciled on the machine. He followed the pre-start directions exactly then, using his good arm, he gave a tug on the crank. Heaving the crank around required a great deal of effort, yet after three full revolutions the engine refused to show any signs that it was ready to start. After a moment's rest he tried again. This time he used both arms. Though he was able to move the crank more easily through several more revolutions it still refused to start. He reviewed the manual start procedures and tried again. Still no luck. It would not start.

Michelle returned and poked her head into the generator room. She held out two cups of hot stew.

"Any luck, Derek?"

"Not yet," reported a very frustrated Derek. "But at least the generator engine isn't frozen up. It seems to turn over pretty good now when I use the hand crank. I've spun it over a few times but it won't even cough so I'm going to have to do a little surgery on it. After we finish that great smelling stew I'd like you to give me a hand if you don't mind."

While they ate, Derek reminisced. "When I was a kid," my older brother always drove old broken-down cars. I was only about 12 years old when I started helping him fix them. Mostly I just handed him wrenches and things like that, but as time went on I helped him do some pretty complicated jobs. By the time I was 16 I could fix almost anything that was wrong with a car. I even did a complete engine rebuild once. It was a tough job, but when I was done, the car ran like new. So, I'm pretty confident that I can get this generator going." They quickly finished the last of the stew and got right to work.

"Okay," explained Derek. "I'm going to remove a spark plug wire from the engine and then have you hold it close to the engine block while I crank the engine over. If we see a spark jump from the wire to the block, that will indicate that the electrical circuit is good. Ready, Michelle? Here goes."

"I see it!" Michelle called out. "I see a fat blue spark jumping from the wire to the block."

"That's great, Michelle! At least it looks like the electrical circuit is good. Now on to step two. I'm going to try to prime the engine by squirting a small amount of gas down the throat of the carburetor. If we have a spark and there's gasoline going into the cylinders then it should kick over. I've started many a balky small engine this way. I've got to go get some gas, be back in a minute," said Derek as he hurried out of the generator room.

Moments Derek returned with a cup of gasoline that he'd filled from the aviation fuel tank in the hangar. He dribbled a small amount of gasoline into the carburetor. "Okay now," said Derek. "I need you to step back from the generator and shine the flashlight on the crank connection while I turn the motor over. Get ready please." While Michelle held the light, Derek firmly placed his feet on the floor, and using both hands, he spun the crank through several revolutions. On the third revolution the engine coughed and fired. It ran for a moment then died. Greatly encouraged, he bent down and tried again. By the second revolution the generator fired up, ran rough for a moment, then settled down and ran perfectly. Both embraced and whooped for joy at the sound of the roaring engine. An instant later Michelle ended their embrace.

"Oh my God! I'm going to try the light switch to see if it works," she shouted. She dashed to the light switch by the door and flipped it on. Bright lights instantly flooded the generator room. They embraced again and shouted louder!

It took them several minutes to calm down. When they did, Michelle suggested that they go inside to see if the radio and TV worked. As they rushed down the length of the hangar towards the main door, Derek flipped wall switches in mid-stride. Each time he hit a switch another bank of ceiling lights came on. By the time they reached the main door, the entire hangar was awash in brilliant light. They thrilled at the sight.

The run to the house seemed to take forever. The moment they burst through the front door they rushed to the grand bedroom. Derek flung the huge door open and headed directly to the short-wave radio. The instant he twisted the 'on' knob, it crackled to life. A moment later rock music filled the room.

Michelle had no such luck with the television. When she turned it on all she got out of it was static. Nothing appeared on the screen. But her disappointment with the television quickly dissipated as she focused her attention on the wonderful beat of the radio music that now filled the room. Both delighted in the experience of feeling close to civilization once again.

"I'm sorry about the television Michelle," Derek said sympathetically. "I guess we're too far from any TV station to get any reception. But at least we have the radio. Isn't that music just great to hear?"

"It sure is!" replied Michelle. She'd already forgotten about the television. "It's just grand to hear music again."

Michelle looked at her watch. "It's about 2:30 now. Most stations broadcast news on the hour. Why don't we lie on the bed for a while and listen to the sounds of civilization until news-time. Maybe we'll hear something about our flight and what happened. Maybe they're still looking for us and we can figure out what to do next."

Robert Campbell

The two lay on the bed enjoying the exquisite pleasure of its comfort. They were overjoyed to hear the sweet music fill the room. The electricity brought them one step closer to civilization. They embraced to the sound of the soft classical music. The intensely pleasurable interlude concluded as both fell into sound restful sleep.

CHAPTER 18

And now, we break into that live report.
"............at this point into the investigation of the
crash of Flight 604. That, as grief-stricken relatives,
most still visibly overcome with grief, continue to seek
information about their loved ones, hoping to bring a
sense of closure to their loss."

"Derek!! Derek!!! Wake up!!" shouted Michelle.
She shook him aggressively.

Derek came awake. "What? What is it? What's
wrong?!" His eyes darted about the room searching for
something that would explain Michelle's urgent cries.

"The plane! Our plane! The crash! They're talking
about the crash on the radio!"

As Derek tried to speak she put her finger to his lips
to make him stop talking. The two listened as the
announcer continued.

"...And now, here's what John Sterling,
Chief Investigator of the Australian Transport
Safety Bureau, had to say at today's briefing.

"As you know, the ATSB has been
continuing its investigation of the crash of

Australian Outback Air flight 604 that occurred approximately two weeks ago. The TC-10 aircraft departed Sydney with the intended destination of Alice Springs. Approximately two and a half-hours into the flight, according to radar records, the aircraft suffered some loss of control, and shortly thereafter, went into an uncontrollable dive. The aircraft impacted the ground and exploded. The wreckage was eventually located near the northwest corner of South Australia's Strzelecki Desert. Destruction of the aircraft was full and complete, leaving the investigation team little to go on as to the cause of the accident. There were no survivors. The force of the crash, and explosion that followed, means that it will likely be months before all deceased passengers can be positively identified.

Unfortunately for the investigation, the Flight Data Recorder and Cockpit Voice Recorder were severely damaged and remain at our headquarters undergoing further study. What, if any, information is recoverable will be released when appropriate.

"Here's a brief rundown of what we do know at this point. Flight 604 had a delayed take off due to a compressor failure—it was replaced and the aircraft departed without incident. Approximately two hours into the flight the aircraft radioed that they were experiencing air conditioning problems. They

requested, and were granted, permission to descend to 16,000 feet in order to properly deal with the situation. Approximately five minutes later, broken-up radio transmissions were received from the stricken aircraft stating that an emergency situation existed on board. However, due to a break up in the radio signals, the exact nature of this emergency was unclear. The radio signals continued to break up and were undecipherable throughout the rest of the flight.

"Radar reports suggest that during the remainder of the flight, the crew appeared to have had only limited flight control over the aircraft. They continued on an erratic course to Alice Springs. A westbound airliner, that had been alerted to watch for the stricken aircraft while in that area, reported seeing a fireball rising up from the desert below. That report came in at the same moment radar contact was lost with the aircraft.

"The Russian built TC-10 was 35 years old. It had a number of foreign owners over the years but had recently been purchased by Australian Outback Air from the, now defunct, Morocco Kingdom Airlines. A month prior to putting the aircraft into service, Australian Outback Air conducted a series of flight inspections, flight tests, and a reconditioning program. No defects were found in the aircraft at that time. However, our team is focusing in

on those 'flight worthiness' inspections for any possible connections to the loss of the aircraft.

Our Maintenance Records Group has already convened and initial reports are now in. *"Although it is early in our investigation, we've already uncovered some discrepancies as to whether airworthy directives were complied with by the multiple foreign owners of the aircraft prior to its sale to Australian Outback Air. Those discrepancies immediately raised a red flag in our investigation. That area of the investigation is hampered by language barriers and the unorthodox record keeping practices maintained by some of the foreign owners and service crews. It is likely that this part of the investigation will take a long time to complete. Meanwhile our accident investigation teams continue to work hard at the accident site. Crews are trying to recover as much of the aircraft as possible in the hopes of putting the puzzle together as to what actually caused the crash of Flight 604. Thank you all."*

The radio broadcast returned to the announcer. *"Well, that's it from here. Back to you live now at the studio."* *"Thanks for that report Adam.........and now to local news. A high-speed chase of a suspected drunk driver ended in a fiery crash just after........"*

Michelle sat in stunned silence for several moments. She put her head in her hands and wept softly. "Turn it off Derek, please turn it off." Derek, choked with emotion, moved closer and held her tenderly.

Though both had already accepted that it was likely that nobody knew they were missing and would probably never search for them, the confirmation of their fears hit them hard. For the first time, it really hit home that there never was, and never would be, a rescue party sent out to search for them. No survivors, they said. No reason for a search party. All passengers and crew perished was what they reported. Each felt more alone than they had ever been in their entire lives. But as they continued their embrace, a warmth and sense of love spread from one to the other. The world didn't matter. They had each other.

CHAPTER 19

Despite the devastating confirmation that rescue crews were no longer searching for survivors, Michelle and Derek did not feel defeated. Both held onto the hope that they would get back to civilization on their own, one way or another.

The next several weeks passed quickly for the pair. They healed well and soon regained their strength and health. But life around the station had been far from boring. Michelle developed an interest in cooking. She prepared meals that were both delicious and creatively prepared when considering the limited supply of ingredients that were available. She was delighted by Derek's reaction, one afternoon, when he entered the house to the grand smell of fresh bread baking in an old fashioned stove-top oven she'd found in the kitchen. She was really proud of herself because she had never made a loaf of bread in her life. It was a stupendous addition to the spaghetti supper she prepared that night.

But Michelle's interests were not limited to cooking. She spent a great deal of time working with Derek. The pair continued examining the hangar and outlying buildings in search of anything that might help them find a way out of their situation. They even floated an idea of somehow repairing the old devastated stake-body truck to drive their way out. Though the idea was quickly abandoned, it was a healthy diversion for them.

Derek and Michelle spent much of their time together inside the hangar. Derek took a keen interest in the airplanes and the contents of the small library near the office alcove. One day, while searching the office alcove, he came across the aircraft maintenance file they'd discovered earlier. This time, as he went through the maintenance documents, he was struck by the curious fact that while the records showed that the twin-engine plane had been used occasionally in the United States from 2007 to 2010, there was not a single document indicating that it had ever been flown again after 2010. And even more curious was the fact that it appeared to have never been flown in Australia at all. Yet the maintenance records showed that the single-engine plane had been used on a regular basis both in the United States and in Australia until a few years ago. But then all record keeping suddenly stopped.

As the days continued to go by, Michelle often found Derek sitting behind the controls of one plane or the other with a flight manual in his hands. Though he found a variety of books and manuals that were fun and interesting to go through, the one book he'd hoped to find simply was not there—a book on how to *actually fly* an airplane. But, nevertheless, the flight manual for the single-engine plane provided him with a glimmer of hope. *Fantasy or not*, thought Derek, *if rescue never*

*comes I might have no other choice but to risk flying us
out of here.*

Derek and Michelle established a routine. They rose
early, ate regular meals, examined the environment
around the station, and tended the garden. It brought
them both great comfort to walk around the station at
night, looking at the warm light flowing from the
windows of the grand bedroom and the hangar. It was
always a pleasure to see the bright lights flooding out
from the hangar. It was their weapon against an enemy
that claimed that they were prisoners of the Outback.
The enemy that claimed they would never get back to
civilization. Defiantly they fought back by creating a
micro civilization of their own--a civilization on their
own terms. And they were determined to fight a greater
battle too. They would return to the real world. Both
knew that one day, very soon, they would have to face a
life-or-death challenge.

They discussed the final challenge more and more as
they days went by. They both knew that they could not
stay at the station forever. Someday the food would run
out or the water would run dry or one of them would get
sick and need medical attention. It was only a matter of
time, a month, two months, or more, but the day would
come. Soon they would have to make that fateful
decision to begin their long trek out across the Outback
in search of civilization.

Derek often spoke about their taking a hike out
beyond the station to a line of high hills that lay off in the
distance. He hoped that their higher elevation and
panoramic view of the Outback, might offer possible

views of settlements off in the distance that couldn't be seen from the station. Once there, he thought, they could camp out at night and look off into the darkness in search of points of light emanating from far off settlements. He figured that if they saw something promising, he would take a compass heading on it and then they would set off towards it, like they did with the flashing light that brought them to the station. Though he didn't look forward to making such a long trek across the forbidding plain, he knew that it offered a far better chance of survival than simply staying put at the station waiting for the unlikely event that someone might stumble across them. Clearly, the station had not been occupied in years, and it might be more years still, before anyone ever came across the well-camouflaged station. Neither he nor Michelle wanted to wait that long for rescue. No, thought Derek, they were going to have to get out of this on their own. Their health and their situation had greatly improved since their trek to the station. Both had confidence. Something would happen soon.

Sweat poured down Derek's forehead. *His eyes stung with a fury. In spite of it, he kept his left hand clamped to the control yoke while his right held the aircraft's throttle fully open. The plane raced down the rough makeshift runway. The airspeed indicator climbed rapidly, forty...forty-five......fifty! The ground rushed faster and faster. The plane shook violently as it tore down the primitive airstrip. Fifty-five...sixty! His knuckles were white. He hauled back on the control wheel. He forced himself to stay in control. "Ease it* *back!" he shouted to himself. "Ease it back more...more. Yes! Come on baby you're coming up...back a little more......Yes! Yes!! We're airborne," he screamed! "We made it, we..........."*

"Derek! Derek!" cried Michelle, as she strolled up to aircraft where it sat silently on the hangar floor.

Her call snapped him out of his daydream. *Someday, maybe someday,* he said to himself. It took him a moment to clear his head. He was surprised at how real it had all seemed a moment ago.

"What's up, Michelle," he called out through the open cockpit door.

She clambered up onto the wing and with the grace of a veteran pilot, slid through the open door and down into the passenger seat. Derek, with a flight manual in his lap, turned and gave her a welcome hug. He was delighted to see her beside him. She was wearing yellow short shorts and a silky white blouse she had selected from the walk-in closet in the bedroom.

"I found the answer," she said excitedly. "I finally found out what this station is all about! Why the grand bedroom is here, why the planes are here, everything!"

"Calm down a minute, Michelle! What have you found, what are you talking about."

Excitedly she held up an unlabeled volume that looked to Derek to be some kind of journal. "I was looking through the bookcase in the house when I came across this book." She placed the dust-covered book on her lap. "She opened the book to reveal a sheaf of papers that was neatly tied with a gold ribbon. "That's when I found *this*!" With great fanfare, she thrust the manuscript into the air proclaiming, "tah-dah!"

Derek smiled. "But how do you know that's the answer to the mystery, it's still tied up."

She laughed, as she untied the ribbon. "Don't be silly, I re-tied it so it would have a better effect when I uncovered it. Didn't you like the drama of that?" Derek remained silent as he watched her delicate beautiful hands lightly pull the ribbon off the sheaf. The ribbon drifted down her silky-smooth legs onto the cockpit floor. She lifted off the blank protective cover sheet revealing a neatly centered header page that read:

Mr. Abraham Winston, Born July 7, 1951
Mrs. Lisa-Marie (Stuart) Winston Born April 19, 1980
Died 2007 (Age 27)
Married: August 16, 2005 (At age 25)

Michelle placed the page at the bottom of the sheaf and moved on to the first page of the document. Unlike the neatly printed header page, much of the manuscript displayed scratchy and shakily scrawled rambling script. It appeared to have been written by someone either under emotional stress or by someone who had been injured.

Michelle pointed to the hand scrawled date 'December 17, 2015' that had been placed at the top of the page. "That means this station was occupied as recently as two years ago. And Mr. Winston, the author, would have been about 67 years old at the time of this entry. Judging from the handwriting changes it looks like he made different entries over a long period up until the time it stops.   And it stops so abruptly. For no apparent reason, he just stopped writing for good."

"For no apparent reason," repeated Derek. "That's a phrase we use a lot around here. You say it explains a lot? Go ahead, let's hear it!"

Michelle could hardly contain her excitement. "Well, before I start, let me explain a little bit." She thought for a moment before continuing. "Actually, I don't know where to begin. What's here isn't so much a journal record written by Mr. Winston —it's more of a love story. And it's a beautiful story too. It's about Abraham and his wife Lisa-Marie. Although he calls her Marie in the journal, he named her airplane the 'Lisa-Marie."

"Marie was so beautiful and so young." She stopped for a minute. With a noticeable quiver to her voice she began again, "And she died of cancer at only 27 years of age. They had been married for only two years. It's so sad. It was really hard to read. It was like a really sad romance novel. I wanted to cry. He must have loved her *soooo* much."

Michelle started to get emotional but quickly regained her composure. She began to recount the story. "Anyway, as I said, it reads kind of like a love story, yet it's really an explanation of what this place is all about. When I opened it, I couldn't stop reading it. It's sad and beautiful at the same time. He writes to her as if she were still alive, sitting right beside him listening to every word. Listen, I'll start at the beginning."

She began reading, "*My Dearest Darling Marie: Things have not been going well of late. I haven't been well these last few months. What bothers me most isn't the frequent pains and exhaustion that I constantly feel. What bothers me is my lapses of memory. It's happening more often now. I forget things that I shouldn't."* The script became more difficult to read. *"I was frightened last week. I came out of the bathroom and couldn't remember where I was. That didn't bother me nearly so much as when I came around again and realized that I had forgotten your name. I'm so sorry my darling. I never ever want that to happen again. But I am more horrified that my condition might get worse and that I could lose all memory of you. I can never let that happen. I'm so bothered by this that I'm writing everything down so I won't ever forget how we met and fell in love and came to this place. I don't want to forget anything about you or anything about us. I must always have you here in my heart. I'll cherish every moment we've ever shared and will continue to share forever."* The script suddenly became much more legible. *"I'm not frightened now. You're here; you're always here. Always. I'm so happy you are here with me. I must keep you here. I must keep you alive. Keep our love alive."*

Derek stopped her for a moment. "He sounds like he's not in very good shape. I wonder if he's getting Alzheimer's disease or something. That would be a terrible thing to happen to someone way out here. Is that what happened?"

"I'm not sure, maybe. But it may be more related to an accident he had. I'll get to that in a little bit." She shuffled the pages and placed them neatly back on her lap. "I won't read it word-for-word from here. I'll just tell you the story."

She looked down at the manuscript that still lay in her lap and picked up the story from where she'd left off.

"From here the journal goes back to his early youth. He recalls how he devoted his entire life to carrying on the family business. Even as a very young man he worked side by side with his father. Early on, he was driven to retain and build upon the huge fortune his father had amassed. He explained how he had spent his whole life running the huge organization. Sadly, his father died at the early age of 45. From that point on, Mr. Winston did everything on his own. He never took a wife. He didn't have a family—no brothers or sisters--no one. The business was his life—his whole life. But most of all he felt that nobody cared for him. Everybody wanted something, he said. Everyone wanted money—*his* money. He laments that nobody in his whole life ever showed that they were concerned about him in any way. No one. No one, that is, until one day he had an automobile accident."

Michelle continued. "In 2005, on an early spring afternoon in Virginia, he accidentally ran his classic old Rolls Royce through a stop sign and crashed into the side of a red Toyota. He wasn't wearing his seatbelt. He was thrown forward, where his head solidly thumped against the windshield. When he came too, he found himself looking into Marie's big beautiful brown eyes. He was immediately taken by the striking beauty of the gorgeous 21-year-old woman. He says he honestly thought he'd died and gone to Heaven and had awakened in the arms of an angel."

I know how he must have felt, though Derek. He gazed at the golden halo that seemed to encircle Michelle's hair, as the sun shone through the cockpit window.

Michelle didn't notice Derek's momentary inattention. She continued, "She had opened his door and had his head cradled in her lap while she tenderly wiped a tiny spot of blood from a very minor scrape on his head. He gazed into her eyes and for the first time in his life he felt someone honestly cared for him. He tells how he could actually feel her concern as if it were something real that he could reach out and touch. He must have been right because the rest of the journal is the part that's really a love story."

"I guess you could say they met by accident," chuckled Derek. Michelle was not amused.

"Shush up. Just listen to the rest of the story," quipped Michelle. "It's really a beautiful story." She gave him a stern look. "If you're ready, now I'll continue."

Derek tried to show his remorse by lowering his head in a theatrical display of shame. Michelle gave him a sharp punch to his arm. She now had his full attention. Derek quietly rubbed his sore arm and without any further theatrics settled in to listen while Michelle continued on with the story.

She looked down at the manuscript, then back at Derek. "And I'm not sorry I punched you!"

Derek believed her. He wouldn't trifle with her emotions again when she was being serious.

"Anyway…he goes on to say how he instantly fell in love with her and knew that she was the girl he wanted to marry. He started to shower her with gifts. His first gift was a brand-new Rolls Royce to replace the Toyota that he had wrecked. She tried to refuse it, but he wouldn't take no for an answer. The gifts continued. He found that she was a graduate student, majoring in Ecology, so he paid all her college expenses. When he found out that she was taking flying lessons, he showed up at the flight school to take flying lessons right alongside her. He hired her a personal flight instructor and paid all the expenses until she got her license. No matter how she tried not to accept his gifts he prevailed and, in the end, he swept her off her feet."

Derek thought for a moment. "Let's see, she would have been 21 when they met and he would have been about 54. Why would she want to marry a man over twice her age?"

"Are you kidding? Didn't you look at him in the wedding picture in the bedroom?" She looked at Derek and smiled. "Didn't you see his strong rugged features with that gorgeous shock of gray hair at the front. He looked strong and mature and that handsome muscular build and powerful chest"

"Ok, Ok. I get the point." Derek looked at the still smiling Michelle. He wasn't sure if she was baiting him or not. "And the fact that he was worth millions didn't hurt I suppose."

"Well, probably not," replied Michelle. "But in this case, if you read the whole manuscript, I think you'll find that the money really didn't matter. I think she truly loved the man."

Michelle got serious again. "It was a fairy tale romance. His age meant nothing to him anymore. He felt young and alive for the first time in his life." She gently patted the manuscript in her lap. "He tells in here how they had a fabulous wedding. They even arrived at the church in a horse drawn coach hauled by six white horses, complete with footmen. Oh, and we were right. The two airplanes were his and her wedding presents. He says he got her the twin-engine for her because she was twice as good a pilot than him. He couldn't get the knack of flying a multi-engine plane, but she excelled at it. So, he bought the single-engine for himself."

"Now here's the most interesting part," she began. "For their honeymoon they got a commercial flight and flew to Australia. Marie had always wanted to go to Australia and she was particularly interested in the Simpson Desert area."

"Then that must be where we are," Derek added.

"Maybe, but the Simpson Desert is huge and the area around it covers thousands of square miles. And he doesn't say exactly where we are, or even if we are actually in the Simpson Desert. So unfortunately, we still don't know for sure where we are located. In any case, they rented a twin-engine plane and they spent two months touring Australia—she flew the plane herself. They spent some time on the East Coast of Australia, traveling north from Sydney up along the coast to

Mossman in Queensland. After that they found their way into South Australia where she wanted to spend some time in the desert area. They rented an old truck with long range fuel tanks and spent weeks touring the Outback. They eventually made their way to this very spot."

"For some reason Marie was taken by this location. I don't know what she saw that made her want to explore it more thoroughly. Maybe it was the ecology of the site or its remoteness, but whatever it was she loved it here. She was like an excited schoolgirl as she ran here and there pointing things out and showing him things that were of great interest to her. At one point she was almost giddy with pleasure. He was getting giddy with pleasure too, but he had something else in mind. He writes so beautifully how he swept her off her feet, placed her softly on the ground, and the two made love. Afterward, while they still lay naked on the ground, she rolled over on top of him, kissed him, and told him that at that moment she was the happiest that she had ever been in her entire life. Her sentiments must have struck him hard because from that moment on this place became special, almost sacred to him. He actually constructed the house on the very spot where they made love among the trees."

Derek thought for a moment about how he, too, had made love under the stars with his true love here at the station. He readily understood how Abraham thought that this place was so special. Michelle must have had the same thought because she stopped for a moment and gave him a quick kiss before continuing.

"Right after their honeymoon visit to Australia, he and Lisa returned to Virginia to live out their lives in happiness. As soon as they returned home she began to work on redecorating their palatial home. She was particularly proud of the bedroom that she'd designed and decorated. And we know she did a grand job because that's it in the house!"

"You mean, that's an exact replica?"

"No, I mean that's *it!* That's the very room from the Virginia mansion that was taken apart and put back together in precisely the same condition it was to start with. But, I'm getting ahead of myself. Let me go on."

"Now the sad part is about to begin. A short time after she finished the house in Virginia, she became sick. It must have been very difficult for Abraham to write about this tragedy because you can almost feel the physical and emotional pain in his script. Anyway, she died after battling cancer for nearly 14 months. He was absolutely devastated. All his money and all his love couldn't save her. He writes how every day after that, he was tortured whenever he saw a young woman. He would see her face, remember his love, and be torn apart again and again. His friends, lawyers, and associates told him to get professional help but he wouldn't or couldn't. He was extremely wealthy and didn't have to answer to anybody so he decided instead to live out his dream as if she were still alive. He sold everything and put it all into trusts. He gave a $20 million-dollar grant to the American Cancer Society and also donated $10 million dollars to the University of Virginia to set up an endowed chair for the Ecology Department. That's where Marie had completed her Master's Degree. Apparently, he still had a huge sum of money left over. He used some of that to build this station and the hangar. He paid workers an exorbitant amount of money to build this place and to keep quiet as to what they built and where it was located. And he had them intentionally build it so that it would be camouflaged as much as possible with the natural cover of the trees and shadows. It must have worked because he gives no indication that anyone ever visited this place from when it was built until the date he wrote this record—that's a period of about twenty years."

They both stopped and reflected on the journal. Each knew that it would be many years before anyone again stumbled upon the station, if ever. And they couldn't wait that long. A moment later Michelle returned to her story.

"Oh, and you'll find this interesting," said Michelle. "Mr. Winston explains in the manuscript that the reason he built the main part of the house so basic and simple is that he wanted to put aside his old life in Virginia. He wanted to be as far away from that life as he possibly could, but he kept one part of Virginia with him. He kept her bedroom. He kept that because that was her favorite place in the mansion. It was there in the bedroom, sitting on the settee, where he sat by her side day and night during her last few weeks before they took her away to the hospital, where she died."

Michelle stopped for a moment and wiped a tear from her eye. Derek reached over to her but she gently pushed his hand aside. She sniffled and picked up from where she left off. She sighed and wiped her cheek again. "He tells how he moved the bedroom completely intact with everything placed in exactly the same spot just as it was the day they took her away to the hospital. Every piece of clothing every hairbrush and cosmetic are exactly where they were the last time she touched them. It's heartbreaking to read about it. He tells how he would turn on the generator then go into the bedroom and tune the radio to receive the classical music she loved so much. "I guess, in his mind, he saw her in her greatest beauty, not in her last days of pain and suffering," added Derek.

"Now let me get back to the building of the station after her death," she continued. "At the same time the station and grand bedroom were being built, he had the airplane hangar constructed. He had the planes shipped over and placed in the hangar. He also purchased that old truck over by the outbuilding. That's actually the one they had originally rented for use on their honeymoon. He had it secretly delivered to the station. He reminisces about his fond memories of how they had used the truck in their original touring of the outback. They even used it to explore this very area where the house is located. He talks about how much fun they had with the truck. They even had a steamy romantic encounter in the truck bed in the middle of the day." She snickered before continuing. "I guess it was just one more memory that he wanted to bring to the station to keep his dream alive."

"Is that the only truck he had here at the station?" Derek asked.

"No, he owns a different truck now. He keeps it here at the station to do work with or to go out into the Outback. He says in the journal that he bought a new red truck--but that would have been a few years ago. He had long-range fuel tanks installed on it. So, he must have been able to travel hundreds of miles at a time. But, obviously, that truck isn't here now. Even though he has the truck, he explains that he used the single-engine airplane to fly out of the station to get supplies several times a year. He thoroughly enjoyed living here and being left alone."

"Now I'll tell you about the accident," she added. "About a month before his last entry, he had some kind of accident. He didn't elaborate. But he did say that he'd badly injured his right leg. He tried to nurse it himself, for some time but he finally realized that he needed real medical help. The injury had become so serious that he wasn't able to fly the airplane anymore. His next-to-the-last entry said that he planned to drive the truck to a hospital instead. He doesn't say where the hospital was, but from the way he writes about the seriousness of the injury, I doubt that he would have been able to drive all the way to Alice Springs alone. I wish he'd said how long a drive it was or which direction he went for help but he doesn't."

"But what happened to him?" Derek asked. "Obviously it's been at least two years since he left the station in search of medical help."

"I'd say it's possible that he drove off and simply didn't reach the hospital," said Michelle. "In his state of mind and medical condition, he could have had an accident or maybe the truck broke down and he became stranded. I don't know exactly why or when he left. He doesn't talk about that in the journal. But I firmly believe that if he could have come back, he would have by now. He loved this place too much to abandon it. It was his life, his whole life. No, I don't think he's ever coming back."

"Is that it? Is that where the journal ends?" Derek asked.

"There is one last entry. The handwriting is clear and legible. He explains that he's always kept her twin-engine plane in perfect condition. She loved that plane and flew it every chance she got in Virginia until she got too sick to fly. Michelle stopped for a moment. "This is a really sad part, and he tells it so eloquently and so beautifully. He explains that he keeps the plane ready to fly because he knows that one day he will feel that his time has come. On that day, he says he will climb into the cockpit of the Lisa Marie, start up the engines, and taxi her out in front of his beloved station. He goes on to say that he'll take off into the golden setting sun, flying on and on until he meets her in paradise where, once again, they can truly share their love. This time for all eternity."

Tears welled up in Michelle's eyes. "He's not coming back Derek. Not ever. I think he knew that himself before he left. And we still don't have a clue as to which way it is to reach civilization. Even as he writes this manuscript, he seems to unconsciously want to keep the location of this site a secret."

Robert Campbell

Michelle placed the manuscript back on her lap, bent her head down, and began to sob softly. Derek reached over and gently comforted her. He knew her emotions had been triggered not just by the beauty and sincerity of the manuscript, but by the realization that their situation was really hopeless now. Their faint hopes that a rescue party would come looking for them were dashed by the radio announcement which said there were no survivors. And now, their last hopes that the station's owner might somehow return, or that someone might stumble across them were dashed. In all the years covered by the manuscript there was not a single word that any outsider had ever come across the station. Mr. Winston's payments to the workers had been a solid investment in insuring his privacy. Just as he had wanted, nobody came. Nobody was ever going to come--the manuscript made that clear. They both knew for certain now that their fate rested in their own hands. They would have to find a way out on their own.

A few minutes later Michelle stopped crying. Derek gently brushed away the tears that steamed down her cheeks. Michelle sniffed a few times then put her hands to her eyes. She rubbed them gently. Still sniffing, she spoke.

"Derek we've got to do something. We've got to try to get out of here. I think it's time we made that hike out to climb those hills out on the horizon. We've got to *do something*. We need to see what's out there beyond them. I'm up to it." She looked pleadingly at into his eyes. "Please, let's do it. Let's start getting ready. We

can leave tomorrow." Derek didn't have to think twice.
He was more than ready!

CHAPTER 20

The afternoon of the second day into their hike, Derek and Michelle reached their destination. Although weary, the pair easily set up camp under a small stand of eucalyptus trees. The shade provided welcome relief from the sun. After a brief rest, the pair stood at the base of the foothills. While Derek surveyed the area looking for the most viable ascent route to the top, Michelle turned and looked back at the far-off station that now lay some 10 miles behind them. She was proud of their achievement. They had reached the base of the hills after a relatively easy march.

Derek's attention was drawn to Michelle. She was standing there gazing at the plain with her hands on her hips. To Derek, Michelle looked like an Outback rancher counting her cattle out on the range. The sight struck him funny, and though he tried, he couldn't keep from laughing. Michelle heard him laugh and spun around. The old work boots she was wearing kicked up a mini cyclone of dust. The boots she'd found in one of the old sheds enhanced the 'rancher' image she projected. She turned to face him. "What's so funny," she asked.

"It's nothing," Derek relied. "It's just that you look just like you belong out here in the Outback surveying your domain."

Michelle put on a frown and came closer. Derek wasn't sure if it was a mock frown or not. He pretended to be scared and stepped back.

"But it's a nice look!" Derek stammered in mock fear. "I mean you really look great with that fine tan and healthy-looking body! No kidding! A beautiful rancher! Yeah, really beautiful! With that great tan against your blond hair, you should be a model for Australia tourism!"

"Okay, I won't kill you now. Maybe I'll wait till later," she joked.

Michelle and Derek looked up at foothills again. Both were encouraged by the fact that although the hills were high, there appeared to be plenty of supports along the way to make the hike fairly safe. "We'll be at the top in no time," Derek replied cheerily. "It's about 4:00 p.m. now and we should make it to the top with daylight to spare." In high spirits, the two picked out the highest hill in the range. It looked to be about 350 feet or so to the top. The hill itself, from their vantage point, looked the most promising. Its rocky surface was peppered with small trees and shrubs and there appeared to be many rocky handholds. Both thought the climbing should be easy. And the reasonably high elevation offered hope that the signal fire they planned to set might meet with success. Their plan to arrive at the base of the hills before sunset had dual benefits. The first was that they'd have some daylight in which to make the ascent in safety. The second, but unplanned benefit, was that the sun's rays began painting the foothills with gorgeous tones of gold, brown, yellow, red, and a twinge of violet. In a matter of moments, it transformed the foothills into a landscape masterpiece on a gigantic scale. The two looked up in awe. It was stunning to view the magnificent foothills that glowed dramatically in front of them.

"Ohhh, that's gorgeous," Michelle marveled. "That's a landscape worthy of the Louvre Museum in Paris."

"I have to admit," responded Derek. "Its beauty is unsurpassed. And maybe its beauty is a sign--like a rainbow means good luck. Maybe this is a sign that things are going to go our way when we climb to the top."

"I hope so," replied Michelle. "We could use a little luck right now."

"No time like the present," chortled Derek. He reached down and grabbed the frame of the backpack and hefted it into position up on his shoulders. Before they left, Michelle gave it a quick going over to be sure that the telephoto lens camera was inside, along with an 8-ounce plastic bottle filled with gasoline for their signal fire. She double checked that the pack contained matches, signal mirror, the tent and some food supplies. Their plan was to climb to the top of the tallest foothill before dark. When darkness fell they planned to search for lights on the horizon. Should that fail they hoped a signal fire might draw attention and rescue. Everything was in order. It was time to go.

With daylight still shining, Derek and Michelle began the ascent. Both were thrilled that the climb towards the top went so easily. But at the halfway point something caught Michelle's attention. She requested a rest. Derek, eagerly agreed.

"Derek, look over there," she called out, pointing to what appeared to be a notch between two of the larger hills a short way off. "Can you hand me the camera?" she asked." Camera in hand, she called to Derek, "It looks like there may be a pass between those hills. Maybe we should check that out before we leave this area tomorrow."

"Let me have a look with the telephoto lens," said Derek. Michelle handed him the camera and he focused in on, what appeared to be, a gap between the hills.

"I think you're right Michelle. It does look like a pass between them. And since we're so close to it, we'd be foolish not to check out the pass as a possible way out of here. In the morning, if we don't see anything from the top, we'll climb back down towards the pass and see if it leads anywhere."

"Sounds like a plan," called Michelle. After a water break and short rest, the two resumed their climb to the summit.

Barely an hour later, the summit finally came into view. Derek reached the top first, followed a moment later by Michelle. She grabbed Derek's outstretched hand for a final boost onto the summit.

In spite of some wrist pain, Derek was elated to be on the top. Ignoring the pain, he quickly rose to his feet.

Robert Campbell

The two stood, side by side, on the angled summit that was crowned with patches of green and brown grasses and a solitary gnarled tree. Their elation at reaching the summit quickly turned to gloom. All they could see in any direction was more of the same endless plain that had tortured them since the crash. They felt utterly cheated. The two were nearly in a state of despair. They sank to the ground and sat wordlessly on the barren summit, staring out at miles and miles of nothingness.

It was some time before either spoke. Eventually Derek forced himself to rise. He groaned as he straightened himself up. "If I only had the energy, I'd pick up a rock and throw it right into the face of that miserable plain. How can there be so much nothing out there?!" he shouted bitterly. "Nothing, there's nothing out there at all. We may as well be the last two people on earth." He let out a loud sigh as he began to think about what he had just said. He knew Michelle was depressed enough and he regretted being so negative. He quickly recovered and added, "but if we're the last two people on earth then I'm damn lucky to be here with you." He painfully knelt down beside her. Michelle leaned over and placed her head against his chest. Derek stroked her hair. For a moment he lost himself in the pleasure of watching her hair glisten as the fading light glinted through it.

"Thanks, Derek. I feel lucky to have you too." With a sigh she added, "I'm so sorry that we didn't see something from up here. But I can't say it comes as a big surprise that there's nothing to see." She quickly added, "Anyway, we still have the night. Maybe tonight when it gets dark we'll be able to see some lights off in the distance. There's still a chance of that!" she added with an unexpected touch of enthusiasm.

Derek let out a halfhearted laugh but gave in to the fact that it was a real possibility. "Okay then," he added. "Let's set up the tent and see what happens. I'll dig out something to eat."

When darkness came they sat side by side carefully scanning the horizon hoping to catch the slightest glimmer of light off in the distance that would indicate civilization. Hour after hour they took turns with the telephoto lens searching for signs of life but all they saw was an ever darkening and barren plain stretching from horizon to horizon.

It was nearly midnight, and pitch black, when Michelle finally suggested that it was time to light the signal fire. Though both knew the fire was an act of futility, neither was willing to speak the words. Reluctantly, Derek rose to his feet and retrieved the bottle of gasoline and a small flashlight from his pack.

"What are we going to burn?" asked Michelle.

"How about that tree?" replied Derek. He shined the beam of light on the solitary tree that clung tenaciously to the barren hilltop.

"No, not that!" cried Michelle. "We should leave it alone. It's kind of like us. It's doing its best to hold onto life up here, all alone in this harsh place. And it's doing well at it. We can too! We can make it too, just like that tree. Please leave it."

Derek readily understood her feelings for the tree and how much it meant to her as a symbol of life

Robert Campbell

overshadowing all its hardships. He quickly offered a
suggestion.

"Well, instead, how about if I pull up a bunch of dry
grass and put it into a pile with any sticks or shrub
branches I can gather up. Along with the gasoline, that
should produce a bright fire."

Michelle was greatly relieved that Derek had agreed
to spare the special tree. "That will be good," she
replied. Warming to the task, she enthusiastically added,
"Come on, Derek I'll help you. We can do this together
and pull up grass. Let's grab all we can and make a really
big fire. It doesn't matter if nobody sees it. We'll be
here to enjoy it ourselves."

"Wait a second," said Michelle. "And we can enjoy
this too," she chortled while holding up a bottle of
Scotch. "I snuck this into our supplies to use in
celebration in case we saw civilization from the top of
the hills. But it looks like that's not going to happen so
we'll just enjoy ourselves anyway!"

Derek beamed with delight. He took the bottle,
broke the seal, and took a long pull of the marvelous
liquid. It glowed a glorious amber color when he shined
the flashlight onto the bottle. "Ah, I needed that," he
chortled, using the back of his hand to wipe his lips.

He handed the bottle back to Michelle. She took a
quick swallow and nearly choked as it burned her throat.
They both laughed once she recovered. Then they went
about the task of gathering grasses to build the fire.

Derek doused the collection of signal fire debris with
the pint of gasoline. Michelle did the honors of throwing
the match that instantly started the blaze. In only a

moment they felt the external warmth from their bonfire and the internal warmth from the scotch as it coursed its way through their bodies. They felt a sense of peace and contentment while they stood hugging each other in the bright yellow glow of the blaze.

The two sat down on the sleeping pad outside the tent watching the flames lick towards the black night sky. Almost in a daze, Derek's eyes followed a large red ember as it slowly lifted itself into the air and floated away. The flying ember caused his mind to shift back to the station and the two aircraft that sat in the hangar. Then he couldn't stop thinking about the airplanes. *The planes are our salvation*, he thought. *They're sitting there just waiting for us to climb in and fly off to safety. If we only knew how to fly!*

Whether from the effects of the alcohol, or simply because his fierce determination had finally risen to the surface, Derek suddenly slammed his fist onto the mat and blurted out, *"That's it!!! That's it Michelle! We're getting out of here! By this time next week, we're going to be sipping Pina Coladas in Sydney!"*

Michelle was startled by his sudden outburst. "What *are* you talking about?" she cried.

Derek jumped to his feet. He started pacing about. **"*I'm going to fly us out of here!*** As soon as we get back to the station I'm going to get that single-engine plane started and I'm going to learn to fly it myself. I've got a little basic knowledge about airplanes and I can do it! Enough is enough. We've been out here long enough," he shouted. "I can do it Michelle, I can learn to fly that plane. All my life I've wanted to fly but I always found an excuse not to do it--not enough time, not enough money, or some other reason. Well now--no more excuses! Tomorrow, we're going back to the station. I'm going to teach myself how to fly that plane and get us out of here."

Michelle was completely taken aback by Derek's sudden change of behavior. Thinking it was most likely due to the effects of the generous quantity of scotch that he'd consumed, she dismissed the idea, and pulled him down onto the mat beside her. "How about taking some of that enthusiasm and converting it into a fun performance instead," she said with a seductive tone that Derek couldn't ignore. In spite of his enthusiasm to discuss his plans to learn how to fly, Michelle's warm caressing hands quickly convinced him to put off the discussion until the morning.

Michelle, too, was feeling the effects of the alcohol. She was feeling mellow. Her excitement built rapidly as she caressed Derek's body. They both were feeling a warm glow of anticipation and the rapidly chilling air did nothing to cool their passion. Later, once inside the tent, the sounds of their pleasure echoed from the summit, but there was nobody to hear the sound and nobody to see their fire.

The morning sun quickly raised the temperature inside the tent where Derek and Michelle still laid naked after the previous evenings pleasurable activities. "Ohh, I've got a headache," moaned Derek.

"It's probably a hangover," said Michelle as she came awake. She groggily looked over at the empty bottle of scotch lying in the corner of the tent. "You'll live."

"Your concern overwhelms me," Derek lamented. He smiled while enjoying the sight of Michelle's beautiful body. "Come on while it's still daylight," he called out with phony enthusiasm, then happily slapped her naked thigh. We have to get going. I'm anxious to get down so we can get back to the station. I want to get right to work on that plane."

Michelle sat up. A beam of sunlight highlighted her bare breast. Derek smiled at the sight.

She looked at him quizzically. "You mean you're really serious. You're really going to try to get the plane running and learn to fly it yourself?"

"Sure, but I'm going to need your help. Like I said last night, I know a little bit about the basics of flying and I've been studying the flight manual for the Warrior for weeks now. But I'll need your help as well. You talk to pilots all the time and pop into the cockpit from time to time. Even though they fly big jets I'm sure you've picked up on a lot of things that happen in the cockpit. Anything that you can come up with will help. You can work with me as we go over controls in the plane and stuff like that, anything at all may prove helpful. With the two of us working together I know we can do it. We'll succeed because we've got one thing on our side that's more important than anything else. We've got *motivation*. We're *well* motivated!"

Michelle was silent for several moments. The idea that had seemed so preposterous to her last night, didn't sound so unrealistic in the light of day. *It might be possible after all,* she thought. They were running out of options. Their only other alternative was to wait until someone stumbled across them at the station...and that was a remote possibility indeed. *Not only that,* she thought, *what if the water at the station dries up like it did at the crash site and at the oasis?* The more she thought about it, the more rational and exciting the idea seemed. "Let's do it!" shrieked Michelle, enthusiastically. Derek pulled her close into a passionate kiss. He was hoping for more than just a kiss but Michelle was too full of excitement to go any further. She was eager to return to the station and wanted to begin the trip back without delay. Derek sighed, but he couldn't blame her. He was anxious to return too. A moment later they hurriedly dressed and broke camp.

A half-hour into the climb back down from the summit, Michelle fought to gain her footing. She almost wished they'd gone back down the way they'd come up. But they needed to check out the possible 'pass' that she'd seen earlier during the ascent. Though the route over towards the possible 'pass' was proving to be a bit dangerous, it was a necessary diversion. Both Derek and Michelle knew that uncovering a pass through the hills might have, as yet, unknown benefits as a survival route.

A few minutes later, Derek spotted a recessed area that offered them a chance to rest and view possible descent routes. The pair took a water break. Derek scanned the horizon then, pointing to a gap over to his right, he called out to Michelle. "Look over there," he said. He motioned down and towards the right. "Over by that gap. Isn't that where you spotted what might be a pass through the range?"

Michelle followed Derek's motioning hand. "Yes, that's it. Good spotting. I'm for checking it out now."

"I agree," said Derek. "But, from here, it looks like it meanders around a bit and it'll certainly take us longer to get back to our campsite. But at least it will give us a chance to see if there really is a pass through the range of hills."

"Great," said Michelle. "So, let's do it. The whole trip won't take more than an hour or two. And we can still get back to our old campsite before the midday sun hits us." Michelle wiped perspiration from her forehead with the back of her forearm. "Wheesh, it's getting hot," she added wearily."

After concluding their short rest, Michelle and Derek set off again, with Derek in the lead position. This time they altered their route and began hiking diagonally downward over toward their destination at the gap. "Michelle looked down nervously. "I didn't mind climbing up because we were always going forward and we had to look up instead of down. I hate having to look down to find my footing. It's a long way to fall. I don't like this at all."

"Don't worry," Derek called upward from ten feet below. "I'm below you to cushion your fall."

"That's not very reassuring! I'd probably land on top of that solid steel head of yours and be killed!" she yelled back. In spite of her nervous comments Michelle continued to find foot holds as she inched her way down towards the precarious gap.

Derek stopped for a moment to catch his breath. A moment later Michelle side-stepped by him. She knew they were close and couldn't wait to take a look over a promising ledge just a little further down the trail. Derek now looked down at Michelle. She was still some twenty feet below him now. Derek saw that Michelle was fatigued as she slipped by him. He called out to her. "Cheer up Michelle. We're just about through the nastiest part of the climb down."

Almost immediately she called back. "Derek, come take a look at this, *we're at the gap!*" Derek hurried to her side. Together they cautiously approached the edge of a rocky ledge. Looking straight down over the ledge, they discovered that it ended with a sheer fifty-foot drop to a rock-strewn gully below.

"This is it Derek! It's just as I thought it would be," Michelle called out happily. She looked up and down the ravine and proclaimed the dry riverbed to be a pass through the range of hills. "We've finally reached the pass through the range!"

Derek, stared down at the rock-strewn pass below. "That's it all right," he confirmed. "But we're not going to be able to get down there from here. We'll have to find another way down."

"You're right," said Michelle. She held onto a small tree and peered over the edge again. She examined the surface below. "Actually, I think it isn't so much a 'pass' as it is a dry riverbed that once cut through here. It's probably been dry for a hundred years or more. It's pretty rocky but we should be able to follow it down to where it opens onto the plain. From there it should be just a short walk back to the campsite."

While Derek sat on a rock wiping the perspiration from his eyes, Michelle wandered over to a nearby ledge. She hoped to spot an easier route down to the riverbed below. Derek watched as she climbed over a boulder and disappeared from view.

A moment later Derek's heart stopped. He heard Michelle scream. "Derek! Derek! Over here! Come quick!" she yelled. Derek scrambled to his feet, scaled the boulder, and raced to where she stood gesticulating frantically at something down in the gully below. She screamed with excitement.

"Derek there's a truck down there! A real truck, not a wreck! Somebody must be down there!" Her arm trembled, as she pointed downwards to a spot between a heap of boulders and a small tree. Derek could feel his heart pounding in his chest. He followed her pointing finger to where he could clearly make out the front end of a truck. He looked almost straight down at the dust covered red truck far below. It was sitting motionless in the narrow rock-strewn gorge with barely a few inches clearance on either side. It looked as if it were wedged in between the rough, rocky, and nearly vertical walls that stood like gigantic tombstones on either side of the canyon-like pass.

Derek stared for a moment in disbelief. His hands shook as he cupped them and yelled at the top of his lungs, "Hello! Hello down there! Is anybody there?! Anybody there?!!"

The only response was the rapidly dissipating echo of his shouts.

"Nobody answers," replied Derek. "Come Michelle, we've got to get down there real fast! Maybe somebody stopped and left the truck to go exploring or something. We've got to get to them before they decide to leave." To speed their descent both dropped their packs on the ground to be retrieved later.

"Here, let's go this way!" said Michelle. She rushed forward skirting around a jagged chunk of rock. "I found a way down just before I saw the truck." Derek turned to follow. "Oh, please hurry Derek! We can't let them get away. We can't!!" She grabbed his arm to turn him around, then raced towards a gap between two large boulders leading down into the pass below. Once through the opening, they clambered down a craggy rock wall face. They readily made use of every hand and foothold available to them, from rocks, to scrubs, to crevices. In their adrenalin fueled rush, they completed the dangerous fifty-foot descent in a matter of minutes. Finally, on the surface of the rock-strewn wash, the truck lay some twenty feet away.

Michelle reached the surface first, yelling even before her feet struck the bottom. "Help! Help! Is anybody there?!" There was no answer. Even as she called, she sensed that something wasn't right about the truck.

Derek sensed it too. With a deep bellow he yelled through cupped hands. "Hallo! Hallo! Is anybody here!" Derek yelled again and again. The pair stood in silence praying for a response that never came.

Derek shook his head dejectedly. "Nobody's here Michelle." He continued to shake his head in disgust. He made his way toward the truck. He picked his way over and around the thousands of stones and rocks that littered the surface of the dry riverbed. Finally, he stood directly in front of the big 4 X 4 truck. "It looks like it's abandoned, Michelle," he sighed in near despair. He hadn't walked more than a few feet forward when it became apparent that something was seriously wrong with the truck. In his initial enthusiasm, he'd failed to notice that the truck was resting at an odd angle with the left front resting nearly on the ground.

Michelle noticed it too as she approached the truck. "It looks like it must have a flat left front tire. Maybe someone left it while they went off to get a spare wheel," she said hopefully. Even as she spoke the words, she knew she was wrong. Up close, they could now see that the left front of the truck had been struck by a huge chunk of rock. It could only have fallen from the near vertical wall that towered above it. The truck had been severely damaged by the strike. The impact had crushed the left front wheel under the frame of the vehicle.

Derek stood looking at the truck with its front end angled onto the ground. "God, if it wasn't for bad luck, we wouldn't have any luck at all." He bent down to look under the truck's front end, but it sat so low he couldn't see anything. "Well this thing isn't going anywhere, that's for sure." He brushed his hand across the dust-covered hood revealing the shiny red paint beneath. "The truck appears to be a late model, but from the look of that heavy dirt and debris all over it I'd guess it's been sitting here a long time, probably for years. Damn! I can't believe our luck."

"Well then we'll just have to make our own luck," said Michelle with an enthusiasm that surprised Derek.

"Come on, let's check out the truck," said Michelle. "Maybe there's something in the truck bed that we can use," she added. "I'll go this way," said Michelle as she squeezed herself into the narrow gap between the canyon-like walls and the front end of the truck.

"You take the low road and I'll take the high road," said Derek. He climbed up onto the hood and jumped over the side of the truck behind the huge chunk of rock that barred his way. Michelle was just rounding the back of the truck when Derek yelled out.

"Stop Michelle! Don't come around this side!! Stay there!!"

His call didn't reach her in time. Her hand shot up to her mouth in an unsuccessful attempt to stifle a loud involuntary gasp.

"Oh my God!" she cried as she caught sight of the remains of a human body that was sticking out from under the front fender of the truck.

Derek spun around in the narrow gap and hurried to Michelle. He embraced her.

"I'm sorry you had to see that. I couldn't see it from the hood. It was only when I jumped down behind the rock that I knew it was there."

Michelle's shock quickly dissipated. "I'm okay now. We've been through enough ourselves. I can take it all right." As they ended their embrace, Michelle looked over his shoulder and down at the remains. "What do you think happened here?" she asked.

Derek looked up around at the steep walls on either side. They were filled with cracks, fissures, and chunks of rock. "I'd guess that the driver found himself caught up on a boulder or rock chunk. He probably got out of the truck to try to free it and that's when that huge boulder tore loose from the slope above. It crushed the front wheel--and him along with it."

"And you're not going to believe this," added Derek. He turned and looked back at the part of the body that could be seen sticking out from under the front end of the truck. He nodded at the remains, "That's our Mr. Winston."

"Mr. Winston, from the station!" Michelle gasped. "How do you know that?"

"It's a pretty likely guess. The truck looks exactly the way he described it in the manuscript that you read to me. Look," he pointed to the side of the truck. "There's the extra-long-range fuel tanks, it's red, and it looks like it's been here for a couple of years." The two slowly inched their way forward to where the body lay crushed under the front wheel of the truck. As they approached the body, both were grateful that the torso was completely out of sight. The body was covered by the truck and the huge chunk of fallen rock that had caused his death.

Michelle stood behind Derek, looking over his shoulder, as he examined the body. He noticed a slight bulge in the left rear pocket of the tough, long, pants that covered what could be seen of the body. He was thankful that the pants remained intact, as he gingerly slipped his fingers into the pocket and withdrew a beaten leather wallet. He opened it as he stood up.

"It's Mr. Winston all right," said Derek. He'd looked at the ID card he found inside. "Look at this, Michelle," said Derek. He handed her a worn, hazy, plastic laminated, driver's license. It was difficult to read the name through the damaged plastic but the picture and name on the license provided clear evidence that it was indeed Mr. Winston.

"This must have been taken in happier times," said Michelle. "Because he looks every bit as handsome in this picture as he does in the wedding picture back at the station."

"Look at this," said Derek. He handed Michelle two more picture IDs. "These are their pilot licenses. He kept her license right along with his own all these years. He really loved her deeply," said Derek, thoughtfully. A moment later Michelle handed him back all the ID's and licenses. Derek returned them all to the wallet.

"I'll turn the wallet in to the authorities as soon as we get back to civilization," he said. He hesitated a moment and reflected on what he'd just said. He was pleased that he said it with such confidence. They *would* make it back—he was certain of it.

"Michelle, how about if you check inside the cab while I cover the body with rocks. It wouldn't be right to leave him here like this."

Michelle opened the door of the cab and climbed inside. The interior was a jumble of clothing, camping supplies, water jugs, and canned goods. It looked like

Mr. Winston had packed, or simply thrown, everything in a heap on the passenger side. *He must have been in a big hurry*, thought Michelle. And from looking at all the supplies in the truck, she assumed that wherever he was going, it was a long way off. Compared to how neat and organized the station had been it seemed to be out of character for Mr. Winston to be so untidy. She had to move an old backpack out of the way in order to reach the glove box. Inside, she found a worn leather pouch containing over $35,000 in cash. "Derek," she called out through the open window. "I've found a wad of money in here. I guess he was going to pay cash for his medical care and supplies with it. He must have thought he was in bad shape to have brought so much money with him."

Derek finished placing a boulder on the pile, stood up and approached the window of the truck. He rested his arms on the windowsill. "I don't think he was thinking rationally Michelle." He pointed out the windshield at the hazardous rock-strewn floor of the pass ahead. "I think he was desperate and drove up through here in a big hurry. That's how he got hung up. Remember when you went through the manuscript with me? It was pretty clear that his physical condition and mental capacities were deteriorating. I think what happened was that he finally realized that he absolutely had to get medical attention—and get it fast. From the looks of the terrible surface conditions of this pass, I figure he took this route out of desperation in order to reach help as soon as possible. We could see as we approached this range that the foothills extend for some distance in either direction. Undoubtedly, his usual route for supplies would have taken him way out and around the range of hills. But by heading this way--hazardous as it is--offered him the chance for a quicker trip. If, he could just make it through. I doubt that he was thinking clearly when he made the decision to try to get through this pass. He took a gamble, unfortunately he lost, and the gamble cost him his life." Derek turned and went back to work.

Michelle put her arm on the windowsill, leaned out and watched Derek work. "What you said makes sense," she said, as she continued to watch him pile up rocks. "And from the look of it, wherever he was going involved a long trip judging from all the food and camping supplies thrown about the cab. I'd guess he was planning on a trip of a three or four days."

Derek stopped working. He stepped up by the window and rested his back against the wall behind him. He thought for a moment. "If he was planning on a trip that would last that long, then his destination must have been around four hundred miles. I figure that in his condition he couldn't hope to make more than a hundred miles a day. Of course, we don't know what kind of terrain he was planning to cover but looking at the oversized wheels he had installed on the truck you can be sure it wasn't super highways that he was planning to drive on. From the terrain we've experienced so far, it's pretty clear he wasn't going to travel very fast. But with the extra long-range fuel tanks on it you we can be pretty certain it's a long way to wherever he was going."

"But where could he have been headed?" asked Michelle.

"Actually, I was hoping you might be able to answer that. Do you have any ideas?"

"No," said Michelle. "And I'm not trying to be difficult, but I lived all my life in Sydney and I know very little about these huge desolate areas of Australia. It's kind of like if you suddenly found yourself stranded in the middle of a desert out in your American west. Would you have any idea what direction to go to find settlements?"

"I see what you mean," said Derek. "As always, we seem to be in the dark as to where we are and where civilization is. But at least this time we can be pretty sure which direction to travel. He was going in this direction because he was heading for medical help where there was a hospital or at least trained medical personnel. That would mean that there must be a settlement of substantial size heading this way. So, when we get the plane up, we're going to fly in this direction," he said, with a big smile on his face.

Derek looked down at the pile of rocks. "It's getting hot now. I better finish this up. I'll be done here in a few minutes." He huffed for air. "We'll move out and head back to the camp site as soon as I'm finished."

"All right," said Michelle. "I'll check out the back of the truck while you finish up." She slipped the pile of bills into her pocket and said, "I'm going to take the money with me. We can turn it into the police along with the wallet."

"Okay, Michelle, that's good," replied Derek. He returned to gathering rocks.

Michelle pulled down on the shiny chrome inside door handle and swung the door open. She had some difficulty squeezing through the narrow opening between the door and the rock wall. Once out of the truck she hoisted herself up into the truck bed. The bed was empty, except for two empty jerry cans full of gasoline that they didn't need, and a spare tire that was bolted to a hold-down clamp. She climbed back down and joined Derek who had just finished putting the last boulder in place.

Derek again wiped the perspiration from his forehead. He looked down at the boulders that he had heaped in place, completely covering the remains of Mr. Winston.

"I think we should say a few words over him Michelle. We owe him our lives. I only wish we could have thanked him in person." Michelle agreed and together they recited as much as Derek could remember of the 23rd Psalm.

After they finished their prayer, Derek looked up at the forbidding walls of the pass that rose sharply on both sides. "I don't like the looks of these walls," he said. "Rocks could come down on us at any time. We need to head down the pass and get out of here as soon as possible. After all we've been through I'd hate to have it all end for us like it did for Mr. Winston. I think we better take anything we need from the truck and get ready to leave right away."

"I've already gone through the truck," said Michelle. "We've got plenty of food back at the station so we won't need any from the truck. And we don't need the camping gear either. I'll just take one of the gallon jugs of water from the cab in case we need it on the way back. Then we'll be ready to leave." She entered the cab for the last time and removed a jug of water.

As the two readied themselves for departure, they began to have second thoughts about following the pass out to where it would reach the plain. The closer they looked at the canyon walls, the more concerned they became. They quickly agreed that it would be too dangerous to use the pass as a route back to camp. Instead, they decided to climb back up the slope from where they had first descended into the canyon. From there, they planned to retrace their steps back to the ledge where they'd first seen the truck from above.

The climb back up the fifty-foot canyon wall was slow but not difficult. In only a short time they reached the top, rested a few minutes, and hiked the short distance to where they had left their packs. Once there, Derek used the water jug from the truck to refill the two smaller containers they'd emptied a few hours earlier. He stored them away in the rucksack and prepared for the hike back down to the camp below. As Derek was shouldering the big pack up onto his back, they heard a loud crack followed by a crash. Both shuddered at the sound. Neither bothered looking over the ledge to verify that another boulder had torn loose from the canyon wall and crashed to the surface below. They knew, for sure now, that climbing out of the canyon had been the right decision after all.

They headed back to the spot where they'd earlier deviated to reach the pass. Once there, they took the route that angled back down to where their original campsite lay. In less than an hour they found themselves, once again, in the cooling shade of the eucalyptus trees. In a matter of minutes, they set up the tent and crawled inside. Derek barely moved once he flopped down onto the sleeping mat. Michelle looked over at the inert Derek. He lay face down beside her. Michelle was tired and weary when she spoke. "Derek," she croaked, "I know you want to get back to the station as soon as possible to work on the plane but I'm really exhausted. Why don't we have a longer rest and wait until it gets really dark before we leave. It'll be a lot cooler then and we'll be more rested." Her words went unheard, Derek was snoring loudly, even as she finished the sentence. Michelle lay down beside him, draped her arm across his slowly heaving chest, and fell fast asleep.

CHAPTER 21

Michelle moaned softly as she squirmed between the luxurious sheets of the huge bed. *What a glorious feeling*, she thought, *to experience a bath tub soak and a soft fresh bed after six hard days of hiking out to the foothills and back.* Without the wonderful bedroom and tub to return to, Michelle thought, she might not have been able to make it back. Suddenly her pleasurable bed rest ended when she realized that the bedside radio was playing soft music. "Wha.... What's that? Derek? ... Derek?" she mumbled. Getting no response from Derek, she stretched her hand over to his side of the bed. He wasn't there. A moment later, after a good stretch, she came fully awake and realized that Derek was no longer in the bed. She didn't have to wonder where he was—she knew. If the radio was on that meant he was already out in the hangar with the generator running while he made preparations to get the Warrior flying. Michelle threw off the sheet. She stood naked on the bedroom floor. She plucked a sheer robe from the end of the bed, put it on, and loosely tied the sash. She'd placed it there the night before, intending to tease Derek after her bath. But things didn't work out.

By the time they climbed into bed together, both were too exhausted to pursue anything but sleep.

Michelle let out a long yawn, then shuffled off to the kitchen. *He can be so obsessive*, she thought. She smiled, as she looked down at the kitchen table. It was strewn with manuals, books, leaflets, and whatever else Derek could get his hands on to figure out how to fly an airplane. Reading, researching, and practicing in the cockpit was now Derek's daily routine. She almost wished she hadn't found the Warrior flight manual.

Maybe I'm being too hard on him, she considered. *Maybe his 'obsession' is really 'motivation.'* She thought for a minute. *Yes, 'motivation' that's the word he used up on the summit back at the foothills. He's says we'll successfully fly out of here because we're 'well motivated.' Maybe he's right at that. He is certainly well motivated. 'Driven' may be a better word, but either way it just might be the driving force that we need to get us out of here. If that's what it takes, I'm going to get just as motivated too.*

Figuring that Derek had probably already been up for hours without eating or drinking, she fixed him a cup of coffee and something to eat. She knew better than to go out to the hangar to suggest that he come back inside to eat—it wouldn't have worked. He was too intent on working on the airplane. All he talked about throughout the hike back to the station was the airplane and how they might get it flying.

While Michelle gathered up what she needed to fix breakfast, she thought about Derek's 'mission' as he called it. She sensed that his desire to get the airplane flying was fueled by more than just their need to get back to civilization. It seemed as if he was unconsciously incorporating their desperate situation into the fulfillment of his lifelong dream of learning how to fly. She smiled, as she recalled the gleam in Derek's eye while they were up on the foothill's summit. He had a faraway look of desire in his eyes when he talked about learning how to fly the airplane. *Maybe he really will fly that plane out of here after all.* It was a great thought, she decided to keep it. It was time to make the coffee.

That's odd, thought Michelle. The sink pump didn't seem to be working. It took ten full pump cycles before the water finally burst from the pump into the coffee pot. Once started, the water continued to flow steadily into the pot. She stopped pumping and dismissed the problem.

Michelle carried the full pot of water over to the stove. She placed it on a burner, struck a match, lit the burner, then went off in search of the instant coffee. Somehow, Derek always managed to put it in a different place every time he used it. Several minutes later, she returned with the jar of instant coffee only to find that the stove burner had gone out. She moved the pot to a different burner, struck a match, and lit it. The burner glowed a healthy blue, but only for a moment before it, too, went out. Successive tries produced the same result. *Oh! Oh,* she thought. *We're out of gas.* She checked the coffeepot and was pleased to find that the water had heated up enough to make the coffee hot before the flame went out. She made a large mug of coffee then headed off to the hangar with the brew in one hand and canned biscuits in the other.

Derek was not in sight when Michelle entered the brightly-lit hangar. All the interior lights were turned on. She looked around the spotless hangar and saw that the cabin door to the Warrior was open. She called out as she approached the plane, but Derek didn't answer. A moment later, she heard the door to the generator room open and saw him emerge looking both dejected and determined.

"Morning Michelle," he called out cheerfully as he spotted the food. "Thanks for bringing me something to eat. I'm starved. I got up a couple of hours ago and came directly out here. I'm really excited about this project. It's going to happen you know."

Michelle believed him even as she asked, "How are things going?"

Derek sighed heavily. "I've had a couple of ideas already, but I haven't had much luck. Let me explain. Our first priority is to get the plane started—we're not going anywhere until that happens. Since the airplane's battery is dead, we can't start the engine using its electric starter. So, then I thought, maybe there's a chance we could start it the old fashioned way."

"Old fashioned way?" asked Michelle.

"You know, by flipping the prop over by hand," explained Derek. "Like they used to do with the old double winger planes sixty or seventy years ago. I know you can still do that on a modern plane but I'm scared to death to try that. I don't want to wind up as confetti all over the hangar. So, I don't want to resort to that method unless it's absolutely, positively, the last option we have."

"But then I had another idea. It suddenly occurred to me that the gasoline generator has a battery that's used to run its starter motor so you don't have to crank the engine over by hand. The only problem is that the generator's battery is dead, and since its case is cracked it can't ever be used again. Anyway, I woke up in the night thinking what a dummy I'd been. If the generator has a 12-volt battery to electrically start it, then it must have a built in 12-volt charger to keep its *own* battery charged up. Whenever the generator runs, the charging circuit would have to send a 'maintenance charge' to the battery. I figured, why not take the 12-volt battery out of the airplane and put it in place of the cracked battery in the generator—that way when I run the generator it should charge the airplane's battery. And if that worked we could even try the radios again."

"What a great idea!" Michelle exclaimed. "Why don't you eat now and try that out as soon as you're done. I'll help you," she said, enthusiastically.

Derek bit into a piece of biscuit. Looking up at Michelle, he asked curiously, "Did you have trouble with the water pump just now?"

"Yes, how did you know that?"

"It happened to me this morning, when I first got up. I went to wash my hands and it took nearly a dozen pumps to get it working. I'm a bit concerned about that. It could be just the leather pump valve inside. I could probably fix that. But what really concerns me is the possibility that the water table is dropping. If that happens we're in real trouble. But," he added cheerfully, "I expect we'll be long gone before that happens. But just to be on the safe side we better clean out one of those empty drums beside the hangar and fill it up with water just in case."

Michelle smiled. "I'll take care of that. And, since you're sure we're going to be out of here by the end of this week anyway, I guess I'll lay another problem on you. The gas has run out in the stove."

Derek seemed unconcerned. "Yeah, well we'll be leaving by the end of the week, or early next week for sure," he added, with confidence. "And 'old Mr. Blazing Sun', can take care of any heating issues we have," he joked. Michelle couldn't help but admire his confidence. Michelle, still in her flimsy robe walked towards the door. "I'm going to get cleaned up and then I'll store some water. I'll leave you to your work." Derek gave her a quick kiss and walked her to the side door. He stood momentarily entranced as he watched her walk back towards the house. He delighted at the sight of the sun shining through her robe as she walked. She looked positively exquisite.

An hour later, Michelle returned to the hangar fully dressed in a 'work outfit.' She found him working in the back seat of the Warrior and looked in. "How's it going now, she asked?"

"If you had asked me that a few minutes ago I'd have told you I was ready to give up," chortled Derek. "But right now, things are looking up. I had an awful time trying to locate the airplane's battery. I searched the engine compartment without success, then the luggage storage area, still without success. As a last resort, I thought to check under the rear seat cushions—and there it was! I'm going to have to take the cushion completely out to get to it. I'd really appreciate it you can help me slide the cushion out." Michelle readily took hold of one end of the seat while Derek slid the cushion out onto the wing. Michelle completed the task by placing the seat onto the hangar floor. With the cushion now out of the way, Derek was able to remove the Warrior's battery hold-down clamp. After a bit of a battle, he managed to haul the battery out of its mounting place. Struggling in the confined space, he finally managed to remove the battery from the aircraft. He placed it carefully onto the hangar floor.

Derek examined the battery. The name of the manufacturer, Gill, was embossed on the side of the battery's case. Aside from the odd pink color of the case, it looked just like a regular 12-volt car battery. Michelle stepped over to look at it. They were both pleased to see that the battery case was in very good condition. Derek was even more pleased when he determined that all the cells were covered with water but just barely so. That was a very good sign. He filled each cell up to the top before carrying it off into the generator room.

Since Derek had already removed the generator's old cracked battery, it took but a minute to install the Warrior's battery in its place. A moment later, he manually hand-cranked the generator into life. Derek and Michelle watched with great satisfaction that the charging light turned 'green' indicating that charging was in effect. Only time would tell if the battery would charge.

Michelle looked down at the battery as it sat charging.

"How long do you think it will take to charge?"

"I'd guess a few hours or so should do it," Derek replied.

Michelle put on a lecherous smile, while running her hands over his sweating bare chest and asked, "Now what could a man and women do with three uninterrupted hours?"

The rhetorical question went unanswered. Michelle led him off towards the house.

A little less than three hours later, Derek was back in the hangar. His impatience had gotten the better of him. He immediately went to work to see if the generator had charged the battery. First, he shut down the generator and let it sit for several minutes. Next, he simply hit the generator's START button. *The generator instantly sprang to life.* The battery was fully charged! A quick call to Michelle brought her running. Derek beamed with delight when Michelle entered the generator room. "The charging worked," he proclaimed. "Now for the best part," said Derek. "Let's get this battery back into the Warrior and see if the plane starts. But I'll need your help to get it back in if you don't mind." With Michelle's help they easily installed the battery back into the rear seat area of the aircraft. But as Michelle struggled to extract herself from her the rear seat she spotted a plasticized card jammed between the two front seats.

She tugged on the card and pulled it out. "Urrgh," cried Michelle as her feet finally settled onto the hangar floor. Derek gave her a big hug then asked her what she had in her hand. "Don't know," she replied. "I found it stuck down deep between the front seats so I picked it up hoping it might be useful." She handed it to Derek while she manipulated her shoulders back into shape.

Derek looked at the card then hugged Michelle. "You've found the Warrior's checklists. I know that the same information is in the manual but this card puts everything we need to know in one place. Now we won't have to flip back and forth through the manual looking for appropriate checklists on a moment's notice. I'm now more confident than ever that we'll be flying out of here in the Warrior. And don't forget that I had one full hour of airplane instruction twenty years ago. I'm practically an expert," he laughed.

Derek finally settled down. It was time to get back on task. His next goal, was to attempt to start the aircraft. and do an engine run-up test. He not only needed to see if the engine would start, but he had to be sure the engine would keep running for an extended period as well. Derek clearly remembered from his first flying lesson, years ago, that it was necessary to check the engine compartment before attempting an engine start. He opened the engine cowling and carefully examined the four-cylinder Lycoming engine that powered the aircraft. He did a quick check of all the wire connections, and noted with satisfaction, that everything still appeared to be tightly attached. Before closing up the engine compartment, he reached over to check the oil. The dipstick showed that the crankcase was at the 'full' mark with remarkably clean oil. "Engine check completed," declared Derek.

"Are you all ready to start the engine now?" Michelle asked.

"Ready as I'll ever be," he replied cheerfully. Before climbing into the plane Derek checked to be certain that the wheel chocks were in place under the main landing gear. He didn't want an accident when they were so close to success. When he was convinced that the plane was properly restrained for the engine run up, Derek climbed up on the wing, grabbed hold of the handle on top of the fuselage, and hoisted himself up into the doorway. Michelle grabbed onto his outstretched arm and joined him on the wing. With the cabin door wide open, Derek swung himself into the cockpit and settled into the left seat. Michelle climbed in beside him.

The airplane was big on the outside, with a wingspan of well over thirty feet, but the cabin was quite small and the cockpit area was rather cramped. Derek made himself comfortable in his seat, then scanned the large array of instruments, switches, and controls that filled the cockpit. For the moment at least, he wasn't overwhelmed by the complexity of the control panel. In fact, he had considerable confidence that he knew what he was doing. He'd spent many hours passing the time by sitting in the cabin of the plane going over the controls trying to figure what each one was and how it might operate. He'd actually memorized the gauge locations and placement of knobs, switches and levers during those weeks he puttered around the hangar waiting for the rescue that never came. At the time he'd done it just for idle amusement. He never thought a time would come when he'd actually be preparing for a real flight.

Michelle maneuvered herself into place, and buckled in. She looked over at him and smiled as he scanned the instrument panel. *This is scary*, she thought, *he actually looks like he knows what he's doing.*

"Okay, this is it!" said Derek, with a tone of seriousness she'd never hear before. "All I'm really concerned about right now is starting the engine. So, we'll just go through the engine start-up list from the plastic card. I'd like you to read down the list for me so I don't miss anything."

Michelle watched while Derek nervously stuck the key into the ignition. She clearly understood his anxiety. Everything was riding on whether or not they could get the plane started. She felt butterflies in her stomach. Derek called that he was ready, then Michelle read off each item on the list while Derek confirmed that each detail was addressed. But he hesitated when she called out the Fuel Tank check item. He looked down at his left foot and noted that the fuel selector switch was in the 'left tank' position. "Okay Michelle," he said. "I checked and both tanks are at the 'one quarter' mark so I'll just leave the fuel selector right where it is. That's plenty of fuel for just an engine run-up test."

"Okay," she replied. "Now we begin the 'Engine Starting" sequence."

Derek went through the list with her, one item at a time. Finally, they neared the end of the list. His parking brake was set, fuel at mixture rich, throttle moved just a

303

little forward of off, and the carburetor heat lever was in the off position.

Michelle read, "Clear the prop!"

Though he felt a little ridiculous, Derek shouted through the small open access window, "*CLEAR!*" That was supposed to warn any bystanders that the engine was going to start and that they should stand clear of the airplane. He smiled sheepishly as he saw that his shout had startled her. "I'm just trying to take everything seriously," he said. "Everything rides on this." Michelle understood.

"Engage starter," she read.

Derek's hand fairly shook as he reached down and placed his hand on the ignition key. His heart pounded in his chest as he took a firm grip on the key and gave it a solid turn.

Michelle's heart too, was pounding in her own chest as the starter engaged. The plane shook as the propeller crossed the windshield again and again without so much as a cough. The prop passed nearly a dozen times before Derek let out an audible sigh and released the key.

Neither spoke as Derek let the starter rest for a moment. For no other reason than to 'just try something,' Derek placed his hand on the T-handle of the engine throttle. He slowly moved it all the way forward and smoothly back again. After two full passes he brought the lever back up a little above the idle position. It was now just opened a 'crack' as the starting procedures indicated.

"One more time," he said softly. "Come on baby, let's go, start for papa." He reached down, grasped the key and gave it a firm turn to the start position. The propeller barely crossed the windshield when the engine roared to life! The plane shook with anticipation.

"*YES! YES! Awhhriiiight!!*" yelled Derek. His cries could hardly be heard over Michelle's squeals of delight as the plane shook wildly. It was unclear whether the shaking was due to the roaring engine or Derek and Michelle's happy antics as they cheered and pounded each other with affectionate delight.

It was several minutes before the elated pair calmed down. Michelle could hardly breathe. Her heart pounded, not with anxiety, but with excitement and relief. The wonderful sound of the roaring airplane engine filled her ears. She was euphoric with the feeling that flying their way out might really happen after all. She looked over at Derek's face. He was still grinning with the pleasure of his success.

"You look like a cat that just ate a canary!" she laughed over the roar of the engine. "You're fabulous!" She reached over and hugged him one last time before getting back to completing the engine run-up. "Okay, I'll begin where we left off!"

According to the procedures Michelle read off, Derek ran the engine up to 1200 RPM, turned the fuel pump off, as indicated on the list, checked that the fuel pressure dropped a bit as it was supposed to, turned the fuel pump back on again and leaned the mixture back for taxi. Throughout the entire procedure the engine ran flawlessly. The only problem came when Derek's enthusiasm got the better of him and he tried to advance the throttle forward to check high speed RPM. Michelle grabbed his hand and yelled to remind him that he might jump the wheel chocks and lose control of the plane. They couldn't afford to run into the hangar walls after all they'd been through. Derek instantly complied and ran the plane back to idle. They sat inside the plane listening to the satisfying sound of the engine for nearly fifteen minutes.

Finally, Derek declared the engine run-up session over. But before he shut the engine down he tried the plane's radio. Not surprisingly, they only got static from the plane's speakers. Still elated with their success, Derek shut the engine down and the two exited the airplane. Once they were back on the hangar floor they talked excitedly about what to do next. They walked hand-in-hand until they stood in front of the wide-open hangar door. They stood transfixed looking out at the barren endless plain that lay before them. Yet, for the first time since their ordeal began, Derek and Michelle saw hope, not defeat, in their future. They finally felt that they had some control back over their lives.

"We need to start clearing a runway right away," said Derek. "I don't think it will be too bad to clear the old runway. After all, Mr. Winston already cleared it once, then used it to fly in and out of here regularly. We should be able to figure out where the original runway used to be, then we'll just clear out any new growth."

"Let's get started right now!" said Michelle.

"I don't think we ought to do it just yet Michelle," said Derek. "Feel the heat." He stepped into the brilliant sunshine and shaded his eyes from the sun. "I think we should wait a few hours for the sun to get lower, then we'll begin clearing the runway. It'll probably take a couple of days at least. I want to make sure the runway is as safe as we can make it. I'm certain I can get the plane off the ground in a reasonable distance but I'm really concerned about the runway being long enough to make a safe landing. If we make it extra-long then we'll have a safety margin just in case I land long."

"What are you talking about?" asked Michelle. "Why do you want to land back here at all? We're going to fly our way out of here, remember?"

"Oh, we'll fly our way out all right," Derek quickly replied. "But first I have to see if I really can fly the plane. As I said, I don't doubt that I can get it up off the ground and make gentle slow turns and stuff, but what I don't know is whether I can get the plane back down on the ground in one piece or not. And I'm not going to take the chance on getting us both killed. I'm going to make one practice takeoff and one landing. If I can do that, we'll both climb back in and fly off until we either run out of gas or find a settlement. In either case the land is god-awful flat out here and we'll find some place to put the plane down."

"Oh no!" protested Michelle. "I'm coming up on that first flight. "We're just going to have to take our chances together!"

Derek protested furiously. "No, Michelle. I can't do that. I couldn't live with myself if I crashed the plane and caused you to be badly hurt—or killed. And besides, what good would it do if I did crash and we *both* were badly hurt? What then? Would we *both* be lying out there in the wreckage suffering for days before we die?

No, no. I can't do that to you. It would kill me if I hurt you like that. If something happens and the plane gets wrecked with just me on board at least you'd still be alive and maybe sometime somebody would stumble across this place and you'd be rescued. Besides, if I crashed and got hurt at least you'd be there to pull me out and fix me up. That way there'd be a chance that I'd recover and we'd still have each other. We could work on another way out of here. We'd think of something. But if we're both killed or trapped in a wrecked plane then all that we've done to save ourselves so far would be lost."

Derek put his arms around her and hugged her tight. "I love you Michelle. I love you more than I've ever loved anyone in my whole life. I just can't take you up with me until I have some idea whether or not I can do a landing without crashing. I'll do *one landing*! Just *one*, I swear to God, *just one*! If I can get back down in one piece we'll load up the plane and take our chances together."

Michelle's eyes filled with tears as Derek spoke. She tried to make him understand that she loved him as much as he loved her. She didn't want to see him killed or badly injured in a twisted wreck in some gallant attempt to fly her to safety. She loved him and she wanted to be with him—no matter what. Her protests were unsuccessful. Derek remained solid and unmoving in his position.

Though Derek insisted that he understood how she felt, he was certain that she didn't believe him. But he really *did* know how she felt, and it hurt him deeply that he couldn't comply with her wish to go along on the potentially deadly first flight.

She just can't comprehend how risky this first flight is, thought Derek. *Damn, my chances of a successful takeoff and landing are minimal at best. Sure, I've played the scene in my mind a hundred times and I always come out a hero. But this time it's no daydream without consequences. This time lives will be at stake. I've read enough about flying to know that it involves exacting and demanding skills. A puff of wind on takeoff, the flip of a wrong switch, or movement of the wrong lever invites death. Newspapers and magazines are full of articles on small plane accidents—and, the pilots that were killed were, more often than not, highly qualified with years of experience and hundreds, sometimes thousands, of hours of flying time in small planes. No, the risk is far too high to take such a chance with Michelle aboard on that first test flight. If something happens, it will happen to me alone. Michelle will have a far greater chance of survival if she remains on the ground unhurt, should the first flight turn into a disaster.*

Michelle pushed Derek away. For the first time since the accident he felt alone—hurt in body and spirit. Michelle turned away from him and left him standing alone. As she walked away Derek started to follow. She heard his footsteps, and in a voice choked with emotion, she called over her shoulder. "Go away and leave me alone." She sobbed as she slowly walked away.

It broke Derek's heart. There was nothing he could do but watch her walk out the hanger door to the house. He didn't follow. He knew she needed space, and time, before they could talk about it again. Clearing the runway would have to wait until tomorrow.

Why did you sleep out here? Why didn't you come into the bedroom?" asked Michelle. She looked down at Derek's twisted form on the fully extended recliner chair.

Derek came awake and groggily replied, "I'd say that was because you screamed '*I hate you! You bastard!*' Then you slammed the door in my face late last night."

"Did I really say that? I'm sorry. I really didn't mean it," she said, as she ran her fingers through his tousled hair.

Derek enjoyed Michele's warm fingers. "I thought you didn't really mean it but I figured it wasn't worth risking my life to find out."

Michelle puts on a contrite frown. "I calmed down after a while and thought about what you had said. You were right. It makes good, logical sense to see if you can get the plane up and down in one piece before we both risk our lives together. I don't like it, but it is logical and makes sense."

Over at the sink, Michelle had difficulty pumping water from the spout. "I think it's getting worse Derek."

Derek forced himself up out of the recliner, stretched and yawned. "I was afraid of that. If it's the water table that's dropping we'll be in for a difficult time if we have to stay here much longer. There'll still be water, but I don't know how we'd ever get it out without the pump.

Anyway, it doesn't matter. We'll be flying our way out of here just as soon as we clear the runway."

"I'm all for that," said Michelle. "But we need to eat something first."

"Yeah, but the stove is out of gas, Michelle. I'll go through the camping supplies and get out some gel-fuel to use with the camp stove."

The camp stove worked well. In short order they finished breakfast, then hurried outside to begin their work before the sun got too hot.

Derek and Michelle stood in front of the big hangar door looking down at the ground. "What we're looking for Michelle," said Derek, "is compacted earth from where the airplane's tires would have rolled out of the hangar onto the plain and out to the end of the runway. If we can see tracks then we'll be able to follow them to where the old runway begins. Then we'll know where to begin clearing the airstrip."

Luck was with them. They had only walked a couple of hundred feet out from the hangar when Michelle called over to Derek. "Come on over here," beckoned Michelle. Derek hurried over.

"Look here," she said, pointing down at a depression in the dry red soil. "I see tire tracks here and after a gentle curve they head straight down that previously cleared area." Derek bent down for a closer look. He followed Michelle's finger to where it revealed the telltale tire marks. He was surprised she spotted them. They were shallow and difficult to see.

"Looks like you've got it, Michelle. They sure look like tire depression marks.

Robert Campbell

Michelle was pleased with herself. She stood up and took a graceful bow. "You're just lucky you have me," she said with a smile.

"And you're lucky too, said Derek. And don't worry. If you lose me, you'll still have my 'back up' available—but you'll have to go to the States to get him," he laughed.

"What are you talking about?" asked Michelle.

"I'm a twin," Derek replied with a big smile. I've got an identical twin brother."

"Two of you?" Michelle asked.

"Yeah, I have an identical twin brother. Didn't I ever tell you that?"

"Oh my God! You've got to be kidding--you are kidding, aren't you? There couldn't possibly be another one of you. The world couldn't stand it."

"Ah, but the world is a better place for it," Derek replied with a smile worthy of a Leprechaun.

"I don't think I believe you. What's your brother's name?"

"Deke," replied Derek.

"Deke and Derek?" Michelle asked incredulously.

"Ditto," Derek replied with a laugh.

"I still don't believe you!" Michelle responded.

"There it is again!" said Derek in a frustrated voice. "When a *kid* says he or she is an identical twin, everyone believes it and says how 'cute' that is. But when *an adult identical twin* says that, people immediately deny that possibility. It's crazy, believe me, I know. More than once I've had to pull out my driver's license and show it to someone who insisted I was Deke."

312

"You really do have a twin brother? And he really looks that much like you?"

"Exactly the same. I spent the first 20 years of my life being called 'twiney' by people who couldn't tell us apart. Some of my dear old aunts still call me that. I *hate* it!"

"When we get back to civilization you'll have to show me a picture of the two of you together because I'm still not convinced."

"Deal," said Derek. "But for now, I guess we better get back to figuring out what we're going to do about this runway. The two looked off into the distance where the runway used to be.

"I don't think it will be too difficult to clear the runway for our purposes," said Derek. He turned towards Michelle. "If you think about it, it's pretty clear that Mr. Winston never completely cleared the runway down to the dirt. If he had done that we wouldn't have had any trouble identifying the old runway bed. I think he purposely kept as much low growth on the runway as possible--just as long as it still allowed for safe landings. He went to great lengths and expense to keep this place from being frequented by visitors. A large, clear landing strip out in the middle of nowhere like this would have drawn attention to itself, like a neon sign in the night."

"That's good news for us," replied Michelle. "If he was able to make takeoff and landings pretty much on the surface of the plain as we see it here, then we should be able to do the same. We'll just have to be sure to remove the big stuff and check for rocks and depressions."

"Okay, then let's get right to it," Derek said with enthusiasm. "I'll go back to the outbuilding and gather up some rakes and shovels. And I'll bring out that big, wheeled garden cart." Derek was back in no time. The pair began the task of clearing an unobstructed path down the old runway bed.

Derek and Michelle were exhausted. They leaned on their shovels for support while they looked back at the completed airstrip. It wasn't great, it wasn't long, but it was done! The piles of rubble and brush that lined both sides of the newly cleared runway stood in mute testimony to their backbreaking efforts. In the rapidly darkening night sky, they looked with pride upon their accomplishment. It was a job well done.

With what little remaining energy they possessed, the two loaded their tools into the garden cart and hauled them off the runway. Though both wanted nothing more than a bath and a bed, there was still much to be done to prepare for the 'trial flight' before their departure in the morning. The two wearily shuffled back towards the house.

CHAPTER 22

Dawn came early for Michelle and Derek. But, despite the protests from their aching bodies, they scrambled out of bed at daybreak. They were anxious to make preparations for their long-anticipated first flight test. They prayed that this would be the day on which they would break out of the Outback. Both felt they had been prisoners long enough. While they hurriedly consumed tea and canned biscuits, the sun began its hot rise into the rapidly brightening morning sky. After quickly finishing breakfast, the pair headed directly out to the hangar.

Upon entering the hangar, Derek gave a cursory glance at the pile of supplies that lay near the hangar door. "You sure the plane will get off the ground with all that weight," teased Derek. In spite of their exhausted state the night before, Michelle insisted that they pack up all their provisions in advance. She was hoping Derek would have a successful trial flight. Then they would quickly load the airplane for their flight out of the station together.

Michelle carefully surveyed the pile. "You may be right about all that weight." She looked Derek over from head to foot, then back at the pile of supplies. "Yes, that is too much weight. Looks like I'm going to have to leave *something* behind. And, after estimating *your* weight, I think that if I leave *you* behind, the weight should be just perfect." She laughed heartily. "And when I get back to civilization *maybe* I'll tell them that I left you behind. Then again, maybe I won't." She smirked. She hoped that Derek would catch her, not too subtle, reference to him leaving *her* behind while he made the first flight *alone*. But Derek didn't get it. Instead, he looked down at the substantial heap of supplies and readily admitted that she had made wise choices in her selection of supplies that they would need.

Derek's thoughts returned to the task at hand. "If all goes well with the test flight," he said, "I'll fill the fuel tanks after I land. And, with full tanks we should be able to fly nearly 300 miles. We've just *got* to find something out there after flying that distance. Even if we don't find people, we'll surely find a road to land on before we run out of fuel. And once we're on a road we can walk the rest of the way out. We'll be fine you'll see."

With high hopes, Derek and Michelle eagerly opened the hangar door and let the brilliant sunlight flood into the interior of the hangar. The sky was bright and clear without a cloud in sight. The gentle breeze that struck their faces seemed to sing out that today was a perfect day for flying. They headed back to the plane.

Derek climbed up onto the wing, opened the cockpit door, and pulled out the plane's checklist card. He handed it to Michelle. "We'll start with the 'walk-around' items first," he said as he stepped back down onto the hangar floor. "Let's move around the outside of the airplane and work our way through the list." Michelle eagerly read off each entry on the card while Derek systematically confirmed that it had been checked. A few minutes later the checklist was done. As a final task, Derek removed the wheel chocks from each of the three wheels. All was in readiness.

"I've got this. I'm good to go now," said Derek, trying to sound confident. He hoped his voice didn't betray his true feelings. He knew all too well that he was taking a dangerous and potentially deadly risk in taking on this flight. He tried to dismiss those self-defeating thoughts. *Think only positive thoughts,* he told himself. He immediately headed for the cockpit, afraid that if he hesitated he might not go through with it. As he was about to climb up into the cockpit he stopped and turned to Michelle. "I'm just going to practice how to steer the plane up and down the runway a couple of times before I actually try for a takeoff. Why don't you come and ride along with me for a while? And maybe you can help me out too." She happily agreed.

Derek smiled as he hoisted Michelle up onto the wing. He felt a sense of relief now that Michelle was accompanying him on the trial runs down the surface of the runway. His spirits picked up. He climbed through the cabin door and over into the left seat. A moment later Michelle settled into the seat beside him with the checklists card. Both reached down and buckled themselves in. Derek fumbled for a time trying to get the pesky lap belt across his waist and latched into its anchor down in the narrow gap between the seats.

"A little nervous?" asked Michelle.

"Nah, I'm used to risking my life every day," he laughed. "I probably never mentioned it but I used to teach high school. I've got some war stories that make flying a plane without instruction seem like a tip-toe through the tulips," he laughed as he buckled up.

Derek reflected on all the time he'd spent sitting in the cockpit through the long, idle weeks they'd spent at the station. He recalled those solitary hours when he studied the aircraft, its controls, instruments, and the Pilot Owners Handbook. He smiled to himself as he replayed in his mind how he'd heroically flown the plane to safety over and over again. *But all that fantasy is over,* he thought. *Now it's for real and all those hours are going to pay off—I hope*!

Derek nervously reviewed the instrument panel with Michelle. Some things were easy to understand, even for a complete novice like himself. He readily identified the engine RPM gauge, compass, turn and bank indicator, air speed gauge, fuel gauge, and alternator gauge. After a few minutes he felt confident about the basic gauges and the artificial horizon gauge that, once in the air, would tell them if the wings were level and where the plane was in relation to the horizon.

When Derek examined the altimeter, Michelle cautioned him not to rely too heavily on it for any precise indication of their altitude. She explained that, from listening to the airline pilots talk, she knew that its accuracy depended upon it being properly set using information given by the airport's tower prior to take off. And since they didn't have any tower information there was a good possibility that the gauge was inaccurate. With no other choice available, they decided that they would have to leave the setting alone and hope that the setting Mr. Winston used last time was still somewhat accurate.

"Now let's move on to the flight controls," Derek said. "We'll start with the rudder pedals and the brakes." Though Derek knew Michelle was likely familiar with how things worked, he felt more confident when he explained things to her out loud. And too, he hoped that if he was wrong about something that she'd be able to correct him.

Derek began by placing his left and right feet onto the left and right rudder pedals. The pedals hung down from behind the instrument panel, much like a brake pedal hangs down on an automobile. With his feet in place on the rudder pedals, he shifted them up slightly until his toes touched a second set of pedals—those were the brakes.

Through his earlier experimentation, he'd discovered that the combination of brake/rudder pedals had an additional function. He'd found that by pushing down on the left or right rudder pedal that, in addition to moving the rudder, that movement simultaneously moved the nose wheel to the left or right, thereby steering the plane while it was on the ground much like the front wheel of a tricycle.

"Okay, on with the controls." Derek continued with his 'lesson.' He explained, more to himself than to Michelle, that pulling back and forth on the control wheel would make the plane climb or descend. Next, he explained that moving the control wheel left or right actuated the ailerons--control surfaces attached to the back edge of the wing--that made the plane bank left or right. As if he were talking to someone who knew nothing about airplanes, he explained how the rudder was used in combination with the ailerons to coordinate turns so the plane would turn and bank simultaneously, the way in which an Indianapolis race car speeds through steeply banked turns on the race track.

"Now here's where I really need some help, Michelle," he said. He moved his hand down between the narrow gap in the seats until his hand rested on the end of a long lever. "I know this controls the flaps. I played around with it before and checked it out. It locks into any one of three positions. Correct me if I'm wrong, but don't the flaps give more lift for better control for landing at slower speed?"

"I'm pretty sure you're right," Michelle responded. "But it's important that you don't add the flaps all at once, at least on the big jets they don't. The flaps come down in stages.

"So, the flaps come down in stages then, but at what speeds do I activate them?" asked Derek.

"Wait a second," said Michelle. She scanned the checklist in her hand. "I remember seeing something in here earlier about flaps." She found the place. "It says here that no flaps are used on takeoff and when landing they must not be extended unless airspeed is below 103 knots. And then it gives the progressive flap speed settings where you add the flaps, in stages, the closer you are to landing." Derek remembered reading that sometime earlier and he was satisfied. "All right. Let's go through the start-up list and I'll taxi out of the hangar."

As Michelle read through the checklist, Derek deftly hit the right buttons and switches. It was time to start the engine. Both held their breath while he turned the ignition key. To their immense satisfaction, the engine fired up instantly and ran smoothly. A minute later Derek brought it back to idle while they completed the checklist.

With the checklist now completed, Derek called out, "We're ready to roll!" He pushed the T-handle throttle gently forward. This time the airplane rolled smoothly towards the hangar door. A minute later, the plane rolled out of the hangar into the sun for the first time in years. Once off the concrete hangar floor, the plane bounced and swayed over the uneven terrain that lay immediately in front of the hangar. Derek found that he had to give the engine more throttle to continue forward movement across the rough surface.

At first, he had a difficult time handling the plane as he fumbled to maintain directional control. Through trial and error, he quickly learned how to use the rudder pedals well enough to maneuver the plane out of the hangar and into position. He lined the airplane up with the starting end of the runway.

"Look at that!" Derek laughed. He spied a pair of pink pantyhose tied to a long pole. A makeshift windsock stuck straight out pointing down the runway. "So that's what you were up to last night when you disappeared for a while," he chuckled.

"I was wondering if you were going to see that," Michelle laughed. Derek gave her a big smile and a 'thumbs up.' He then turned his attention away from the windsock and concentrated on the runway that lay directly ahead of him. He idled the engine back so they could converse more easily without the roar of the engine.

"Here's the plan," said Derek. "I'm ready to practice now. I'll run the plane up and down the runway a few times so I'll be able to keep it going straight when I take off. After that, I'll drop you off up at the hangar and try for a solo flight. After I land, hopefully in one piece, we'll load up our gear, fill the fuel tanks, and fly away from here." Michelle nodded her head in understanding.

Derek lifted his feet off the brakes and pushed the throttle slowly forward. The plane lurched and swayed as it slowly built up speed down the newly cleared runway. Despite their efforts to improve the runway, it was far from smooth. Derek found it difficult to keep the plane going in a straight line over the uneven surface. "It's a lot harder to steer this thing than I thought." shouted Derek. The aircraft wandered all over the runway as he fought to steer it in a straight line down the airstrip. "It's bad enough that the field makes it hard to keep the wheel straight but I have this tendency to use the control yoke like a car's steering wheel."

Michelle poked Derek on the arm and motioned for him to stop. He pulled back on the throttle, applied the brakes, and brought the airplane to a stop with the engine idling smoothly.

"Why don't you just take your hands off the yoke completely. Try steering it with just your feet, then you won't be struggling with your impulse to turn the yoke like a steering wheel."

"I'll give it a try," said Derek. He took both hands off the control column and advanced the throttle. Derek held the aircraft's taxi speed constant on the next practice run down the runway. His 'feel' for using only his feet to direct the Warrior improved dramatically. On his next try he completed a nearly perfect straight line run down the entire length of the runway. Michelle congratulated him on the nice job he'd done.

"Thanks for the confidence," Derek replied with a smile. "I'll just do this last trial taxi run, then I'll drop you off and I'll go for a real takeoff." He dearly hoped his 'motivation' was enough to carry him through when the time came to really take off. Sweat was already forming on his brow. And, the tension he felt in the pit of his stomach made him wonder if this was such a good idea after all. While the engine continued idling, Derek scanned the instruments and checked over the controls. Everything seemed in order. He looked over at Michelle.

"I think I'm ready for a dress rehearsal," declared Derek. "So, on this final taxi run let's go through the procedures just as if I were actually going to take off. After that, I'll make a wide turn at the end of the runway and line up for takeoff. That's when I'll drop you off."

Michelle looked over at Derek. She was about to protest being left behind again. He held up his hand. "Please, Michelle, don't. We've already been through this. You know it has to be this way. It's logical, it makes sense, it's for the best. I'll come back five minutes later, pick you up and we'll do a takeoff--for real."

Michelle badly wanted to object, but Derek had been so firm in his resolve that she knew returning to the argument would accomplish nothing. In fact, she thought rehashing the argument would probably put him under greater stress and anxiety than he already was. And that could lead to disaster. She resigned herself to letting him do the first dangerous takeoff and landing alone.

"Yes, it's logical, it's for the best," she sighed.

Derek nodded his approval, placed his hand on the throttle and eased it full forward. The engine roared to full throttle. The plane shook as it started rolling forward across the uneven surface, but Derek held it straight down the runway. As speed built up he kept shifting his glance between the view out the windshield and airspeed indicator to be sure that he stayed under 55 knots, the speed at which the checklist indicated would be takeoff speed. *Got to watch that air speed*, he kept reminding himself, as the instrument's dial climbed. He coached himself on his progress. The aircraft's speed continued to increase--35 knots, now 40 knots. *I'm still holding her really straight*, he said half aloud--*I'll go for a really high-speed taxi run.*

The engine's roar filled the cockpit. As the taxi speed increased, the shaking and rocking sensation was replaced by a rapid vibration. Derek's confidence grew. He watched himself continue in a straight run down the runway despite the constant increase in speed. In spite of the stress, he managed to keep his sweating hands loosely gripped to the control wheel. He could feel the tension and anxiety in his body building more and more as the airspeed rose. The runway raced at the windshield faster and faster. *Got to watch that airspeed! Got to keep those hands on the control yoke. Check out my airspeed...it's 45, now 50!*

Derek's eyes darted towards Michelle. *God, she's beautiful.* His eyes shot back to the air speed indicator— he was virtually at takeoff speed. His emotions rushed as the tension built. *I should take off right now and bring her with me.* His thoughts raced between his love for Michelle and doing the *logical thing.*

The tension was intense. Derek forced his thoughts back to the airplane. *Getting closer, watch that speed, coming up on 55, still straight. God! It's 60! He could feel the aircraft begin to lift off the runway.* Derek's emotions were racing. *"Go or no-go?"* In one frantic second, he made a fateful decision.

"Hang on Michelle," Derek screamed. "We're going for it!" An instant later he pulled back smoothly on the control wheel and the plane lifted off the runway.

Derek's outburst took Michelle completely by surprise. She squealed with delight as the plane, now free of the runway, lifted gracefully into the air. She had been taken completely off guard by his unexpected behavior.

In spite of his smiling face, Derek's grip on the control wheel was now so tight that his knuckles were white. He yelled over the roar of the engine. "I know it was stupid but we're in this together. If something happens now, it will happen to us while we're side by side."

"Let's not make something happen right now, just keep on flying, you're doing great," yelled Michelle, with a bigger grin than Derek's.

Derek instantly put his full attention back to the task of very gently climbing the airplane out and away from the station. He looked out the window and saw that they were still barely a hundred feet in the air. He pulled back further on the control wheel to increase his rate of ascent. He continually monitored the climb, splitting his attention between the airspeed indicator and the view of the horizon out the windshield. Even as he looked out the window he could hardly believe that they were airborne.

Feels like our climb is too steep, thought Derek. His eyes shot to the airspeed indicator. It was falling. His mind raced. *God, what do I do? Throttle's already at full. The nose. I'll push forward on the controls. That will lower the nose. That should increase our speed.* Derek pushed forward on the control yoke. Though it only took a moment for the speed to increase to Derek it seemed as if it had taken hours. He brushed the sweat out of his eyes and checked the airspeed again. He was greatly relieved to see that it now read 79 knots. *That's better*, he thought. *That's exactly the ideal climb speed that was given on the checklist—damn I'm good!* He chuckled nervously to himself. *I'm getting to be a pro at this.*

Derek looked out the side window and back over his shoulder at the station. It was rapidly slipping out of his view. He was astounded at how difficult it was to see it from the air. Even at a low altitude the big hangar, with its dull gray and rust streaked roof, blended naturally in among the trees and heavy undergrowth. It was no wonder nobody ever stumbled across it. "You did it, Derek, you really did it!" yelled Michelle, as the plane continued its gentle but steady climb. "But watch your altitude, you're vacillating a lot," she cautioned. Derek worked to comply by cutting back on the throttle and working the control wheel more gently.

"What do you think of that Michelle? We did it!"

"Awesome," Michelle cheered! She had a wide grin plastered to her face.

Derek suddenly became serious. "But now we've got to get her down again and land it in one piece. The landing is the hard part. You scared?"

"No," she lied.

"That's good," replied Derek. Though he didn't believe her, he appreciated her encouragement. "I have to tell you, I don't know what I'm going to do next. I hadn't planned this takeoff." He glanced at the altimeter. It read 700 feet and climbing. "I'm going to keep climbing straight ahead out and away from the station for a while. At 1000 feet I'm going to try to level off and see if I can hold us at a steady altitude. Then I'll try to make one big circle over the area of the station. Hopefully from so high up we'll be able to see something that might lead us towards civilization." Derek eased the throttle back slightly. "Engine seems to be running fine right now." Derek called to Michelle. "It's important that we keep the station in sight. If we get lost we'll really be in trouble."

The climb out from the station had gone far better than Derek could have hoped. He felt a wave of relief now that they were at a safe altitude. A few minutes later he breathed a heavy sigh of relief when he read the altimeter.

"One thousand feet," Derek called out. He slowly pushed the control yoke forward in an attempt to bring the nose down to achieve level flight. Holding the altitude steady still eluded him. The more he moved the control wheel forward and back, the more their altitude fluctuated. Michelle readily noticed the constant changes in altitude.

"Derek, I think you're too tense. It seems like you're over-reacting to every movement of the plane. Try a lighter touch and be more gentle, it may help."

"That's exactly what my flight instructor said to me during my one and only flying lesson, from what seems like 100 years ago now," chuckled Derek. He took her advice and let go of the wheel, one hand at a time, and flexed them. He took a moment to flex his shoulders and arms as well.

"God, you're right. I can't believe how tense I am." Derek repositioned himself in the seat. "I'll try to relax and see what happens. I'm going to have to learn how to maintain level flight if we're going to have any chance of a safe landing." He gripped the wheel again, this time more gently.

Derek's attention turned to getting the plane back on the ground in one piece. "I'm going to make a wide, slow turn now," he announced. "That's going to bring us back to the station and we can search for any signs of civilization on the way back. Hang on," he said with a grin. "Here we go!" Though both kept a keen lookout for signs of civilization, the search proved fruitless.

Once the turn was completed, Derek brought the airplane around and lined it up with the runway which now lay barely three miles out. By now he'd found a good way to maintain level flight. Instead of fixating upon the altimeter dial to stay at a constant altitude, he found that he was able to do a better job by getting a visual reference of the horizon through the windshield. By keeping the visual reference steady, he was able to keep his altitude more constant.

The runway lay dead ahead now. The thrill of having made a safe take off and climb up to altitude was starting to wear off, as evidenced by the grim look on Derek's face. He surveyed the view below.

"Michelle," Derek called out. "It's time we started figuring out how to land. This is a one-shot deal. No practice landings, I'm going to put everything into making a slow steady descent. With all that low scruffy scrub before and after the runway, we've got plenty of runway length. I think we'll be all right. With you handling the checklists and calling out instrument readings I really think we can do this. At the worst, I'll just come in long and slow and when we're just above the runway I'll stall it out." Michelle was ready. Like Derek, she too, had memorized the checklists.

CHAPTER 23

Minutes passed like seconds. The runway loomed ahead. Now at 700 feet and two miles out, Derek began his slow descent. As the plane reached 500 feet Michelle called out. "We're below 90 MPH, time for the first notch of flaps." Derek pulled up the flap lever one click. He reduced the throttle and brought the airspeed down to 70 knots.

"Only a mile out now," Derek called out nervously. The runway approach was getting very close. He reduced the throttle to continue the descent. Derek was getting agitated. The nose of the airplane was down. To continue on that way, the plane would fly nose down directly into the runway. It was time for flaps!

At that moment, Michelle called out. "Speed 67 knots, altitude 200 feet, time for second notch of flaps." Derek responded immediately by pulling up the flaps lever to the second position. He was greatly relieved as the aircraft's nose immediately popped up and he felt more in control of the aircraft. Barely 100 feet above the runway, Derek blinked a rivulet of sweat out of his eyes. He tried to maintain focus on the approach end of the runway now. He was losing altitude fast and guessed he was barely 75 feet off the ground. "Airspeed 65," Michelle called out. "Stall speed coming up! Be careful! You're coming in awfully steep! Time for the last notch of flaps!" she yelled. Derek immediately pulled up the final notch of flaps.

"Almost....almost time!" Derek cried. His heart was in his throat. He had to flare. That was the final maneuver before touchdown that provides for a safe roll-out upon landing. Derek knew from his, one and only, flying lesson that the flare was the last critical move. An error on flare could end in disaster. "Got to hold off for just a few more seconds!" he yelled. His arms ached to pull back on the controls that would start the flare. But he held steady as the ground lunged up at them. "Now!" Derek yelled. He pulled back on the controls to initiate the flare. The nose came up but the plane continued to sink rapidly towards the ground.

"Too fast! I'm coming down too fast!" he yelled. With no time left to react, Derek felt the main gear of the plane hit hard on the runway. He never heard the stall warning blare it's shrieking signal as the plane bounced and lurched back into the air. He instinctively reacted by shoving the control wheel hard forward. But that caused the plane's nosewheel to the impact the runway! The plane bounced heavily and was thrown back up into the air again. Derek's natural instinct was to push the control wheel forward again. But his final overcorrection, sent the nose of the plane plunging downward onto the runway--nosewheel first. The force of the impact blew the front tire and deformed the nosewheel landing strut. The propeller slammed into the ground—the roar of the

331

engine instantly ceased, only to be replaced by the horrific sound of the aircraft grinding its nose wheel strut across the cracked red earth. The damaged aircraft continued sliding down the runway, out of control. The plane continued forward in a slow slew off to the left of the runway. The awful noise of the botched landing was followed by complete silence amid a large red-dust cloud around the wrecked plane.

The dust settled. It was a full minute before either spoke. Derek finally broke the silence. His voice was weak and choked with emotion.

"Are you okay, Michelle?" He reached over and touched her arm.

Michelle slowly raised herself up off the control panel. "Yeah, I think so," she replied though she was clearly shaken by the disastrous landing.

"Thank God!" Derek replied with a heavy sigh.

"I'm just grateful we're alive," she said weakly. "Let's get out now." The two departed the aircraft, stepped back and examined the plane. Both were amazed at how little damage had been done. Although it had settled in a nose-down attitude, there with little damage other than a bent nose gear landing strut, a blown tire, and a badly bent propeller. Both stared in wonder. Derek, unhurt, helped Michelle to a sitting position on the ground. Though she had no clear injuries, she massaged the back of her neck and held her scraped knee. Derek sat down beside her. A moment later the hopelessness of their situation set in. Barely able to hold back tears, Michelle spoke. "We're stuck here now.

We're here forever and the water's running out. I'm frightened Derek."

"No! No, Michelle. We're not stuck. I said we're getting out of here, and that's just what we're going to do.

"But you can see that the plane is wrecked!" protested Michelle. She pointed to the mangled propeller and nose gear.

"I know that," Derek reluctantly agreed.

Michelle looked at Derek as if he'd just had the sense knocked out of his head. "You *are* crazy!? You just *crashed* this plane."

"But I didn't *crash* this plane," Derek said in his own defense. "I just made a *bad landing*. In aviation they say any landing you can walk away from is a good one. Well, we're completely unhurt. Not bad for a first attempt. Besides, all we have to do is make *one more* landing."

"Well you're not doing it in this one," Michelle declared with stern disapproval. Derek rose to his feet and gave the nose of the airplane a closer examination. "And don't even *think* about trying to fix this one," she added.

"You're right about that, Michelle. No, we're not going to fly out of here in this plane. Even I readily admit that it would require the services of a professional aircraft mechanic who had access to replacement parts, if this plane was ever to fly again. Derek's comments sounded heavy with disappointment. Michelle sensed his pain. She joined him at the front of the plane. The two embraced for a moment of comfort and reflection.

Derek slowly ended the embrace and stepped back. He turned his attention to the damaged Warrior. A curious look spread across his face. Michelle sensed he was formulating some kind of plan in his mind. The look on his face slowly began to change. Michelle could have sworn that a smile was beginning to break out on his face. *Whatever he's planning*, thought Michelle, *it must be starting to come together. And I don't think I'm going to like it.*

Michelle looked at Derek quizzically. He'd turned and looked off at the distant hangar. There was no mistaking it. A huge grin began to stretch across his face. Michelle was baffled. She followed his gaze from the Warrior to the hangar. Suddenly it came to her!

"No! No! You wouldn't! You can't possibly be thinking....!"

"Oh yes I am!" Derek replied. His spirits suddenly soared. He lunged forward and threw his arms around the stunned Michelle. "We're going to do it! We're going to fly the twin-engine out of here. And we'll do it right away!! All I have to do is to get it started and ready for flight and we'll be out of here!"

Michelle could hardly believe it. "But you can't be serious! Look behind you! Look at that plane! And that's only a single-engine! How can you possibly expect to fly a twin-engine plane?"

Undeterred by Michelle's doubt Derek, bursting with excitement, tried to explain. "Remember that flight manual you found for the Lisa Marie when we first arrived at the station? At that time, we dismissed it out of hand, simply because we never conceived of ever having to be forced into a situation where we would actually have to try to fly our way out of here in that plane. I didn't take it seriously at the time because I never thought that things would ever come to that. But now that time has come! It's real and I'm super motivated. I know we can do this together. For weeks now, even as we prepared the Warrior for flight, I've been studying that twin-engine flight manual searching for any information that might help us fly out of here. True, there was little information to help fly the Warrior but there was a ton of useful data in the manual about flying and flight principles. And, even better, the Pilot Owner's Manual also has all the checklists for preflight, engine start, takeoff, and landing checklists as well. I found charts and systems diagrams that provide guides for stall speed, and landing speeds and configurations. It's all there Michelle, it's all there! I've gone over that manual a bunch of times. But now I'll go over it in precise detail. And it won't take long. I'm almost ready now.

Derek's enthusiasm seemed unbounded. Michelle listened as he repeated his insistence that all that was necessary was to get the plane up off the ground. "All we have to do is one takeoff and make *one* landing where the plane stays in one piece and we're golden! I know we'll reach civilization given the range *that* plane can fly! And this time, they'll be no fooling around with practice flights--we get in and we go! I know I can get the plane up in the air, that's the easy part. And as far as landing it again, you can see for yourself that it's as flat as a pancake in every direction, probably for a million miles. At worst, all I have to do to land is to just fly as slow and as close to the ground as possible. Then I just chop the throttles and slide on a dirt roadway till we stop. With all this flat land around we should be able to settle to the ground and land in one piece. We can do it! Look at the Warrior. It's not all that bad. All we have to do is set it down on the ground. I just made an error by not flaring properly. I hit the runway too fast and that caused the bouncing that botched the landing. I'll make *absolutely sure* it doesn't happen again. What do we have to lose?"

Despite Michelle's protests and reasonable arguments against it, he remained enthusiastic. Michelle looked at him quizzically once again. "Are you sure you didn't bash your head against something during that *crash* that you still call a landing?" She tilted her head and looked him in the eye. "You're really serious and you really want to try it don't you?"

"Sure, as hell do!" he blurted out, grinning wider than ever. "Besides, what else do we have going down! Come on let's go over to the hangar and look over the Lisa Marie." Derek took Michelle's hand and led her off to the hangar. Michelle reluctantly went along.

"Well if you didn't crack your head, then I must have," she replied. "Because you sound so convinced that you can do it that I'm starting to believe it too. I shudder to think what you must have gotten into when you were a kid--your mother should have supervised you better!" She shook her head in resignation. She couldn't believe she was actually going to give in to Derek's crackpot idea. "But first," said Michelle, we're going to go back to the main house and take a good long rest before we do anything at all about flying the Lisa Marie." Her demanding tone indicated how seriously she took the matter. Derek sensed that he'd better not press the issue. Silently, he took Michelle's hand. Both walked shakily back towards the house.

CHAPTER 24

After Michelle's enforced 'two-day rest and recovery period' Derek was ready to tackle the flight of the Seneca. Though the time off was supposed to be a 'rest' period Derek, spent almost every minute studying the Seneca's flight manual and checklists. In fact, after only a day and a half into the scheduled two-day rest period Derek's impatience got the better of him. Though it was past noon and already getting hot, he convinced Michelle to walk out to the hangar and gather together the things that they would need for their flight out. Michelle didn't want to admit it but she, too, was getting restless and anxious. She willingly ended the rest period. She and Derek ignored the burning sun and eagerly headed off to the hangar.

The moment they entered the hangar Derek, once again, pulled off the huge silk cover that had protected the airplane for nearly two and a half decades. He stood with Michelle marveling at the beautiful aircraft. He reminded Michelle that the plane was virtually brand new. And, the fact that Mr. Winston had periodically run up the engines probably meant that they should start easily once the battery was charged up.

Michelle couldn't help but be impressed by Derek's enthusiasm and conviction that the plane that stood before them would be their salvation. As she reflected on this latest challenge, she remembered how uneasy she'd felt when Derek had first come up with the idea of using the Warrior to fly them out—yet he'd very nearly done that. If only they had just loaded up the Warrior in the first place they could have kept flying onward to safety. They might well have reached civilization by now, she lamented. But this time, the two resolved that they wouldn't make that mistake again.

Michelle stood at Derek's side looking up at the gleaming airplane. She glanced over to see his beaming smile. She knew he was hooked. He'd been reading the Seneca's Flight Manual every waking moment since their ill-fated attempt with the Warrior. Even as they had walked together towards the hanger Derek kept his head buried in the flight manual. But there was no time for reflection now. It was time to prepare for the flight.

Derek and Michelle spent a considerable time sorting through their provisions and camping supplies as they made the plane ready for flight. Michelle was exhausted from working in the hot hangar. She turned to Derek and placed her arms around his waist. She could tell from his perspiration-soaked shirt that he, too, needed a break.

"You know, I'm beginning to believe that you can do this after all," said Michelle. "But I'm not up to the challenge just yet. I need more rest and some lunch, and so do you. So, let's go back into the house and recuperate for a while more after that crash.....oops, I mean *landing* we had the other day." Derek reluctantly complied. After closing the hangar door, he picked up the Seneca's Flight Manual. Michelle snatched it right out of his hand. She knew he planned to read it as he walked. "You need more rest, not more studying," she cautioned. The two strolled wearily up to the house.

The heat of the day was in full force. Both welcomed the cooler air inside the house. Derek headed directly to the sink. "I could use a good douse of water over my head," he said. Grabbing the pump handle he began working it vigorously without result. It took nearly two dozen pumps before a small amount of water began running out of the spout. "It looks like the pump needs some attention," he added. I'm certain that there's still water down there. I'm betting it's the old pump seal that's worn out. That's what's making it so hard to get the water up from the well. I think I can fix it." He looked around the room and added with affection, "It just wouldn't be right to leave this place without making it work again. Someday someone else may stumble across this place, and if they do, the water from this pump will probably save their lives like it did ours. I'll leave a quart of water behind so the pump can be primed."

In spite of her desire to get Derek to rest, she knew he was right about the water situation. She nodded in agreement. Looking around the room she, too, felt a special attachment to the place that had saved their lives and become their home. Though she dearly wanted to return to Sydney, to her friends and family, she knew that she would always hold this place dear to her heart.

"While you take care of the pump I'm going to clean up the place," said Michelle with pride. "I want it to look as clean and inviting as when we first came through the door." She looked around the room again and smiled. "It's really a magical sort of place. It's the stuff of dreams, like out of a romance novel. I think I'm actually going to miss this house." Derek put his arms around Michelle's waist and kissed her gently.

Less than an hour later Derek yelled out, "hey Michelle, check this out!"

Michelle emerged from the grand bedroom carrying a pile of clothes. "Great work!" she cheered as Derek pumped a strong steady flow of water into the sink.

"How'd you do that?"

"Just like I thought, the valve inside was worn out. I found a piece of leather out in the hangar and I cut out a new piece to match the old. It works fine now."

"And we'll be looking fine when we fly out of here tomorrow," Michelle added. She held up the clothes she'd brought into the room with her. "I thought we should dress up for the flight." She held up a white, neatly folded, short sleeved shirt and a clean pair of navy blue dress shorts for Derek. "And this!" She held up a multi-colored striped tie.

"Shorts and a tie?" asked Derek.

"You'll look cute!" Michelle giggled. "With this outfit you'll look like an Australian businessman. I wish there was a better selection of clothes for you but Mr. Winston didn't stock any suits in his dresser."

"And what are *you* going to wear?" asked Derek.

"I'm going to wear *this*!"   She held a beautifully sheer peach chiffon dress up against her body.

Derek, dried his hands and pulled Michelle towards him. "I think you should try it on right now," he said with a twinkle in his eye. "Here let me get those hot old clothes off you."   Derek swept her up into her arms and carried through the huge open door of the grand bedroom. In spite of his passion, he laid her down upon the bed with a smooth, delicate touch as if he were putting a sleeping child to bed.   With loving desire, he lay down beside her. Work on the Lisa Marie would wait till tomorrow.

Morning came very early for Derek.   He was up and out of bed and working in the hangar even before sunup. In the predawn darkness he focused the beam of his dimming flashlight onto the generator start-up panel. It only took a moment for him to crank it to life. The machine started immediately and quickly settled down into a smooth steady idle. A minute later he turned on the hangar lights. The brilliant glow of the overhead lights illuminated the gleaming twin engines of the Lisa Marie.   Derek stood transfixed staring at the beautiful aircraft pondering their upcoming fate, barely a few hours away.   A moment later he was shaken out of his reverie by Michelle's entrance into the hangar.

"Morning pretty lady!" he cheerfully called out as she came into view.   As always, she looked gorgeous in her Outback shorts. She managed to make them look fashionable by keeping them rolled up high on her thigh. Derek noticed that she was carrying the clothes she'd picked out for their flight out. The chiffon dress lay on top. His mind snapped a pleasing mental picture of how great she'd look in it.

"Is this flight going to leave on time today mister?"

"You bet it is!" Derek replied. He pretended to look at his nonexistent wristwatch. "Leaving at exactly 2:00 p.m." he joked. "I'd like to leave earlier but we still have a lot of work to do. And that's assuming that the engines start properly. But I'm really hopeful. I want to be sure we get as much daylight flying in as possible. I wouldn't dare attempt flying into the night." He turned and looked over his shoulder at the gleaming white Lisa Marie. "I figure a plane like this will probably fly for four or five hours on full tanks. And I know they're filled, I already checked that. I'd guess that I'll fly around 160 miles an hour so we should be able to cover around five hundred miles in safety. And for safety purposes I won't push it. I'll try to keep our speed at no more than 140 miles an hour. But even at that speed we'll cover a great area and we'll surely see some signs of civilization."

"Providing we fly in the right direction," Michelle corrected, without meaning to say it. "But," she quickly added, "at least we have a decent idea that north is the way out." She looked down at the pile of camping equipment that hadn't yet been loaded. "We'd better load this stuff up *first thing*," she insisted. "This time after we take off, I want to keep on going!"

"That's exactly what I had in mind," Derek replied.

"We've got an awful lot of stuff in the cabin already," said Michelle. "We better be careful when we load it up so that's it's properly balanced. Weight distribution is critical in airplanes."

"Since you're the airline expert here, I'll defer to your expertise, My Lady," said Derek, bowing gracefully. "What do you recommend?" he asked, dropping the big heavy rucksack to the hangar floor. It landed with a thud that echoed through the nearly empty hangar.

Michelle pointed to the large baggage door in the nose of the aircraft. "We should probably put our remaining supplies in there. That should balance us pretty well. Michelle twisted a chrome latch on the storage compartment door and lifted it wide open. "Hey, look what I found in here Derek!" She reached inside and withdrew two boxes that had been stored there. Michelle read the label off one of the boxes. "They're aviation headsets. It says they're manufactured by David Clark, Worcester, Massachusetts, USA."

"Here, let me see," asked Derek. She handed him one of the boxes. "These are brand new, I wonder why they were stored in there. You'd think they would have been up inside the cabin." Derek unpacked his headset and tried it on. "What do you think, Michelle, do I look like a real pilot with these on?"

"I don't know about that. But I'm all for *anything* that will make you a better pilot than your first attempt," she teased. "Think about it. You crashed 100% of the times you flew," she laughed.

"But remember, we walked away without a scratch. So, I guess I'm a decent pilot at that," retorted Derek.

Derek turned his attention back to the headset. "With these, it'll be a lot easier for us to talk while we fly this time. It was really loud in the single-engine. I can only imagine that it's twice as loud in the twin. I'm happy you found them." Derek removed the headset and wound the long cord around the earphones.

"Oh, and look at this," said Michelle as she pointed into the open luggage compartment. When I fished the headsets out of the compartment I spotted a hatch at the back that's labeled Battery Compartment."

Derek happily craned his neck looking up into the compartment. "Nice find, Michelle," he called out. "That's cool. It saves me time trying to locate the battery. Before you load anything in there I'll change out the battery."

"Sounds good," replied Michelle. "Let's work loading the rear compartment then."

"Be with you in a minute," Derek called out. "I forgot something at the house. I want to go get it before we take off."

Michelle barely heard Derek's muffled response. "What'd you say? Can't hear you," she called out. A moment later, she pulled her head out of the baggage storage compartment. But all she saw was Derek's behind as he slipped out of view through the hangar door.

Michelle's gaze lingered. She phased out for a moment contemplating how great Derek's butt looked in the shorts he was wearing. An instant later her pleasant daydream popped. She got right back to work loading the rear baggage compartment.

345

"Sorry I took so long. I had to find something," Derek called out. He approached the plane just as Michelle finished loading a heavy five-gallon can of water into the rear storage compartment. Michelle closed the compartment and declared that all baggage was aboard and properly stowed.

Both were hungry after the early morning's work. Michelle offed to fix up something to eat. Checking to see that she was out of sight, Derek reached into his shirt and pulled out an old, yellowed envelope he'd secretly retrieved from the house. He stuffed it in the pilot side door pocket of the Seneca. After making one final check to be sure that everything was securely in place, he slammed the door shut and walked around to the front of the plane. It was time to work on charging the Seneca's battery.

Michelle returned to find Derek standing on a ladder with his head stuck deep inside the front storage compartment. "I'm back," she called out cheerfully.

"Great!" Derek yelled back. "Good timing. Can you give me a hand over here for a minute please?" Michelle lay down the food she'd brought and met him at the ladder. He was struggling to keep hold of the airplane battery that was slipping from his grasp. Michelle's quick assistance enabled him to lay the battery carefully on the ground.

"What's the trouble?" asked Michelle. She sidled up beside him.

"Just as we thought earlier, the battery is dead. But fortunately, the cells still have water covering the plates.

That's great news. But now I have to see if it will take a charge like the Warrior's did. I'll start the charging as soon as we eat this little breakfast feast you prepared," he joked. Both were famished. The food and drink quickly disappeared.

Breakfast done, Derek picked up the heavy 12-volt battery and hauled it down to the generator room. Michelle assisted as Derek made the proper connections and restarted the generator so the charging process could begin. "That does it," Derek announced. "I'm guessing but I'd say it should be fully charged in three or four hours. Since we can't do anything about starting the engines till the battery is fully charged we ought to check out the Lisa Marie.

The Seneca, as always, was an impressive sight with the morning sun shining on her nose.
They strolled up to the plane. "Wow, it sure is a lot bigger than the Warrior," said Michelle.   Derek reached up and grabbed hold of the smooth shiny wingtip and ran his hand over the surface of the wing.

"It's a handful of airplane, I'll grant you that," he sighed. "But I don't think it will be all that bad once we put our minds to it. I've practiced the procedures so many times it feels natural. Come on, let's climb aboard and check her out."

Derek climbed up onto the big wing, turned and stretched out his arm to give Michelle a lift up.   He entered the cockpit first and climbed and settled down into the left side pilot's seat.   Michelle lowered herself into the passenger seat beside him.

Derek examined the complicated panel before him. "It sure has a lot more things on the control panel than the Warrior but at least a lot of the stuff is the same--just more of it. Basically, the instruments on the left side of the panel are for the left engine. And the instruments on the right side of the panel are for the right engine, so it's really not that bad. And I'm pretty familiar with a lot of it already," he said confidently.

"Look here," said Derek, pointing out gauges on the instrument panel." He held the Pilot Owner's Handbook open to the double-wide page that displayed the entire instrument panel and controls. All instruments and controls were clearly labeled. "Here's the turn and bank indicator, compass, airspeed, artificial horizon, and rpm indicators for each engine and flap controls—and a whole lot more," declared Derek. He reached over to the center console and placed his hands on the twin throttle levers. "See a lot of the stuff is the same." He reached down between the seats and lifted the flap-setting lever. "Even the flaps are in the same place." He pointed at the red white and blue Piper Aircraft logo that stood out prominently in the center of the control wheels. "Both planes are made by Piper Aircraft so it makes sense that a lot of things would be just the same. I still honestly think that we can safely get this plane up off the ground. I know that getting it back down again in one piece will be a lot tougher but we'll do it.

Derek hoped his up-beat tone masked his true feelings. He was still unsure of his ability to fly the big aircraft. Even though he'd played around in the cockpit for many hours during their stay at the station, he was far more intimidated by the complexity of the aircraft than he wanted Michele to know. He remembered their earlier bargain not to hide anything from each other. *But this time*, he thought, *I'd better keep this to myself.*

"Michelle, do you want to spend some time going over all the start-up, takeoff, and landing procedures with me while we wait for the battery to charge?" asked Derek. She willingly responded to Derek's request by reaching for the takeoff checklist procedures card. It was stored in her door pocket. As she bent forward to retrieve the card she spotted a plug-in connection on the lower right corner of the control panel.

"Derek, look here," she said, pointing to a connection labeled *Headset.* "This must be where we plug in the headphones. Check and see if you have one on your side too."

Derek scanned the panel in front of him and quickly located the same marked connections on the far-left side of the control panel. "Bingo! Got it. We're in business," he chortled. "We'll have to check them out as soon as we get power to the plane. Remind me later. I put them in the back seat on top of the dress clothes."

"Sounds good," said Michelle.

"Let's get to it then," said Derek. The two began a methodical review of the procedures as best as they could understand them. Derek quickly discovered the value of Michelle's aircraft knowledge. Her familiarity with some of the abbreviations and confusing terms on the checklist helped them identify a number of critical items. All went well until they came to a disagreement over what to do about the landing gear after takeoff. They

349

discussed and debated whether or not to raise the gear after they got airborne. Michelle argued that it would be very risky to play around with the landing gear. But Derek insisted that the risks would be greater in leaving them down. He reasoned that raising the gear would reduce the likelihood of going into a stall. And he was particularly insistent that with the gear raised they would use less fuel. Fuel, he stressed, was of critical importance to them. Although the fuel check Derek made earlier indicated both tanks were full, he was still concerned. Since they didn't have any idea where settlements might be, they might have to fly much longer and further than Mr. Winston did to reach civilization. He was certain they'd need every drop of fuel they had. In the end, Michelle relented. They would raise and lock the landing gear after takeoff.

An hour later, the checks were completed and practice time was over. Derek looked out the windshield of the airplane into the bright sunshine. "Time's flying by Michelle," he said. "We're all finished in the cockpit with the takeoff and landing procedures. We'd better get out now and do a complete preflight inspection on the outside of the airplane. Once we get the battery back in I want run up the engines and take off immediately. Let's hop out of here and begin that preflight inspection," declared Derek.

Michelle exited the plane first with her checklists card in her hand. "Well, let's get started," said Derek. "You call off the items like before and I'll check them out." The two walked to the front of the airplane.

Their spirits were high as they moved around the plane methodically checking it over. Everything seemed to be going well as they worked their way down the list. The engines, in particular, were pristine. The oil on the dipsticks looked brand new and the readings were precisely at the proper levels indicated on the preflight checklist. When they reached the landing gear check Michelle spotted a problem.

"Looks like we're going to need air in the left tire," Michelle called out.

"No problem," Derek replied. The compressor is still hooked up. I'll run it up and fill the tire. A few minutes later the job was done. But as an added safety precaution he checked and filled the other tires as well. Derek stepped back away from the plane, and with a look of extreme satisfaction, pronounced the preflight a complete success. "How we doing for time?" he asked, putting his arm around Michelle's waist.

"That depends on what you have in mind," she said, playfully pushing him aside. She looked at her watch. "The battery has been on the charger for nearly three hours now."

Derek thought for a moment. "It should be charged by now. Let's check it out."

A minute later they stood looking down at the battery sitting on the generator room floor; everything appeared normal. Derek knelt down beside it and unhooked the charging wires from the terminal posts. He used a hydrometer he'd found on the workbench to check the charge of the battery. Much to his dismay, the device showed almost all the cells were dead. *"Damn! It*

351

doesn't work!" he shouted. *"It didn't take the charge! The damn battery is no good! And it's' been on there for nearly four hours!"*

"Damn! Damn!" Derek cursed. He threw his hands up in the air. "Every time it seems like something is going our way, life gives us another boot in the butt. Ahhh....crap," he sighed, as he sank to the ground.

Suddenly Michelle's face lit up. "I've got a great idea!" she burst out. "Why don't we just take the battery out of the Warrior and put it into the Seneca?! We know that one is fully charged."

"Gahhh! Of course. I feel like a dummy!" Derek shouted. He jumped to his feet, grabbed Michelle by the waist, and planted a big fat wet kiss on her cheek. "I should have thought of that in the first place. You're a genius! At least we know *that* battery works. And best of all it's also a 12-volt battery so that should work out perfect. Let me grab some tools and we'll go get it right now!"

"Wait a second," said Michelle. "Let me grab the garden cart. We'll use it to carry the battery. It's a long walk out to the plane and I don't want you to go spilling battery acid all over that handsome chest of yours."

Michelle returned with the garden cart. The two hurried off towards the Warrior. Derek was impatient. He barely held himself back from breaking into a run as they hurried towards the plane. His impatience finally got the better of him. In a burst of inspiration, he swept Michelle off her feet and plunked her down into the garden cart. Her legs dangled over the front.

"You deserve chauffeur service My Lady after that great suggestion of yours," Derek laughed. He grabbed hold of the handles and headed at a fast trot towards the wrecked Warrior that lay nearly a half-mile off. Michelle laughed with delight while Derek jogged towards the plane. Their spirits were soaring at the prospect of getting the battery out of the Warrior. Suddenly Derek yelled out. "You said you've never been to Disney World, Michelle! So, I'm going to take you on Mr. Toad's Wild Ride! Hang on!" he yelled. He put on a sudden burst of speed and raced wildly ahead, throwing the cart into crazy turns."

"Ahhhh!" screamed Michelle. "Slow down, you're going to kill me! Stop! Stop! Stooo....."

Michelle's cries were cut off in mid-scream when the cart's right wheel struck a rock during a wild turn. She was sent flying out of the overturned cart. Derek felt a slam to the chest as his body caught a hit from the cart's handle. It sent him somersaulting into the air. An instant later he found himself lying face down in the hot red dirt.

Derek slowly pushed himself up. Forcing himself to sound amused by the event, he called out to Michelle. "What a ride that was!" he laughed. But all he heard was silence. His stomach sickened an instant later when he realized that she hadn't answered. Gripped by fear, he jumped to his feet. He raced to the overturned cart where Michelle lay unmoving, face up in the blazing sun. She wasn't breathing! His heart pounded like a freight train. He fell to his knees and hovered over her. He could barely find his voice to call out her name.

"Michelle, Michelle," he croaked. There was no response.

Derek was devastated. He was certain she'd broken her neck and died in the fall. *"I'm sorry, I'm sooo sorry, Michelle. Please, please forgive me,"* he pleaded.

Just as Derek thought he was going to die from sorrow, Michelle's chest began to quiver. An instant later he heard a loud '*pafff*!!' Michelle expelled the breath she'd been struggling to hold during her attempt to play dead. She burst into hysterical laughter.

"I got you! And I got you good!" she screamed delightedly. She was barely able to get up she was laughing so hard. "Oh Michelle, I'm *sooo sorry!*" she mocked. She continued laughing.

Derek was dumbstruck by the twist of events.

"Oh, this is so great!" Michelle sputtered out between fits of laughter. "I've spent so many times these last few weeks dealing with your silly jokes. This time it was my turn to torment you with a joke. *I love it!*"

Michelle's laugher finally slowed. She revealed that she was about to burst from holding her breath while he hovered over her. Looking over at Derek's shocked expression, she gleefully taunted him, "Ah, poor baby. You can make jokes but you can't take them."

Derek was beginning to recover. He struggled to his feet. "Well I don't think that was funny at all Michelle!" he said, moving to her side. "But maybe I did deserve that after all," he mused.

He let out a great sigh of relief and took Michelle into his arms. "But you don't know what you just did to me just then. You don't know how I felt." He put on his most serious face. "Why if anything had happened to you I wouldn't have gotten over it for at least several...*minutes!*"

Michelle frowned and shoved him away. "You're impossible," said Michelle. She brushed herself off and headed towards the wrecked Warrior. "And I hope you get run down by a road-train," she called off over her shoulder as she marched on. Derek wisely decided to let her walk ahead while he brought up the rear with the garden cart.

Michelle quickly recovered. After only a short distance she stopped to let him catch up. By the time they reached the plane they were both laughing hysterically about the incident.

It took Derek only a few minutes to remove the 12-volt battery from the damaged airplane. They loaded it into the garden cart and made a quick return trip to the hangar. Once there, Derek gave the battery the 'hydrometer' test just to be sure that it was fully charged. Both were thrilled when the test showed a 'full charge' in all the cells. Derek hurried off to install the battery in the Lisa Marie. Michelle was pleased to hear him report that the battery fit perfectly in place. "All set," said Derek. "All we have to do now is to make a final check to see if we've got everything we need; then, if all goes well the engine will start, and we'll be headed home. A few minutes later they rechecked their baggage and determined that all was in readiness. Derek made sure to place the camera, along with the big telephoto lens, onto the rear seat where it would be within easy reach. He jumped down from the wing and let out a big sigh.

"We've done all we can with practicing of takeoff and landing procedures; the plane's all checked out and the weather is perfect. I guess it's time to crank it up and get out of here. What do you say?"

Michelle didn't answer. She just placed her arms around Derek, gave him a hug, and placed her soft, warm head on his shoulder. He could feel both their hearts beating rapidly with anticipation. *Or is it fear,* he thought.

A moment later Michelle ended their embrace. "I'm all ready, but this time let's start by removing the wheel chocks," she laughed.

"Deal," said Derek. He ducked under the wing out of sight. A moment later he emerged from under the aircraft, wheel chocks in hand. He placed them off to the side.

"We're okay now," said Derek. "Let's get aboard and see if we can get the old girl started. We'll change into the dress clothes you brought while the engines warm up," he added with a note of enthusiasm.

"Oh, and I'll grab the headsets," said Michelle. "We'll need them, don't you think?" A minute later, headsets in hand, Michelle was ready.

"Okay," said Derek. "Let's climb aboard My Lady!"

CHAPTER 25

Derek and Michelle climbed up onto the wing and entered the cabin. Derek settled into the left seat and got into a comfortable position. Michelle methodically buckled herself in. "A little early for that isn't it?" Derek asked. "We haven't even gotten the engines started yet," he chuckled.

Michelle turned to Derek with a mock serious expression. "It's never too early with *you at* the controls," she laughed. "Remember I've flown with you before."

"We need to get serious now," chided Derek. "It's time to see if we can get this plane airborne." Michelle reached down and retrieved the checklists card. She placed her finger on the 'engine start' sequence. "Before we get started do you want to put these on?" She held up the headsets.

"No, not yet. Let's see if we can get the engines started first," Derek replied.

"Okay then, here we go," she said cheerfully. "I'll just start at the top the list and go down."

"Master switch ON," Michelle called out.

"ON, and we've got power," he blurted out. The two watched and listened with approval as a number of the cockpit dials started to quiver into action and begin to emit sounds of powering up. The battery swap worked! A quick check of the radios was unsuccessful, only static emerged from the speakers. Undaunted, they moved slowly and carefully down the list, Derek's concern grew as they found themselves having to skip some of the checklist items that they didn't fully understand. Still, they continued moving through the list. Derek located the fuel tank lever. It was supposed to be set onto the fullest tank but since both tanks were full, he left the selector lever on the right-hand tank where it had already been set. They continued down the list. Derek, turned on the switches, engaged the fuel pumps, alternators, and manipulated a variety of other switches until they came to the last item on the checklist.

"Now comes the big one," Michelle sighed. "Clear and start left engine." She held her breath as Derek located the start button for the left engine.

"CLEAR" yelled Derek, even though he knew nobody else was near the propellers. He reached to his left and pressed the 'start' button. His heart raced as the propeller crossed over the engine cowl once…twice….three times, without starting. Michelle could easily read the disappointment spreading across his face.

Derek sighed deeply. "Ahhh. Well I didn't expect it to start immediately anyway," he said shaking his head. "I hope the problem isn't with priming the engine. We had to skip that step. And I have no clue how to do that anyway.

"That's okay," responded Michelle. "Let's just try it again."

"All right then. Here goes," Derek huffed. His finger hesitated for a moment. It hung motionless over the start button. Finally, he pressed it down and held it there. Again, the propeller crossed the engine cowl once....twice... three times... four times....and then it roared into life!

"*YES*!" Derek yelled.

Michelle cheered loudly and vigorously clapped her hands while Derek grinned from ear to ear. It took them a moment to calm down and contain their excitement. But, Michelle could no longer communicate with Derek over the roar of the engine. To get his attention she waved her headset in the air and motioned to him to put on his own headset. He got the message and gave a 'thumbs up' sign of acknowledgement. Like Michelle, he put on the headset and plugged it in. They were delighted when the headsets worked flawlessly. With good communications now established, Michelle returned to the long checklist of items to start the right engine. As before, Derek performed each task and moved on to the next. Finally, Michelle reached the last and final item on the 'right' engine checklist. Her heart was beating like a drum. She willed herself to make the final call out. "Okay, here we go," she croaked. "Clear and start right engine."

Derek's palms were itching and his heart was racing as he shouted, "CLEAR" and hit the 'start' button for the right engine. The prop crossed over the right engine cowl once...twice...three times...four times, without effect. Derek kept his finger tightly down on the start button. The prop continued to flip through cycle after cycle without exhibiting any signs of starting.

Finally, Derek released the start button. He let out a heavy sigh. "I'm going to let the starter rest a minute before I try it again. I don't want to damage the starter motor by overheating it."

The two sat in silence as the left engine continued running smoothly. A full two minutes later Derek hit the start button for the right engine again. The propeller worked through more and more revolutions without starting. Clearly frustrated, he released the button. He looked over at Michelle. Clearly, she was anxious and concerned as well.

He turned his gaze back to the control panel and hit the start button again. *Come on start*, he pleaded, as the prop cranked across the cowl over and over without effect. *You can't let us down now. Come on! Come on! Start!* The engine stubbornly refused to start. Out of the corner of his eye he caught a glimpse of Michelle looking over at him. He wished he could hide his face from her because he knew it mirrored his growing concern that the engine might never start at all. In frustration he released the start button.

Derek waited a few minutes then wordlessly began working the throttle control for the right engine back and forth several times. He moved the fuel mixture setting up and down, and then back to the full rich setting. His frustration was beginning to turn to anger. He hit the start button again. The propeller continued crossing the engine cowl without any signs of starting. Michelle watched as his agitation heightened exponentially after each failed attempt. He tried again and again with the same dismal result—it would not start.

Derek put his head forward and rested it against the padded control panel for several moments. Sweat dripped down his forehead. He sat up straight, wiped the sweat from his eyes, and prepared to start the engine again.

"Maybe you should give it a rest," Michelle suggested.

Derek let out a long breath. "Not yet. Let me give it another try." He reached up and put his hand on the right throttle and worked it up and down through several cycles. Again, he hit the start button. Again, the propeller crossed the cowl over and over without effect. Derek was getting more upset after each revolution. "Damn, damn, come on, start!" he yelled. "Do it. Do it. Come on! Come on!"

In spite of his furious rants, the engine stubbornly refused to kick into life. His fury heightened as the engine steadfastly refused to offer even the slightest sign that it was ever going to start. As each effort offered less and less hope, he finally let out a deep sigh of despair. He flopped his weary frame against his seat back. Rivulets of sweat poured down his face.

"Ahhh...." Derek moaned. "I am so sick of this emotional roller coaster we're on," he complained, over the noise of the left engine. "This damn engine isn't going to start. It's just like I said before. Every time it looks like something might be going our way something else goes wrong to crush hopes and spirits."   In frustration, Derek let out a heavy sigh and laid his head down on the control panel again.

"Maybe the starter just needs a rest Derek," Michelle said hopefully. "Maybe it's getting overheated now and isn't developing full power or something."

Derek was physically and emotionally spent. He picked his head up off the panel, leaned back, and stared at the ceiling of the plane. He was clearly frustrated with the plane, himself, and their situation.

"I'm going to shut the left engine down now," said Derek. He chopped the throttle, shut off the engine switches and let the engine die. The silence in the cabin was overwhelming. Where only a few minutes earlier they were cheering in celebration, now they sat in crestfallen silence. The hopeful roar of the second engine--their hope for survival--was gone.

The two sat in the deafening silence for several minutes before Derek finally spoke. His voice was choked with frustration and emotion. He practically whispered, "There's no way we're getting out of here today, Michelle. It's nearly late afternoon already. "We may never get out of here." He let out another heavy sigh.

"So, what are you going to do?" Michelle asked, trying to hold back tears.

"I don't know," Derek sighed. He shook his head dejectedly. "I'm at a complete loss, Michelle. I just don't have any idea what to do right now."

Michelle sat with her head down, unmoving in her seat.

"Come on," Derek said weakly. "Let's get out. There's nothing more we can do today." He unbuckled his seatbelt. "I've really had it. I'm going into the house and have a few beers. Maybe by morning I'll figure something out."

Michelle maneuvered out of her seat and climbed out onto the wing. She jumped onto the hangar floor. A minute later Derek followed. Even as he hit the floor she could read the signs of frustration, disappointment, and disgust that were etched in his face. While he headed towards the hangar door, Michelle hung back.

"Aren't you coming?" asked Derek.

"No, you go on ahead. I....I think I'll stay out here for a while. I don't feel like going inside." Nodding, he walked slowly out of the hangar towards the house.

He was barely out of sight when Michelle began to cry. She, too, was suffering greatly from the emotional roller coaster they continued to ride. *It's not fair* she sobbed. *We're good people. We don't deserve this. When is it ever going to end?* She sat down on the wing near the cabin door and sobbed softly. A few minutes later she stood at the big open hangar door, rivulets of tears still streaking her face. She stood on the threshold where their micro civilization ended and the harsh reality of the torturous Outback reigned supreme. She pondered their fate. Suddenly a strange, yet wonderful feeling, sweep over her. For an instant she thought someone was calling her name. She looked around. She listened carefully. *No...no...it was nothing after all.* She looked

363

out again at the clear blue sky—it was such a perfect day to fly. Then, out of nowhere a gentle breeze brushed her cheeks and dried her tears leaving a comforting chill where the tears had been. She felt as if her cheek had just been kissed. But it wasn't the kind of kiss a man might give a woman. It was more the kind of kiss a woman might give to another woman. It had the feel of two lifelong friends and soul mates parting ways, with each heading off towards an unknown and exciting future. Then as quickly as it occurred, the fleeting feeling passed. She was left with a feeling of great warmth and comfort from the encounter. Feeling at peace, she stood gazing off into the sky contemplating what had been and what might yet come to pass.

It was sometime later that Michelle finally turned her eyes, and thoughts, back to the present. She turned and walked back to the Lisa Marie--she shone pure white. When Michelle got closer she stretched out her hand, reached up, and touched the cowl of the right engine. The smooth polished surface felt lovely to her touch. With a sigh, she placed her arms over the top of the cowl and let her head and chest rest against the side of the cowling. A sweet warmth spread from the cowl through her body. It felt good. It felt spiritual.

She began talking, almost whispering, to the airplane. "I'm sorry darling," she said softly. "I'm sorry for the way Derek spoke to you. Please forgive him. He's just a man. When things don't go their way, they think rudeness and fury will fix everything. I'm sorry."

Michelle slowly stood and stepped back from the gleaming aircraft. She looked at the plane with pride. "I don't know what's going to happen to us, Marie. But thanks. Thanks for all you've done, for all you've given us." Michelle felt tears welling up in her eyes. "I wish you and I could have shared some time together when you were alive. I would have liked that very much." She brushed a tear off her cheek. Her voice choked as she brushed back more tears and whispered, "God took you too soon." Her tears fell softly on the airplane. It was several minutes before she stepped back away from the plane. But not before she placed a soft kiss on the warm white cowling.

Michelle was beginning to feel weary and depressed. She wandered aimlessly about the hangar. Though she wanted to go to the house to rest, she didn't want to face Derek. *I can't let him see me like this*, she thought. *Besides, he'll be better off if I leave him alone for a while. He's probably feeling as bad as I am and doesn't want me to see him either*. In need of a place to rest, she climbed up onto the wing and pulled open the cockpit door.

As she entered the aircraft she noticed the headset she'd left behind was still on her seat. Not wanting to deal with it, she wearily slipped across into in the pilot's seat, sank down into it and closed her eyes.

A few minutes later Michelle opened her eyes, and for reasons she couldn't explain, decided to try to start the balky right engine. Stretching over the passenger seat, she retrieved the engine startup checklist. They had practiced it so many times now she felt she knew it by heart. It only took a moment to go through the list down to the last item. All that was left was to press the 'start' button.   She placed her finger on the button and hesitated. She sat for a moment in deep thought. *Marie, my friend. I feel I've known you all my life. I've worn your cloths, slept in your bed, and felt your pain. I feel almost as if we're sisters.   You've kept us alive and, through you husband, have taken care of us. After all you've done for us it doesn't seem right to ask you for anything more.   But I'd be ever grateful Marie if you could help us out here.   Please darling.   Please help us.* Michelle hit the right engine start button. The propeller barely crossed the cowl when it roared into life! Michelle was in shock. She wept with tears of joy.

Derek had already downed two beers and was getting ready to start a third when he heard the roar of an aircraft engine coming from the hangar.   *Now what's she up to*, he thought. *She shouldn't be doing that. She'll burn out the starter motor for sure when she tries to start that freaking right engine. I'd better get out there.* He started to rise, then flopped back into his chair. *"Ah, to hell with it anyway."* He picked up another can of beer and took a long swallow.

Michelle could barely contain her delight as the right engine continued to roar steadily and smoothly. Without delay, she flew down the checklist, cracked the throttle on the left engine and hit the start switch. The propeller crossed the cowl only twice before, it too, roared into life.

Accompanied by a loud *'phhfffftttt,'* a huge spray of beer shot from Derek's mouth when he heard the unmistakable roar of a *second* engine.   He leaped from his seat, knocking over his chair in his rush to the door. He tore through the hangar door and was met by a wildly grinning Michelle. She was standing at the opened rear door of the plane wearing little more than a smile.   He raced up to her just as the chiffon dress she was holding over her head slid softly into place. Derek swept her into his arms and whirled her around in celebration.   She squealed with delight.

"How in the hell did you do that? I could have sworn that the engine would never start!"

"It's a secret between us girls," Michelle giggled cryptically.

She hurriedly grabbed Derek's dress clothes from the back seat of the plane. "Here, like we agreed! Get dressed and look good. Let's go!"

She didn't have to repeat herself. Derek stripped off his dirty clothes and got dressed in a matter of seconds.

"Don't forget this!" said Michelle.   She thrust a necktie into his hands. He threw it around his neck.

"I'll tie it inside." The two scrambled into the airplane.

"You're a miracle worker," said Derek.   The two hurriedly buckled themselves in and plugged in their headsets.

"Can you hear me?" Derek asked as he spoke into his mike.

Michelle adjusted her headset. "Loud and clear."

"Okay. I'll taxi us out of here. I know it's way later in the afternoon than we planned to leave but there's no way we're going to lose this chance now. The engines are running and she sounds sweet and we're all loaded up. Let's rock and roll." Michelle readily agreed. It was takeoff time. "Keep a good lookout for me as we taxi out of the hangar so we don't hit anything," said Derek excitedly. He released the hand brake and the plane started to roll slowly towards the open hangar door. "This is a big plane and it's hard for me to judge the location of the wingtips." A moment later, under Michelle's careful guidance, the plane emerged into the daylight ready for its first flight in over two decades.

"Hold up a minute," said Michelle. "Let me jump out for a second to close up the hangar. It wouldn't be right to just leave it wide open." Derek agreed. He brought the plane to a halt and set the brake while Michelle hurriedly removed her headset, unbuckled, and swiftly exited the airplane.

Only a minute later, she was back, buckled in, and ready to go. Derek released the brake and eased the throttles forward once again. The big plane jounced and rocked along erratically while Derek fought to steer it across the uneven terrain towards the runway. He caught sight of the pink pantyhose 'windsock.' It was limply pointing north.

"Looks like I'm going to have to taxi all the way down to the other end of the runway so I can take off into the wind," said Derek. He used the rudder pedals to turn the plane onto the cleared section of the airstrip. "Good thing too. I need the practice. This thing steers like a bear," he mused. He found that he had to work the rudder pedals aggressively to control the plane's direction.

Michelle forced herself to keep from commenting on the erratic course Derek took as he struggled to maneuver the plane down the length of the runway. But by the time he reached mid-field she could see that his skill had greatly improved. She let out a silent sigh of relief.

"What time you got?" asked Derek as the plane rocked down the uneven runway.

Michelle looked down at her wrist. "Oh my gosh, I don't have my watch. I don't know what happened to it. I'm sorry."

"That's okay, it doesn't really matter," said Derek, trying to calm her down. "We've got a clock on the panel anyway, we'll just use that. Besides, we're going to take off, no matter what." He glanced up. "From the position of the sun I'd guess we've got about two and a half hours till sunset. We should be able to cover about 300 miles before we have to land. But I'm almost certain that we'll be able to find civilization or at least spot a road that leads somewhere over that distance."

Michelle reflected on what Derek had just said but she thought it better not to enlighten him with specifics on the vastness of the Outback territory. She knew that even seasoned small plane pilots had become lost in the Outback after following endless roads till they ran out of fuel. She shuddered as she recalled that few had ever successfully walked their way out.

Derek taxied the plane over and beyond the cleared section of runway. A minute later he completed a turn that swung the plane around towards the departure end of the runway. Though he was all lined up for takeoff, he was a good two hundred yards back from the cleared section of runway. He left the engines idling and set the parking brake.

"How come you're stopping here?" asked Michelle. "Aren't you going to begin from the cleared section of the runway?"

"I don't know how much runway we're going to need," he explained. "But we'll certainly need more distance to take off than in the Warrior. I'm concerned that the cleared section of runway won't be long enough and I don't want to take any chances. I'm afraid that if we start the roll at the very beginning of the cleared section that we'll run out of runway and hit the uncleared section at high speed. That could be disastrous. But this way we'll run through the rough part at a lower speed and hit the higher speeds on the cleared section."

"Sounds like a decent plan to me," said Michelle. "I'm ready to go if you are."

Derek's pulse was racing. He took several deep breaths to calm himself down. Finally, he was ready. "Let's do it," Derek called back.

Michelle held the intimidating takeoff checklist in her trembling hands. Neither knew if they would be able to understand or even complete all of the checks now that the engines were up and running. Derek quickly gave up on attempting to follow every direction on the long and confusing checklist. In frustration he said, "Michelle, we'll just have to keep on going down the list doing the best we can. The ones we can't figure out we'll just have to skip. What other choice do we have? We can't just give up, turn off the engines, and walk back to the station and wait until someone stumbles across us in our old age.

No, we've run out of options here. I say the engines are running, we need every second of daylight, and we've done the best we can with the checklists. If we just go to full throttle down the runway and pull back on the control wheel the plane *will get airborne*. Then we say a prayer and hope for the best! If we can get into the air, I can keep us in the air."

Michelle considered the plan. Without a spoken word, the final decision had been made. The pair sealed their mutual decision with a kiss. It was time to go.

Derek placed his hands on the twin throttles and concentrated fully on the runway ahead. Stress was already building. He wiped perspiration out of his eyes. Pressure built as he considered that every second that passed meant more fuel was being burned and that they would have less daylight flying time. The fact that darkness was less than three hours away weighed heavily on his mind. He took a deep breath and made a sign of the cross. Then, in a single fluid motion, he sent his hand to the throttles and smoothly pushed them hard against their stops. He kept careful watch that both engines had equal revolutions to maintain straight and level flight. Michelle bent her head down in silent prayer as the plane rumbled forward. A moment later her eyes flashed to the instrument panel. She focused on the airspeed indicator, ready to call out the airspeeds for Derek. The plane slowly picked up speed. It jounced heavily over the grassy clumps that covered the terrain. Moments later they reached the cleared section of the runway. The plane's speed picked up dramatically over the smoother surface they had worked so hard to clear.

"Speed's increasing fast now--coming up on 60 knots now," called Michelle.

Derek didn't answer. He kept his eyes fixed on the runway that was rushing up at him. *Got to keep it straight. Don't drift*, he chided himself. He manipulated the rudder pedals. An involuntary smile sprang to his face as the nose of the wrecked Warrior flashed by. Its cowling intake seemed to be smiling right back at him. *Thanks for the encouragement, my friend; I can use some right now*, he thought. He flashed a quick salute to the old Warrior, then tightened his hands on the controls.

Derek's smile quickly vanished when he focused his attention back out the windshield. They were nearly out of runway! An instant later, Michelle yelled, "we're at 80 MPH – that's takeoff speed." Derek couldn't respond. The end of the cleared section of the runway was getting closer by the second! His eyes shot from the windshield to the airspeed indicator. It now read 85MPH. *"God, this is going to be close,"* he whispered *"Don't want go beyond the cleared stretch."* Derek immediately pulled back on the control wheel. With barely yards to spare, the plane smoothly lifted into the air. Derek and Michelle let out a huge collective sigh of relief and an instant later they filled the cabin with screams of joy. In spite of their celebratory antics Derek held the aircraft in a smooth gentle climb.

Derek glanced out the side window. He had no words to describe the immense sense of relief that washed over him. He thrilled as he watched the ground fall away from the airplane. *Too early to congratulate myself*, he thought. His eyes snapped back to the view out the windshield. A moment later Michelle called out, "Time to raise the landing gear!" Derek immediately flipped the Landing Gear lever into the up position.

'*Bleep! Bleep! Bleep!*' rang through the cockpit.

"What the hell is that!" yelled Derek. "What did I do?!"

"Oh my God!" Michelle exclaimed. "There's an emergency light flashing on the panel."

"What is it! What is it!" he yelled.

Her heart was in her mouth. "It says 'Landing Gear Unsafe'," she yelled back.

"I don't know what to do!" Derek exclaimed. "All I can do is to keep climbing till we get can some altitude." Seconds later the pair felt a dull 'thud.' Derek felt adrenaline racing through his veins. "Shit! This is bad!" he yelled.

"*Oh my God! I know what that is!*" cried Michelle. She felt an enormous sense of relief. A moment later she started laughing.

Derek was incredulous. *My God, she's lost it*, he thought. "Michelle! Michelle!" Derek yelled. He pounded her shoulder. "Get a grip girl! Get a grip!" Michelle laughed all the louder.

"Get a grip yourself!" she managed to get out between fits of laughter. "Don't you know what that was?"

Derek shot a glance at Michelle. He was completely baffled.

Her laughter slowed as she explained. "You remember how you gave me such a hard time when I suggested leaving the gear down. Well God's punishing you for that. Didn't you notice that the beeping sound stopped and the lights went out after there was a slight 'thump'? That meant the landing gear was fully up and the gear doors were closed. The audio signal and 'Landing Gear Unsafe' light apparently comes on to warn you that the gear is in transition and that it's unsafe to land while the gear is still coming up. I didn't figure it out till after the gear came up and the sound stopped. Then an instant later those three green lights came on." She pointed to the lights low on the panel that Derek had been too busy to notice. "They confirm that the gear is up and locked."

Derek let out a heavy sigh of relief. "I was so tensed up I never heard the sound turn off after the gear came up. I'm just glad you figured that out. Hell, I was ready to drop it back onto the runway!" Derek reached up and wiped the sweat off his brow. He paid rapt attention to the horizon while he maintained a climbing attitude.

"Well thank God there was nothing wrong," Derek replied. "I'm a wreck enough already."

"Well that really boosts my confidence in you," Michelle added with a smile.

"Just kidding, Michelle. I'm cool. I'm the big guy. Mr. Big, that's me. I'm in control," he chuckled.

Derek settled down and held the plane in the smooth climb. A minute later he called out, "Five hundred and climbing." He let out an audible sigh of relief. "Now that we're over the gear fiasco that almost cost me a heart attack, I think I actually like flying this plane."

The altimeter registered 1,000 feet and climbing. Derek decided to risk a slight turn to the left. He was surprised at how much heavier and sluggish the controls were compared to those in the Warrior. In spite of that, he maintained fairly good control. He smoothly banked the plane and began the gentle turn that would bring them on a direct heading to the foothills to the north.

The plane was fast. It seemed like only minutes had passed when they reached the foothills. Derek checked the altitude.

"I'm going to keep her here at 1200 feet when we pass over the foothills," said Derek. "We should still be able to see the truck down in the gully. The bright red cab should be easy to pick out even from this altitude. Let me know when you spot it and we'll note the compass heading."

Less than a minute later Michelle called out, "I see it!" She pointed out her side window. "Down there. Just off to the right."

Derek craned his neck to see. "Nah, I can't see it from my side Michelle. The engine cowling and wing are blocking my view."

"Okay, just turn to the right a little bit."

He moved the control wheel to the right.

"That's it. We're right over it," said Michelle. She reached over and pointed to the compass. The heading reads pretty close to due north. That's the way the truck was heading."

"And that's the way we're heading too," said Derek. "It won't be long now," he added enthusiastically. "I think I'm going to keep our altitude low for the whole flight. We seem to be flying well now. If I try for a higher altitude that might mean we'd have to make some changes or engine settings and I really don't want to deal with that. I'm a firm believer in the old adage that says '*if it ain't broke, don't fix it.*"

In spite of Derek's enthusiasm, Michelle looked out the window with concern. Though the sun was getting lower in the sky, she tried her best to be upbeat. "Looks like we still have at least a couple of hours of daylight left, don't you think?"

Derek craned his neck as he looked at the sun. "Guess you're about right." He checked the airspeed indicator. "Our speed reads 160 so if we do have two hours we'll cover about 320 miles." Derek continued, "and I'll need every minute of those two hours to practice controlling this plane the best I can. I've still got to work on holding a steady altitude. Especially when it comes time to make the long smooth descent for the landing."

Derek shot Michelle a hopeful smile. She smiled back then switched her view out the side window. She watched as the foothills smoothly slipped out of view behind the aircraft. While Michelle continued sweeping the horizon for signs of civilization, Derek concentrated on maintaining a steady altitude and constant heading. Although his studies of the manuals and procedures guides gave practical knowledge to get airborne, the real-life application of the actual hands-on flying skills was terrifying. But as minutes became hours he started to get the feel of the aircraft. In-flight practice of small turns and altitude changes gave him more confidence. It wasn't 'good' flying by any stretch of the imagination. But it was flying. Good or bad flying, their lives were in his hands.

For what seemed like the thousandth time, Derek shifted his gaze out the window as the plane droned on. He shook his head in disgust as he looked at the desolate scene below through the transparent whirl of the propellers. "You still don't see anything? Nothing at all?" he asked petulantly, even though he knew Michelle would have reported any signs of civilization immediately.

Derek didn't wait for an answer. He continued lamenting, "I can't believe this awful place. We've been up for over two hours and all we've seen is the same monotonous flat plane. Just endless patches of scrub grass, crazy rock outcroppings, a few pathetic trees, and that never-ending red dirt. How I hate this place."

Michelle lowered the heavy telephoto camera from her face. She turned to Derek, her face grim. "I'm not exactly having the time of my life either you know" she shot back. "My arms ache, my head aches, and I hate looking at that endless flat plane just as much as you."

Michelle's outburst took Derek by surprise. He felt ashamed of his behavior. It was clear that their lack of success in spotting any signs of civilization was taking its toll on them both.

"I'm sorry Michelle. I didn't mean to upset you."

Michelle, on the verge of tears, put the camera down on her lap. "I'm sorry too Derek. I didn't mean to snap back at you so." She took off her headset, put her face in her hands and massaged her cheeks and eyes. "It's so frustrating that it hurts. It's going to be dark soon and we're no better off than when we left—maybe worse off.

And no matter what I do I can't get anything out of this radio. No communications go out or come back in. We haven't even see a single sign of life and we can't even go back to the station because we'd never find it again." She brushed back tears from her cheek.

Derek reached out and took her hand in his. He gave it a gentle squeeze. "Aw, it was all my fault. I didn't mean to be so testy. The truth is, I'm getting worried about how late it's getting. We're going to have to put down real soon. The sun's getting pretty low. We have a half-hour, probably less before we have to land. Why don't you take a rest for a while? You've been struggling with that heavy camera almost the full two hours. Michelle readily accepted Derek's suggestion. She lay back in the seat, closed her eyes and rested.

While Michelle rested, Derek scanned the instrument panel. The fuel gauges immediately caught his attention. Both tanks registered considerably below the half empty mark. They were using a lot more fuel than he'd expected. He suspected that he might have improperly adjusted the fuel mixture controls. That would have caused more fuel consumption. He momentarily considered moving the mixture setting less 'rich' but dismissed the idea. No, thought Derek, that's far too risky. The engines are running perfectly, I'd best leave them alone.

Derek's concern about the fuel level jogged his mind back to the first time he switched from the right tank over to the left tank. He thought he'd have a heart attack when he flipped the fuel selector lever over to make the required hourly fuel tank switch over. He feared the engines would die. But to his complete surprise, absolutely nothing happened, the engines kept running. And both engines continued running flawlessly when he switched the lever back again an hour later. Small successes boosted his spirits. Now that the fuel problem was no longer an issue, he turned his attention back to the horizon, searching fruitlessly for civilization.

After a ten-minute rest, Michelle opened her eyes. She was dismayed to see that the sun was sinking alarmingly lower in the sky. Without hesitation, she picked up the telephoto camera and hefted it back up to her face.

Derek looked over at Michelle. She strained to hold up the heavy camera. Though he admired her persistence, he knew it was just too late. It was time to land.

"I'm sorry Michelle but you may as well put the camera away. I'm going to have to put her down now," he sighed. "It's going to get dark very quickly. I'm going to have to start descending so we can find a place to land. Better give your seatbelt a tug," he added, then prepared to push the control wheel forward.

"Wait! Wait a second Derek," Michelle called out. "Hold it right there. Don't do a thing. I think I see something on the horizon."

Derek pulled back on the control wheel to stop the descent. "You sure?" he asked hopefully.

"Pretty sure," Michelle replied. She kept the camera pressed to her face.

"What is it? What do you think you see out there?"

"Shush! Just keep flying there—in that direction."
She pointed a few degrees of north.

Derek turned the control wheel. The big Seneca
gently banked and picked up the new heading.

"I'm sure I see something off on the horizon. I can't
be sure but something doesn't look right. Something
seems to be out of place. I think it's something that could
be man-made."

Derek strained to see what it was that Michelle was
looking at but detected nothing on the horizon. "I don't
know Michelle," he said. "Nothing in this place ever
looks like it belongs here. It's so wild and weird. I'm
sure you're looking at something all right but it'll
probably turn out to be some weird rock formation. I
think I better get right into a descent and look for a
landing spot."

"No. Please Derek. Let's get a little closer. It can't
be more than ten minutes off at this speed."

Derek looked out the window at the sinking sun.
"Ah, I guess a few more minutes won't hurt," he replied
reluctantly. "But that's all. We've got to get down while
there's still decent light available. We can't blow it all
now." Michelle put the camera down for a moment and
blew Derek a kiss. "Thanks!" she said with a smile.

Derek did not share Michelle's enthusiasm. While
she focused her attention on the unknown shapes on the
horizon, he focused his attention on the terrain below.
He searched intently for a suitable landing spot. But,
clearly the terrain, for miles in every direction, was flat
and featureless. He figured that things weren't so
desperate after all. He'd give Michelle a little more time.

But now nearly ten minutes had passed since Michelle had first reported the shapes on the horizon. His concern about finding a landing site deepened by the second.

Finally, he could wait no longer. "Michelle, this is it," he called out. "I'm going to…….."

He was cut off in mid-sentence. Michelle exclaimed, "Derek, they're buildings! I can see buildings! There's a series of structures. There's one big one and a bunch of smaller ones. They can't be anything else!" Excitedly, she poked him on the arm. "Look. Look out there." She pointed out the windshield dead ahead.

Though he was dubious, Derek shifted his gaze to follow her finger. "My God. I think you're right. Even without the lens they really do look like buildings. You're a lifesaver. I'm proud of you!" Derek could hardly control his enthusiasm. He lunged over and planted a kiss on her cheek.

"Yikes! Careful" yelled Michelle as plane went into an unexpected descent. Derek had accidentally pushed the control wheel forward. "Okay! Okay! Just don't get us killed while thanking me for saving our lives!" she laughed, shoving him away. "Get back on the controls! Fly now! Play later!"

"Is that one of your company's slogans" he chuckled.

Derek's high spirits quickly evaporated as he nervously scanned the sky. He suddenly became deadly serious. "We're still about six or seven miles out and the light is fading pretty quickly. I'll head towards the structures for just a couple of more minutes—then we land wherever we can. No matter what! Agreed?"

"Agreed," Michelle fired back. She immediately hefted the telephoto lens back to her face. An instant later she yelled, "I see a road!!!" She dropped the camera into her lap. "Down there! To the right!" She excitedly jabbed her finger downward.

Derek immediately banked the plane to the right. "I see it!" he shouted. "It doesn't look like much but it's very long and very straight and we're out of time and choices!" He immediately increased the bank of the aircraft. "We'll have to forget the town for now. I'm going to make a quick descending turn away from it so I can line us up on that road." He pushed the control wheel forward, increasing their rate of descent. "This turn's going to bring us around a couple of miles outside of town. Then I can line up on the road before we touch down," he explained. "The road is straight as an arrow right here and I want as much landing room as I can get."

Derek was afraid that Michelle might be frightened by their rate of descent, but she said nothing as the altimeter continued spiraling downward. A few minutes later he brought the plane onto a heading that lined them up with the road below.

The altimeter read 500 feet and falling. Derek made a final course correction. He struggled to line the plane up into position for the road landing. His concern deepened. The twin-engine plane was no fighter plane. Changes in altitude and lateral movements were challenging. He prayed that there was room for error. And now he was beginning to feel, the now familiar, pounding of his heart. It was time to prepare for the landing. "Michelle, grab your Landing Checklist and get ready for the landing procedures like we practiced earlier," he said curtly.

Michelle said nothing, she knew Derek was stressed. She pulled out the checklist from the door pocket, then tightened her seatbelt. Derek followed her lead and retightened his own seatbelt as well. "Ready, for landing call outs," Michelle acknowledged, then flashed a smile of confidence at him. Derek caught it even amid his stress. He flashed a 'thumbs up' sign in return.

Thank God, the road is long, wide, and straight, with only low bushes lining the roadway, Derek said to himself. *I couldn't ask for a better landing site.* Derek stared intently out the windshield as he continued the descent. It was time to make his landing approach on the road. "Our speed is 110 MPH," he called out. Michelle worked her way down the checklist with Derek confirming each item was completed.

A moment later Michelle called out, "landing gear down!" Derek grabbed the landing gear lever and engaged it into the 'gear down' position. Both felt the drag as the gear extended, the thump as the gear locked into place, and the thrill of seeing all three 'gear down and locked' lights illuminate on the panel. He paid rapt attention as Michelle continued working down the list throughout the descent. Time blurred as she called for the first notch of flaps and then the second. Even as Derek felt more control over the aircraft, the roadway was coming up fast. He struggled to maintain his slow, steady approach while simultaneously keeping the wings level.

Michelle called for the last notch of flaps then checked his airspeed. She called out, "Your speed on the final approach should be 95 MPH." Derek checked, he was precisely on the mark.

But, as the landing approached, Michelle saw that further tension was showing on Derek's face. His knuckles tensed as he tightly gripped the throttles. She placed her soft warm hand on top of his and squeezed it gently. *Please God. Please let us make it,* she silently prayed.

Derek lifted Michelle's hand to his lips. He kissed it. "Check your seatbelt again," he said. A moment later he released her hand, placed his own back on the throttle, and reduced power. He needed to correct his attitude as the plane slowed and the nose fell. He felt the tension building stronger by the moment. The road filled the windshield as it rose up to meet the aircraft. He shook his head. A rivulet of sweat stung his eye. Though he ached to brush it away, he focused his attention on the imminent landing. He tightened his grip on the control yoke. *Damn, if I don't loosen up on the wheel I'm going to squeeze hand prints right into the wheel itself. Got to settle down,* he told himself, got *to relax more.*

Derek's hand fairly shook as he throttled back to 90 MPH. It was essential to stay above the plane's stall speed of 68 miles per hour. *Got to be careful now,* he told himself. *I just hope to God nobody is coming down the road at us.* Derek could feel the color draining from his face. *Airspeed 90--we'll be down in seconds! He shot a glance out the side window and chopped the throttles. The plane was down to 20 feet above the runway. Derek pulled the control wheel back into a flare. Oh God, sinking too fast! Too fast! No, no. I'm going to do it again!* The aircraft's speed dropped down to 88 MPH. Stall speed was rapidly approaching.

The plane's main gear hit solidly on the center of the roadway and momentarily bounced back into the air. Derek fought his urge to shove the control wheel hard forward. *That's what wrecked the Warrior! Can't do that again! An instant later the plane bounced down again onto the red dusty roadway. The hit was greatly reduced this time. Derek held the control wheel full back now and this time the plane remained on the road. The STALL WARNING horn blared.* Derek felt as if his heart was pumping pure adrenaline. He forced himself to stay in control as the plane tore down the roadway.

Seconds later the nose wheel came down onto the make-shift runway. *My God! We're down. Can't lose it now. Got to keep it straight,* thought Derek. His concentration intensified as he worked the rudder pedals. He knew the landing wouldn't be pretty but the roadway was wide and he was determined. He managed to keep the plane heading straight down the road. *Brakes! Time for brakes!* His feet shot up to the brake pedals. *Can't jam them. Gentle pressure at first or I'll blow the tires. That's it, easy now. I've got a very long runway ahead of me. I'll use it all if I have to.* He felt an intense sense of relief as the plane began to slow down.

A whirlwind of red road dust filled the air behind the big plane. Even as the plane rolled to a stop, an enormous dust cloud enveloped the aircraft. Derek's mind was in overdrive after the successful landing. He had the good sense to taxi the plane off the roadway onto the dead flat area to the side of the plane. He had no desire to see their plane wrecked in the night by a vehicle barreling down the road and striking it.

A moment later, with visibly shaking hands, Derek reached over and pushed the master switch into the off position. The engines rotated slowly into silence. But the silence was deafening! Wordlessly Derek removed his headset. He dropped them onto his lap. Michelle did the same. The pair sat in stunned silence for several moments. Derek could barely speak when he finally croaked, "Shouldn't we be cheering or something like that?"

Michelle placed her hands on her chest while she struggled to find her voice. "I don't know about you," she struggled between breaths. "But I'm not going to do anything until I massage my heart back into beating again."

Color was starting to return to Derek's face. "How about if I massage your chest for you," he offered as the sparkle came back into his blue eyes.

"I know what you've got in mind," said Michelle. She reached down and unbuckled her seatbelt. "And you're not doing anything until I climb out of here and kiss the ground!"

"It'll be my pleasure to join you in that endeavor," laughed Derek. But first I need to go through the 'post landing shut down' checklist. It would be disaster to run the battery dead before we can restart the plane tomorrow. Barely a minute later they unbuckled their seatbelts, exited the airplane, and jumped off the wing onto the ground.

"My God! I never thought I'd be happy to be back on the surface of the outback again," exclaimed Derek.

Michelle turned to Derek. "My legs are so shaky I'll fall down if you don't give me a big hug!"

"I'll hug you all right, but it will be so *you* can hold *me* up," said Derek with a smirk. The pair embraced. Each felt the other's heart still pounding from the stress and thrill of the landing.

As they embraced, Derek looked over Michelle's shoulder at the darkening scene that lay behind her. The road, he thought, could barely be called a road at all. Now that they were down on the surface he could see that, although it may have once been used with some frequency, it was now little more than an old desert road. It looked like it hadn't been used in a very long time.

"I'm afraid we're not exactly on a major highway," Derek said as he gently ended their embrace. "Take a look behind you."

Michelle was unable to hide her disappointment and deep concern as she looked down the pathetic roadway. "Well it doesn't look like much," she said trying to sound hopeful. "But out here in the Outback we have lots of small settlements that don't see much traffic."

The pair moved away from the airplane and looked intently at the dismal scene that lay down the road. In the lowering twilight all they could see was the dark outline of a darkened complex of buildings at the top of a rise. And they lay nearly a mile off from the airplane.

"It's pretty dark and quiet up there," Derek noted. "There's no lights at all. Nothing from the buildings, nothing from vehicle headlights. I hate to say it, Michelle, but from here it sure looks like a ghost town you'd see in an old western movie back home."

"It's not really dark yet," Michelle said hopefully. "Clearly it's just a small settlement. Maybe they use kerosene lamps and we just can't see them shining yet. Come on Derek, let's start hiking up there. There must be someone around."

"I'd better get our flashlights out of the plane," said Derek. A moment later he returned with two flashlights. Flashlights in hand, the pair headed up the rapidly darkening road.

They had been walking less than fifteen minutes when the final rays of light disappeared. Neither said a word. They switched on their flashlights and continued on toward the darkened structures in the distance. Sometime later Derek finally broke the silence. He put his hand on Michelle's shoulder and called for rest.

The pair stopped. Michelle was glad that it was dark. She didn't want Derek to see the tears that were welling up in her eyes. Derek didn't have to see the tears. He knew they were there. She sobbed softly as he hugged her. He knew that by now she too was certain that the settlement was deserted.

"It's no use Michelle, you know that," said Derek, trying to comfort her. "Whatever it is up there is deserted. It's dark enough now that if anybody were there we'd have seen some sign of life by now. Even an old kerosene lamp would show up in this darkness."

388

Michelle's sobs slowly subsided. Derek released her from his embrace and wiped the tears from her face.

"I'm sorry Derek," she sniffed. "I really thought I'd found a settlement. A real one, I mean. I feel so down and discouraged."

"You've got to be kidding." Derek replied. "You saved our lives. You spotted this settlement and then the road leading to it. If you hadn't found that road I don't think I'd have been able to get the plane down undamaged. Right now, the way things are, all we have to do is to take off again in the morning and follow this road one way or the other. It's got to lead somewhere. Come here my little Indian scout." He hugged her tight for a moment. Then to cheer her up he said, "What the heck, we've walked all this way. Why not just keep going a little longer and see what this place is before we go back?"

"Sure, why not?" said Michelle softly.

"Ah cheer up," said Derek enthusiastically. He put his arm around her waist and the two headed up the road towards the darkened buildings.

Fifteen minutes later they stood in the middle of a dismal, rutted, dirt street looking up at a large abandoned building. In the dimming beam of his light, Derek noted that many of the outside wood panels had fallen off the building and much of the rusted corrugated roof was missing. He played his light over some of the twisted corrugated sections of roofing that lay about the street.

"I'm going to take a closer look, said Derek." He moved toward the building, stepping over and around scraps of twisted and rusted pieces of steel and piping

389

until he stood in front of the building's main door. He flashed his beam onto an all but illegible sign. He brushed some dirt off the rusted old sign exposing some of its letters. "Can't make out much," he said. "But it looks like part of the word 'mining' on the sign. This must be what's left of some old mining company.

"It's probably an old played-out opal mine," Michelle replied. "There's a number of them scattered around the Outback in South Australia." She looked around in dismay. "These abandoned mines are really dangerous Derek. Why don't you come back away from there?" Derek heeded her advice. He slowly worked his way away from the derelict structure until he reached Michelle. They stood in silence gazing down the dark street.

"Looks like they had some houses for their workers at one time," said Derek. "I can see a number of deserted structures that are in worse shape than the main building. They turned and walked further down the street towards another large structure that seemed to stand in the middle of the street. When they got close enough, it became apparent that the street ended at a dilapidated old building.

"Well this is it," said Derek. "The road is just a dead-end." He scanned the ghostly street and sighed, "I guess there's no use wasting any more time here. There's nothing here for us at all. What do you say we just head back?"

"Yeah, let's head back. There's no sense wasting our flashlights any longer," said Michelle wearily. Almost as if to confirm its own weariness, her flashlight dimmed and went out just as she finished her sentence. Derek took Michelle's hand. The pair headed back down the road guided by the dim glow of his flashlight. On their way back to the aircraft they discussed their plans for an early morning departure. By the time they reached the plane they were feeling better again. In spite of the day's failure, they were eager to be on their way again. They felt certain that the next day would find them back at civilization.

Michelle was starved when they finally reached the plane. "We've got a freeze-dried lasagna dinner left in our food supplies, are you interested?"

"Sure," Derek eagerly responded. "I'll get the stuff out of the plane and set up the tent then I'll help you get supper ready." Michelle had just finished filling a pot of water when she heard Derek announce that the stove was lit and ready to go. He was still kneeling by the stove when she aimed the dimming flashlight beam at him. "I think there's just about enough light left in this to cook supper, then we're out of luck. That's all the batteries we have," she sighed.

"Ah, but we don't need any more batteries Michelle," Derek chimed in cheerfully. "No more camping out. Tomorrow we reach civilization. I just know it!"

Michelle watched as Derek rose to his feet and stretched his handsome frame. At the same moment his attention was drawn to Michelle's beauty which was enhanced by the sexy dress she wore. He couldn't hold back a lecherous comment. "Oh, and by the way," Derek added as he stood by the stove. "You're likely to spoil your beautiful dress making that lasagna. That would be an awful shame. You want to look your best when we land tomorrow. Don't you think you should take it off? Just to keep it clean, I mean," he added with a sheepish grin.

"Funny you should say that," replied Michelle with an energetic and enticing grin. Then, in a single motion, she slipped out of her dress. She stood nearly naked before him, her body bathed in the warm glow of the stove. She moved silkily towards him and fingered the buttons on his shirt. "I was just thinking the same thing about your fancy white shirt and that pretty little tie and those neat tight shorts of yours. It would be a shame to get them all soiled," she said, while unbuttoning his shirt.

"Lasagna can wait, I think we should just skip to desert first," Derek laughed. Michelle readily agreed to his suggestion. After a long, harrowing day fraught with adventure and danger the pair found pleasure and hope in each other's arms. Neither cared any longer for supper. They kissed, then crawled into the tent. The night sky echoed with the sounds of their love.

CHAPTER 26

The next morning Michelle awoke to find Derek already up and dressed. Through the tent opening she spotted him hunched under the right wing examining the landing gear. A moment later he emerged from under the wing. "Just checking the landing gear," he hollered to her. "I was afraid that after the hard hit we took on landing, it might have broken something. But everything looks fine as far as I can tell. Still, I want to check everything over one more time before we fly out of here. After that, we'll load up the plane, and we'll be ready for departure."

Michelle emerged from the tent and called back, "We're not going anywhere till we eat. We never did get to eat last night and we may be flying for hours." Derek was starved. He eagerly jogged over to the tent to join Michelle for a much-needed breakfast. Though both were anxious to be underway, they lingered over breakfast laughing as they recalled their previous evening's escapades. But the time passed quickly. It wasn't long before the rising sun signaled that it was time for departure.

"Looks like it's time to pack up and be on our way," said Derek. He stood up and stretched. "Sun's up enough now so I've got enough light to do the preflight inspection and give that landing gear a final check. As soon as I do that I'll come back and we'll pack up the camping gear and load everything into the plane." He leaned over and kissed Michelle. A moment later he vanished under the plane.

Well, that's everything," yelled Michelle, as she closed the rear cabin door. When Derek didn't answer she walked around the other side of the plane looking for him. She spied him some distance down the road. "Oh, there you are!" she yelled out. "What are you doing down there?"

"Oh nothing, I'll be along in a minute," he called back. He stood in the middle of the desolate road looking off into the distance, his hand shielding his eyes from the sun's brilliant glare. He shook his head in dismay as he surveyed the inhospitable terrain around him. In disgust, he kicked his boot into the dry crumbly surface of the road. A cloud of dust rose up from the surface as if to show its own disgust for his intrusion. The dust, carried by a gentle breeze, drifted up into his face. A moment later he suffered a minor fit of coughing. The dust had gotten its revenge.

Derek continued gazing off at the horizon while he contemplated how deadly their situation would become if the engines didn't start. He cursed softly to himself as he looked around at the harsh steaming and desolate surroundings. The forbidding Outback seemed to be taunting every living thing to survive in its murderous grasp. Even the scrub brush and grasses that proliferated seemed barely able to survive its evil dare. No trees, no shelter, no water—just a desiccated deserted mining town. How can anything live out here, he mused? Finally, he just shrugged his broad shoulders, turned and walked back to the plane, tying his necktie as he walked. It was time to leave.

Derek's cloud of depression quickly dissipated when he approached the airplane. Michelle was standing beside the Lisa Marie, her hair glowing in the bright sun. She looked fantastic in the chiffon dress that she was wearing again this morning. "You look great, he said with a smile as he reached the plane. "And, I even tied my tie for you," he proclaimed.

"We'll be the envy of everyone when we land," Michelle chortled. She reached out and straightened his tie. Derek put his arms around her and pulled her soft body against his own. "Mmmm," she cooed. "I've got a little secret to share with you." She squirmed amorously against him. "I'm naked under this dress."

Derek's hands moved smoothly over the soft fabric of the dress. His smile of approval ensured that she wasn't just teasing him. "Now what could be on your mind, I wonder? But, there's no time for that now," she giggled. "But don't worry, I've got a little 'happy landings' surprise for you the second we put our feet back on the ground." She flipped her hair back across her shoulders. She laughed as she backed away from his extended arms. "Shouldn't we be going now?"

"You're right," he said reluctantly. "It's time to go My Lady! This flight is now loaded and ready for departure. We'll be arriving on time in exactly three hours from now. Of course, I can't exactly guarantee *where* we'll be arriving *at*. But, at least we'll be on time, seeing as we've only got about three hours of fuel left!" He laughed at his own joke then climbed up onto the wing. He extended his hand to help her up into the plane. "Come My Lady, we've got a schedule to keep," chortled Derek. The two disappeared into the cockpit.

Derek settled into the left seat and busied himself adjusting his seatbelt and headset while Michelle did the same. "After we get the engines running," explained Derek, "we'll do the takeoff just like last time. As soon as I get us lined up on the roadway I'll go full throttle till we hit takeoff speed--then I'll pull back and pray. It worked well for us last time and I'm sure hoping it will work even better this time. We've got a smooth, soft runway of unlimited distance. I'm hoping for a smooth, easy takeoff. Oh, and please be sure to remind me to keep switching tanks every half hour."

"Oh my gosh," said Michelle. "That reminds me. I forgot to tell you that I found my watch while you were down the road. It was on the floor of cabin under some supplies. It must have fallen there when we were hurrying to load the supplies. My parents gave it to me when I graduated from the Flight Academy. It means the world to me." Derek admired the fine-looking watch. "Okay," she continued. "I've got my watch and I'm ready to go," she declared.

"Now what direction will we head once we're airborne?" Michelle asked.

"Since the road is a dead-end heading east, I figure we'll follow it back to the west until it either ends or comes out someplace," Derek replied. "What do you think?"

"I don't think we have any other choice. Besides, if the road ends here then people must have come from *somewhere* and it can only have been from the other end of the road," replied Michelle, pointing to the west. "Let's go. I'm ready when you are," she added as she held up the Engine Start checklist."

Derek smiled and signaled a thumbs up. The two quickly worked their way through the engine start list, but Michelle stopped when she reached the last item— the 'Start Left Engine' call out. Derek, surprised by her sudden silence, looked over at her. She seemed to be in deep thought. He was surprised to see a tear starting to form in the corner of her eye.

"Something wrong, Michelle?"

"No, it's nothing," she replied. She returned her attention to the procedure list and read, "Start *Left Engine.*" As Derek moved his hand towards the engine start button Michelle suddenly reached over and stopped him.

She turned towards him. "Derek, if she doesn't start right away please don't be upset with her. Please be kind to her. Please treat her like a lady." Derek was taken by surprise by her tone--she seemed to be pleading to him.

"Of course," he replied softly. He readily sensed that she had become attached to the plane and that for some reason it now seemed to hold a special meaning for her. He respected her for that. He reached out and affectionately ran his hand across the padded top of the control panel. "I'll be gentle and kind—I promise you that."

Holding his breath, he pressed the start button. After the second pass of the propeller the engine fired up sending welcome vibrations through the aircraft. Both beamed with delight while Michelle completed the checklists down to the *right engine* start sequence. Neither spoke as Derek reached over and put his finger on the right engine start button. His finger hovered over the button for a moment. The he turned unexpectedly towards Michelle.

"Michelle, I'd like you to do this engine." He gave her a smile of understanding. "I don't know what you did last time but I think you've got something special going with the Lisa Marie. I'd really appreciate it if you'd do the honors and see if you can get this lovely lady started for us."

Michelle appreciated his thoughtfulness. She leaned over, pressed the button and listened with intense joy as the engine instantly roared into life.

"You're the greatest, Michelle!" Derek roared back. He lunged over and kissed her full on the lips.

Derek grinned wildly. He released the brake and pushed the throttles smoothly forward. The plane taxied easily over the dry red earth. He made a slow turn that lined the aircraft up into takeoff position down the center of the road. After completing the checklists, he made one last check to see that the controls were free and that the engines were running smoothly.

All was in readiness. Michelle had the takeoff procedures on her lap. Derek looked over at Michelle and with a big grin called out, *"let's rock and roll!"* He smoothly pushed the throttles full against their stops.

Even through the protection of the headset, Derek could hear the powerful roar of the engines racing at full throttle. He was so delighted to hear them running again that the roar was music to his ears. *Sounds to me like Beethoven's Ode to Joy,* he thought, as the plane rapidly picked up speed down the improvised dirt runway.

Derek was pleased with himself that he'd been able to hold the plane straight and level all the way up to takeoff speed. Seconds later he pulled back gently on the controls and the big Seneca, once again, climbed smoothly into the sky. He carefully watched the airspeed climb to 125 miles per hour. A moment later Michelle activated the gear-up lever. She flashed Derek a smile of success as the gear came up and the three green 'gear up and locked' lights winked on.

Derek continued his slow steady climb. He finally leveled out at a reasonably steady altitude of 2,500 feet at 150 miles per hour and picked up a westerly heading to follow the road. Though Derek couldn't explain it, for some reason he seemed at peace with himself and with the plane. *She almost feels alive in my hands,* he thought as he fingered the control wheel. In his reverie, his thoughts slipped back to that 'one-and-only' flying lesson he'd had back in high school. He recalled how his instructor said that he really seemed to have 'a natural talent' for flying. Derek was beginning to think it was true. A relaxed smile came across his face. He listened to the aircraft's engines humming flawlessly as she climbed swiftly into the sky.

Derek felt elated to be safely back in the air with the Lisa Marie at his fingertips. "I can't believe it," he said into the headset. He turned and smiled at Michelle. "Our Lisa Marie seems to be as excited as we are to be back in the air." She smiled and nodded in agreement as they continued cruising westward. Even his thoughts of the inevitable upcoming landing, dangerous as it might be, didn't dampen his spirits. He was beginning to understand Michelle's attachment to the beautiful plane. Smiling happily, he turned his attention back to flying the plane.

A quick check of the instrument panel showed that Derek was still managing to maintain a reasonably steady altitude of between 2,500 and 2,600 feet. But he found that the controls were heavy and tiring to work. He knew that adjusting the trim tabs would make the controls far less difficult to work, but he also knew that it would be a huge risk to play around with them when the airplane was operating perfectly. He chose to leave everything alone. They'd already made one safe takeoff and landing. If he left everything alone he felt sure that he could do it again. *We won't take any unnecessary risks*, he told himself. *What a joke*, he thought, *this entire adventure is a huge risk necessary or not.*

But even though Derek was managing to keep the plane somewhat stable, he knew that he was just barely keeping it in the sky. The entire escapade was a huge risk. But they had no choice. This was their emergency 'last ditch effort' at survival. But so far, they were beating the odds. And that was good enough for him. His thoughts again returned to flying the aircraft. He looked out of his side window down at the old dirt road below they'd been following in a westerly direction. It stretched endlessly far off into the horizon. He just hoped to God that it led somewhere and that he could keep the plane safely airborne.

Michelle looked at her watch. She noted that they had been following the road for a nearly an hour, yet the terrain below remained as inhospitable as ever. And they still hadn't come across a single sign of life. She took a moment to remind Derek that it was time to switch fuel tanks, then hefted the big telephoto camera up to her eye and scanned the horizon.

Michelle had no sooner put the camera to her face than she cried out. "Derek! I see something! I think the road is finally ending! And it looks like it ends at a crossroad!" she added excitedly.

"Can you tell if it's a more traveled road than this one," Derek quickly asked.

"Not yet," said Michelle as she continued to stare through the lens. "But we'll know in about ten minutes, that's for sure. Just keep following the road below us."

Though only a few minutes had passed, Derek asked Michelle for a third time if she could tell if the approaching road appeared to be a traveled one.

"No, Derek! I keep telling you the same thing—no I can't tell yet. You're starting to sound like a little kid in a car who keeps asking, 'Are we there yet?'"

"Well you said ten minutes, Michelle. It sure seems longer than that."

"Don't worry," said Michelle. "When I know for sure, you'll be the first person I tell. I promise. Just calm down and take it easy."

Michelle felt a pang of guilt. *I shouldn't be so hard on him. If he had the telephoto lens instead of me I'd probably be pestering him worse than he is me.* She was just about to apologize when something came into view.

"Ah, here's the news you've been looking for Derek! I can see it much better now. It's a road all right. It runs north south and it's a much better road than the one we're following. It's dirt but it's clearly wider," she said enthusiastically. She was elated with her find.

Several minutes later, Derek brought the Seneca through a wide, gentle turn while they surveyed the road below. Even from 1,000 feet above the surface they could tell that even though it didn't appear to be used frequently, it was a road that was clearly used. Things were finally looking up. Derek beamed with delight.

"Which way do we go, Michelle? You're the Australian. Any ideas?"

"Obviously let's forget the old mine road that continues through the intersection. Let's follow the new better-traveled road. It looks to be heading northwest. So, let's go that way."

"Why northwest?" asked Derek.

"If we head south we'll just be doubling back into the area we just came from," said Michelle without hesitation.

"Northwest it is then!" Derek gently banked the plane and started following the new road.

They'd been flying for less than half an hour when Michelle screamed. "Derek!!! Look. Look at that!" She excitedly pointed to a dial on the control panel.

"The dial moved. The needle is twitching back and forth!"

"Oh-oh, is that bad?" Derek asked, anxiously.

"No, you silly person! That's good! Very good! That dial is one of the radio navigation instruments. I don't know exactly how they work but if the dial moved then it means we're passing near a navigation beacon. That means we're getting close to civilization!"

"Thank God!" said Derek, obviously relieved. "You scared me with that one. I thought we were having engine trouble or something. Anyway, that's just great! But how close are we to an airport and which direction do we go from here?"

"I don't know those answers, Derek. But I do know that we seem to be on the right track by following this road. Let's just keep going. Don't change anything. Maybe we'll see someone driving on the road. We can land way out in front of them, wait for them to catch up with us, then flag them down and ask for help."

"Whatever you say, My Lady," chortled Derek. "Whatever you're doing, you're doing it right. I'm with you." Both were elated by the turn of events but were distracted by them as well—neither remembered to check the fuel gauges.

Michelle put down the camera and nervously checked her watch. They'd been flying northwest for over half an hour. She was beginning to wonder if her decision to head northwest was the right one after all. She looked down at the terrain below. Things were getting greener now and there was a lot more vegetation. Occasional clumps of trees dotted the landscape but still there was no sign of any traffic on the road below.

"How are you doing," asked Michelle.

"I'm doing just great. We've just got to see something any minute."

Michelle hoped Derek was right. She checked her watch and noted that fifteen more minutes had passed, and still there was nothing in sight on the roadway. Though her arms ached, Michelle hefted the telephoto camera off her lap.

"Okay, here we go again," Michelle sighed. She lifted the camera up to here eye. Less than a minute later she was rewarded by a grand sight to the north.

"*Derek, I see another road ahead!*" she shouted. "I'm sure it's a real road with real traffic. It intersects with the one we're following. Can you see it way up ahead? It runs east-west." She excitedly pointed it out through the windshield. We can't be far from civilization now. It won't look like much to you when you see it, but here in the Outback that's what they call a major highway, even though it's still dirt. Oh, God. I can hardly wait. We'll be there in a few minutes!"

The minutes seemed like hours. The pair strained their eyes to get a better view of the road. Ever so slowly, it came into full view. Michelle squealed with delight at the sight below—it was a real roadway after all. Tears of joy streamed down her face. She pulled off her headset and kissed Derek profusely.

Despite Michelle's unbounded enthusiasm, he anxiously looked out the window at the rapidly approaching dirt road. "I know you're excited about it, but it still looks like a seldom used old dirt road to me."

Michelle was not put off in the slightest by Derek's lack of enthusiasm. "I know it's dirt Derek, but it has the look of being well traveled, you'll see." She craned her neck to keep the road in view as Derek continued circling.

"You really think that's well-traveled?" asked Derek skeptically."

"Of course," Michelle explained, "this far into the Outback 'well-traveled' may mean only one vehicle every few hours," she laughed.

"Or every few days, maybe?" Derek added. Realizing that his attempt at humor wasn't helping, Derek put his skepticism aside. "Okay, seriously now. You've convinced me," he said. "You've been right every time so far, so let's go with it. Which direction should we head now?"

"Just follow that road as it heads to the northwest. I'm certain we'll see traffic very soon. "All right," sighed Derek. He turned the control wheel to the left and began a turn that would take them onto a northwest heading. Michelle put the camera back up to her face.

No sooner had Derek begun the turn than Michelle shouted. "Derek, I see something!"

"What do you see?" asked Derek, while he picked up the northwest heading. "I think I see something coming down the road. It's putting up a big plumb of dust," she said excitedly.

That bit of information got Derek's immediate attention. A minute into the turn he spotted the distant but unmistakable cloud of dust moving towards them, way off on the horizon. He banked the plane still further until he picked up the road's heading. A moment later they were heading straight down the road towards the rapidly rising dust cloud.

Less than five minutes later the cause of the dust cloud came into view. The two cheered in unison as a huge, four trailer long, road-train roared beneath the Lisa Marie followed by a huge cloud of dust.

"Awh right!" screamed Derek. He pulled off his headset and returned Michelle's earlier barrage of kisses. Derek's enthusiasm was getting the better of him until Michelle pushed him away, reminding him that they were still up in the air and most definitely *we're not on the ground yet*.

Derek quickly calmed down. He turned his attention back to flying the plane. He was about to suggest that they over-fly the truck and land some distance in front of it to flag it down when Michelle called out that she could see plumbs of smoke way off on the horizon. She was certain it was a plant or mine of some kind and suggested that it was from there that the truck had come. Almost as if to confirm her theory another plum of dust rose from the road ahead followed a short time later by another road-train truck.

"The plant, or whatever it is, looks to be about ten miles out and a short distance off the main road," said Michelle. "How about if we keep following the road a little longer until we're close enough to see if there's a small town or......"

"*Oh no!*" wailed Derek, cutting her off in mid-sentence. "*I can't believe it! We've been paying so much attention to what's outside I never remembered to check the fuel gauges! Damn!*" He tapped the fuel gauges praying that they were wrong. "Both gauges are really low! I think it's possible that we're all right, but clearly, we have *zero* margin for error. We have to land *right now*. The roadway looks really long and perfectly straight. And best of all I don't see any more trucks on the horizon. I say we should land now." Michelle immediately agreed.

"It's time to tighten up your seat belt Michelle," Derek called. He then began a gentle turn that would line him up with the roadway below. He held the nose down throughout the gentle turn as he prepared to land. He watched as the altimeter quickly spiraled downward towards 500 feet. Derek carefully surveyed the upcoming roadway. "We're lucky Michelle," said Derek. "It looks like the road runs straight for miles and its surface looks good. My only concern is that I keep us heading straight down the road when we touch down."

Derek again glanced out the side window at the terrain below. "The scrub brush is healthier and thicker here. That could be a problem if I drift off the center of the roadway." He gestured to Michelle to look below. "And I don't like the look of those occasional clumps of trees way down the road. They seem to be far enough back from the roadway right here, but we've got a couple of miles before I can actually set her down. We'll have to keep a sharp eye out as we make the final approach." He glanced at the gas gauges, shaking his head in dismay. *We're probably flying on fumes by now*, he thought. *But I'm not going to take any chances. I'm going to have to make this a one-shot landing.*

Derek glanced at the altimeter. *Got to be alert now*, he thought. *Can't trust the accuracy of the altimeter from here on until touchdown. Damn, this is going to be a tough one.* Derek began his planned long and slow approach. He was stressed to the breaking point. *If things start to go bad,* he thought, *I'll just stall us out when we're just a few feet off the roadway and just ride it out till we stop.* But Derek held his nerve as Michelle called out each of the approach and landing checklist items. He slowly and smoothly brought the airspeed down to 115 MPH when Michelle called for 'gear down.' The cockpit filled with the sound of the gear transitioning down and locking into place. Both heaved a sigh of relief the moment the three green 'Gear Safe" lights came on. Their descent speed increased. Derek needed more control. He called out to Michelle for the first notch of flaps. Moments later, as his airspeed dropped further, he called for the second notch. He quickly felt more control of the aircraft. *Got to lower the speed more*, he told himself. Derek made the proper settings as they continued their descent. *I've got plenty of time and plenty of runway*, he told himself. *Got to keep it low and slow, low and slow.* His airspeed dropped to 100 MPH. He was on short final now…less than a minute before touchdown. Perspiration dripped from his forehead as he watched the roadway racing towards the windshield. "Watch it, Derek!" shouted Michelle. "There's a clump of trees off to your left. They're pretty close to the roadway," she warned. Derek fired a glance out the side window of the rapidly sinking aircraft.

"Crap! I see 'em! I just hope we can clear them," he said as he fought to keep the wings level and the plane going straight. "Almost down now," he blurted out. "Airspeed 95, 90,……we'll stall any second now!"

Derek's body was now covered in sweat. He called to Michelle. "We've got no choice now we're committed to land now!" Both knew that the most critical phase of the approach, the flare, was just seconds away. "No, no! I'm sinking too fast again," Derek cried out. "Hold on Michelle! I'm still too fast! It's too late to do anything about it. God damn it! Damn! Damn!" Derek yanked the engine throttles full back and an instant later he pulled the control wheel full back. The Stall Warning horn blared and the annunciation panel button glared bright red. "Hold on Michelle!" he yelled.

The bloody hell!! What's that damn nut doing!" exclaimed the old man. He watched the Seneca hit hard onto the roadway directly in front of his house then bound wildly back up into the sky. He painfully rose from an old and battered overstuffed chair mumbling aloud, "Why I can do a better job landing than that with my hands tied behind my back. And me with two bum knees to boot."

In spite of the pain in his legs he hobbled off the tree covered porch of his ramshackle station. He hurried down the short driveway just in time to see the plane hit the road then bound once more back into the air. An instant later he saw it hit solidly again onto the road. This time it stayed there, racing forward followed by an ever-growing rooster tail cloud of dust.

"Bloody fools, they're going to kill themselves!" he yelled. A moment later he headed as fast as he could towards the beat up old Holden truck he kept parked in the driveway.

I've got her! I've got her!" exclaimed Derek, as he gained control over the racing plane. His heart continued racing while he worked the rudder pedals to keep the Lisa Marie going down the center of the road. "We made it!!! Michelle, we made it!!" he yelled as the plane finally began to slow.

Michelle was bursting with emotion. She shouted for joy even as tears streamed down her face. Derek firmly applied the brakes and slowed the plane to a stop into a shrub covered field just off the side of the road. The instant the plane halted, Derek hit the master switch to shut down the engines. He ripped off his headset and gasped for air. An instant later he lunged over and threw his arms around Michelle. The two showered each other with kisses and tears as their ordeal of fear, tension, and isolation burst like a bubble. A moment later they recovered their senses and began whooping for joy. As they yelled and pounded each other in congratulatory affection, neither heard nor saw the old Holden truck skid wildly to a stop amid a cloud of dust just behind the airplane. The old man cringed as he listened to the screams emanating from the aircraft. He jumped down from the cab, nearly falling as he hobbled towards the plane as fast as his legs would carry him. His mind raced with the thought of the suffering people on board. *Oh my God! Listen to those screams. They must be hurt bad!*

The dust from the truck hadn't even settled before the pair scrambled boisterously out of the plane. Michelle continued to scream with delight as she hit the ground. An instant later she joyfully flung her dress over her head, letting it fall to the ground exposing her naked body. "Ah God!!" yelled Derek. He flung his strong arms around her and pulled her towards him. His strong fingers caressed her gorgeous naked bottom.

"*Arrggghhhh!*" screamed Michelle in ecstatic joy.

Oh God! Listen to that. Them poor souls must be in awful pain," thought the old man. He painfully forced his legs to carry him around to the other side of the plane. "I'm coming, help is here!" he yelled as he rounded the tail of the aircraft.

Startled by the sound of another human's voice Michelle spun around.

"Oh my God! A person! A real live person!" she screamed. She was delirious with joy, as she caught sight of the scruffy old man hobbling quickly forward. Caught up in the intense joy and thrill of finally reaching civilization she forgot her nakedness. In a blur of motion, she raced up to him with her golden hair flowing behind. She wildly threw her arms around the old man, showering his tired weather-beaten face with tears and kisses of pure joy.

"Oh my God!" stammered the old man. He stopped dead in his tracks. "I done died and gone to Heaven!" He stood stark still in utter disbelief. "God's gone and sent an angel down to gather me up," he sputtered.

An instant later Michelle turned beet red as she realized what she'd done. Derek ran the few steps to her side, with the dress in his outstretched hand. Hugely embarrassed, Michelle grabbed the dress and darted behind Derek to gain cover. Michelle was utterly mortified. She'd never been so embarrassed in her entire life. She thought she'd die as she slipped the dress back on nearly as fast as she'd removed it. It was a full minute before she was able to speak. With great embarrassment she blurted out a profuse apology.

"She doesn't do that to every stranger she meets," laughed Derek. He extended his hand to the old man. It took a moment for the man to react. Derek grasped the man's firm callused hand in his own. He pumped it vigorously until the old man finally came around.

"I'm sorry," Derek apologized. "My name's Derek and this is Michelle," he said, motioning behind him. "We've been lost in the Outback and you're the first living sole we've seen in months. I'm afraid Michelle got carried away with her greeting."

"Bloody hell young man," the old man finally blurted out. "Bloody hell, if that ain't the best God damn greetin' I've ever had in all my 81 years. And you want

412

to apologize for that? Bloody hell! If God took me right now I'd die the happiest I been in nearly a century," he chuckled as he shook his head. He still wasn't sure if he'd been dreaming.

A moment later, a meek and apologetic Michelle emerged from behind Derek. "I'm Michelle," she whispered, extending her hand towards the man. The old man visibly shook with emotion as he took her slender hand. He closed his big weathered hand around hers as gently as if he were caressing the tiny hand of a newborn child. Michelle was instantly soothed by the man's gentleness.

"I'm so sorry," Michelle finally got out.

The man kept his hand in hers for a nearly a minute before he finally spoke. "No. *I* thank *you* darlin'," he said softly. "I'll remember this pleasure till my dying day. And at my age," he chuckled, "it ain't that long. Thank you, dear lady," he added with a surprisingly graceful bow that ended as he kissed the top of her hand.

As the man let Michelle's hand slip gently out of his, he turned and looked at the pair, then at the plane. "I'm relieved to see that you nice people ain't hurt. But what's going on with that landing. I thought you'd crashed. I jumped into my truck and raced down the road after I saw you slam down onto the road and back up again.

"We did crash," Derek responded solemnly. "A couple of months ago our airliner crashed in some desolate area of the Outback."

The old man looked questioningly at Derek. He scratched his mop of gray scraggly hair. "Heard about that." He thought for a minute. "But that ain't possible,"

413

he continued. "Everyone on board that plane died. It crashed in a fireball in a swamp hundreds of miles from here."

"It's a long story," Derek responded. "I'll tell you all about it later, but first can you help us get to a phone mister.....?"

"Oh. I'm sorry about that," he replied. "I kinda lost track there for a minute. Mick's my name, Mick Adams. I'm a transplant here. I come for Arizona originally. Been here nearly 60 years. Came to make my fortune," he chuckled. "Didn't do all that bad though. Had a good job with the mining company for thirty odd years. Got me a little station back yonder," he said, pointing down the road. "And I got me one of them cell phones back at the station. Marilyn, that's my daughter, she give it to me so she can keep pestering me. She don't like me livin' so far outside of town. Especially since my wife, Vera, passed away. That was some ten years ago now. But I love it out here and livin in the old station cause it keeps her memory alive for me." Derek looked on as Mick's eyes went off into a faraway look. "Gonna miss it so bad when the bank takes it over in a few months. Can't afford to live here no more. Don't know where I'm gonna go but wherever it is I'll never forget Vera. She meant everything to me," he said passionately.

"I'm so sorry for your loss, Mick," Derek said in sincere sorrow. "You may not believe it but I honestly understand your feelings and pain." Mick gave off a huge sniff then wiped his nose on the sleeve of his dusty plaid shirt. Derek quickly sensed that it was time to move the conversation away from Mick's sorrow. It was

Mick that changed the topic. "Anyways, as I was sayin, I like it out here and I'm gonna stay. It's quiet and nobody bothers me much—except for when someone crashes a plane on my front door," he chuckled, looking at the plane. "We can go back there an you can use my phone to get help.

"That'd be just great," said Derek. "I guess that landing was more like a crash, now that you mention it," he added sheepishly. "You see, the plane doesn't belong to me. We kind of borrowed it to get back to civilization. It was our only way out. Even though I never learned how to fly, we took the risk that I could get us up and back down again in one piece."

The old man surveyed the undamaged plane. "Well in that case, ya' done good," he replied with a hearty laugh. "She's such a beauty." Clearly feeling better now, he smiled and walked over to the wing. He reached out and stroked the gleaming white wingtip. "Used to fly myself till my knees give out on me. Course that was a long time back. Had a twin-engine of my own once," he added with obvious pride. "She wasn't as nice as this one but she was still a real beauty. My wife, she used to fly with me back in those days. Those were good days. Then after my Vera died...well..." his voice trailed off. He sighed softly then turned away from Derek, immersing himself in beautiful memories. A moment later, Mick brushed back a tear and cast a longing look at the Lisa Marie. The old man recovered quickly. "I can take you back to my station, so you can make your calls, but you can't leave this beauty out here unattended. No sir. Can't do that," he added as he ran his hand along the smooth shiny surface of the fuselage.

A big smile spread across the old man's face. "Say, I'd be mighty happy to store her for you in my hangar back at my station. Had to sell my own twin years ago but I still got my hangar. I'd be honored if you'd let me keep her there for you for a while till you can arrange to get her back home."

"That's a deal," said Derek, extending his hand to Mick. He watched the old man's face light up with pleasure before adding, "Would you like to start her up and taxi her back to your hangar?"

Derek swore the old man's face looked 20 years younger as he enthusiastically accepted the offer. They decided that Derek and Mick would run the plane back to the station while Michelle drove the truck out in front as a precaution in case other vehicles came down the road. Mick and Derek walked Michelle over to the truck. Mick gave her a few simple directions to find his station which was barely a mile away. A minute later she started up the truck's motor, then watched as Mick and Derek headed back to the Lisa Marie to run-up her engines.

Derek let Mick climb into the cabin first so he could slide over into the pilot's seat. But before sitting in his own seat Derek retrieved the yellowed envelope he'd put in the door pocket earlier in the day just before takeoff. He stuffed it inside his shirt.

A minute later Derek settled into the co-pilot seat. He couldn't help but smile when he saw the look on Mick's face as he sat in the pilot's seat tenderly running his hand over the control panel. "This takes me back, Derek. It surely does. I did so love to fly," he mused.

"Kind of like it myself," replied Derek. "At least I can say that now that we're safely back on the ground." Derek retrieved the engine start-up list from the cabin floor. The two went through the engine start procedures and the Lisa Marie's engines roared into life.

Beep… Beep…..Beep, blared the truck's horn. Michelle was getting impatient. She couldn't understand what in the world was taking so long for Derek and Mick to start the airplane's engines. Just as she was about to get out of the truck to check on what was going on, she heard the Lisa Marie's engines start up. She delighted to the sound of both engines running up.

As Derek watched, Mick advanced the throttles and swung the airplane smoothly around. He rolled forward onto the road and lined the plane up behind the truck.

Seeing that Mick and Derek were ready to roll, Michelle gave a wave out the truck's window. As soon as Mick acknowledged her signal, she put the truck into gear and moved forward. It was a strange procession. Michelle drove the old pickup truck, followed by the big-twin engine with its propellers kicking up an enormous dust cloud as they moved down the dirt highway. Fortunately, no road-trains or other traffic hampered their progress.

Derek was impressed by the old man's expertise in taxiing the plane. In spite of the pain he must have felt in his knees, he skillfully maneuvered the plane down the roadway then into the driveway of his station. With barely enough room for the plane to fit between two tall trees along the driveway he masterfully directed the plane through the opening and into the open hangar behind the station. Just as Derek was about to go through the engine shut down list, both engines sputtered and died. Derek's heart skipped a beat--the plane had just run out of fuel.

A moment later Derek exited the cockpit and climbed to the ground. He sensed that Mick's knees were hurting. He held up his arm to help him down.

"Here let me give you a hand," Derek called out.

Mick, perched atop the wing, stood cringing in pain.

"I'm okay. Don't have to worry about me none. Them are pains of joy young man. It's been a long time since I've had the fun of being in a plane, let alone getting the chance to start up and taxi a beauty like this one." Derek helped Mick off the wing.

Once again back on the ground, Mick looked up at the Lisa Marie, then back at Derek with a questioning look on his face. "Say if you two survived that awful crash, how'd you wind up way out here months later?" Derek wasn't sure Mick would believe the story but he decided to tell him anyway. He first explained his theory of how they survived the fall to the earth after the explosive decompression. If Mick thought he was lying or crazy he didn't show a hint of disbelief. Instead, his reaction was rather the opposite. The fantastic story seemed to fire his imagination. He enthusiastically urged Derek to continue.

Mick's eagerness to hear the rest of the story inspired Derek. He described their terrible experience trekking across the outback to where they found the fantastic abandoned station with its airplanes locked away in the vault-like hangar. Mick's interest grew more intense as Derek revealed the mystery of the station.

At Mick's urging, Derek went on. He explained how they had spent many weeks resting, recuperating, and waiting for a rescue that never came before finally trekking across the outback to the foothills where they made the decision to fly their way out.

Though Mick continued listening intently, Derek was afraid he was beginning to sound like a veteran World War II pilot telling battle stories. But Mick didn't care. He listened closely while Derek described the Warrior's first flight. He certainly didn't have any trouble believing Derek's description of their previous harrowing landings in the Warrior and the Lisa Marie.

When Derek finally finished, Mick stood in stunned silence. A minute later a huge grin spread across Mick's face. "Damn if that ain't a hell of a tale. Sounds like you done made yourselves a *flyabout*," he laughed.

"What's a *'flyabout*,'" asked Derek.

"Well, ya' see a 'walkabout' is a long walking journey around the Outback that Australian bush boys have to make in order to prove their manhood." Derek already knew that but he kept silent and let Mick continue. "Hah," Mick laughed, "looks like you young people just did the same thing, only instead of 'walking about' the Outback, you chose to 'fly about' the Outback instead!" The old man laughed heartily. Derek, releasing months of stress, joined in. Warm and friendly laughter filled the air.

Well now," Mick continued, "I guess you'll be looking to get back home after you make your phone calls. Where you looking to go?" he asked.

"We'll be heading back to Sydney as soon as we can," replied Derek.

Mick laughed. "Can't help ya' that much Derek. That's a hell of a ways from here," he chuckled. "But I can take you to town though and from there you might be able to get transportation to Birdsville in a day or two. Hell, you may get lucky and might be able to charter a plane in town. They got a small field just north of here. One of the pilots might help you out if he thinks he can get the right price out of you," he laughed. "And once you get yourselves to Birdsville you can get back to Sydney easy enough. But if you get stuck in town and need a place to stay, it'd be my pleasure to have you and your young lady stay as long as you like at my place. It ain't much, as my daughter reminds me all the time, but I'd be pleased to put you up. And I'd be honored to watch that beautiful airplane for you while you're gone."

"Transportation to town would be just fine Mick. And if we need a place to stay for the night, we'd be honored to accept your invitation. I can't tell you how much we appreciate your help already." He looked up at the airplane. "I know you'll take good care of the Lisa Marie until I can make arrangements with her owners to get her back." Derek couldn't help but run his hand across the fuselage one last time before they shut the plane up into storage.

Derek felt a strange sense of loss as he helped Mick pull the big hangar door closed. A moment later they turned and headed towards the house. Derek had only walked a few yards when he felt compelled to turn around. He stood gazing at the huge hangar door. *This doesn't feel right*, he thought. *It's like I just read a great book and closed it just before I reached the end* he mused. He stood a full minute looking at the door before Mick brought him out of his daze.

"You all right?" he inquired.

"Yes. Yes, I'm all right," he replied weakly. "It's been a long hard journey." He turned back towards the house.

The old man put his leathery hand on Derek's shoulder as they walked.

"A hard journey indeed," Mick responded sympathetically. "Let's get inside. I'm sure you and Michelle have some important calls to make. Your adventure ain't over yet."

Derek walked on silently. A moment later Michelle came running towards him, her arms spread wide and her hair flying out behind her like spun gold. A broad grin spread across his face. He flung his arms open in anticipation of her embrace. As they held each other tight, Derek thought about the scratchy envelope stuffed inside his shirt—an anxious smile spread across his face. Michelle wasn't able to see his smile. Nor did she hear him whisper softly; "Our adventure isn't over, Michelle. It's just beginning."

CHAPTER 27

Derek was mindless of the wild taxi ride as the cab driver jerkily weaved in and around Sydney's busy downtown traffic. *God,* he thought, *has it really only been a week since we've returned to civilization.* He stared out the window in a daze while his mind re-ran the hectic events of the last week—the news media, the phone calls to his parents, his twin brother, and to the University. So much had gone on and he'd had so little time to stay in touch with Michelle. He quickly put those harried thoughts aside and focused on his upcoming lunch with Michelle. He'd missed her deeply. But he knew that she, too, had been overwhelmed with activities of her own since their return. He looked at his watch. A smile of anticipation spread across his face.

"Just a few more minutes now and we'll be together again," Derek announced to no one in particular. The cab driver didn't respond. Instead he took a sharp right turn. A moment later the cab jerked to a halt. Derek could hardly control his anticipation. He quickly paid the cab driver with a healthy tip, flung open the door, and jumped out of the taxi.

Screeeachhh!!!" filled the air. Derek's heart jumped to his throat as he caught sight of a huge truck, tires smoking, charging directly at him. He watched in horrified slow motion as the Mercedes Benz emblem on the hood of the truck came to a stop barely six inches from his chest. His whole body shook as he stumbled shakily to the curb. He never heard the unending hail of curse words the driver hurled at him as he restarted the stalled truck and sped off.

God! thought Derek. *I survive falling three miles from the sky without a parachute; a crash landing in a plane I don't know how to fly, then I almost get myself killed crossing the street. Got to remember that they drive on the wrong side of the road,* he chided himself. He stood unsteadily looking up at the world-famous Sydney Opera House. The awe-inspiring structure housed the famous 5-star Bennelong Restaurant that was situated under the astonishing 'glass sails' of the opera house. Derek had chosen the fabulous location because he'd promised to take Michelle out to the finest restaurant in Sydney once they got back to civilization. And, as promised, he wore the white shirt, shorts, and necktie that Michelle had picked out for him at the station.

The doorman, alert to Derek's narrow escape from the truck, opened the door wide and held it there while he passed through. Seeing that the maitre d' was occupied, he walked directly into the dining room where he saw Michelle waiting. As he approached the table he couldn't help but remark how gorgeous she looked in the peach chiffon dress, she'd promised to wear. And

Michelle smiled, with pleasure, at what she called Derek's Aussie businessman's outfit. He eagerly bent over and gave her a long lingering kiss, much to the distress of some stoic patrons seated nearby. His greeting was returned just as eagerly.

He noticed that Michelle was wearing sunglasses. He tilted his head as he looked at her. "I'm not sure," said Derek, "but rather than disguising that pretty face of yours from an admiring public, I think those glasses just make you look like you're a famous person who's trying to dodge the press. Having any luck?"

"I don't think being famous is all that it's cracked up to be," Michelle mused. "I'll be glad when all this dies down. I just want to get on with my life again."

"I know what you mean," Derek sighed. "This has been a wild week for me too. But at least with me the press can't find me very easily. Anyway, it will all blow over soon. They'll get their story and, in a few days, we'll be ancient history to them. They'll move on to something else. Nothing is as old as old news," he added hopefully.

The two spent nearly two hours lingering over their meal. They laughed and cried as they recalled a hundred wacky, wild, and terrifying experiences they'd shared during their adventure. Things nearly got out of hand when Michelle told Derek about her phone call to her fiancé. She had called him many times since her return but all she'd gotten was his answering machine. The story of what happened when she finally reached him in person caused the two to laugh hysterically. Though she didn't laugh about it at the time, she thought the story was hilarious when she told it to Derek.

She explained to him how John, who had just gotten back from a ten-day trip to New Zealand, hadn't yet checked his phone messages and wasn't aware that she had survived the plane crash. Nor had he caught any of the news stories of their miraculous survival before he answered the phone. As far as he knew, she was dead. When she finally reached him in person he'd answered the phone with a hoarse '*Yeah, hello. Who is it?*' When Michelle excitedly shouted, '*John it's me—Michelle,*' there was stunned silence on the other end.' "Michelle?" he'd repeated quizzically. It was then that Michelle heard a young woman's voice ring out clearly in the background. '*Who the hell is Michelle!*' the woman shouted. '*You always screw up our sex! It's been this same crap for six months. You always got to answer a phone call after it's taken half the night to get that puny thing ready. Now hang up!*' the woman screamed. A moment later Michelle knew that John finally realized that it was *her*, on the line—she heard a loud retching sound followed by the same woman's voice screaming, "*You bastard! You just puked all over me......*" The phone went dead.

Michelle's initial shock at learning that her fiancé had been womanizing for the past six months, even as they planned their wedding, changed to fury. She never called him back and John never attempted to reach her. The wedding was off, *permanently!*

Tears streamed down Derek's cheek as he listened to the story. But he didn't tell Michelle that they were tears of joy, not tears of laughter. He thrilled to the thought that Michelle was free of John. It was a great ending to their reunion.

Their luncheon date came to a close all too quickly. Derek looked at his watch and realized that it was time to go. "I've got to catch my plane back to the states," said Derek, checking his watch again. "I can't believe the chaos there is at home and at the university. My whole family went nuts when they heard the news about our miraculous survival. Everyone's dying for me to get home. And things at work are a mess. I'd been working on a big financial grant for my department before I left and it was nearly approved when I came to Australia. But when I didn't come back, the school was forced to withdraw the grant application. That could have a devastating effect on the department. I'm going to have to work my brains out to get the grant resubmitted. What a mess," he mused. He shook his head in disgust.

Derek needn't have explained his situation to Michelle. She knew full well the chaos he was facing—she'd just spent the entire week trying to get her own life back together. Between the fuss her family and the press had made over her return she hadn't had a moment's peace. She understood Derek's need to return home to straighten out his personal and professional life. And she knew that she'd miss him dearly. She just prayed that he would return to Australia as he promised.

Derek quickly paid the enormous bill, left a generous tip, then led Michelle out the main entrance of the restaurant. The doorman gave an elegant bow to

Michelle as she emerged onto the street. Michelle blushed as he surveyed her beautiful face, smiled and said, "It's been an honor to you have you dine with us Miss Sherry."

Derek didn't feel slighted when the doorman failed to recognize him as a fellow survivor of the crash. He could easily understand how the man's attention focused on Michelle rather than himself. Can't blame him for that, he thought, as he admired the lovely blush tone that graced Michelle's face.

With a snap of his fingers and a sharp wave of his hand, the doorman directed a specific gleaming cab to the curb. He suspected he had chosen the most perfect cab in the line for Michelle. The cab stood waiting for several minutes without protest as Derek and Michelle, choked with emotion, tried their best to say goodbye. Derek hoped the tears welling up in his eyes didn't show. He finally ended their embrace with a stern affirmation of his promise that he would return to Australia just as soon as he possibly could.

A moment later the doorman sensed that the moment was right. He silently swooped into place and opened the cab's door allowing Michelle to enter. After assuring himself that she was safely settled into the cab, he closed the door, checked that it was secure, and motioned to the driver. The cab pulled smoothly away from the curb and merged with the busy afternoon traffic.

Michelle craned her neck looking over her shoulder as Derek quickly receded from view. She tried her best to hold back her tears as she slowly turned her view forward. She glanced up into the rearview mirror and caught the driver's eyes. She could tell that the he had been courteously waiting until she was ready to speak.

"Where would you like to go?" he asked politely.

Michelle cleared her throat for a moment. "Please take me to the Medical Building on Elizabeth Street," she said. Choking back tears, she looked back once again, in a failed attempt to glimpse Derek one last time.

"That would be my pleasure Miss Sherry," the driver added with a smile.

I guess Derek was right, thought Michelle. She removed her sunglasses. People will recognize me anyway. She took a deep breath, released it, and settled back into the seat for the rest of the trip.

Derek lost sight of the cab the moment it left the curb. Though Michelle's cab had already disappeared from view, he continued gazing aimlessly at the traffic. A moment later the doorman sensed that Derek was ready to return to the world around him. He snapped his fingers and called a slightly worn cab into place. He opened the rear door and Derek stepped in.

"Where to mate?" the driver quipped as he swung the car away from the restaurant.

Derek pulled a weathered business card out of his shirt pocket, examined it thoughtfully and said, "Corner of Liverpool, and Castelreagh." The cab driver cut a hard left and began threading his way through the heavy downtown traffic. A moment later, Derek sank down into the seat contemplating what might happen when he reached his destination.

428

Derek slipped into deep thought throughout the short ride. He was shaken out of his reverie when the driver brought the cab to an abrupt halt in front of a large office building. He quickly paid the bill. This time he used extreme caution before exiting the cab. He carefully checked to see that he got out on the side that gave him direct access to the sidewalk.

The cab shot off into the traffic, leaving Derek standing on the corner. He stared for a moment at the huge office building that stood in front of him. It was an imposing sight with its shiny black marble façade and mirrored glass windows. Impressive polished stainless-steel letters spelled out 'Kline and Smithson Attorneys at Law' across its main entrance. Derek reached into his coat pocket and pulled out the yellowed envelope he'd placed there earlier. *I'm more nervous now than I was when I tried to land the Warrior*, thought Derek. He swallowed hard, stepped forward, and entered the building.

CHAPTER 28

Derek felt elated as he pushed his way through the throngs of passengers at Sydney Airport. *Oh God, it's so great to be back*, he thought. He hurried out to the curb towing his bags behind him. *Was it only three months ago that I left? Seems more like a year.* A cab driver spotted Derek. He wheeled the car right up in front of him, jumped out and took hold of his bags. While Derek entered the cab, the driver hastily stuffed the luggage into the trunk. A moment later he slammed the trunk shut with a solid *'thunk'* then went around to the front of the car. He'd barely gotten into the driver's seat when Derek eagerly fired off an address. The driver, sensing Derek's impatience and hoping for a generous tip, immediately hit the gas pedal, sending the cab darting into an opening in the traffic.

After a speedy, and sometimes hair-raising ride, the cab pulled to a stop in the downtown business district. Though the short trip had taken little time, Derek's impatience made it seem agonizingly slow.

Derek quickly paid the fare, along with a very generous tip and exited the cab. As he hastily turned away, he called over his shoulder and shouted into the cab's open window. "If you can, wait for me. Keep the meter running. I may be as long as an hour or two but I'll make it very worth your while if you do." With that he dashed off down the street.

A few minutes later he stood on the street looking up at the office building in front of him. It looked the same as it did the last time he'd seen it with the words 'Kline and Smithson Attorneys at Law,' still spelled out in stainless steel letters over the entrance. His heart thumped heavily in his chest as he stood on the curb trying to summon up enough courage to enter.

Derek sighed heavily. *Well, this is it. I've burnt my bridges behind me and there's no turning back now.* He stretched himself to his full height and stepped forward, convinced that he was doing the right thing.

As Derek went through the revolving door to the building, he recalled the in-flight phone call he'd made to their offices just a few hours earlier. He prayed that the answer they promised they'd have for him this afternoon was the one he was hoping for.

Two hours later, an ecstatic Derek emerged from the building. He dashed to the curb where he'd been previously dropped off. He spotted the cab, now parked across the street, and tried to get the driver's attention. The cab driver had no trouble locating him. He saw Derek frantically waving a sheaf of papers in the air to get his attention. *I don't know if he's dancing or flagging me down,* he laughed to himself. An instant later, he pulled away from the curb, made a U-turn, and headed towards his enthusiastic fare. "G'day," the cab driver called over his shoulder as Derek thumped into the seat.

"A good day indeed, my friend. A good day indeed!" Derek practically shouted back. "Take me to the Bennelong Restaurant. I've got a date with an angel!"

The cab driver smiled to himself as he visualized the fat tip that was certainly coming his way. An instant later the cab merged into traffic and Derek was on his way. His excitement was clearly evident. He impatiently fidgeted throughout the cab ride. He could think of nothing but Michelle and their future as the cab driver skillfully maneuvered the taxi around the busy noontime traffic. For the tenth time in the last three minutes, Derek checked his watch. *She'll be there already*, he thought. He was glad he had called beforehand to tell her he would likely be delayed.

He was lucky to have reached her when he called from the law offices. He had caught her just as she was about to leave the house for the day. He'd nearly missed her. He smiled to himself as he recalled her excited and enthusiastic response when she found out that he was already back in town. He wasn't supposed to arrive for another two days yet, but he used his minor celebrity status to pressure the airline into letting him change his flight to an earlier one.

"We'll be there in less than five minutes now," the cab driver called over his shoulder. He easily sensed Derek's impatience. He watched through the rear-view mirror as Derek constantly cheeked his watch throughout the entire trip.

432

Finally, the cab pulled up in front of the Bennelong Restaurant. Derek didn't even bother to ask how much the fare was. He just thrust an enormous bill at the driver. "Keep it," he called over his shoulder. He flung open the door and leaped to the curb. He didn't even think to close the door behind him as he ran towards the big wood-carved restaurant door.

"Bloody hell," said the cab driver as he stared at the bill in disbelief. "A couple of more fares like that and I can retire!" He grinned happily as he snapped the bill and ran his fingers over its surface. A moment later he slammed the back door shut, spun his cab around, and raced back towards the law offices. He was hoping that Derek wasn't the only happy client coming out of the building.

It was a good thing that the doorman was alert. He barely had time to fling the door open as Derek hurtled towards him. He cringed at the thought of a customer being knocked senseless against *his* door when *he* was on duty.

The alert maitre'd, in his immaculate tuxedo, intercepted Derek as he rushed through the elegant lobby towards the dining room. He tactfully stepped out in front of Derek and gently, yet firmly, placed his fingertips onto Derek's chest.

"Excuse me sir, do you have a reservation?" he asked with greater courtesy than Derek deserved.

"Ah…..no, I mean yes," Derek replied, bobbing his head trying to look around the rotund maitre'd in search of Michelle.

"And that would be under the name of......?" he asked, while continuing to serve as a roadblock.

"Michelle," Derek blurted out just as he caught sight of her sitting alone at a table. She was nearly hidden by the lush elegant furnishings that gave the restaurant its famous atmosphere. Her ears immediately picked up Derek's cry. She waved cheerfully. A look of recognition came to the maitre d's' face. "Ah yes. But of course, Miss Sherry's table," he said, sounding like a perfect gentleman. He stepped gracefully aside and let Derek rush by.

Even as he hurried across the dining room, still clutching his sheaf of papers, Derek sensed something different about Michelle. As he focused on her face he could see that she was as beautiful as ever. But there was something more, something special, about her appearance. Though he couldn't put his finger on it, he sensed that her face had a special warmth and radiance that he'd never seen before. Whatever it is, he thought, it makes her look more beautiful than ever.

Michelle was seated at a table that was fully draped with a colorful tablecloth and nicely shaded by a palm tree. She was not wearing sun glasses this time. He hoped some normalcy had returned to her life. Though he couldn't see much of her, he was thrilled by what was in view. He lunged across the table and gave her an embarrassingly long kiss. Several moments passed before the happy pair finally separated.

Derek could hardly contain his joy. He pulled out a chair and sat down across from her, placing his sheaf of papers on the table beside him. He excitedly told her how much he had missed her and profusely apologized for not staying in better contact over the last few months. He had barely gotten into his seat when the wine steward approached the table asking for their drink order. Derek hastily ordered a bottle of fine wine.

Before Derek had a chance to share his news with Michelle, the wine steward returned. Derek tasted and approved the wine. The steward then poured two long stem glasses full of the exquisite red wine. Michelle took a couple of sips from her glass then watched in fascination as Derek hurriedly downed his full glass.

"I needed that," said Derek as he caught his breath. The bracing and refreshing drink calmed him down. "God, you look great Michelle," I missed you terribly."

"I missed you too," said Michelle. She flashed him a radiant smile. "So, what's this great news you want to tell me?"

"Not yet," said Derek. "When I called you earlier today you said on the phone that you had some really important news to share with me. So, I'll let you go first," said Derek, in spite of his nearly overwhelming desire to share his own news first. "I haven't given you a chance to say hardly anything yet. My news can wait. You go ahead."

Michelle studied Derek's face for a moment then her expression changed. She appeared to be in deep thought but couldn't seem to figure out exactly how to say what was on her mind. She opened her mouth as if to speak then stopped—she was at a loss for words. Finally, she just gave up.

"No, you go ahead Derek. I know you're excited about something. You should tell me your news first." She looked down at the papers that lay by Derek's elbow. "Come on now. Tell me what you've got there?"

indent

Michelle's prompt was all Derek needed. He couldn't hold back his enthusiasm any longer.

"You won't believe it, Michelle." He practically shouted as he reached down and picked up the legal documents. "But here's the proof--it's true!" He held them up for her to see. "I know I should have told you about this earlier but it was all too fantastic. I didn't know if it would ever really hold up in court. I didn't know if we had a real claim. But we did!"

"What *are* you talking about?"

"The *will* Michelle, *Mr. Winston's will!*"

Michelle shook her head. "I don't follow you."

"Let me explain." He went on eagerly. "It all started back at the station a couple of days before we attempted to fly out of the station in the Warrior. I was looking in the bookcase one last time for something that might help us find our location. Then I stumbled across *this*!" He pushed an old yellowed envelope towards her. "Open it up, Michelle, take it out and look at it."

As he continued his story, Michelle removed a number of yellowed sheets of paper from the envelope and began examining them.

"I found it wedged down in a corner at the back of the bottom shelf. It had fallen down behind some books. Out of curiosity, I opened it and found that it contained a will with some instructions as to what to do if anyone should find it. If you check the date, you'll see it was written years ago."

Derek watched as Michelle scanned the document. He continued, "I was astounded when I read it. I've just come back from a meeting at the law offices of 'Kline and Smithson Attorneys at Law,' here in Sydney. And this will, as explained to me by Mr. Winston's personal attorney, is essentially a 'bearer instrument' in that everything that's listed in the will is to go to whoever finds it. And that's *us*! In it, he leaves us the station, its contents, the hangar and both airplanes, plus a $500,000 cash gift if we honor his wishes as stated in the will!"

"You can't be serious!" Michelle blurted out. Her facial expression was one of excitement yet disbelief. "You're kidding, aren't you?!"

"No, I'm not!" continued Derek. "And there's more! There's a yearly living expenses for us for years to come. *But, as I said*, the will holds *only if certain conditions are met*—and I'll get to those in a minute."

"I wanted so badly to tell you about the possibility of our inheriting the station, the planes, and all that money when I first found the will. But it all seemed so fantastic, so impossible. So many times, while we were stranded in the Outback, we had high hopes that things would finally go our way only to have those hopes dashed before our eyes time after time. I just didn't want to put either of us through that again. So, I resolved to hold off telling you until I found out for sure if we had a legal claim before I broke the news to you. I'm so very sorry. In retrospect, it seems mean of me not to have shared the hope with you, but I thought we'd both been through enough. I was afraid that might be just a cruel joke to top off our ordeal with yet another shattered hope."

Michelle looked over the pages for several minutes before putting them down. "But surely this will couldn't stand up in court. Wouldn't lawyers think that he wasn't of….what do they call that….'sound mind?' After all he was living in a fantasy world and his health failing. Surely he wasn't thinking clearly."

"Ah, but Mr. Winston was thinking very clearly indeed when he had this document prepared. It happened during, what may have been, his last trip back to civilization. That was at least several years *before he left* on his ill-fated search for help in the truck we found. In fact, when I first read the will I wondered how he could possibly have written such an impressive legal document on his own. I got the answer to that question, and a lot more, when I went to his lawyer's office a few days after we got back from the Outback."

Derek continued. "The reason I went to them in the first place was that I found the firm's business card in the bottom of the envelope that contained the will. Anyway, it was during the first week we got back that I went to see them. I spoke with one of the partners. Actually, it was Mr. Kline himself. He was an elderly man but still very much active in the firm. I talked with him for a long time. He's the one who actually wrote the will and he confirmed that the will is genuine, legal, and binding."

Michelle's face lit up. "So, it's really true? I can't believe it!" She paused a moment then continued. "But how did all this happen. I mean, didn't he already have a will?"

"Let me explain," Derek began. "It seems that the founding partner of the firm, Mr. Jonathan Kline, was a long-time friend of Mr. Winston. They were college roommates at Harvard University many years ago. Mr. Kline was in the Law School and Mr. Winston was in the School of Business. After graduation, Mr. Kline passed the bar exam and set up a lucrative private practice of wealthy clients. Mr. Winston, with his rapidly growing business empire, became his very first client. Mr. Winston and Mr. Kline remained friends and business associates for many years. Mr. Kline confided in me that he and Mr. Winston remained the best of friends throughout all the years that he knew him. He thought the world of him.

Anyway, their long-term friendship entered a new phase when Mr. Kilne decided to leave the United States to set up a law practice here in Sydney. Although they remained in touch through mail and occasional telephone communication, it wasn't until years later that they rekindled their friendship. That happened when Mr. Winston and his new wife, Lisa, came to Australia on their honeymoon. He looked up Mr. Kline and they readily renewed their friendship. Lisa apparently had an infectious personality. Mr. Kline took an instant liking to her, as did Mrs. Kline, and they became close friends. The two couples saw a lot of each other before the Winston's returned to the states."

Derek stopped for a moment and took a drink of wine. "But then soon after they returned home, Lisa got sick." He hesitated for a moment before continuing. "Mr. Kline told me how badly he and his wife felt when they heard about her illness. They were devastated when, only a short time later, Mr. Winston called and gave them the news that Lisa had died. During the call he was clearly distraught. He talked at length to the Kline's about coming back to Australia to live alone in the area of the Outback that Lisa had loved so much. He said it was the only way he could relieve himself of his pain and suffering.

At first Mr. Kline just listened, thinking that the plan was just a whim that would fade away after he'd dealt with his grief. But the plan didn't fade away. Months passed and Mr. Winston was suffering badly. He contacted the Kline's again. He consolidated his United States holdings and moved himself and his absolutely enormous fortune permanently to Sydney. His grief was strong but he had a plan and he needed Mr. Kline's help.

Mr. Kline was no stranger to the pain of the loss of a loved one. He had suffered a personal tragedy himself when one of his sons was killed in an automobile accident just as he was about to become a full partner in his firm. Like Mr. Winston, the loss of someone so dear hit him hard. Though he eventually got over his loss, he had great empathy for Mr. Winston's pain and suffering. He committed himself to helping him in any way he could. And, although he didn't agree with Mr. Winston that becoming a hermit in the Outback was the answer, he understood his grief.

So, in the end he agreed to help him make arrangements to ship his airplanes to Australia and to arrange for construction of his fantasy station and airplane hangar. He kept to Mr. Winston's strict instructions that the location of his station was to remain a closely guarded secret—even from Mr. Kline himself." His lawyer oversaw all the engineering particulars and hiring of construction specialists to build the complex station. He even contracted with a Virginia historic building restorer to dismantle, transport, and reconstruct Lisa's fabulous bedroom onsite at the Outback station. Arrangements were made for all materials and belongings for the secret construction project, including the dismantled bedroom, to be delivered to a single staging point outside of Sydney. But that's where Mr. Kline's role ended. Mr. Winston took care of moving the materials and work crews, as secretly as possible, to the actual building site in the Outback. Its physical location was never revealed to Mr. Kline.

"I found out that while Mr. Winston spent years alone in the Outback appearing to live the life of a hermit shunning contact with the outside world, he did remain in contact with Mr. Kline. He and his firm, managed Mr. Winston's enormous portfolio of investments. So, in reality he managed to keep control of his remaining substantial wealth in a way that allowed him to live out his fantasy lifestyle and to maintain the expensive airplanes. "Ah," said Michelle as a look of understanding spread across her face. "So, he didn't just disappear. He kept in touch with Mr. Kline to take care of his finances."

"That's right," Derek went on. "In fact, he kept in regular contact with Mr. Kline whenever he went out for

441

supplies a couple of times a year. Mr. Kline told me that one day he got an unexpected call from Mr. Winston. He was greatly surprised because he requested a *personal* visit regarding some financial issues. That was highly unusual because previously he had only been in contact over the phone for investment issues, and then only to transfer funds or check on investments. In any case, he told him that he was in the city only for a few days and that he wanted to make out a new will.

"Mr. Kline said that when he met him at his Sydney hotel room he was pleasantly surprised by his excellent physical and mental condition. He, in no way, resembled a hermit, he was in good health and very rational. Nevertheless, he pleaded with him to give up his fantasy world and return to live back in Sydney where he would be safe and could live peacefully. But he steadfastly refused. He insisted that, aside for the short time he enjoyed with his wife before she died, the years he had spent alone in the Outback had been the happiest years of his life. He explained to his friend that he honestly felt Lisa's presence within him. Whether he was at the station or roaming around the Outback that she so loved, he knew she was there. He talked lovingly, almost spiritually, how he'd pretended that Lisa was in another room, or outside in the garden, or in taking care of the Lisa Marie." He was completely rational, albeit lonely, in love, and at peace where he lived. He said Mr. Winston was clearly of sound mind, even if his personal life choices may have been at odds with others.

"Finally, he got to the reason why he had called the in-person meeting. He explained that he was concerned about what would happen to the station's contents and his wife's beautiful plane when he died. He wanted Mr. Kline to write him a new will." Derek took another drink of wine, then continued on. "Mr. Kline explained to me that Mr. Winston said he fully expected to live out the rest of his life at the station and that he knew that some day he would die out there. Perhaps it was another of his fantasies, but he hoped that after he died, whoever found his body might be a person like himself. He hoped it would be someone who had good reason to remove himself from the real world--someone who wanted and needed to live alone, in peace, to resolve the loss of a loved one. He hoped that such a person might appreciate the station and respect it and take care of it much the way he had done. But he was also a realist. He knew full well that such a scenario was very unlikely. Still, he was deeply concerned. He didn't want to see the things his Lisa loved so much destroyed through neglect or greed. So, he had Mr. Kline draw up a sort of 'bearer instrument will' that spelled out certain conditions to ensure that the beneficiary would respect the Lisa Marie and the contents of the station. He made provisions that, should the beneficiary choose not to remain living alone in the Outback, a remote possibility at best, that he would be taken care of financially. *But only if he agreed to preserve his wife's possessions in a dignified manner.* And he granted the sole right to make the decision, as to what a 'dignified manner' meant, up to Mr. Kline's law firm."

"Mr. Winston must have pleaded his case well because he got Mr. Kline to write up the will exactly the way he wanted it," said Derek. He touched the yellowed document that lay on the table. "I guess it's not all that surprising that Mr. Kline gave in to his wishes. He told me that Mr. Winston was a tough and convincing man with a commanding personality. He always got what he wanted. He was a strong but fair man who always did things his own way."

"Mr. Kline told me that he saw Mr. Winston only one more time. They met at a truck dealership a few days after their first meeting. Mr. Winston had asked Mr. Kline to arrange for the purchase of a sturdy new truck for him. It was to be equipped with long-range fuel tanks and big Outback style tires on it. We know now, of course, that he made it back to the station in the red truck and that a few years later he wound up out in the ravine where he died." Derek continued, "Before leaving the dealership Mr. Kline pleaded with him, one more time, to return to Sydney or at least to tell him the location of the hidden station so he could check up on him, but he refused. There was nothing more he could do. He handed Mr. Winston a copy of the new will, the one here on the table, and watched him climb resolutely, but happily, into the cab of the truck and head northwest out of the city."

"Mr. Kline told me that as he watched him drive off he was certain that he would never see him again. His fears were well founded because all communications stopped after he left that day. He was certain that the worst had happened when Mr. Winston didn't make his usual phone calls around the time he should have come back for his semiannual supply runs."

"First weeks went by, then months, then a year, without a word from him. Finally, Mr. Kline decided that it was time to act. So, in spite of Mr. Winston's express demands that he be left alone, Mr. Kline decided that he would try to find him to check up on his condition. He told me that he spent thousands of dollars to conduct an aerial search to find the hidden station but the search was unsuccessful. That's not surprising because not only was the station purposefully camouflaged, nobody knew where it was because he'd apparently required all the contractors to agree in the contract to keep the station's location strictly secret. The enormous bonuses to ensure their silence worked well indeed. Mr. Kline never knew, until now, the location of the station.

Then as the years passed without any further contact Mr. Kline knew for certain that Mr. Winston had died. He wasn't surprised at all when I showed up in his office with the will in my hand. Actually, he appeared to be quite relieved. At last he knew what had happened to his dear friend. And he seemed comforted by the news that we had given him a proper burial. He told me that he planned to grant his friend his last wish—to be left alone. There will be no effort to recover Mr. Winston's remains. He'll rest there in peace." Derek became somber and didn't speak for several minutes.

Finally, Derek began again. "But let me get back now and finish the story. Mr. Kline was enthralled by my story of how we found the station and how we felt that Mr. Winston and his wife Lisa played such an important role in our survival. He was very pleased by the story and he was certain that Mr. Winston would have approved of the way in which we honored his wife and the station during our ordeal."

"After that, I spent a long time talking with him about me, and you, but mostly about *you*," he added sheepishly. He's looking forward to getting a chance to meet you in person. Then he asked me what use we had in mind for the contents and use of the station and the airplanes. I had no problem laying out my plan— hopefully *our* plan before him. He continued. "After I explained the plan, he readily agreed that it would certainly satisfy the 'dignified use' directive in the will. But he told me it would take at least three months to process the will before they could properly access the estate and give a final judgement on whether or not we were the legal beneficiaries. I got a call from him a week ago that we *absolutely* qualify as the beneficiaries— that's what brought me back early. All they need now is to process our claim on the estate and to get our signatures on some documents.

"You mean it's all settled? We really are inheriting everything?" Michelle asked, though she was still a bit bewildered by Derek's ramblings.

Michelle quickly gathered her senses. She looked quizzically at Derek. "So, what's this about the dignified use of the contents of the station? What did you tell them you had in mind for us to do with the station and the planes?"

Derek's heart began to beat as hard as it did when he crash-landed the Warrior months before. He stammered, trying to get the words out. He hesitated for a moment

446

then began again. "I had a long talk with Mick before we left his place. He told me about his sadness that he was just about to lose his home to the bank, and how much he envied Mr. Winston and his ability to live, unbothered, in the Outback while honoring his wife. Remember, he too, lost his own wife and dearly wanted to enjoy his own last years in peace with his wife's memories. His fantasy so closely matched that of Mr. Winston that my heart went out to both of them. And then when we got to the will's provision about 'dignified' use of the station, I couldn't help but think of Mick. So, I suggested that we would turn over the station to Mick Adams.

I discussed the matter in detail with Mr. Kline. I told him about my idea of leaving the station in Mick's care for as long as he wishes to be there. And I suggested providing Mick with a new truck, and radio communications, while he serves as a paid caretaker of the station. But part of the plan is that Mick would have to agree to accept 'check-in visits' from his daughter on a regular basis. I told him that I'd take care of all the fly-in, fly-out expenses for her visits. And I even suggested making financial provisions for him to bring along a friend or companion for safety and to prevent loneliness. Since Mick had given me his cell phone number before we left, Mr. Kline had no trouble reaching him as I sat in his office. Mick, who had just been notified by the bank that he was losing his home, was staggered by our offer. Although he's already agreed to the provisions, I'm not sure he actually believes this is really happening. But Mr. Kline immediately made arrangements for one of his partners to visit him in person to take care of all the legal details so he'll know it's real. In the end, Mr. Kline was especially pleased to find that Mick's needs and desires so closely matched Mr. Winston's dream that someone, like himself, would find joy at the station. I think this brings needed closure to Mr. Kline about the loss of his good friend, Mr. Winston.

Derek continued. "I also told him that we'd use some of the money to repair the Warrior and ferry it back, along with the Lisa Marie, to Sydney where *Mr. Derek Hunter and Mrs. Michelle Hunter*," that's us he beamed, "plan to start our own Outback flying taxi service. We can even give tourists flying tours over the Outback—we can give them their own *'flyabout'!*" he laughed. Suddenly Derek got intensely serious. He took a deep breath, reached out and took her hand gently in his and said softly, "That is, if you approve of the idea......and if you'll have me."

Michelle began to cry. Tears of joy streamed down her face as she rose and leaned across the table to kiss Derek.

"Of course, I will," she finally got out through the tears. "If you'll have *us*," she added, half laughing half crying.

"*Us*?" asked Derek.

"Yes, me and our *twin girls*, silly," she sobbed. "That's what I've been trying to tell you the past hour but I didn't know how!"

Derek was in joyous shock as he now saw what had been hidden by the table. Michelle looked radiantly beautiful as she showed her three and a half months of pregnancy.

He moved out from behind the table and hugged her tight. "Well that's going to change our plans," he quickly added between kisses. "No more taxi service for us. We'll go right into setting up our own *airline*." He patted her belly gently as he chortled, "we've got two of our best pilots in the hangar already. And we know they've got great flying genes. Just look at their father," he laughed. Michelle, punched him, not too softly, in the belly. A moment later she relented and joyfully kissed him.

THE END

Robert Campbell

About the Author

Although the author of *Flyabout*, Dr. Robert Campbell, has enjoyed his career as a Computer Science professor, he's also enjoyed a lifelong interest in all areas related to aviation. In order to write with accuracy and precision about the flying sequences in the novel, he became a student pilot and learned to fly a single-engine Piper Warrior and a twin-engine Piper Seneca. A colleague of his, a fully certified DC-10 Captain, served as a consultant for the airline accident sequences. Dr. Campbell, a USAF veteran, and his wife Alice, left Boston for the sun and fun of Florida where he still enjoys taking flying lessons.